A W. E. B. Du Bois Reader

A W. E. B. Du Bois Reader

edited by Andrew G. Paschal
introduction by Arna Bontemps

Collier Books
Macmillan Publishing Company
New York

Maxwell Macmillan Canada
Toronto

Maxwell Macmillan International
New York   Oxford   Singapore   Sydney

Collier Books   Maxwell Macmillan Canada, Inc.
Macmillan Publishing Company   1200 Eglinton Avenue East
866 Third Avenue   Suite 200
New York, NY 10022   Don Mills, Ontario M3C 3N1

Macmillan Publishing Company is part of
the Maxwell Communication Group of Companies.

Library of Congress Cataloging-in-Publication Data
Du Bois, W. E. B. (William Edward Burghardt), 1868–1963.
    [Selections.   1993]
    A W. E. B. Du Bois reader / edited by Andrew G. Paschal;
introduction by Arna Bontemps.
        p.   cm.
    Originally published: New York: Macmillan, [1971].
    Includes bibliographical references.
    ISBN 0-02-002351-0
    1. Afro-Americans.   2. Africa.   I. Paschal, Andrew G.   II. Title.
E185.97.D73A25   1993   92-30128   CIP
973'.0496073—dc20

Macmillan books are available at special discounts for bulk purchases for
sales promotions, premiums, fund-raising, or educational use. For details,
contact:

Special Sales Director
Macmillan Publishing Company
866 Third Avenue
New York, NY 10022

First Collier Books Edition 1993

10 9 8 7 6 5 4 3 2 1

Printed in the United States of America

Acknowledgments

FOR PERMISSION TO publish these writings of W. E. Burghardt Du Bois, acknowledgments are made and grateful appreciation extended to Mrs. Shirley Graham Du Bois. Any reprint or other use without her permission is unauthorized.

"Of Africa," "New Creed for American Negroes," and "Africa's Mighty Past" from *Dusk of Dawn*, copyright, 1940, by Harcourt Brace Jovanovich, Inc.; copyright, 1968, by Shirley Graham Du Bois. Reprinted by permission of the publisher.

"The Rape of Africa," "The Dark Workers of the World," and "On the Revolt of San Domingo" from *Black Folk—Then and Now* by W. E. Burghardt Du Bois. Copyright 1939 by Holt, Rinehart and Winston, Inc. Copyright © 1967 by W. E. Burghardt Du Bois. Reprinted by permission of Holt, Rinehart and Winston, Inc.

"The Present Economic Problem of the American Negro" is reprinted with the permission of *The National Baptist Voice*.

"Africa and America" is from *John Brown*, copyright 1962 by International Publishers. "American Negroes and Africa's Rise to Freedom," "Negroes and the Third World," and "China and Africa" are from *The World and Africa*, copyright 1965 by International Publishers Co., Inc. These are reprinted by permission of International Publishers Co., Inc.

"Realities in Africa" is reprinted by special permission from *Foreign Affairs*, July, 1943, copyright 1943 by the Council on Foreign Relations, Inc., New York.

"Pan-Africanism: A Mission in My Life" is reprinted with permission from the April 1955 issue of *United Asia*.

"Behold the Land!" appeared in Vol. 4, No. 1 (First Quarter) of *Freedomways*; "India's Relation to Negroes and the Color Problem" appeared in Vol. 5, No. 1; and "Africa and the French Revolution" in Vol. 1., No. 2. All are used by permission of *Freedomways*.

"Where Do We Go From Here" appeared in the May 20, 1933, issue of *Afro*, and is reprinted by permission of Afro-American Newspapers.

"Will the Church Remove the Color Line?" copyright 1931, Christian Century Foundation, is reprinted by permission from the December 9, 1931, issue of *The Christian Century*.

"The Negro in Literature and Art" is reprinted by permission from the September, 1913, issue of *The Annals* of the American Academy of Political and Social Science.

Reprinted by permission from the following issues of the *Guardian* are: "The Future of All Africa Lies in Socialism," December 22, 1958; "The Vast Miracle of China Today," June 8, 1959, and "The War to Preserve Slavery," February 15, 1960.

Used by permission from the following issues of *The Pittsburgh Courier* are: "A Negro Book-of-the-Year Club," August 15, 1936; "On Discussion" and "What Have You Read?" August 22, 1936.

I would also like to express my appreciation to the presidents of Negro colleges and universities, Fisk, Howard, and Talladega, for permission to use commencement addresses delivered at those institutions.

And to all those, too numerous to mention, who have in some way assisted or cooperated in this effort, my sincere thanks.

TO

THE MEMORY

OF

MY FATHER AND MOTHER

William Valentine—
Nellie Ann

Preface

A GREAT LIFE is likely to be misunderstood, yet its worth to humanity lies in understanding, and understanding can be accomplished only by a careful study of the life—a study of all the words, written and spoken, the thoughts, the ideas and ideals, the mannerisms and behaviorisms, as well as all that others may have thought of that life. In the case of William Edward Burghardt Du Bois, this task is rendered easier than in most cases, because as Dr. St. Clair Drake has said, "His was a life 'experimentally lived and self-documented'—a restless seeking, ever searching quest, a life journey which began in New England, carried him over the whole world, and ended—by his own choice—on the Guinea Coast." But in all this, above it all, he had his eyes on eternity —a profound perspective of posterity, a deep concern for what his life may mean to unborn generations.

Since his death in Africa in 1963, a growing interest has been manifested in his life and works, and the prospects of a thorough study and understanding of his life and philosophy seem ever more imminent. During 1968, the centenary of his birth, much was done to honor his memory and to revive his life and personality by presenting his works to the reading public. On his birthday, February 23, his autobiography was released by International Publishers. This work, *The Autobiography of W. E. B. Du Bois: A Soliloquy on Viewing My Life from the Last Decade of Its First Century*, was completed months before his death and is, therefore, more complete than his previous autobiography, *Dusk of Dawn: An Essay Toward an Autobiography of a Race Concept* (1940), a new edition of which was published by Schocken Books, who had also brought out a new 1967 edition of his *The Philadelphia Negro: A Social Study* (1899); and in 1969 the same publishers issued a new edition of his *Darkwater: Voices from Within the Veil* (1920).

In addition to the two autobiographical works above, there are three other items in this category: *W. E. B. Du Bois—A Recorded Autobiography*, interviewed by Moses Asch (1961), and published by Folkways Records and Service Corporation; and two autobiographical articles, "The Shadow of Years" in *Darkwater: Voices from Within the Veil*, and "My Evolving Program For Negro Freedom" in *What the Negro Wants*, edited by Rayford W. Logan, published by the University of North Carolina Press in 1944. These autobiographical works furnish a rather comprehensive and vivid interpretation of the man and the epoch of his life and labors—a concise and moving story of that life "experimentally lived and self-documented."

What have others thought of that life? Already, at least four book-length biographies have been published and a half dozen other works in which his life has received treatment of one or more chapters. And, of course, various phases of his life are subjects of numerous articles of journals, magazines and newspapers in this country and abroad. Of these biographical works, three are here recommended as positive contributions to an understanding of his life: *100 Years of Negro Freedom*, by Arna Bontemps, Dodd, Mead & Company, 1965; *His Day Is Marching On*, by Shirley Graham Du Bois, J. B. Lippincott Co., 1971; and *Cheer the Lonesome Traveler: The Life of W. E. B. Du Bois*, by Leslie Alexander Lacy, Dial Press, 1970.

Arna Bontemps, who introduces this work, is a product of the Negro Renaissance of the twenties and first came to the attention of the reading public through *The Crisis* literary contest conducted by Dr. Du Bois, then editor of the magazine. Mr. Bontemps' poem "Nocturne at Bethesda" won one of the poetry contests. In later years, Dr. Du Bois closed one of his lectures with stanzas from this poem of Mr. Bontemps',

referring to him as "our own poet, great, but little known."
In this work, *100 Years of Negro Freedom*, written to com-
morate the centennial of the Emancipation Proclamation,
the author devotes several chapters to the life of Du Bois,
as the predominate figure of that epoch of freedom. The
chapters on his boyhood and student days are revealing and
add significantly to our basic understanding of the man, his
times and his philosophy of life.

Shirley Graham Du Bois, his wife and great companion
during that last historical decade, knows more about him than
any other living person. Mrs. Du Bois' *His Day Is Marching
On* reflects the impact of his life on the young men and
women of her generation in America and in Africa. The work
must aid a more profound understanding of his life and philosophy. Leslie Alexander Lacy's *Cheer the Lonesome Traveler* is a work for children, and in this respect is a pioneer
effort. In this field more must be done generally, to cope with
the cultural ignorance of youth, inherited from their elders.
In addition to these, also recommended is *Black Titan:
W. E. B. Du Bois*, an anthology by the editors of *Freedomways*: John H. Clarke, Esther Jackson, Ernest Kaiser, and
J. H. O'Dell, Beacon Press, 1970. This is a collection of
articles and essays appreciative of the life and works of Dr.
Du Bois by writers and scholars whom his life influenced. It
is an enlargement of the special Du Bois memorial issue of
Freedomways (Winter 1965); also, it contains selections from
the writings of Du Bois.

A thorough study of autobiographical and biographical
works is not only necessary but imperative to an understanding of his life and philosophy. His life—the philosophy which
grew out of it—was formed during the last two decades of the
nineteenth century and the first two decades of the twentieth;
that philosophy was put to test during the third decade—the
depression years—and the result of that test, easily detected
within the pages of this work, is crucial for white and black
relations and the cultural development of the two peoples, in
America and in Africa.

Had white leaders accepted his invitation to study the
American Negro, had they cooperated with this effort, had

white and black leaders not opposed and obstructed his program for economic cooperation and cultural development
and solidarity for American Negroes, white and black relations would, perhaps, be infinitely better than they now are
because these relations would be based on intellectual and
moral growth and development and not on the absence of
such growth and development, so characteristically true today. Perhaps such thinking has not yet come to the minds
of many of these leaders, who have bent knees to the "God-
dess of Technology" and taken the long and fatal road down
to Vietnam! Yet the only relationship of human beings that
is abiding and satisfying is a relationship that is *human*. This
is the message of the life of William Edward Burghardt
Du Bois, and it is the message of that worldwide revolution
confronting mankind today. Mankind's problem is economic,
yet basically, it is an intellectual and moral problem which
can be solved only by an intellectual and moral approach.
Could the economic plight of the world's majority possibly
be what it is had man's relationship of the past not been predominantly *inhuman*—a relationship of slave-trading and
slavery, of lying and cheating, robbing, raping, murder and
lynching, and exploitation, prevalent to this day? Now, if
these negatives of humanity are sublimated with an over-
awing technology, if the basic relationship is not changed, are
we likely to have a securely happy people of *human beings
who are human?*

For this reason—because of the character and personality
his life represented—since his death in 1963, some writers
and enterprises that are "promoting" black history have been
inclined either to omit his name or to assign it a secondary
place; however, in no sense can the name be omitted or
assigned less than a prime position in the promotion of black
culture, and when this is not done, it should arouse suspicion
as to the motive which prompts the "promoting." But this
attitude cannot long mislead while his works are available to
the reading public.

This collection of essays, lectures, articles, notes and excerpts covers the span of his active life of seven decades and
has been compiled because of relevancy to the present scene.

It does not pretend to be a complete collection of this classi-
fication of his works, as such an undertaking would require
several volumes the size of the present one; however, the collection is highly representative of over a hundred such items.

When first conceived several years ago, it was to be simply
a collection of a half dozen or more commencement addresses
to Negro graduates—a book for youth. In its present expanded form it remains, primarily, a work for youth, but also
for the elders. There is essentially no generation gap between
youth and its elders; as a generation of youth has ever been
and always will be, in character and personality, what its
elders were before and what the elders have made it. While
there is no generation gap between younger and older blacks,
there is, however, a generation chasm, wide and deep, which
separates both groups from their glorious and living past; because of this, the character and personality of the elders is
mirrored in black youth today. This is the chasm this work
seeks to bridge, connecting all blacks with their living past,
and in so doing to galvanize them in that bond of ancient
African confraternity, which is the very essence of man's
existence and the method by which civilization moves forward. There can be no real separation of the generations which
is not at once fatal to our cultural development and survival.
Therefore, I have not hesitated to recommend it as a work
for all ages, especially for the black youth of America, to the
honor and glory of their elders—the fathers and mothers
whose toil and tears have made possible this Great Day of
Youth, that the fathers and mothers of today will make possible even a greater day for the oncoming generation.

Let black youth realize that the all-prevailing character
and personality of W. E. Burghardt Du Bois were based on
his relentless search for truth and the courage to express the
truth once he had found it; selflessness and sacrifice and
an abiding faith in and ceaseless effort for the uplift of the
masses of men. Let black youth embrace that character and
personality, and by example convey the message of his life
to all youth. With such character and personality, black
power could never mean solely the power of black people to
advance themselves; but rather power to be used in that great

crusade, that sustaining crusade, for humanity, for a higher humanity, embracing all mankind. This, after all, is the point of differentiation between black power and white power, for black power will never exploit an individual or a group of individuals simply because it has the knowledge or the power to do so, for its own advancement—and may it never have the greed to wish to do so. And just as W. E. Burghardt Du Bois was outspoken and forthright in his views, so black power could never adopt a strategy of deceit and conceit, of vindictiveness and revenge, or of a conspiracy of silence relative to the great and challenging issues of life.

This, his black power thesis, the product of his sterling character and dynamic personality, as set forth in this anthology, may not be the final word on the subject, but those who will think of it can ill afford not to consider his vast contribution. For this reason and in this spirit the work is presented to this generation and those to come.

In this sustained effort to understand his life and philosophy, collections of his writings already published and those to be published must be given due consideration. Outstanding in this class is the collection he himself compiled—*An ABC of Color: Selections from over a Half Century of the Writings of W. E. B. Du Bois* (1896-1958); this work of his was published the year of his death (1963) by the Seven Seas Publishers of East Berlin, Germany, and has since been issued in a new edition by International Publishers, New York. These are mostly excerpts from his writings rather than a complete text of articles, and are highly significant because they indicate the importance which he attached to certain of his expressions. Another excellent collection, *W. E. B. Du Bois—A Reader*, edited by Meyer Weinberg, was published early in 1970 by Harper & Row. Although bearing a like title, the present work represents altogether different material, except for several exceptions worthy of an encore; therefore, these two readers make useful companion volumes. Especially, will the articles on segregation and mixed and separate schools in this collection strengthen the arguments of the section on "Segregation versus Integration—Race Solidarity and

Economic Cooperation," in the present work. Yet another companion, with mostly different selections of (Du Bois') writings: *The Selected Writings of W. E. B. Du Bois*, edited by Walter Wilson with an Introduction by Stephen J. Wright, a Mentor book, The New American Library, Inc., 1970. This anthology contains chapters and passages from some of Du Bois' important books, as *The Philadelphia Negro, The Souls of Black Folk, John Brown, Darkwater, Black Reconstruction*, etc., and may prove to be an asset to the reader when these books are not readily available; the work also contains other writings, especially those of his later years. J. B. Lippincott is also the publisher of a volume of correspondence of W. E. B. Du Bois (up to 1934) edited by Herbert Aptheker. A second volume may be expected soon. Another important collection in two volumes recently off the press, *W. E. B. Du Bois Speaks: Speeches and Addresses*, Volume I, 1890–1919, and Volume II, 1920–1963, edited and with an Introduction by Dr. Philip S. Foner and a tribute by Dr. Martin Luther King, Jr., Pathfinder Press, 1970. Volume I has twenty-four selections, with several exceptions, not published in other collections. It is noteworthy for its introduction by the editor, Dr. Foner, who gives a fair and favorable appraisal of Dr. Du Bois, without straining to locate faults in his scholarship and personality, seemingly so characteristically true of some of the white writers who have undertaken to write of him.

To facilitate reading and reference, this anthology has been arranged in four major divisions: Afro-America, Africa, The Darker Races, and Youth: Afro-America and Africa. In the first division, "Afro-America," items are arranged as they treat of the African background, culture, history, literature and art, race pride, race solidarity and economic cooperation; under the second major division, "Africa," arrangement is in the order of African culture, colonialism and independence; in the third major division, "The Darker Races," are items dealing with the impact of the color line in the Americas, Africa and Asia; the fourth and final division,

"Youth: Afro-America and Africa" comprises mostly commencement addresses to Negro graduates, delivered to the all-black-segregated school system of Washington, D.C.—rated one of the best school systems of the country—and to the Negro colleges and universities of the South—Fisk, Howard, Johnson C. Smith, Dillard and Talladega College. In these commencement addresses the speaker consistently hammers on those guiding ideals of youth—truth and beauty, honesty and goodness, work and knowledge, selflessness and sacrifice, integrity—manhood and womanhood—and love for and interest in the uplift of the masses of the race. From reading these addresses, there can be no shadow of doubt of the speaker's sincere and abiding profound interest in youth, for these are masterpieces of logic and rhetoric designed to inspire to strive and to arouse to study, to thought and to action.

The fact that W. E. Burghardt Du Bois during his lifetime never spoke to Negro graduates at commencements in any of the northern schools (with their all-Negro student bodies but with white administrators, principals, and mostly white teachers) is highly significant—crucial in its implications for this generation and for the cultural, or human, development of black and white people in the United States. Had there been only these schools of the North, undoubtedly we would not have these his words of wisdom, inspiration and guidance for black youth today and tomorrow—the youth of Afro-America and Africa.

Finally, in his *The Souls of Black Folk* (1903) and *The Gift of Black Folk* (1924) the author opens and closes the works with the "Forethought" and "Afterthought," the "Prescript" and "Postscript." Use has been made of his invention in this collection of his writings. Du Bois opens the anthology with his words in the "Forethought" and closes it with the "Afterthought." Likewise, each grouping is introduced with a "Prescript" and closed with a "Postscript"—excerpts, more or less laconic passages, from his books and writings elsewhere. At times, these selections seem to strengthen the thesis of the group or enhance the spirit; generally, they are mildly but significantly critical, and in them, too, Du Bois is generally addressing his words to the two peoples: black—"Voices from Within the Veil," and white—"Voices from Without the Veil." But it matters not to whom he speaks; it is never unprofitable to listen—*carefully*—to what is said.

Chicago, Illinois   ANDREW G. PASCHAL
January, 1971

Contents

Introduction

ARNA BONTEMPS

THE YEARS W. E. B. Du Bois spent at Fisk University as an undergraduate left a lasting impression on him and on the college. This was clearly apparent when he returned to the campus in May of 1958 to celebrate the seventieth anniversary of his class's graduation and to receive belatedly the Phi Beta Kappa key his college had been unauthorized to grant him in his own time. In the course of academic rituals a moment became grave with memories.

Seventy years. Seventy-three years, to be exact!

He had come up the hill from the Nashville railroad station in a horsedrawn carriage with poetry on his lips and laughter in his eyes. An hour or two later a bell rang, and he joined the rush to the dining hall. Confronted there by a glorious girl, he suddenly lost his breath. Her name was Lena Calhoun, and we now know that she was the grandmother of Lena Horne. In any case, a decade later, after New York and Boston, Berlin and Paris, Du Bois still remembered her (as he confessed in one of his essays) as the most beautiful girl he had ever seen. Naturally, when he became editor of the school paper, she was one of the students he invited to submit a contribution. She consented, and in due time he published her first literary effort, an essay on the subject "Babies."

His college days, like the rest of his long life, are thoroughly, often delightfully, documented. If we cannot account for every golden day of that happy period, we can certainly account for every month. We know, for example, what a fearful bout he had with typhoid fever in the autumn of his first year and the nickname the students gave him when, pale and thin, he was able to get up and resume his activities. We know when he began to grow "burnsides" and something about the impression this made on his classmates.

And we can follow through his columns, his articles, stories, and editorials in the Fisk Herald, the awakening of his interests and the budding of his thought.

Oddly enough, the quality that stands out in his earliest writing is humor. He was a laughing boy, and he enjoyed nothing so much as poking fun. His column "Sharps and Flats," while it ran, was devoted to nothing else, and one discovers as a sidelight that even a joke told in dialect didn't bother him when the point it made was sharp and valid. In fact, one of the things Du Bois cherished in connection with his attendance at a Southern college after his New England upbringing was the exposure it gave him to the richness of Negro folk expression as well as folk experience. He treated it all gently, sometimes lovingly.

In his youth Du Bois formed the habit of celebrating his birthdays by writing little testimonials to himself, as it were. "I am striving to make my life all that life may be," he stated in one of these. If this strikes us as a trifle serious in one so young, so ostensibly carefree, we may wish to recall that he was born just three years after the Civil War, that the span of his life was itself a kind of documentary of the first *100 Years of Negro Freedom*, that these personal memos were in an odd sense annual reports on the rise and progress of his race in America. It was as if he watched the unfolding of a play within a play, the drama of his own career within the epic of his people.

It was as a college student, apparently, that he acquired his lifelong fondness for allegory as a literary form and became impressed with the power of the symbol. Time and again as a campus writer and later as editor of *The Crisis*, the files of these publications reveal, he produced in this genre pieces which never failed to make their point and some of which, as his posthumous *ABC of Color* shows, can stand very well as literature.

His use of the symbol, however, has little if anything to do with the so-called symbol-mongering of some schools of literary criticism. To him the symbol was a weapon of unmeasured capability in the nonviolent struggle against oppression. This was as true of the symbolic act as of the word. We don't have to be told what he wished to signify when he named the Niagara Movement, or when he selected Harpers Ferry as the place to hold its second and crucial meeting, and we may be equally sure that his use of the parable, the symbol, the allegory, though not always so obvious, not always explained, did not necessarily end with these. It may therefore be worth our time to read further.

References to life behind the Veil ran through Du Bois' early essays like a refrain, anticipating by more than half a century the serious and provocative point about the Negro's *invisibility* in American life that has intrigued the best of our younger writers in this present decade. His statement about the Negro's *two-ness*, growing out of the racial situation, is echoed today as *ambivalence* and treated by a younger generation of writers as a discovery, but it has not been stated more clearly than it was by Du Bois in the *Atlantic Monthly* in 1897.

His subsequent career is now history. His writings, covering the long span, are a treasure trove from which can be reclaimed nearly a century of penetrating insight and arresting statement. To disciples, such as the compiler of the *A W. E. B. Du Bois Reader*, Du Bois became a national resource to be excavated and mined somewhat as builders mined marble from the ruins of antiquity. Thus a part of the vital past is preserved.

Forethought

The Black Problem:—
"Voices from Within the Veil"—
Intellectual-Moral Training-Development

THE ASSUMPTIONS of the anti-segregation campaign have been all wrong. This is not our fault, but it is our misfortune. When I went to Atlanta to teach in 1897, and to study the Negro Problem, I said, confidently, that the basic problem is our racial ignorance and lack of culture. That once the Negroes know civilization, and the whites know Negroes, then the problem is solved. This proposition is still true, but the solution is much further away than my youth dreamed. Negroes are still ignorant, but the disconcerting thing is that white people on the whole are just as much opposed to Negroes of education and culture, as to any other kind, and perhaps more so. Not all whites, but the overwhelming majority.

Our method, then, falls flat. We stop training ability. We lose our manners. We swallow our pride, and we beg for things. We agitate and get angry. And with all that we face the blank fact: Negroes are not wanted; neither as scholars nor as business men; neither as clerks nor as artisans; neither as artists nor as writers. What can we do about it? We cannot enforce the law, even if we get them on the statute books. So long as overwhelming public sanction justifies and defends color segregation, we are helpless and without remedy. We are segregated. We are cast back upon ourselves.

W. E. Burghardt Du Bois in Defense of Negro Solidarity and Economic Cooperation in 1934, from *The Crisis* editorial "On Segregation."

The White Problem:—
"Voices from Without the Veil"—
Intellectual-Moral Thought and Action

When, now, a nation of reasonable human beings faces such a contradiction and paradox, the danger to their culture is great. The greater danger lies not in the so-called "problem" of race, but rather in the integrity of national thinking and the ethics of national conduct. Such a nation, if it persists in its logical contradictions, is bound to develop fools and hypocrites: fools, who in the presence of plain facts, cannot think straight; and hypocrites who in the face of clear duty, refuse to do the right thing and yet pretend to do it. . . .

What is going to become of a country which allows itself to fall into such an astonishing intellectual paradox? NOTHING BUT DISASTER! Intellectual and ethical disaster in some form must result unless immediately we compel the thought and conscience of America to face the facts of this so-called racial problem.

W. E. Burghardt Du Bois on Race Relations in the United States—1928, from "Race Relations in the United States," *The Annals of the American Academy of Political and Social Science,* November, 1928.

Selfishness Versus Humanity
The Problem of Humanity—
The "Voice of Voices"

There still persists among American Negroes the more or less clear idea that universal selfishness is going to be the salvation of the Negro race; that is, if every Negro gets all he can for himself, and makes the most of himself, the Negro problem is going to be settled. Such sublimated selfishness settles nothing, either for white people or black. In every successful scheme for the uplifting of men must come something of sacrifice and devotion. There is no other way. . . .

There is a feeling in the minds of many good people that civilization can only be saved through racial superiority. Thus, one must pick out the gifted races or gifted individuals and let them conduct human culture for their own benefit. Every attempt of this sort leads to disaster. There is no denying that we need the genius of unusually gifted persons, but we need this not simply for themselves or for such as approach them in ability; but for all people. There is no doubt but what races, who at definite times lead the world in accomplishment, can advance and preserve civilization. But again not simply for themselves, for all mankind. Because if science proves one thing, it is the fact that superior human gifts are never confined and made permanent in one family or one race. They vary inexplicably from person to person, and the genius which the world needs is just as apt to be found today among Hottentots and Papuans, among Indians and Negroes, as among French and Germans. All that is needed is opportunity and training. The object of culture, then, is this universal training, and the attempt to confine ability to one group by brute force is against nature.

From "A Forum of Fact and Opinion" in the *Pittsburgh Courier*, August 8, 1936.

PART ONE

Afro-America

I. *Africa and America—*
The African Background

Prescript
Who Made America? (1924)

WHO MADE AMERICA? Who made this land that swings its empire from the Atlantic to the Sea of Peace and from Snow to Fire—this realm of New Freedom, with Opportunity and Ideal unlimited?

Now that its foundations are laid, deep but bare, there are those as always who would forget the humble builders, toiling wan mornings and blazing noons, and picture America as the last reasoned blossom of mighty ancestors; of those great and glorious world builders and rulers who know and see and do all things forever and ever, amen! How singular and blind! For the glory of the world is the possibilities of the commonplace and America is America because it shows, as never before, the power of the common, ordinary, unlovely man. This is real democracy and not that vain and eternal striving to regard the world as the abiding place of exceptional genius with great black wastes of hereditary idiots.

We who know may not forget but must forever spread the splendid sordid truth that out of the most lowly and persecuted of men, Man made America. And what Man has here begun with all its want and imperfection, with all its magnificent promise and grotesque failure will some day blossom in the souls of the Lowly.

From the "Prescript" to *The Gift of Black Folk*, 1924, p. 33.

Of Africa—Autobiographical (1940)

What is Africa to me? Once I should have answered the
question simply: I should have said "fatherland" or perhaps
better "motherland" because I was born in the century when
the walls of race were clear and straight; when the world
consisted of mutually exclusive races; and even though the
edges might be blurred, there was no question of exact definition and understanding of the meaning of the word. One of
the first pamphlets I wrote in 1897 was on "The Conservation
of Races" wherein I set down as the first article of a proposed
racial creed: "We believe that the Negro people as a race
have a contribution to make to civilization and humanity
which no other race can make."

Since then the concept of race has so changed and presented so much of contradiction that as I face Africa I ask
myself: what is it between us that constitutes a tie which I
can feel better than I can explain? Africa is, of course, my
fatherland. Yet neither my father nor my father's father ever
saw Africa or knew its meaning or cared overmuch for it. My
mother's folk were closer and yet their direct connection, in
culture and race, became tenuous; still, my tie to Africa is
strong. On this vast continent were born and lived a large
portion of my direct ancestors going back a thousand years
or more. The mark of their heritage is upon me in color and
hair. These are obvious things, but of little meaning in themselves; only important as they stand for real and subtle differences from other men. Whether they do or not, I do not
know nor does science know today.

But one thing is sure and that is the fact that since the
fifteenth century these ancestors of mine and their other descendants have had a common history; have suffered a common disaster and have one long memory. The actual ties of
heritage between the individuals of this group vary with the
ancestors that they have in common and many others: Europeans and Semites, perhaps Mongolians, certainly American
Indians. But the physical bond is least and the badge of color

relatively unimportant save as a badge; the real essence of this kinship is its social heritage of slavery; the discrimination and insults; and this heritage binds together not simply the children of Africa, but extends through yellow Asia and into the South Seas. It is this unity that draws me to Africa.

When shall I forget the night I first set foot on African soil? I am the sixth generation in descent from forefathers who left this land. The moon was at the full and the waters of the Atlantic lay like a lake. All the long slow afternoon as the sun robed herself in her western scarlet with veils of misty cloud, I had seen Africa afar. Cape Mount—that mighty headland with its twin curves, northern sentinel of the realm of Liberia—gathered itself out of the cloud at half past three and then darkened and drew clear. On beyond flowed the dark low undulating land quaint with palm and breaking sea. The world grew black. Africa faded away, the stars stood forth curiously twisted—Orion in the zenith—the Little Bear asleep and the Southern Cross rising behind the horizon. Then afar, ahead, a lone light shone, straight at the ship's fore. Twinkling lights appeared below, around, and rising shadows. "Monrovia," said the Captain. . . .

Christmas Eve, and Africa is singing in Monrovia. They are Krus and Fantimen, women and children, and all the night they march and sing. The music was once the music of mission revival hymns. But it is that music now transformed and the silly words hidden in an unknown tongue—liquid and sonorous. It is tricked out and expounded with cadence and turn. And this is that same rhythm I heard first in Tennessee forty years ago: the air is raised and carried by men's string voices, while floating above in obligato, come the high mellow voices of women—it is the ancient African art of part singing, so curiously and insistently different.

So they come, gay appareled, lit by transparency. They enter the gate and flow over the high steps and sing and sing and sing. They saunter round the house, pick flowers, drink water and sing and sing and sing. The warm dark heat of the night steams up to meet the moon. And the night is song. . . .

As I look back and recall the days, which I have called

great—the occasions in which I have taken part and which
have had for me and others the widest significance, I can
remember none like the first of January, 1924. Once I took
my bachelor's degree before a governor, a great college president, and a bishop of New England. But that was rather
personal in its memory than in any way epochal. Once before
the assembled races of the world I was called upon to speak
in London in place of the suddenly sick Sir Harry Johnston.
It was a great hour. But it was not greater than the day when
I was presented to the President of the Negro Republic of
Liberia.

Liberia had been resting under the shock of world war into
which the Allies forced her. She had asked and been promised a loan by the United States to bolster and replace her
stricken trade. She had conformed to every preliminary requirement and waited when waiting was almost fatal. It was
not simply money, it was world prestige and protection at a
time when the little republic was sorely beset by creditors and
greedy imperial powers. At the last moment, an insurgent
Senate peremptorily and finally refused the request and the
strong recommendation of President Wilson and his advisers,
and the loan was refused. The Department of State made no
statement to the world, and Liberia stood naked, not only
well-nigh bankrupt, but peculiarly defenseless amid scowling
and unbelieving powers.

It was then that the United States made a gesture of courtesy; a little thing, and merely a gesture, but one so unusual
that it was epochal. President Coolidge, at the suggestion of
William H. Lewis, a leading colored lawyer of Boston, named
me, an American Negro traveler, Envoy Extraordinary and
Minister Plenipotentiary to Liberia—the highest rank ever
given by any country to a diplomatic agent in black Africa.
And it named this Envoy the special representative of the
President of the United States to the President of Liberia, on
the occasion of his inauguration; charging the Envoy with a
personal word of encouragement and moral support. It was a
significant action. It had in it nothing personal. Another ap-
pointee would have been equally significant. But Liberia rec-

ognized the meaning. She showered upon the Envoy every
mark of appreciation and thanks.

From "The Concept of Race" in *Dusk of Dawn,* 1940, pp.
116–23.

John Brown—Africa and America (1909)

"That it might be fulfilled which was spoken of the Lord by
the prophet saying, Out of Egypt have I called My son."

The mystic spell of Africa is and ever was over all America. It has guided her hardest work, inspired her finest literature, and sung her sweetest songs. Her greatest destiny—
unsensed and despised though it be—is to give back to the
first continents the gifts which Africa of old gave to America's fathers' fathers.

Of all inspiration which America owes to Africa, however,
the greatest by far is the score of heroic men whom the
sorrows of these dark children called to unselfish devotion
and heroic self-realization: Benezet, Garrison and Harriet
Stowe; Sumner, Douglass and Lincoln—these and others, but
above all, John Brown.

John Brown was a stalwart, rough-hewn man, mightily yet
tenderly carven. To his making went the stern justice of a
Cromwellian "Ironside," the freedom-loving fire of a Welsh
Celt, and the thrift of a Dutch housewife. And these very
things it was—thrift, freedom and justice—that early crossed
the unknown seas to find asylum in America. Yet they came
late, for before them came greed, and greed brought black
slaves from Africa.

The Negroes came on the heels, if not on the very ships of
Columbus. They followed De Soto to the Mississippi; saw
Virginia with D'Ayllon, Mexico with Cortez, Peru with
Pizarro; and led the western wanderings of Coronado in his
search for the Seven Cities of Cibola. Something more than a
decade after the Cavaliers, and a year before the Pilgrims,
they set lasting foot on the North American continent.

These black men came not of their own willing, but be-

cause the hasty greed of new America selfishly and half
thoughtlessly sought to revive in the New World the dying
but unforgotten custom of enslaving the world's workers. So
with the birth of wealth and liberty west of the seas, came
slavery, and a slavery all the more cruel and hideous because
it gradually built itself on a caste of race and color, thus
breaking the common bonds of human fellowship and weaving artificial barriers of birth and appearance.

The result was evil, as all injustice must be. At first the
black men writhed and struggled and died in their bonds, and
their blood reddened the paths across the Atlantic and around
the beautiful isles of the Western Indies. Then as the bonds
gripped them closer and closer, they succumbed to sullen
indifference or happy ignorance, with only here and there
flashes of wild red vengeance.

For, after all, these black men were but men, neither more
nor less wonderful than other men. In build and stature, they
were for the most part among the taller nations and sturdily
made. In their mental equipment and moral poise, they
showed themselves full brothers to all men—"intensely
human"; and this too in their very modifications and peculiarities—their warm brown and bronzed color and crisp curled
hair under the heat and wet of Africa; their sensuous enjoyment of the music and color of life; their instinct for barter
and trade; their strong family life and government. Yet these
characteristics were bruised and spoiled and misinterpreted in
the rude uprooting of the slave trade and the sudden trans-
plantation of this race to other climes, among other peoples.
Their color became a badge of servitude, their tropical habit
was deemed laziness, their worship was thought heathenish,
their family customs and government were ruthlessly over-
turned and debauched; many of their virtues became vices,
and much of their vice, virtue.

The price of repression is greater than the cost of liberty.
The degradation of men costs something to the degraded
and those who degrade. While the Negro slaves sank to list-
less docility and vacant ignorance, their masters found themselves whirled in the eddies of mighty movements: their system of slavery was twisting them backwards toward darker

ages of force and caste and cruelty, while forward swirled swift currents of liberty and uplift.

They still felt the impulse of the wonderful awakening of culture from its barbaric sleep of centuries which men call the Renaissance; they were own children of the mighty stirring of Europe's conscience which we call the Reformation; and they and their children were to be prime actors in laying the foundations of human liberty in a new century and a new land. Already the birth pains of the new freedom were felt in that land. Old Europe was begetting in the new continent a vast longing for spiritual space. So there was builded into America the thrift of the searchers of wealth, the freedom of the Renaissance and the stern morality of the Reformation.

Three lands typified these three things which time planted in the New World: England sent Puritanism, the last white flower of the Lutheran revolt; Holland sent the new vigor and thrift of the Renaissance; while Celtic lands and bits of lands, like France and Ireland and Wales, sent the passionate desire for personal freedom. These three elements came, and came more often than not in the guise of humble men—an English carpenter on the *Mayflower*, an Amsterdam tailor seeking a new ancestral city, and a Welsh wanderer. From three such men sprang in the marriage of years, John Brown.

To the unraveling of human tangles we would gladly believe that God sends special men—chosen vessels which come to the world's deliverance. And what could be more fitting than the human embodiment of freedom, Puritanism and trade—the great new currents sweeping across the back eddies of slavery, should give birth to a man who in years to come pointed the way to liberty and realized that the cost of liberty was less than the price of repression? So it was. In bleak December, 1620, a carpenter and weaver landed at Plymouth—Peter and John Brown. This carpenter Peter came of goodly stock, possibly, though not surely, from that very John Brown of the early sixteenth century whom bluff King Henry VIII of England burned for his Puritanism, and whose son was all too near the same fate. Thirty years after Peter Brown had landed, came the Welshman, John Owen, to Windsor, Conn., to help in the building of that commonwealth, and near him settled Peter Mills, the tailor of Holland. The great-grandson of Peter Brown, born in Connecticut in 1700, had for a son a Revolutionary soldier, who married one of the Welshman's grandchildren and had in turn a son, Owen Brown, the father of John Brown, in February of 1771. This Owen Brown a neighbor remembers "very distinctly, and that he was very much respected and esteemed by my father. He was an earnestly devout and religious man, of the old Connecticut fashion; and one peculiarity of his impressed his name and person indelibly upon my memory: he was an inveterate and most painful stammerer—the first specimen of that infirmity that I had ever seen, and, according to my recollection, the worst that I had ever known to this day. Consequently, though we removed from Hudson to another settlement early in the summer of 1807, and returned to Connecticut in 1812, so that I rarely saw any of that family afterward, I have never to this day seen a man struggling and half strangled with a word stuck to his throat, without remembering good Mr. Owen Brown, who could not speak without stammering, except in prayer."

In 1800, May 9th, wrote this Owen Brown: "John was born, one hundred years after his great-grandfather. Nothing else very uncommon."

From *John Brown*, 1909, pp. 15–20

On the Revolt of San Domingo (Toussaint L'Ouverture) (1939)

Not only did the scourge of fever increase but signs of distrust and rebellion multiplied among the blacks. The news of restored slavery in Martinique and Guadeloupe leaked out. "No general of an army has ever been in such an unfavorable situation. The troops which arrived last month have ceased to exist. The rebels are attacking the valley every day; they open fire, which can be heard in Le Cap. It is impossible for me to defend myself; my regiments have diminished, and I have no means for carrying on the defence or for utilizing the

advantages which they offer me." (Vinogradov, The Black
Consul, p. 213).

The tom-toms rolled darkly in the hills. By September the
revolt was in full sway. Even the mulattoes deserted the
French. Earlier in the spring of the same year Toussaint
died or was murdered at Fort Joux. He had not been allowed
the services of a physician because as his jailor explained,
"The health of Negroes is in no way similar to the health of
Europeans." After studied humiliations and deprivation he
was found dead April seventh.

Thus perished the greatest of American Negroes and one
of the great men of all time, at the age of fifty-six. A French
Planter said, "God in his terrestrial globe did not commune
with a purer spirit." Wendell Phillips said, "You think me a
fanatic, for you read history, not with your eyes, but with
your prejudices. But fifty years hence, when Truth gets a
hearing, the Muse of history will put Phocion for the Greek,
Brutus for the Roman, Hampden for the English, La Fayette
for France; choose Washington as the bright consummate
flower of our earliest civilization; and then, dipping her pen
in the sunlight, will write in the clear blue, above them all,
the name of the soldier, the statesman, the martyr, Toussaint
L'Ouverture."

Sonthonax, a wily Jacobin, who knew him, said, "Toussaint is the real leader of the Negroes, and the white inhabitants, who have been conciliated, regard him as a friend.
Sometimes I feel that this fanatic man is inflamed with an
unquenchable fire of love for humanity." Wordsworth wrote:

> There's not a breathing of the common wind
> That will forget thee: Thou hast great allies;
> Thy friends are exultations, agonies,
> And love, and Man's unconquerable mind.

In 1802 and 1803 nearly forty thousand French soldiers
died of war and fever. Leclerc himself died in November,
1803. Rochambeau succeeded to his command and was
promised soldiers by Napoleon; but already in May, 1803,
Great Britain started a new war with France and communica-

tion between France and San Domingo was impossible. The
black insurgents held the land; the British held the Sea. In
November, 1803, Rochambeau surrendered and white authority died in San Domingo forever.

The effect of all this was far-reaching. Napoleon gave up
his dream of an American empire and sold La. for a song.
"Thus all of the Indian Territory, all of Kansas and Ne-
braska, Iowa and Wyoming, Montana and the Dakotas, and
most of Colorado and Minnesota and all of Washington and
Oregon States, came to us as the indirect work of a despised
Negro.

"Praise, if you will, the work of Robert Livingstone or a
Jefferson, but today let us not forget our debt to Toussaint
L'Ouverture, who was indirectly the means of America's ex-
pansion by the Louisiana Purchase of 1803."

From *Black Folk—Then and Now*, 1939, pp. 175–76

American Negroes and Africa's Rise to Freedom (1958)

In the United States in 1860 there were some 17,000,000
persons of African descent. In the eighteenth century they
had regarded Africa as their home to which they would eventually return when free. They named their institutions "African" and started migration to Africa as early as 1815. But the
American Negroes were soon sadly disillusioned: first their
immigrants to Liberia found that Africans did not regard
them as Africans; and then it became clear by 1830 that
colonization schemes were a device to rid America of free
Africans so as to fasten slavery more firmly to support the
Cotton Kingdom.

Negroes therefore slowly turned to a new ideal: to strive
for equality as American citizens, determined that when Africa needed them they would be equipped to lead them into
civilization. Meantime, however, American Negroes learned
from their environment to think less and less of their fatherland and its folk. They learned little of its history or its

present conditions. They began to despise the colored races along with the white Americans and to acquiesce in color prejudice.

From 1825 to 1860 the American Negro went through hell. He yelled in desperation as the slave power tried to make the whole union a slave nation and then to extend its power over the West Indies; he became the backbone of the abolition movement; he led thousands of fugitives to freedom; he died with John Brown and made the North victorious in the Civil War. For a few years he led democracy in the South until a new and powerful capitalism disfranchised him by 1876.

Meantime a great change was sweeping the earth. Socialism was spreading; first in theory and experiment for a half century and then at last in 1917 in Russia where a communist state was founded. The world was startled and frightened. The United States joined 16 other nations to prevent this experiment which all wise men said would fail miserably in a short time. But it did not fail. It defended its right to try a new life, and staggered on slowly but surely began to prove to all who would look that communism could exist and prosper.

What effect did this have on American Negroes? By this time their leaders had become patriotic Americans, imitating white Americans without criticism. If Americans said that communism had failed, then it had failed. And this of course Americans did say and repeat. Big business declared communism a crime and communists and socialists criminals. Some Americans and some Negroes did not believe this; but they lost employment or went to jail.

Meantime, many thoughtful white Americans, fearing the advance of socialism and communism not only in Europe but in America under the "New Deal," conceived a new tack. They said the American color line cannot be held in the face of communism. It is quite possible that we can help beat communism if in America we begin to loosen if not break the color line.

The movement started and culminated in a Supreme Court

decision which was a body blow to color discrimination, and certainly if enforced would take the wind out of the sails of critics of American democracy.

To Negroes the government said, it will be a fine thing now if you tell foreigners that our Negro problem is settled; and in such case we can help with your expenses of travel. A remarkable number of Negroes of education and standing found themselves able to travel and testify that American Negroes now had no complaints.

Then came three disturbing facts: (1) The Soviet Union was forging ahead in education and science and it drew no color line. (2) Outside the Soviet Union, in England, France and all West Europe, especially Scandinavia, socialism was spreading: state housing, state ownership of railroads, telegraphs and telephones, subways, buses and other public facilities; social medicine, higher education, old age care, insurance and many other sorts of relief; even in the United States, the New Deal was socialism no matter what it was called. (3) The former slave South had no intention of obeying the Supreme Court. To the Bourbon South it was said: don't worry, the law will not be enforced for a decade if not a century. Most Negroes still cannot vote, their schools are poor and the black workers are exploited, diseased and at the bottom of the economic pile. Trade unions north as well as south still discriminate against black labor. But finally a new and astonishing event was the sudden rise of Africa.

My own study had for a long time turned toward Africa. I planned a series of charts in 1900 for the Paris Exposition, which gained a Grand Prize. I attended a Pan-African conference in London and was made secretary of the meeting and drafted its resolutions.

In 1911 the Ethical Culture Societies of the world called a races congress in London and made Felix Adler and me secretaries for America. In 1915 I published my first book on African history and there was much interest and discussion. In 1919 I planned a Pan-African Congress, but got little support. Blaise Diagne of Senegal, whose volunteers had saved France from the first on-slaughter of the Germans in World War I, induced Clemenceau to allow the Congress despite the opposition of the United States and Britain. It was a small meeting, but it aroused a West African Congress the next year which was the beginning of independence of Ghana and Nigeria.

In 1921 I called a second Pan-African Congress to meet in London, Paris and Brussels. This proved a large and influential meeting, with delegates from the whole Negro world. The wide publicity it gained led to the organization of congresses in many parts of Africa by the natives. Our attempt to form a permanent organization located in Paris was betrayed but I succeeded in assembling a small meeting in London and Lisbon in 1923. I tried a fourth congress in Tunis but France forbade it. At last in 1927 I called the Fourth Pan-African Congress in New York. It was fairly well attended by American Negroes but few Africans. Then the Second World War approached and the work was interrupted.

Meanwhile methods changed and ideas expanded. Africans themselves began to demand more voice in colonial government and the Second World War had made their cooperation so necessary to Europe that at the end actual and unexpected freedom for African colonies was in sight.

Moreover there miraculously appeared Africans able to take charge of these governments. American Negroes of former generations had always calculated that when Africa was ready for freedom, American Negroes would be ready to lead them. But the event was quite opposite. The African leaders proved to be Africans, some indeed educated in the United States, but most of them trained in Europe and in Africa itself. American Negroes for the most part showed neither the education nor the aptitude for the magnificent opportunity which was suddenly offered. Indeed, it now seems that Africans may have to show American Negroes the way to freedom.

The rise of Africa in the last 15 years has astonished the world. Even the most doubting of American Negroes have suddenly become aware of Africa and its possibilities and particularly of the relation of Africa to the American Negro. The first reaction was typically American. Since 1910 American Negroes had been fighting for equal opportunity in the

United States. Indeed, Negroes soon faced a curious paradox.

Now equality began to be offered; but in return for equality, Negroes must join American business in its domination of African cheap labor and free raw materials. The educated and well-to-do Negroes would have a better chance to make money if they would testify that Negroes were not discriminated against and join in American red-baiting.

American Negroes began to appear in Africa, seeking chances to make money and testifying to Negro progress. In many cases their expenses were paid by the State Department. Meantime Negro American colleges ceased to teach socialism and the Negro masses believed with the white masses that communism is a crime and all socialists conspirators.

Africans know better. They have not yet all made up their minds what side to take in the power contest between East and West but they recognize the accomplishments of the Soviet Union and the rise of China.

Meantime American Negroes in their segregated schools and with lack of leadership have no idea of this world trend. The effort to give them equality has been over-emphasized and some of our best scholars and civil servants have been bribed by the State Department to testify abroad and especially in Africa to the success of capitalism in making the American Negro free. Yet it was British capitalism which made the African slave trade the greatest commercial venture in the world; and it was American slavery that raised capitalism to its domination in the nineteenth century and gave birth to the Sugar Empire and the Cotton Kingdom. It was new capitalism which nullified Abolition and keeps us in serfdom.

The Africans know this. They have in many cases lived in America. They have in other cases been educated in the Soviet Union and even in China. They will make up their minds on communism and not listen solely to American lies. The latest voice to reach them is from Cuba.

Would it not be wise for American Negroes themselves to read a few books and do a little thinking for themselves? It is not that I would persuade Negroes to become communists, capitalists or holy rollers; but whatever belief they reach, let it for God's sake be a matter of reason and not of ignorance, fear, and selling their souls to the devil.

From *The World and Africa*, 1965, pp. 334–38

Postscript
Negroes and the Third World (1961)

. . . they [Negroes] are advancing rapidly today and it is clear that they have a chance to trade wide breaks in the American color line for acquiescence in American and Western European control of the world's colored peoples. This is shown by the pressure on them to keep silence on Africa and Asia and on white working class movements, and in return accept more power to vote, abolition of separation in education, dropping of "jim crow" units in our military forces and gradual disappearance of the Negro ghetto in work and housing. . . . It is fair to admit that most Negroes, even those of intelligence and courage, do not fully realize that they are being bribed to trade equal status in the United States for the slavery of the majority of men. When this is clear, especially to black youth, the race must be aroused to thought and action and will see that the price asked for their cooperation is far higher than need be paid, since race and color equality is bound to come in any event.

From *The World and Africa*, 1965, pp. 267–68, originally published in the *Guardian*, 1961.

II. Black Culture—"The Black Power Concept"—"A Negro Self-Sufficient Culture in America"

Prescript
The "Gift of the Spirit" (1903 and 1924)

WE THE DARKER ones come even now not altogether empty-handed: there are today no truer exponents of the pure human spirit of the Declaration of Independence than the American Negroes; there is no true American music but the wild sweet melodies of the Negro Slave; the American fairy tales and folk-lore are Indian and African; and, all in all, we black men seem the sole oasis of simple faith and reverence in a dusty desert of dollars and smartness. Will America be poorer if she replace her brutal dyspeptic blundering with light-hearted but determined Negro humility? or her coarse and cruel wit with loving jovial good-humor? or her vulgar music with the soul of the Sorrow Songs?

Merely a concrete test of the underlying principles of the great republic is the Negro Problem, and the spiritual striving of the freedmen's sons is the travail of souls whose burden is almost beyond the measure of their strength, but who bear it in the name of an historic race, in the name of this the land of their fathers' fathers, and in the name of human opportunity.

From "Of Our Spiritual Strivings" in *The Souls of Black Folk*, 1903, pp. 11–12

THIS THEN IS the Gift of Black Folk to the new World. Thus in singular and fine sense the slave became master, the bond servant became free and the meek not only inherited the earth but made that heritage a thing of questing for eternal youth, of fruitful labor, of joy and music, of the free spirit and of the ministering hand, of wide and poignant sympathy with men in their struggle to live and love which is, after all, the end of being.

From "The Gift of the Spirit" in *The Gift of Black Folk,* 1924, p. 340

The Conservation of Races (1897)

The American Negro has always felt an intense personal interest in discussions as to the origins and destinies of races: primarily because back of most discussions of race with which he is familiar, have lurked certain assumptions as to his natural abilities, as to his political, intellectual and moral status, which he felt were wrong. He has, consequently, been led to deprecate and minimize race distinctions, to believe intensely that out of one blood God created all nations, and to speak of human brotherhood as though it were the possibility of an already dawning tomorrow.

Nevertheless, in our calmer moments we must acknowledge that human beings are divided into races; that in this country the two most extreme types of the world's races have met, and the resulting problems as to the future relations of these types are not only of intense and living interest to us, but form an epoch in the history of mankind.

It is necessary, therefore, in planning our movements, in guiding our future development, that at times we rise above the pressing, but smaller questions of separate schools and cars, wage-discrimination and lynch law, to survey the whole question of race in human philosophy and to lay, on a basis of broad knowledge and careful insight, those large lines of policy and higher ideals which may form our guiding lines and boundaries in the practical difficulties of every day. For it is certain that all human striving, no matter how intense and earnest, which is against the constitution of the world, is vain. The question, then, which we must seriously consider is this: What is the real meaning of Race; what has, in the past, been the law of race development, and what lessons has the past history of race development to teach the rising Negro people?

When we thus come to inquire into the essential difference of races we find it hard to come at once to any definite conclusion. Many criteria of race differences have in the past been proposed, as color, hair, cranial measurements and language. And manifestly, in each of these respects, human beings differ widely. They vary in color, for instance, from the marble-like pallor of the Scandinavian to the rich, dark brown of the Zulu, passing by the creamy Slav, the yellow Chinese, the light brown Sicilian and the brown Egyptian. Men vary, too, in the texture of hair from the obstinately straight hair of the Chinese to the obstinately tufted and frizzled hair of the Bushman. In measurement of heads, again, men vary; from the broad-headed Tartar to the medium-headed European and the narrow-headed Hottentot; or, again in language, from the highly-inflected Roman tongue to the monosyllabic Chinese. All these physical characteristics are patent enough, and if they agreed with each other it would be very easy to classify mankind. Unfortunately for scientists, however, these criteria of race are most exasperatingly intermingled. Color does not agree with texture of hair, for many of the dark races have straight hair; nor does color agree with the breadth of the head, for the yellow Tartar has a broader head than the German; nor, again, has the science of language as yet succeeded in clearing up the relative authority of these various and contradictory criteria. The final word of science, so far, is that we have at least two, perhaps three, great families of human beings— the whites and Negroes, possibly the yellow race; and that other races have arisen from the intermingling of the blood of these two. This broad division of the world's races which men like Huxley and Raetzel have introduced as more nearly true than the old five-race scheme of Blumenbach, is nothing more than an acknowledgment that, so far as purely physical characteristics are concerned, the differences between men do not explain all the differences of their history. It declares, as Darwin himself said, that great as is the physical unlikeness of the various races of men their likenesses are greater, and upon this rests the whole scientific doctrine of Human Brotherhood.

Although the wonderful developments of human history teach that the grosser physical differences of color, hair and bone go but a short way toward explaining the different roles which groups of men have played in Human Progress, yet there are differences—subtle, delicate and elusive, though they may be—which have silently but definitely separated men into groups. While these subtle forces have generally followed the natural cleavage of common blood, descent and physical peculiarities, they have at other times swept across and ignored these. At all times, however, they have divided human beings into races, which, while they perhaps transcend scientific definition, nevertheless, are clearly defined to the eye of the Historian and Sociologist.

If this be true, then the history of the world is the history, not of individuals, but of groups, not of nations, but of races, and he who ignores or seeks to override the race idea in human history ignores and overrides the central thought of all history. What, then, is a race? It is a vast family of human beings, generally of common blood and language, always of common history, traditions and impulses, who are both voluntarily and involuntarily striving together for the accomplishment of certain more or less vividly conceived ideals of life.

Turning to real history, there can be no doubt, first, as to the wide-spread, nay, universal, prevalence of the race idea, the race spirit, the race ideal, and as to its efficiency as the vastest and most ingenious invention for human progress. We, who have been reared and trained under the individualistic philosophy of the Declaration of Independence and the laissez-faire philosophy of Adam Smith, are loath to see and loath to acknowledge this patent fact of human history. We see the Pharaohs, Caesars, Toussaints and Napoleons of history and forget the vast races of which they were but epitomized expressions. We are apt to think in our American impatience, that while it may have been in conglomerate America *nous avons changé tout cela*—we have changed all that, and have no need of this ancient instrument of progress. This assumption of which the Negro people are especially fond, can not be established by a careful consideration of history.

We find upon the world's stage today eight distinctly differentiated races, in the sense in which History tells us the word must be used. They are, the Slavs of Eastern Europe, the Teutons of middle Europe, the English of Great Britain and America, the Romance nations of Southern and Western Europe, the Negroes of Africa and America, the Semitic people of Western Asia and Northern Africa, the Hindoos of Central Asia and the Mongolians of Eastern Asia. There are, of course, other minor race groups, as the American Indians, the Esquimaux and the South Sea Islanders; these larger races, too, are far from homogeneous; the Slav includes the Czech, the Magyar, the Pole and the Russian; the Teuton includes the German, the Scandinavian and the Dutch; the English include the Scotch, the Irish and the conglomerate American. Under the Romance nations the widely-differing Frenchman, Italian, Sicilian and Spaniard are comprehended. The term Negro is, perhaps, the most indefinite of all, combining the Mulattoes and Zamboes of America and the Egyptians, Bantus and Bushmen of Africa. Among the Hindoos are traces of widely differing nations, while the great Chinese, Tartar, Korean and Japanese families fall under the one designation—Mongolian.

The question now is: What is the real distinction between these nations? Is it the physical differences of blood, color and cranial measurements? Certainly we must all acknowledge that physical differences play a great part, and that, with wide exceptions and qualifications, these eight great races of to-day follow the cleavage of physical race distinctions; the English and Teuton represent the white variety of mankind; the Mongolian, the yellow; the Negroes, the black. Between these are many crosses and mixtures, where Mongolian and Teuton have blended into the Slav, and other mixtures have produced the Romance nations and the Semites. But while race differences have followed mainly physical race lines, yet no mere physical distinctions would really define or explain the deeper differences—the cohesiveness and continuity of these groups. The deeper differences are spiritual, psychical, differences—undoubtedly based on the physical, but infinitely transcending them. The forces that bind together the Teuton nations are, then, first, their race identity and common blood; secondly, and more important, a common history, common laws and religion, similar habits of thought and a conscious striving together for certain ideals of life. The whole process which has brought about these race differentiations has been a growth, and the great characteristic of this growth has been the differentiation of spiritual and mental differences between great races of mankind and the integration of physical differences.

The age of nomadic tribes of closely related individuals represents the maximum of physical differences. They were practically vast families, and there were as many groups as families. As the families came together to form cities the physical differences lessened, purity of blood was replaced by the requirement of domicile, and all who lived within the city bounds became gradually to be regarded as members of the group; i.e., there was a slight and slow breaking down of physical barriers. This, however, was accompanied by an increase of the spiritual and social differences between cities. This city became husbandmen, this, merchants, another warriors, and so on. The *ideals of life* for which the different cities struggled were different. When at last cities began to coalesce into nations there was another breaking down of barriers which separated groups of men. The larger and broader differences of color, hair and physical proportions were not by any means ignored, but myriads of minor differences disappeared, and the sociological and historical races of men began to approximate the present division of races as indicated by physical researches. At the same time the spiritual and physical differences of race groups which constituted the nations became deep and decisive. The English nation stood for constitutional liberty and commercial freedom; the German nation for science and philosophy; the Romance nations stood for literature and art, and the other race groups are striving, each in its own way, to develop for civilization its particular message, its particular ideal, which shall help to guide the world nearer and nearer that perfection of human life for which we all long, that "one far off Divine event."

This has been the function of race differences up to the present time. What shall be its function in the future? Manifestly some of the great races of today—particularly the Negro race—have not yet given to civilization the full spiritual message which they are capable of giving. I will not say that the Negro race has as yet given no message to the world, for it is still a mooted question among scientists as to just how far Egyptian civilization was Negro in its origin; if it was not wholly Negro, it was certainly very closely allied. Be that as it may, however the fact still remains that the full, complete Negro message of the whole Negro race has not as yet been given to the world: that the messages and ideal of the yellow race have not been completed, and that the striving of the mighty Slavs has but begun. The question is, then: How shall this message be delivered; how shall these various ideals be realized? The answer is plain: By the development of these race groups, not as individuals, but as races. For the development of Japanese genius, Japanese literature and art, Japanese spirit, only Japanese, bound and welded together, Japanese inspired by one vast ideal, can work out in its fullness the wonderful message which Japan has for the nations of the earth. For the development of Negro genius, of Negro literature and art, of Negro spirit, only Negroes bound and welded together, Negroes inspired by one vast ideal, can work out in its fullness the great message we have for humanity. We cannot reverse history; we are subject to the same natural laws as other races, and if the Negro is ever to be a factor in the world's history—if among the gaily-colored banners that deck the broad ramparts of civilization is to hang one uncompromising black, then it must be placed there by black hands, fashioned by black heads and hallowed by the travail of 200,000,000 black hearts beating in one glad song of jubilee.

For this reason, the advance guard of the Negro people—the 8,000,000 people of Negro blood in the United States of America—must soon come to realize that if they are to take their just place in the van of Pan-Negroism, then their destiny is *not* absorption by the white Americans. That if in America it is to be proven for the first time in the modern world that not only Negroes are capable of evolving individual men like Toussaint, the Saviour, but a nation stored with wonderful possibilities of culture, then their destiny is not a servile imitation of Anglo-Saxon culture, but a stalwart originality which shall unswervingly follow Negro ideals.

It may, however, be objected here that the situation of our race in America renders this attitude impossible; that our sole hope of salvation lies in our being able to lose our race identity in the commingled blood of the nation; and that any other course would merely increase the friction of the races which we call race prejudice, and against which we have so long and so earnestly fought.

Here, then, is the dilemma, and it is a puzzling one, I admit. No Negro who has given earnest thought to the situation of his people in America has failed, at some time in life, to find himself at these cross-roads; has failed to ask himself at some time: What, after all, am I? Am I an American or am I a Negro? Can I be both? Or is it my duty to cease to be a Negro as soon as possible and be an American? If I strive as a Negro, am I not perpetuating the very cleft that threatens and separates Black and White America? Is not my only possible practical aim the subduction of all that is Negro in me to the American? Does my black blood place upon me any more obligation to assert my nationality than German or Irish or Italian blood would?

It is such incessant self-questioning and the hesitation that arises from it, that is making the present period a time of vacillation and contradiction for the American Negro; combined race action is stifled, race responsibility is shirked, race enterprises languish, and the best blood, the best talent, the best energy of the Negro people cannot be marshalled to do the bidding of the race. They stand back to make room for every rascal and demagogue who chooses to cloak his selfish deviltry under the veil of race pride.

Is this right? Is it rational? Is it good policy? Have we in America a distinct mission as a race—a distinct sphere of action and an opportunity for race development, or is self-obliteration the highest end to which Negro blood dare aspire?

If we carefully consider what race prejudice really is, we find it, historically, to be nothing but friction between different groups of people; it is the difference in aim, in feeling, in ideals of two different races; if, now, this difference exists touching territory, laws, language, or even religion, it is manifest that these people cannot live in the same territory without fatal collision; but if, on the other hand, there is substantial agreement in laws, language and religion; if there is a satisfactory adjustment of economic life, then there is no reason why, in the same country and on the same street, two or three great national ideals might not strive together for their race ideals as well, perhaps even better, than in isolation. Here, it seems to me, is the reading of the riddle that puzzles so many of us. We are Americans, not only by birth and by citizenship, but by our political ideals, our language, our religion. Farther than that, our Americanism does not go. At that point, we are Negroes, members of a vast historic race that from the very dawn of creation has slept, but half awakening in the dark forests of its African fatherland. We are the first fruits of this new nation, the harbinger of that black tomorrow which is yet destined to soften the whiteness of the Teutonic to-day. We are the people whose subtle sense of song has given America music, its only American fairy tales, its only touch of pathos and humor amid its mad money-getting plutocracy. As such, it is our duty to conserve our physical powers, our intellectual endowments, our spiritual ideals; as a race we must strive by race organization, by race solidarity, by race unity to the realization of that broader humanity which freely recognizes differences in men, but sternly deprecates inequality in their opportunities of development.

For the accomplishment of these ends we need race organizations: Negro colleges, Negro newspapers, Negro business organizations, a Negro school of literature and art, and an intellectual clearing house, for all these products of the Negro mind, which we may call a Negro Academy. Not only is all this necessary for positive advance, it is absolutely imperative for negative defense. Let us not deceive ourselves at our situation in this country. Weighted with a heritage of moral iniquity from our past history, hard pressed in the economic world by foreign immigrants and native prejudice, hated here, despised there and pitied everywhere; our one haven of refuge is ourselves, and but one means of advance, our own belief in our great destiny, our own implicit trust in our ability and worth. There is no power under God's high heaven that can stop the advance of eight thousand thousand honest, earnest, inspired and united people. But—and here is the rub—they *must* be honest, fearlessly criticizing their own faults, zealously correcting them; they *must* be *earnest*. No people that laughs at itself, and ridicules itself, and wishes to God it was anything but itself ever wrote its name in history; it *must* be inspired with the Divine faith of our black mothers, that out of the blood and dust of battle will march a victorious host, a mighty nation, a peculiar people, to speak to the nations of earth a Divine truth that shall make them free. And such a people must be united; not merely united for the organized theft of political spoils, not united to disgrace religion with whoremongers and wardheelers; not united merely to protest and pass resolutions, but united to stop the ravages of consumption among the Negro people, united to keep black boys from loafing, gambling and crime; united to guard the purity of black women and to reduce that vast army of black prostitutes that is today marching to hell; and united in serious organizations, to determine by careful conference and thoughtful interchange of opinion the broad lines of policy and action for the American Negro.

This, is the reason for being which the American Negro Academy has. It aims at once to be the epitome and expression of the intellect of the black-blooded people of America, the exponent of the race ideals of one of the world's great races. As such, the Academy must, if successful, be

(a) Representative in character.
(b) Impartial in conduct.
(c) Firm in leadership.

It must be representative in character; not in that it represents all interests or all factions, but in that it seeks to comprise something of the *best* thought, the most unselfish striving and the highest ideals. There are scattered in forgotten nooks and corners throughout the land, Negroes of some considerable training, of high minds, and high motives, who are unknown to their fellows, who exert far too little influence. These the Negro Academy should strive to bring into touch with each other and to give them a common mouthpiece.

The Academy should be impartial in conduct; while it aims to exalt the people it should aim to do so by truth—not by lies, by honesty—not by flattery. It should continually impress the fact upon the Negro people that they must not expect to have things done for them—they *must do for themselves*; that they have on their hands a vast work of self-reformation to do, and that a little less complaint and whining, and a little more dogged work and manly striving would do us more credit and benefit than a thousand Force or Civil Rights bills.

Finally, the American Negro Academy must point out a practical path of advance to the Negro people; there lie before every Negro today hundreds of questions of policy and right which must be settled and which each one settles now, not in accordance with any rule, but by impulse or individual preference; for instance: What should be the attitude of Negroes toward the educational qualification for voters? What should be our attitude toward separate schools? How should we meet discriminations on railways and in hotels? Such questions need not so much specific answers for each part as a general expression of policy, and nobody should be better fitted to announce such a policy than a representative honest Negro Academy.

All this, however, must come in time after careful organization and long conference. The immediate work before us should be practical and have direct bearing upon the situation of the Negro. The historical work of collecting the laws of the United States and of the various States of the Union with regard to the Negro is a work of such magnitude and importance that no body but one like this could think of undertaking it. If we could accomplish that one task we would justify our existence.

In the field of sociology an appalling work lies before us. First, we must unflinchingly and bravely face the truth, not with apologies, but with solemn earnestness. The Negro Academy ought to sound a note of warning that would echo in every black cabin in the land: *Unless we conquer our present vices they will conquer us*; we are diseased, we are developing criminal tendencies, and an alarming large percentage of our men and women are sexually impure. The Negro Academy should stand and proclaim this over the housetops, crying with Garrison: *I will not equivocate, I will not retreat a single inch, and I will be heard*. The Academy should seek to gather about it the talented, unselfish men, the pure and nobleminded women, to fight an army of devils that disgraces our manhood and our womanhood. There does not stand today upon God's earth a race more capable in muscle, in intellect, in morals, than the American Negro, if he will bend his energies in the right direction; if he will

> Burst his birth's invidious bar
> And grasp the skirts of happy chance,
> And breast the blows of circumstance,
> And grapple with his evil star.

In science and morals, I have indicated two fields of work for the Academy. Finally, in practical policy, I wish to suggest the following *Academy Creed*:

1. We believe that the Negro people, as a race, have a contribution to make to civilization and humanity, which no other race can make.

2. We believe it the duty of the Americans of Negro descent, as a body, to maintain their race identity until this mission of the Negro People is accomplished, and the ideal of human brotherhood has become a practical possibility.

3. We believe that, unless modern civilization is a failure, it is entirely feasible and practicable for two races in such essential political, economic and religious harmony as the white and colored people of America, to develop side by side in peace and mutual happiness, the peculiar contribution which each has to make to the culture of their common country.

4. As a means to this end we advocate, not such social equality between these races as would disregard human likes and dislikes, but such social equilibrium as would, throughout all the complicated relations of life, give due and just consideration to culture, ability, and moral worth, whether they be found under white or black skins.

5. We believe that the first and greatest step toward the settlement of the present friction between the races—commonly called the Negro Problem—lies in the correction of the immorality, crime and laziness among the Negroes themselves, which still remains a heritage from slavery. We believe that only earnest and long continued efforts on our part can cure these social ills.

6. We believe that the second great step toward a better adjustment of the relations between the races, should be a more impartial selection of ability in the economic and intellectual world, and a greater respect for personal liberty and worth, regardless of race. We believe that only earnest efforts on the part of the white people of this country will bring much needed reform in these matters.

7. On the basis of the foregoing declaration, and firmly believing in our high destiny, we, as American Negroes, are resolved to strive in every honorable way for the realization of the best and highest aims, for the development of strong manhood and pure womanhood, and for the rearing of a race

ideal in America and Africa, to the glory of God and the uplifting of the Negro people—1897.

From *Negro Social and Political Thought*, edited by Howard Brotz, 1966, pp. 483–92

The Talented Tenth (1903)

The Negro race, like all races, is going to be saved by its exceptional men. The problem of education, then, among Negroes must first of all deal with the Talented Tenth; it is the problem of developing the Best of this race that they may guide the Mass away from the contamination and death of the Worst, in their own and other races. Now the training of men is a difficult and intricate task. Its technique is a matter for educational experts, but its object is for the vision of seers. If we make money the object of man-training, we shall develop money-makers but not necessarily men; if we make technical skill the object of education, we may possess artisans but not, in nature, men. Men we shall have only as we make manhood the object of the work of the schools— intelligence, broad sympathy, knowledge of the world that was and is, and of the relation of men to it—this is the curriculum of that Higher Education which must underlie true life. On this foundation we may build bread winning, skill of hand and quickness of brain, with never a fear lest the child and man mistake the means of living for the object of life.

If this be true—and who can deny it—three tasks lay before me; first to show from the past that the Talented Tenth as they have risen among American Negroes have been worthy of leadership; secondly, to show how these men may be educated and developed; and thirdly, to show their relation to the Negro problem.

You misjudge us because you do not know us. From the very first it has been the educated and intelligent of the Negro

people that have led and elevated the mass, and the sole
obstacles that nullified and retarded their efforts were slavery
and race prejudice; for what is slavery but the legalized survival of the unfit and the nullification of the work of natural
internal leadership? Negro leadership, therefore, sought from
the first to rid the race of this awful incubus that it might
make way for natural selection and the survival of the fittest.
In colonial days came Phillis Wheatley and Paul Cuffe striving against the bars of prejudice; and Benjamin Banneker, the
almanac maker, voiced their longings when he said to
Thomas Jefferson, "I freely and cheerfully acknowledge that I
am of the African Race, and in colour which is natural to
them, of the deepest dye; and it is under a sense of the most
profound gratitude to the Supreme Ruler of the Universe,
that I now confess to you that I am not under that state of
tyrannical thraldom and inhuman captivity to which too
many of my brethren are doomed, but that I have abundantly
tasted of the fruition of those blessings which proceed from
that free and unequalled liberty with which you are favored,
and which I hope you will willingly allow, you have mercifully received from the immediate hand of that Being from
whom proceedeth every good and perfect gift.

"Suffer me to recall to your mind that time, in which the
arms of the British crown were exerted with every powerful
effort, in order to reduce you to a state of servitude; look
back, I entreat you, on the variety of dangers to which you
were exposed; reflect on that period in which every human
aid appeared unavailable, and in which even hope and forti-
tude wore the aspect of inability to the conflict, and you
cannot but be led to a serious and grateful sense of your
miraculous and providential preservation, you cannot but
acknowledge, that the present freedom and tranquility which
you enjoy, you have mercifully received, and that a peculiar
blessing of heaven.

"This, sir, was a time when you clearly saw into the injustice of a state of Slavery, and in which you had just appre-
hensions of the horrors of its condition. It was then that your
abhorrence thereof was so excited, that you publicly held
forth this true and invaluable doctrine, which is worthy to be

recorded and remembered in all succeeding ages: 'We hold these truths to be self evident, that all men are created equal; that they are endowed with certain inalienable rights, and that among these are life, liberty and the pursuit of happiness.' "

Then came Dr. James Derham, who could tell even the learned Dr. Rush something of medicine, and Lemuel Haynes, to whom Middlebury gave an honorary A.M. in 1804. These and others we may call the Revolutionary group of distinguished Negroes—they were persons of marked ability, leaders of a Talented Tenth, standing conspicuously among the best of their time. They strove by word and deed to save the color line from becoming the line between the bond and free, but all that they could do was nullified by Eli Whitney and the Curse of Gold. So they passed into forgetfulness.

But their spirit did not wholly die; here and there in the early part of the century came other exceptional men. Some were natural sons of unnatural fathers and were given often a liberal training and thus a race of educated mulattoes sprang up to plead for the black men's rights. There was Ira Aldridge, whom all Europe loved to honor; there was that voice crying in the Wilderness, David Walker, and saying:

"I declare it does appear to me as though some nations think God is asleep, or that he made the Africans for nothing else but to dig their mines and work their farms, or they cannot believe history, sacred or profane. I ask every man who has a heart, and is blessed with the privilege of believing —Is not God a God of justice to all his creatures? Do you say he is? Then if he gives peace and tranquility to tyrants and permits them to keep our fathers, our mothers, ourselves and our children in eternal ignorance and wretchedness to support them and their families, would he be to us a God of Justice? I ask, O, ye Christians, who hold us and our children in the most abject ignorance and degradation that ever a people were afflicted with since the world began—I say if God gives you peace and tranquility, and suffers you thus to go on afflicting us, and our children, who have never given you the least provocation—would he be to us a God of Justice? If you will allow that we are men, who feel for each other, does not the blood of our fathers and of us, their children, cry aloud to the Lord of Sabaoth against you for the cruelties and murders with which you have and do continue to afflict us?"

This was the wild voice that first aroused Southern legislators in 1829 to the terrors of abolitionism.

In 1831 there met that first Negro convention in Philadelphia, at which the world gaped curiously but which bravely attacked the problems of race and slavery, crying out against persecution and declaring that "Laws as cruel in themselves as they were unconstitutional and unjust, have in many places been enacted against our poor, unfriended and unoffending brethren (without a shadow of provocation on our part), at whose bare recital the very savage draws himself up for fear of contagion—looks noble and prides himself because he bears not the name of Christian." Side by side this free Negro movement, and the movement for abolition, strove until they merged into one strong stream. Too little notice has been taken of the work which the Talented Tenth among Negroes took in the great abolition crusade. From the very day that a Philadelphia colored man became the first subscriber to Garrison's "Liberator," to the day when Negro soldiers made the Emancipation Proclamation possible, black leaders worked shoulder to shoulder with white men in a movement, the success of which would have been impossible without them. There was Purvis and Remond, Pennington and Highland Garnet, Sojourner Truth and Alexander Crummell, and above all, Frederick Douglass—what would the abolition movement have been without them? They stood as living examples of the possibilities of the Negro race, their own hard experiences and well-wrought culture said silently more than all the drawn periods of orators—they were the men who made American slavery impossible. As Maria Weston Chapman once said, from the school of anti-slavery agitation "a throng of authors, editors, lawyers, orators and accomplished gentlemen of color have taken their degree! It has equally implanted hopes and aspirations, noble thoughts, and sublime purposes, in the hearts of both races. It has prepared the white man for the freedom of the black man, and it has made the black man scorn the thought of enslavement, as does a white man, as far as its influence has extended. Strengthen that noble influence! Before its organization, the country only saw here and there in slavery some faithful Cudjoe or Dinah, whose strong natures blossomed even in bondage, like a fine plant beneath a heavy stone. Now, under the elevating and cherishing influence of the American Anti-slavery Society, the colored race, like the white, furnishes Corinthian capitals for the noblest temples."

Where were these black abolitionists trained? Some, like Frederick Douglass, were self-trained, but yet trained liberally; others like Alexander Crummell and McCune Smith, graduated from famous foreign universities. Most of them rose up through the colored schools of New York and Philadelphia and Boston, taught by college-bred men like Russworm, of Dartmouth, and college-bred white men like Neau and Benezet.

After emancipation came a new group of educated and gifted leaders: Langston, Bruce and Elliot, Greener, Williams and Payne. Through political organization, historical and polemic writing and moral regeneration, these men strove to uplift their people. It is now the fashion of to-day to sneer at them and to say that with freedom Negro leadership should have begun at the plow and not in the Senate—a foolish and mischievous lie; two hundred and fifty years that black serf toiled at the plow and yet that toiling was in vain till the Senate passed the war amendments; and two hundred and fifty years more the half-free serf of to-day may toil at his plow, but unless he have political rights and righteously guarded civic status, he will still remain the poverty-stricken and ignorant plaything of rascals, that he now is. This all sane men know even if they dare not say it.

And so now we come to the present—a day of cowardice and vacillation, of strident wide voiced wrong and faint hearted compromise; of double-faced dallying with Truth and Right. Who are to-day guiding the work of the Negro people? The "exceptions" of course. And yet so sure as this Talented Tenth is pointed out, the blind worshippers of the Average cry out in alarm: "These are the exceptions, look here at

death, disease and crime—these are the happy rule." Of
course they are the rule, because a silly nation made them the
rule: Because for three long centuries this people lynched
Negroes who dared to be brave, raped black women who
dared to be virtuous, crushed dark-hued youth who dared to
be ambitious, and encouraged and made to flourish servility
and lewdness and apathy. But not even this was able to crush
all manhood and chastity and aspiration from black folk. A
saving remnant continually survives and persists, continually
aspires, continually shows itself in thrift and ability and character. Exceptional it is to be sure, but this is its chiefest
promise; it shows the capability of Negro blood, the promise
of black men. Do Americans ever stop to reflect that there
are in this land a million men of Negro blood, well-educated,
owners of homes, against the honor of whose womanhood no
breath was ever raised, whose men occupy positions of trust
and usefulness, and who, judged by any standard, have
reached the full measure of the best type of modern European culture? Is it fair, is it decent, is it Christian to ignore
these facts of the Negro problem, to belittle such aspiration,
to nullify such leadership and seek to crush these people back
into the mass out of which by toil and travail, they and their
fathers have raised themselves?

Can the masses of the Negro people be in any possible way
more quickly raised than by the effort and example of this
aristocracy of talent and character? Was there ever a nation
on God's fair earth civilized from the bottom upward? Never;
it is, ever was and ever will be from the top downward that
culture filters. The Talented Tenth rises and pulls all that are
worth the saving up to their vantage ground. This is the
history of human progress; and two historic mistakes which
have hindered that progress were the thinking first that no
more could ever rise save the few already risen; or second,
that it would better the unrisen to pull the risen down.

How then shall the leaders of a struggling people be trained
and the hands of the risen few be strengthened? There can be
but one answer: The best and most capable of their youth
must be schooled in the colleges and universities of the land.
We will not quarrel as to just what the university of the

Negro should teach or how it should teach it—I willingly admit that each soul and each race-soul needs its own peculiar curriculum. But this is true: A university is a human invention for the transmission of knowledge and culture from generation to generation, through the training of quick minds and pure hearts, and for this work no other human invention will suffice, not even trade and industrial schools.

All men cannot go to college but some men must; every isolated group or nation must have its yeast, must have for the talented few centers of training where men are not so mystified and befuddled by the hard necessary toil of earning a living, as to have no aims higher than their bellies, and no God greater than Gold. This is true training, and thus in the beginning were the favored sons of the freedmen trained. Out of the colleges of the North came, Cravath, Chase, Andrews, Bumstead and Spence to build the foundations of knowledge and civilization in the black South. Where ought they to have begun to build? At the bottom, of course, quibbles the mole with his eyes in the earth. Aye! truly at the bottom, at the very bottom; at the bottom of knowledge, down in the very depths of knowledge there where the roots of justice strike into the lowest soil of Truth. And so they did begin; they founded colleges, and up from the colleges shot normal schools, and out from the normal schools went teachers, and around the normal teachers clustered other teachers to teach the public schools; the colleges trained in Greek and Latin and mathematics, 2,000 men; and these men trained full 50,000 others in morals and manners and they in turn taught thrift and the alphabet to nine millions of men, who to-day hold $300,000,000 of property. It was a miracle—the most wonderful peace-battle of the nineteenth century, and yet to-day men smile at it, and in fine superiority tell us that it was all a strange mistake; that a proper way to found a system of education is first to gather the children and buy them spelling books and hoes; afterward men may look about for teachers, if haply they find them; or again they would teach men Work, but as for Life—why, what has Work to do with Life, they ask vacantly.

Was the work of these college founders successful; did it

stand the test of time? Did the college graduates, with all their fine theories of life, really live? Are they useful men helping to civilize and elevate their less fortunate fellows? Let us see. Omitting all institutions which have not actually graduated students from college courses, there are to-day in the United States thirty-four institutions giving something above high school training to Negroes and designed especially for this race.

Three of these were established in the border States before the War; thirteen were planted by the Freedmen's Bureau in the years 1864–1869; nine were established between 1870 and 1880 by various church bodies; five were established after 1881 by Negro churches, and four are state institutions supported by United States' agricultural funds. In most cases the college departments are small adjuncts to high and common school work. As a matter of fact six institutions—Atlanta, Fisk, Howard, Shaw, Wilberforce and Leland, are the important Negro colleges so far as actual work and number of students are concerned. In all these institutions, seven hundred and fifty Negro college students are enrolled. In grade the best of these colleges are about a year behind the smaller New England colleges and a typical curriculum is that of Atlanta University. Here students from the grammar grades, after a three years' high school course, take a college course of 136 weeks. One-fourth of this time is given to Latin and Greek; one-fifth, to English and modern languages; one-sixth, to history and social science; one-seventh, to natural science; one-eighth to mathematics, and one-eighth to philosophy and pedagogy.

In addition to these students in the South, Negroes have attended Northern colleges for many years. As early as 1826 one was graduated from Bowdoin college, and from that time till to-day nearly every year has seen elsewhere, other such graduates. They have, of course, met much color prejudice. Fifty years ago very few colleges would admit them at all. Even to-day no Negro has ever been admitted to Princeton, and at some other leading institutions they are rather endured than encouraged. Oberlin was the great pioneer in the work of blotting out the color line in colleges, and has more **Negro** graduates by far than any other Northern college.

The total number of Negro college graduates up to 1899 (several of the graduates of that year not being reported), was as follows:

			Negro Colleges			White Colleges
Before '76	------		137 ------	------		75 ------
'75–80	------		143 ------	------		22 ------
'80–85	------		250 ------	------		31 ------
'85–90	------		413 ------	------		43 ------
'90–95	------		465 ------	------		66 ------
'95–99	------		475 ------	------		88 ------
Class Unknown	------		57 ------	------		64 ------
TOTAL	------		1,940 ------	------		389 ------

Of these graduates 1,079 were men and 250 were women; 50 per cent of Northern-born college men come South to work among the masses of their people, at a sacrifice which few people realize; nearly 90 per cent of the Southern-born graduates instead of seeking that personal freedom and broader intellectual atmosphere which their training has led them, in some degree, to conceive, stay and labor and wait in the midst of their black neighbors and relatives.

The most interesting question, and in many respects the crucial question, to be asked concerning college-bred Negroes, is: Do they earn a living? It has been intimated more than once that the higher training of Negroes has resulted in sending into the world of work, men who could find nothing to do suitable to their talents. Now and then there comes a rumor of a colored college man working at menial service, etc. Fortunately, returns as to occupations of college-bred Negroes, gathered by the Atlanta conference, are quite full— nearly 60 per cent of the total number of graduates.

This enables us to reach fairly certain conclusions as to the occupations of all college-bred Negroes. Of 1,312 persons reported, there were:

	PER CENT	
Teachers, _____	___53.4__	xxxxxxxxxxxxxxxxx
Clergymen, _____	___16.8__	xxxxxx
Physicians, etc., _____	___ 6.3__	xxx
Students, _____	___ 5.6__	xx
Lawyers, _____	___ 4.7__	xx
In Govt. Service, _____	___ 4.0__	x
In Business, _____	___ 3.6__	x
Farmers and Artisans, _____	___ 2.7__	x
Editors, Secretaries and		
Clerks _____	___ 2.4__	
Miscellaneous, _____	___ .5	

Over half are teachers, a sixth are preachers, another sixth
are students and professional men; over 6 per cent are farmers, artisans and merchants, and 4 per cent are in government
service. In detail the occupations are as follows:

OCCUPATIONS OF COLLEGE-BRED MEN

TEACHERS:
      Presidents and Deans, _____ 19
      Teachers of Music, _____ 7
      Professors, Principals and Teachers, _____675 Total 701

CLERGYMEN:
      Bishop, _____ 1
      Chaplains, U.S. Army, _____ 2
      Missionaries, _____ 9
      Presiding Elders, _____ 12
      Preachers, _____197 Total 221

PHYSICIANS:
      Doctors of Medicine, _____ 76
      Druggists, _____ 4
      Dentists, _____ 3 Total 83

STUDENTS, _____ 74

LAWYERS, _____ 62

CIVIL SERVICE:
      U.S. Minister Plenipotentiary, _____ 1
      U.S. Consul, _____ 1
      U.S. Deputy Collector, _____ 1

U.S. Gauger, _____	1	
U.S. Postmasters, _____	2	
U.S. Clerks, _____	44	
State Civil Service, _____	2	
City Civil Service, _____	1	Total 53

BUSINESS MEN:

Merchants, etc., _____	30	
Managers, _____	13	
Real Estate Dealers, _____	4	Total 47

FARMERS, _____ 26

CLERKS AND SECRETARIES:

Secretary of National Societies, _____	7	
Clerks, etc. _____	15	Total 22

ARTISANS, _____ 9

EDITORS, _____ 9

MISCELLANEOUS, _____ 5

These figures illustrate vividly the function of the college-bred Negro. He is, as he ought to be, the group leader, the man who sets the ideals of the community where he lives, directs its thoughts and heads its social movements. It need hardly be argued that the Negro people need social leadership more than most groups; that they have no traditions to fall back upon, no long established customs, no strong family ties, no well defined social classes. All these things must be slowly and painfully evolved. The preacher was, even before the war, the group leader of the Negroes, and the church their greatest social institution. Naturally this preacher was ignorant and often immoral, and the problem of replacing the older type by better educated men has been a difficult one. Both by direct work and by direct influence on other preachers, and on congregations, the college-bred preacher has an opportunity for reformatory work and moral inspiration, the value of which cannot be overestimated.

It has, however, been in the furnishing of teachers that the Negro college has found its peculiar function. Few persons realize how vast a work, how mighty a revolution has been thus accomplished. To furnish five millions and more of ignorant people with teachers of their own race and blood, in one generation, was not only a very difficult undertaking, but a very important one, in that, it placed before the eyes of almost every Negro child an attainable ideal. It brought the masses of the blacks in contact with modern civilization, made black men the leaders of their communities and trainers of the new generation. In this work college-bred Negroes were first teachers, and then teachers of teachers. And here it is that the broad culture of college work has been of peculiar value. Knowledge of life and its wider meaning, has been the point of the Negro's deepest ignorance, and the sending out of teachers whose training has not been simply for bread winning, but also for human culture, has been of inestimable value in the training of these men.

In the earlier years the two occupations of preacher and teacher were practically the only ones open to the black college graduate. Of later years a larger diversity of life among his people has opened new avenues of employment. Nor have these college men been paupers and spendthrifts; 557 college-bred Negroes owned in 1899, $1,342,862.50 worth of real estate (assessed value), or $2,411 per family. The real value of the total accumulations of the whole group is perhaps about $10,000,000, or $5,000 apiece. Pitiful, is it not, beside the fortunes of oil kings and steel trusts, but after all is the fortune of the millionaire the only stamp of true and successful living? Alas! it is, with many, and there's the rub.

The problem of training the Negro is to-day immensely complicated by the fact that the whole question of the efficiency and appropriateness of our present systems of education, for any kind of child, is a matter of active debate, in which final settlement seems still afar off. Consequently it often happens that persons arguing for or against certain systems of education for Negroes have these controversies in mind and miss the real question at issue. The main question, so far as the Southern Negro is concerned, is: What under the present circumstance, must a system of education do in order to raise the Negro as quickly as possible in the scale of civilization? The answer to this question seems to me clear: It must strengthen the Negro's character, increase his

knowledge and teach him to earn a living. Now it goes
without saying, that it is hard to do all these things simultaneously or suddenly, and that at the same time it will not do
to give all the attention to one and neglect the others; we
could give black boys trades, but that alone will not civilize a
race of ex-slaves; we might simply increase their knowledge
of the world, but this would not necessarily make them wish
to use this knowledge honestly; we might seek to strengthen
character and purpose, but to what end if this people have
nothing to eat or to wear? A system of education is not one
thing, nor does it have a single definite object, nor is it a mere
matter of schools. Education is that whole system of human
training within and without the school house walls, which
molds and develops men. If then we start out to train an
ignorant and unskilled people with a heritage of bad habits,
our system of training must set before itself two great aims—
the one dealing with knowledge and character, the other part
seeking to give the child the technical knowledge necessary
for him to earn a living under the present circumstances.
These objects are accomplished in part by the opening of the
common schools on the one, and of the industrial schools on
the other. But only in part, for there must also be trained
those who are to teach these schools—men and women of
knowledge and culture and technical skill who understand
modern civilization, and having the training and aptitude to
impart it to the children under them. There must be teachers,
and teachers of teachers, and to attempt to establish any sort
of system of common and industrial school training, without
first (and I say *first* advisedly) without *first* providing for the
higher training of the very best teachers, is simply throwing
your money to the winds. School houses do not teach themselves—piles of brick and mortar and machinery do not send
out *men*. It is the trained, living human soul, cultivated and
strengthened by long study and thought, that breathes the
real breath of life into boys and girls and makes them human,
whether they be black or white, Greek, Russian or American.
Nothing, in these latter days, has so dampened the faith of
thinking Negroes in recent educational movements, as the
fact that such movements have been accompanied by ridicule

and denouncement and decrying of those very institutions of higher training which made the Negro public school possible, and make the Negro industrial schools thinkable. It was Fisk, Atlanta, Howard and Straight, those colleges born of the faith and sacrifice of the abolitionists, that placed in the black schools of the South 30,000 teachers and more, which some, who depreciate the work of these higher schools, are using to teach their own new experiments. If Hampton, Tuskegee and the hundred other industrial schools prove in the future to be as successful as they deserve to be, then their success in training black artisans for the South will be due primarily to the white colleges of the North and the black colleges of the South, which trained the teachers who to-day conduct these institutions. There was a time when the American people believed pretty devoutly that a log of wood with a boy at one end and Mark Hopkins at the other, represented the highest ideal of human training. But in these eager days it would seem that we have changed all that and think it necessary to add a couple of saw-mills and a hammer to this outfit, and, at a pinch, to dispense with the services of Mark Hopkins.

I would not deny, or for a moment seem to deny, the paramount necessity of teaching the Negro to work, and to work steadily and skillfully; or seem to depreciate in the slightest degree the important part industrial schools must play in the accomplishments of these ends, but I *do* say, and insist upon it, that it is industrialism drunk with its vision of success, to imagine that its own work can be accomplished without providing for the training of broadly cultured men and women to teach its own teachers, and to teach the teachers of the public schools.

But I have already said that human education is not simply a matter of schools; it is much more a matter of family and group life—the training of one's home, of one's daily companions, of one's social class. Now the black boy of the South moves in a black world—a world with its own leaders, its own thoughts, its own ideals. In this world he gets by far the larger part of his life training, and through the eyes of this dark world he peers into the veiled world beyond. Who guides and determines the education which he receives in his world?

His teachers here are the group-leaders of the Negro people—
the physicians and clergymen, the trained fathers and mothers, the influential and forceful men about him of all kinds;
here it is, if at all, that the culture of the surrounding world
trickles through and is handed on by the graduates of the
higher schools. Can such culture training of group-leaders be
neglected? Can we afford to ignore it? Do you think that if
the leaders of thought among Negroes are not trained and
educated thinkers, that they will have no leaders? On the
contrary a hundred half-trained demagogues will still hold the
places they so largely occupy now, and hundreds of vociferous busy-bodies will multiply. You have no choice; either you
must help furnish this race from within its own ranks with
thoughtful men of trained leadership, or you must suffer the
evil consequences of a headless misguided rabble.

I am an earnest advocate of manual training and trade
teaching for black boys, and for white boys, too. I believe
that next to the founding of Negro colleges the most valuable
addition to Negro education since the war, has been industrial training for black boys. Nevertheless, I insist that the
object of all true education is not to make men carpenters, it
is to make carpenters men; there are two means of making
the carpenter a man, each equally important: the first is to
give the group and community in which he works, liberally
trained teachers and leaders to teach him and his family what
life means; the second is to give him sufficient intelligence
and technical skill to make him an efficient workman; the
first object demands the Negro college and college-bred men
—not a quantity of such colleges, but a few of excellent
quality; not too many college-bred men, but enough to leaven
the lump, to inspire the masses, to raise the Talented Tenth to
leadership; the second object demands a good system of
common schools, well-taught, conveniently located and properly equipped.

The Sixth Atlanta Conference truly said in 1901:

"We call the attention of the Nation to the fact that less
than one million of the three million Negro children of
school age, are at present regularly attending school, and
these attend a session which lasts only a few months.

"We are to-day deliberately rearing millions of our citizens in ignorance, and at the same time limiting the rights of citizenship by educational qualifications. This is unjust. Half the black youth of the land have no opportunities open to them for learning to read, write and cipher. In the discussion as to the proper training of Negro children after they leave the public schools, we have forgotten that they are not yet decently provided with public schools.

"Propositions are beginning to be made in the South to reduce the already meagre school facilities of Negroes. We congratulate the South on resisting, as much as it has, this pressure, and on the many millions it has spent on Negro education. But it is only fair to point out that Negro taxes and the Negroes' share of the income from indirect taxes and endowments have fully repaid this expenditure, so that the Negro public school system has not in all probability cost the white taxpayers a single cent since the war.

"This is not fair. Negro schools should be a public burden, since they are a public benefit. The Negro has a right to demand good common school training at the hands of the States and the Nation since by their fault he is not in position to pay for this himself."

What is the chief need for the building up of the Negro public school in the South? The Negro race in the South needs teachers to-day above all else. This is the current testimony of all who know the situation. For the supply of this great demand two things are needed—institutions of higher education and money for school houses and salaries. It is usually assumed that a hundred or more institutions for Negro training are to-day turning out so many teachers and college-bred men that the race is threatened with an over-supply. This is sheer nonsense. There are to-day less than 3,000 living Negro college graduates in the United States, and less than a 1,000 Negroes in college. Moreover, in the 164 schools for Negroes, 95 per cent of their students are doing elementary and secondary work, work which should be done in the public schools. Over half of the remaining 2,157 students are taking high school studies. The mass of so-called "normal" schools for the Negro are simply doing elementary common school work, or, at most, high school work, with a little instruction in methods. The Negro colleges and the postgraduate courses at other institutions are the only agencies for the broader and more careful training of teachers. The work of these institutions is hampered for lack of funds. It is getting increasingly difficult to get funds for training teachers in the best modern methods, and yet all over the South, from State Superintendents, county officials, city boards and school principals comes the wail, "We need *teachers!*" and teachers must be trained. As the fairest minded of all white Southerners, Atticus G. Haygood, once said: "The defects of colored teachers are so great as to create an urgent necessity for training better ones. Their excellencies and their successes are sufficient to justify the best hopes of success in the effort, and to vindicate the judgment of those who make large investments of money and service, to give to colored students opportunity for thoroughly preparing themselves for the work of teaching children of their people."

The truth of this has been strikingly shown in the marked improvement of white teachers in the South. Twenty years ago the rank and file of white public school teachers were not as good as the Negro teachers. But they, by scholarships and good salaries, have been encouraged to thorough normal collegiate preparation, while the Negro teachers have been discouraged by starvation wages and the idea that any training will do for a black teacher. If carpenters are needed it is well and good to train men as carpenters. But to train men as carpenters, and then set them to teaching is wasteful and criminal; and to train men as teachers and then refuse them a living wage, unless they become carpenters, is rank nonsense.

The United States Commissioner of Education says in his report for 1900: "For comparison between the white and colored enrollment in secondary and higher education, I have added together the enrollment in high schools and secondary schools with the attendance in colleges and universities, not being sure of the actual grade of work done in the colleges and universities. The work done in the secondary schools is reported in such detail in this office, that there can be no doubt of its grade."

He then makes the following comparisons of persons in every million enrolled in secondary and higher education:

	WHOLE COUNTRY	NEGROES
1880	4,362	1,289
1900	10,743	2,061

And he concludes: "While the number in colored high schools and colleges had increased somewhat faster than the population, it had not kept pace with the average of the whole country, for it had fallen from 30 per cent to 24 per cent of the average quota. Of all colored pupils, one (1) in one hundred was engaged in secondary and higher work, and that ratio has continued substantially for the past twenty years. If the ratio of colored population in secondary and higher education is to be equal to the average for the whole country, it must be increased to five times its present average." And if this be true of the secondary and higher education, it is safe to say that the Negro has not one-tenth his quota in college studies. How baseless, therefore, is the charge of too much training! We need Negro teachers for the Negro common schools, and we need first-class normal schools and colleges to train them. This is the work of higher Negro education and it must be done.

Further than this, after being provided with group leaders of civilization, and a foundation of intelligence in the public schools, the carpenter, in order to be a man, needs technical skill. This calls for trade school. Now trade schools are not nearly such simple things as people once thought. The original idea was that the "Industrial" school was to furnish education, practically free, to those willing to work for it; it was to "do" things—i.e.: become a center of productive industry, it was to be partially, if not wholly, self-supporting, and it was to teach trades. Admirable as were some of the ideas underlying this scheme, the whole thing simply would not work in practice; it was found that if you were to use time and material to teach trades thoroughly, you could not at the same time keep the industries on a commercial basis and make them pay. Many schools started out to do this on a large scale and went into virtual bankruptcy. Moreover, it was found also that it was possible to teach a boy a trade mechanically, without giving him the full educative benefit of the process, and, vice versa, that there was a distinctive educative value in teaching a boy to use his hands and eyes in carrying out certain physical processes, even though he did not actually learn a trade. It has happened, therefore, in the last decade that a noticeable change has come over the industrial schools. In the first place the idea of commercially remunerative industry in a school is being pushed rapidly to the background. There are still schools with shops and farms that bring in an income, and schools that use student labor partially for the erection of their buildings and the furnishing of equipment. It is coming to be seen, however, in the education of the Negro, as clearly as it has been seen in the education of the youths the world over, that it is the *boy* and not the material product, that is the true object of education. Consequently the object of the industrial school came to be the thorough training of boys regardless of the cost of the training, so long as it was thoroughly well done.

Even at this point, however, the difficulties were not surmounted. In the first place modern industry has taken great strides since the war, and the teaching of trades is no longer a simple matter. Machinery and the long processes of work have greatly changed the work of the carpenter, the iron worker and the shoemaker. A really efficient workman must be to-day an intelligent man who has had good technical training in addition to thorough common school, and perhaps even higher training. To meet this situation the industrial schools began a further development; they established distinct Trade Schools for the thorough training of better class artisans, and at the same time they sought to preserve for the purpose of general education, such of the simpler processes of the elementary trade learning as were best suited therefor. In this differentiation of the Trade School and manual training, the best of the industrial schools simply followed the plain trend of the present educational epoch. A prominent educator tells us that, in Sweden, "In the beginning the economic conception was generally adopted, and everywhere manual training was looked upon as a means of preparing the children of the common people to earn their living. But gradually it came to be recognized that manual training has a more elevated purpose, and one, indeed, more useful in the deeper meaning of the term. It came to be considered as an educative process for the complete moral, physical and intellectual development of the child."

Thus, again, in the manning of trade schools and manual training schools we are thrown back upon the higher training as its source and chief support. There was a time when any aged and worn-out carpenter could teach in a trade school. But not so to-day. Indeed the demand for college-bred men by a school like Tuskegee ought to make Mr. Booker T. Washington the firmest friend of higher training. Here he has as helpers the son of a Negro senator, trained in Greek and the humanities, and graduated at Harvard; the son of a Negro congressman and lawyer, trained in Latin and mathematics, and graduated at Oberlin; he has as his wife, a woman who read Virgil and Homer in the same class room with me; he has as college chaplain, a classical graduate of Atlanta University; as teacher of science, a graduate of Fisk; as teacher of history, a graduate of Smith—indeed some thirty of his chief teachers are college graduates, and instead of studying French grammars in the midst of weeds, or buying pianos for dirty cabins, they are at Mr. Washington's right hand helping him in a noble work. And yet one of the effects of Mr. Washington's propaganda has been to throw doubt upon the expediency of such training for Negroes, as these persons have had.

Men of America, the problem is plain before you. Here is a race transplanted through the criminal foolishness of your fathers. Whether you like it or not the millions are here, and here they will remain. If you do not lift them up, they will pull you down. Education and work are the levers to uplift a people. Work will not do it unless inspired by the right ideals and guided by intelligence. Education must not simply teach work—it must teach life. The Talented Tenth of the Negro race must be made leaders of thought and missionaries of culture among their people. No others can do this work and the Negro colleges must train men for it. The Negro race, like all other races, is going to be saved by its exceptional men.

From *The Negro Problem*, 1903, pp. 33–75

The Field and Function of the American Negro College (1933)

Delivered at the Fifty-second Anniversary of the General Alumni Association of Fisk University and the Forty-fifth Anniversary of the graduation of Dr. Du Bois from Fisk, June, 1933.

Once upon a time some four thousand miles east of this place, I saw the functioning of a perfect system of education. It was in West Africa, beside a broad river; and beneath the palms, bronze girls were dancing before the President of Liberia and the native chiefs, to celebrate the end of the Bush Retreat and their arrival at marriageable age.

There under the Yorubas and other Sudanese and Bantu tribes, the education of the child began almost before it could walk. It went about with mother and father in their daily tasks; it learned the art of sowing and reaping and hunting; it absorbed the wisdom and folk lore of the tribe; it knew the lay of land and river. Then at the age of puberty it went into the Bush and there for a season the boys were taught the secrets of sex and the girls in another school learned of motherhood and marriage. They came out of the Bush with a ceremony of graduation, and immediately were given and taken in marriage.

Even after that, their education went on. They sat in council with their elders and learned the history and science and art of the tribe and practiced all in their daily life. Thus education was completely integrated with life. There could be no uneducated people. There could be no education that was not at once for use in earning a living and for use in living a life. Out of this education and out of the life it typified came, as perfect expressions, song and dance and saga, ethics and religion.

Nothing more perfect has been invented than this system of training youth among primitive African tribes. And one sees it in the beautiful courtesy of black children; in the modesty and frankness of womanhood, and in the dignity and courage of manhood; and too, in African music and art with its world-wide influence.

If a group has a stable culture which moves, if we could so conceive it, on one general level, here would be the ideal of our school and university. But, of course, this can never be achieved by human beings on any wide stage.

First and most disconcerting, men progress, which means that they change their home, their work, their division of wealth, their philosophy. And how shall men teach children that which they themselves do not know or transmit a philosophy or religion that is already partly disbelieved and partly untrue? This is a primal and baffling problem of education and we have never wholly solved it. Or in other words, education of youth in a changing world is a puzzling problem with every temptation for lying and propaganda. But this is but the beginning of trouble. Within the group and nation significant differentiations and dislocations appear, so that education of youth becomes a preparation not for one common national life but for the life of a particular class or group; and yet the tendency is to regard as real national education only the training for this group which assumes to represent the nation because of its power and privilege, and despite the fact that it is usually a small numerical minority in the nation. Manifestly in such case if a member of one of the suppressed groups receives the national education in such a land, he must become a member of the privileged aristocracy or be educated for a life which he cannot follow and be compelled to live a life which he does not like or which he deeply despises.

This is the problem of education with which the world is most familiar and it tends to two ends: It makes the mass of men dissatisfied with life and it makes the university a system of culture for the cultured.

With this kind of university, we are most familiar. It reached in our day perhaps its greatest development in England in the Victorian era. Eton and Harrow, Oxford and Cambridge, were for the education of gentlemen—those people who inherited wealth and who by contact and early training acquired a body of manners and a knowledge of life and even an accent of English which placed them among the well-bred; these were taken up and further trained for the particular sort of life which they were to live; a life which pre-supposed a large income, travel, cultivated society; and activity in politics, art, and imperial industry.

This type of university training has deeply impressed the world. It is foundation for a tenacious legend preserved in fiction, poetry, and essay. There are still many people who quite instinctively turn to this sort of thing when they speak of a university. And out of this ideal arose one even more exotic and apart. Instead of the university growing down and seeking to comprehend in its curriculum the life and experience, the thought and expression, of lower classes; it almost invariably tended to grow up and narrow itself to a sublimated elite of mankind.

It conceived of culture, exquisite and fragile, as a thing in itself, disembodied from flesh and action; and this culture as existing for its own sake. It was a sort of earthly heaven into which the elect of wealth and privilege and courtly address, with a few chance neophytes from the common run of men, entered and lived in a region above and apart. One gets from this that ideal of cloistered ease for Science and Beauty, partaken of by those who sit far from the noise and fury, clamor and dust of the world, as the world's aristocrats, artists and scholars.

And yet, the argument against such an ideal of a university is more an argument of fact than logic. For just as soon as such a system of training is established or as men seek to establish it, it dies. It dies like a plant without room, withering into fantastic forms, that bring ridicule or hate. Or it becomes so completely disassociated from the main currents of real life that men forget it and the world passes on as though it was not for it and had not been. Thus the university cut off from its natural roots and from the mass of men becomes a university of the air and does not establish and does not hold the ideal of universal culture which it sought, in its earlier days, to make its great guiding end.

How is it now that failure to reach this, often if not always, kills the university? The reasons to me seem clear. Human culture in its broadest and finest sense can never be wholly the product of the few. There is no natural aristocracy of man, either within a nation or among the races of the world, which unless fed copiously from without can build up and maintain and diversify a broad human culture. A system, therefore, of national education which tries to confine its benefits to preparing the few for the life of the few, dies of starvation. And this every aristocracy which the world has ever seen can prove a thousand times. There are two ways in which this can be remedied: The aristocracy may be recruited from the masses, still leaving the aim of education as the preparation of men for the life of this privileged class. This has been the desperate effort of England and in this way English aristocracy has kept its privilege and its wealth more successfully than any modern or ancient land. But even here the method fails because the life of the English aristocrat is after all not the broadest and fullest life.

It is only, therefore, as the university lives up to its name and reaches down to the mass of universal men and makes the life of normal men the object of its training, it is only in this way that the marvelous talent and diversity and emotion of all mankind pours up through this method of human training and establishes a national culture and a national art. Herein lies the eternal logic of democracy.

Thus in the progress of human culture you have not simply a development that produces different classes of men, because classes may harmonize more or less and above the peasant, the artisan and the merchant may exist a leisured class; a class culture may be built, which may flourish long and wide. But the difficulty goes further than the narrowness and ultimate sterility of this plan. Dislocations come within these classes. Their relations to each other may change and break and the foundations upon which the cultured class has been built may crumble. In this case your system of human training becomes not only a system for the supposed benefit of the privileged few, but cannot, indeed, carry out its function even for them. Its system of learning does not fit the mass of men nor the relations of its constituents to that mass.

One can see examples of this the world over. In Kenya, which used to be German East Africa, there are millions of black natives and a few thousand white Englishmen who have seized and monopolized the best land, leaving the natives scarcely enough poor land for subsistence. By physical slavery, economic compulsion or legal sanction, the natives work the land of the whites. On the recent discovery of gold, the natives were dispossessed of their own land in favor of white miners.

What kind of education will suit Kenya? The minority of landed aristocracy will be taught by tutors in Africa and then go to the great English schools and universities. The middle class of immigrant Indian merchants will learn to read and write and count at home or in elementary schools. The great mass of the black millions will be taught something of the art of agriculture, something of the work of artisans, perhaps some ability to read and write, although whether this should be in English or merely in the native tongue is the question. But on this foundation there can grow in Kenya no national university of education, because there are no national ideals. No culture, either African or European, can be built on any such economic foundation. Education in Kenya is a misnomer.

Thus the university, if it is to be firm, must hark back to the original ideal of the Bush School. It must train the children of a nation for life and for making a living. And if it does that, and insofar as it does it, it becomes the perfect expression of the life and the center of the intellectual and cultural expression of its age.

I have seen in my life three expressions of such an ideal; all of them imperfect, all of them partial, and yet each tending toward a broad and singularly beautiful expression of universal education. My first sight of it was here at Fisk University in the fall of 1885 when I arrived as a boy of seventeen. The buildings were few, the cost of tuition, board, room and clothes was less than $200 a year; and the college numbered less than twenty-five. And yet the scheme of education as it existed in our minds, in the class room, in the teaching of professors, in the attitude of students, was a thing of breadth and enthusiasm with an unusual unity of aim. We were a small group of young men and women who were going to transform the world by giving proof of our own ability, by teaching our less fortunate fellows so that they could follow the same path, by proclaiming to the world our belief in American democracy, and the place which Negroes would surely take in it. In none of these propositions did there exist in our minds any hesitation or doubt. There was no question as to employment and perfectly proper employment for graduates, for the ends which we had in view. There was no question of our remaining in school for no good or earnest student ever left.

Above all, to our unblinking gaze, the gates of the World would open—were opening. We never for a moment contemplated the possibility that seven millions of Americans who proved their physical and mental worth could be excluded from the national democracy of a common American culture. We came already bringing gifts. The song we sang was fresh from the lips that threw it round the world. We saw and heard the voices that charmed an emperor and a queen. We believed in the supreme power of the ballot in the hands of the masses to transform the world. Already the North was breaking the Color Line and for the South we were willing to wait.

I saw the same thing a few years later in Harvard University at the end of the nineteenth century. Harvard had broadened its earlier ideals. It was no longer simply a place where rich and learned New England gave the accolade to the social elite. It had broken its shell and stretched out to the West and to the South, to yellow students and to black. I had for the mere asking been granted a fellowship of $300.00—a sum so vast to my experience that I was surprised when it did not pay my first year's expenses. Men sought to make Harvard an expression of the United States, and to do this by means of leaders unshackled in thought and custom who were beating back bars of ignorance and particularism and prejudice.

There were William James and Josiah Royce; Nathaniel Shaler and Charles Eliot Norton; George Santayana; Albert Bushnell Hart, and President Eliot himself. There were at least a dozen men—rebels against convention, unorthodox in religion, poor in money, who for a moment held in their hands the culture of the United States, typified it, expressed it, and pushed it a vast step forward. Harvard was not in 1888 a perfect expression of the American soul, or the place where the average American would have found adequate training for his life work. But perhaps it came nearer that high eminence than any other American institution had before or has since.

Again a few years later, I saw the University of Berlin. It represented in 1892 a definite and unified ideal. It did not comprehend at once the culture of all Germany, but I do not believe that ever in modern days and certainly not at Fisk or Harvard did a great university come so near expressing a national ideal. It was as though I had been stepping up from a little group college with a national outlook to a national institution which came near gathering to itself the thought and culture of forty million human beings. Every great professor of Germany, with few exceptions, had the life ambition to be called to a Chair in the Friedrich Wilhelm's Universitaet zu Berlin. I sat beneath the voice of a man who perhaps more than any single individual embodied the German ideal and welded German youth into that great aggressive fist which literally put Deutschland ueber Alles! I remember well Heinrich von Treitschke. With swift flying words that hid a painfully stuttering tongue, he hammered into the young men who sat motionless and breathless beneath his voice, the doctrine of the inborn superiority of the German race. He told us few foreigners to our faces, that we felt and acknowledged our inferiority. And out and around that university for a thousand miles, millions of people shared in its ideal teaching, and did this in spite of caste of birth and poverty, jostling wealth because they believe in an ultimate unity which Bismarkian state socialism promised. They sang their national songs and joined in national festivals with enthusiasm that brought tears to the onlooker. And it made you realize the ideal of a single united nation and what it could express in matchless poetry, daring science and undying music.

Yet in each of these cases, the ultimate ideal of a national much less a universal university was a vision never wholly attained, and in the very nature of the case it could not be. Fisk had to be a Negro university because it was teaching Negroes and they were a caste with their own history and problems. Harvard was still a New England provincial institution and Berlin was sharply and determinedly German. Their common characteristic was that starting where they did and must, they aimed and moved toward universal culture.

Now with these things in mind, let us turn back to America and to the American Negro. It has been said many times that a Negro university is nothing more and nothing less than a university. Quite recently one of the great leaders of education in the United States, Abraham Flexner, said something of that sort concerning Howard University. As President of the Board of Trustees, he said he was seeking to build not a Negro university but a University. And by those words he brought again before our eyes the ideal of a great institution of learning which becomes a center of universal culture. With all good will toward them that speak such words it is the object of this paper to insist that there can be no college for Negroes which is not a Negro college and that while an American Negro university, just like a German or a Swiss university may rightly aspire to a universal culture unhampered by limitations of race and culture, yet it must start on the earth where we sit and not in the skies whither we aspire. May I develop this thought?

In the first place, we have got to remember that here in America, in the year 1933, we have a situation which cannot be ignored. There was a time when it seemed as though we might best attack the Negro problem by ignoring its most unpleasant features. It was not and is not yet in good taste to speak generally about certain facts which characterize our situation in America. We are politically hamstrung. We have the greatest difficulty in getting suitable and remunerative work. Our education is more and more not only being confined to our own schools but to a segregated public school system far below the average of the nation with one-third of our children continuously out of school. And above all, and this we like least to mention, we suffer a social ostracism which is so deadening and discouraging that we are compelled either to lie about it or to turn our faces toward the red flag of revolution. It consists of the kind of studied and repeated and emphasized public insult of the sort which during all the long history of the world has led men to kill or be killed. And in the full face of any effort which any black man may make to escape this ostracism for himself, stands this flaming word of racial doctrine which will distract his effort and energy if it does not lead him to spiritual suicide.

We boast and have a right to boast of our accomplishment between the days that I studied here and this Forty-fifth Anniversary of my graduation. It is a calm appraisal of fact to say that the history of modern civilization cannot surpass if it can parallel the advance of American Negroes in every essential line of culture in these years. And yet when we have said this we must have the common courage honestly to admit that every step we have made forward has been greeted by a backward step on the part of the American public in caste intoleration, mob law, and racial hatred.

I need but remind you that when I graduated from Fisk there was no "Jim Crow" car in Tennessee and I saw Hunter of '89 once sweep a brakeman aside at the Union Station and escort a crowd of Fisk students into the first-class seats for which they had paid. There was no legal disfranchisement and a black Fiskite sat in the Legislature; and while the Chancellor of Vanderbilt University had annually to be reintroduced to the President of Fisk, yet no white Southern group presumed to dictate the internal social life of this institution.

Manifestly with all that can be said, pro and con, and in extenuation, and by way of excuse and hope, this is the situation and we know it. There is no human way by which these facts can be ignored. We cannot do our daily work, sing a song, or write a book or carry on a university and act as though these things were not.

If this is true, then no matter how much we may dislike the

statement, the American Negro problem is and must be the center of the Negro American university. It has got to be. You are teaching Negroes. There is no use pretending that you are teaching white Americans or that you are teaching citizens of the world. You are teaching American Negroes in 1933, and they are the subjects of a caste system in the Republic of the United States of America and their life problem is primarily this problem of caste.

Upon these foundations, therefore, your university must start and build. Nor is the thing so entirely unusual or unheard of as it sounds. A university in Spain is not simply a university. It is a Spanish university. It is a university located in Spain. It uses the Spanish language. It starts with Spanish history and makes conditions in Spain the starting point of its teaching. Its education is for Spaniards, not for them as they may be or ought to be, but as they are with their present problems and disadvantages and opportunities.

In other words, the Spanish university is founded and grounded in Spain, just as surely as a French university is French. There are some people who have difficulty in apprehending this very clear truth. They assume, for instance, that the French university is in a singular sense universal, and is based on a comprehension and inclusion of all mankind and of their problem. But it is not, and the assumption that it arises simply because so much of French culture has been built into universal civilization. A French university is founded in France; it uses the French language and assumes a knowledge of French history. The present problems of the French people are its major problems and it becomes universal only so far as other peoples of the world comprehend and are at one with France in its mighty and beautiful history.

In the same way, a Negro university in the United States of America begins with Negroes. It uses that variety of the English idiom which they understand; and above all, it is founded, or it should be founded on a knowledge of the history of their people in Africa and in the United States, and their present condition. Without white-washing or translating wish into facts, it begins with that; and then it asks how shall these young men and women be trained to earn a living and

live a life under the circumstances in which they find themselves or with such changing of those circumstances as time
and work and determination will permit.

Is this statement of the field of a Negro university a denial
of aspiration or a change from older ideals? I do not think it
is, although I admit in my own mind some change of thought
and modification of method.

The system of learning which bases itself upon the actual
condition of certain classes and groups of human beings is
tempted to suppress a minor premise of fatal menace. It
proposes that the knowledge given and the methods pursued
in such institutions of learning shall be for the definite object
of perpetuating present conditions or of leaving their amelioration in the hands of and at the initiative of other forces and
other folk. This was the great criticism that those of us who
fought for higher education of Negroes thirty years ago
brought against the industrial school.

The industrial school founded itself and rightly upon the
actual situation of American Negroes and said: "What can be
done to change this situation?" And its answer was: A training in technique and method such as would incorporate the
disadvantaged group into the industrial organization of the
country, and in that organization the leaders of the Negro
had perfect faith. Since that day the industrial machine has
cracked and groaned. Its technique has changed faster than
any school could teach; the relations of capital and labor
have increased in complication and it has become so clear
that Negro poverty is not primarily caused by ignorance of
technical knowledge that the industrial school has almost surrendered its program.

In opposition to that, the proponents of college training in
those earlier years said: "What black men need is the broader
and more universal training so that they can apply the general principles of knowledge to the particular circumstances
of their condition."

Here again was indubitable truth but incomplete truth. The
technical problem lay in the method of teaching this broader
and more universal truth and here just as in the industrial

program, we must start where we are and not where we wish to be.

As I said a few years ago at Howard University both these positions had thus something of truth and right. Because of the peculiar economic situation in our country the program of the industrial school came to grief first and has practically been given up. Starting even though we may with the actual condition of the Negro peasant and artisan, we cannot ameliorate his condition simply by his learning a trade which is the transient technique of a passing era. More vision and knowledge is needed than that. But on the other hand, while the Negro college of a generation ago set down a defensible and true program of applying knowledge to facts, it unfortunately could not completely carry it out and it did not carry it out because the one thing that the industrial philosophy gave to education, the Negro college did not take and that was that the university education of black men in the United States must be grounded in the condition and work of those black men!

On the other hand, it would be of course idiotic to say, as the former industrial philosophy almost said, that so far as most black men are concerned education must stop with this. No, starting with present conditions and using the facts and the knowledge of the present situation of American Negroes, the Negro university expands toward the possession and the conquest of all knowledge. It seeks from a beginning of the history of the Negro in America and in Africa to interpret all history; from a beginning of social development among Negro slaves and freedmen in America and Negro tribes and kingdoms in Africa, to interpret and understand the social development of all mankind in all ages. It seeks to reach modern science of matter and life from the surroundings and habits and aptitudes of American Negroes and thus lead up to understanding of life and matter in the universe.

And this is a different program than a similar function would be in a white university or in a Russian university or in an English university, because it starts from a different point. It is a matter of beginnings and integrations of one group which sweep instinctive knowledge and inheritance and current reactions into a universal world of science, sociology, and art. In no other way can the American Negro college function. It cannot begin with history and lead to Negro history. It cannot start with sociology and end with Negro sociology.

Why was it that the Renaissance of literature which began among Negroes ten years ago has never taken real and lasting root? It was because it was a transplanted and exotic thing. It was a literature written for the benefit of white people and at the behest of white readers, and starting out primarily from the white point of view. It never had a real Negro constituency and it did not grow out of the inmost heart and frank experience of Negroes; on such an artificial basis no real literature can grow.

On the other hand, if starting in a great Negro university you have knowledge, beginning with the particular, and going out to universal comprehension and unhampered expression, you are going to begin to realize for the American Negro the full life which is denied him now. And then after that comes a realization of the older object of our college—to bring this universal culture down and apply it to the individual life and individual condition of living Negroes.

The university must become not simply a center of knowl- edge but a center of applied knowledge and guide of action. And this is all the more necessary now since we easily see that planned action especially in economic life is going to be the watchword of civilization.

If the college does not thus root itself in the group life and afterward apply its knowledge and culture to actual living, other social organs must replace the college in this function. A strong, intelligent family life may adjust the student to higher culture; and, too, a social clan may receive the graduate and induct him into life. This has happened and is happening among a minority of privileged people. But it costs society a fatal price. It tends to hinder progress and hamper change—it makes education propaganda for things as they are. It leaves the mass of those without family training and without social standing—misfits and rebels who despite their education are uneducated in its meaning and application. The only college which stands for the progress of all—mass as well as aristocracy—functions in root and blossom as well as in the overshadowing and heaven filling tree. No system of learning—no university—can be universal before it is German, French, Negro. Grounded in inexorable fact and condition, in Poland or Italy, it may seek the universal and haply it may find it—and finding it bring it down to earth and to us.

We have imbibed from the surrounding white world a childish idea of progress. Progress means bigger and better results always and forever. But there is no such rule of life. In six thousand years of human culture, the losses and retrogressions have been enormous. We have no assurance that twentieth century civilization will survive. We do not know that American Negroes will survive. There are sinister signs about us, antecedent to and unconnected with the great depression. The organized might of industry north and south is relegating the Negro to the edge of survival and using him as a labor reservoir on starvation wage. No secure professional class, no science, literature nor art can live on such sub-soil. It is an insistent deep-throated cry for rescue, guidance, and organized advance that greets the black leader today and the college that trains him has got to let him know at least as much about the great black miners strike in Alabama as about the age of Pericles. By singular accident—almost by compelling fate—I drove by as I came here yesterday—the region where I taught a country school over forty years ago. There is no progress there. There is only space, disillusion, and death beside the same eternal hills. There where I first heard the Sorrow Songs are the graves of men and women and children who had the making of a fine intelligent upstanding yeomanry. There remains but the half-starved farmer, the casual laborer, the unpaid servant. Why in a land rich with wealth, muscle, and colleges?

To the New Englander of wealth and family Harvard and Yale are parts and only parts of a broad training which the New England home begins and a State Street or Wall Street business ends. How fine and yet how fatal! There lies root and reason for the World War and the Great Depression. To the American Negro, culture must adjust itself to a different family history and apply itself to a new system of social caste and in this adjustment comes new opportunity of making education and progress possible and not antagonistic.

We are on the threshold of a new era. Let us not deceive ourselves with outworn ideals of wealth and servants and luxuries, reared on a foundation of ignorance, starvation and want. Instinctively, we have absorbed these ideals from our twisted white American environment. This new economic planning is not for us unless we do it. Unless the American Negro today, led by trained university men of broad vision, sits down to work out by economics and mathematics, by physics and chemistry, by history and sociology, exactly how and where he is to earn a living and how he is to establish a reasonable life in the United States or elsewhere, unless this is done the university has missed its field and function and the American Negro is doomed to be a suppressed and inferior caste in the United States for incalculable time.

Here, then, is a job for the American Negro university. It cannot be successfully ignored or dodged without the growing menace of disaster. I lay the problem before you as one which you must not ignore.

To carry out this plan, two things and only two things are necessary—teachers and students. Buildings and endowments may help, but they are not indispensable. It is necessary first to have teachers who comprehend this program and know how to make it live among their students. This is calling for a good deal, because it asks that teachers teach that which they have learned in no American school and which they never will learn until we have a Negro university of the sort that I am visioning. No teacher, black or white, who comes to a university like Fisk, filled simply with general ideas of human culture or general knowledge of disembodied science, is going to make a university of this school. Because a university is made of human beings, learning of the things they do not know from things they do know in their own lives.

And secondly, we must have students. They must be chosen for ability to learn. There is always the temptation to assume that the children of privileged classes, the rich, the noble, the white, are those who can best take education. One has but to express this to realize its utter futility. But perhaps the most dangerous thing among us is for us, without thought, to imitate the white world and assume that we can choose students at Fisk because of the amount of money of which their parents have happened to get hold of. That basis of selection is going to give us an extraordinary aggregation. We want by the nicest methods possible, to seek out the talented and the gifted among our constituency, quite regardless of their wealth or position, and to fill this university and similar institutions with persons who have got brains enough to take fullest advantage of what the university offers. There is no other way. With teachers who know what they are teaching and whom they are teaching and the life that surrounds both the knowledge and the knower, and with students who have the capacity and the will to absorb this knowledge, we can build the sort of Negro university which will emancipate not simply the black folk of the United States, but those white folk who in their effort to suppress Negroes have killed their own culture—men who in their desperate effort to replace equality with caste and to build inordinate wealth on a foundation of abject poverty have succeeded in killing democracy, art, and religion.

Only a universal system of learning, rooted in the will and condition of the masses and blossoming from that manure up toward the stars, is worth the name. Once builded it can only grow as it brings down sunlight and star shine and impregnates the mud. The chief obstacle in this rich land endowed with every national resource and with the abilities of a hundred different peoples—the chief and only obstacle to the coming of that kingdom of economic equality which is the only logical end of work, is the determination of the white world to keep the black world poor and make themselves rich. The disaster which this selfish and short-sighted policy has brought lies at the bottom of this present depression, and too, its cure lies beside it. Your clear vision of a world without wealth, of capital without profit, of income based on work alone, is the path cut not only for you but for all men.

Is not this a program of segregation, emphasis of race and particularism as against national unity and universal humanity? It is and it is not by choice but for force; you do not get humanity by wishing it nor do you become American citizens simply because you want to. A Negro university from its high ground of unfaltering facing of the Truth, from its unblinking stare at hard facts does not advocate segregation, apart, hammered into a separate unity by spiritual intolerance and legal sanction backed by mob law, and that this separation is growing in strength and fixation; that it is worse today than a half century ago and that no character, address, culture or desert is going to change it, in our day or for centuries to come. Recognizing this brute fact, groups of cultured, trained, and devoted men gathering in great institutions of learning proceed to ask: What are we going to do about it? It is silly to ignore and gloss the truth; it is idiotic to proceed as though we were white or yellow, English or Russian. Here we stand. We are American Negroes. It is beside the point to ask whether we form a real race. Biologically we are mingled of all conceivable elements, but race is psychology, not biology; and psychologically we are a unified race with one history, one red memory, and one revolt. It is not ours to argue whether we will be segregated or whether we ought to be a caste. We are segregated; we are a caste. This is our given and at present unalterable fact. Our problem is: How far and in what way can we consciously and scientifically guide our future so as to insure our physical survival, our spiritual freedom and our social growth? Either we do this or we die. There is no alternative. If America proposes the murder of this group, its moral descent into imbecility and crime and its utter loss of manhood, self-assertion, and courage, the sooner we realize this the better. By that great line of McKay: "If we must die, let it not be like hogs." But the alternative of not dying like hogs is not that of dying or killing like snarling dogs. It is rather conquering the world by thought and brain and plan; by expression and organized cultural ideals. Therefore, let us not beat futile wings in impotent frenzy, but carefully plan and guide our segregated life, organize in industry and politics to protect it and expand it, and above all to give it unhampered spiritual expression in art and literature. It is the council of fear and cowardice to say this cannot be done. What must be can be and it is only a question of Science and Sacrifice to bring the great consummation.

What that will be, none knows. It may be a great physical segregation of the world along the Color Line; it may be an economic rebirth which insures spiritual and group integrity amid physical diversity. It may be utter annihilation of class and race and color barriers in one ultimate mankind, differentiated by talent, susceptibility and gift—but any of these ends are matters of long centuries and not years. We live in years, swift flying, transient years. We hold the possible future in our hands but not by wish and will, only by thought, plan, knowledge, and organization. If the college can pour into the coming age an American Negro who knows himself and his plight and how to protect himself and fight race prejudice, then the world of our dream will come and not otherwise.

> The golden days are gone. Why do we wait
> So long upon the marble steps, blood
> Falling from our open wounds? and why
> Do our black faces search the empty sky?
> Is there something we have forgotten?
> Some precious thing we have lost,
> Wandering in strange lands?

What we have lost is the courage of independent self-assertion. We have had as our goal—American full citizenship, nationally recognized. This has failed—flatly and decisively failed. Very well. We're not dead yet. We are not going to die. If we use our brains and strength there is no way to stop our ultimate triumph as creators of modern culture—if we use our strength and brains.

And what pray stops us but our dumb caution—our fear, our very sanity? Let us then be insane with courage.

> Like a mad man's dream, there came
> One fair, swift flash to me
> Of distances, of streets aflame,
> With joy and agony;
> And further yet, a moonlit sea

Foaming across its bars
And further yet, the infinity
Of wheeling suns and stars.

From the *Fisk News*, Vol. 6, No. 10, June, 1936

A Negro Nation Within the Nation (1935)

No more critical situation ever faced the Negroes of America than that of today—not in 1830, nor in 1861, not in 1867. More than ever the appeal of the Negro for elementary justice falls on deaf ears.

Three-fourths of us are disfranchised; yet no writer on democratic reform, no third party movement says a word about Negroes. The Bull Moose crusade in 1912 refused to notice them; the LaFollette uprising in 1924 was hardly aware of them; the Socialists still keep them in the background. Negro children are systematically denied education; when the National Education Association asks for Federal aid to education it permits discrimination to be perpetuated by the present local authorities. Once or twice a month Negroes convicted of no crime are openly and publicly lynched, and even burned; yet a National Crime Convention is brought to perfunctory and unwilling notice of this only by mass picketing and all but illegal agitation. When a man with every qualification is refused a position simply because his great-grandfather was black there is not a ripple of comment or protest.

Long before the depression Negroes in the South were losing "Negro" jobs, those assigned them by common custom— poorly paid and largely undesirable toil, but nevertheless life-supporting. New techniques, new enterprises, mass production, impersonal ownership and control have been largely displacing the skilled white and Negro worker in tobacco manufacturing, in iron and steel, in lumbering and mining, and in transportation. Negroes are now restricted more and more to common labor and domestic service of the lowest paid and worst kind. In textile, chemical and other manufactures Negroes were from the first nearly excluded, and just as slavery kept the poor white out of profitable agriculture, so freedom prevents the poor Negro from finding a place in manufacturing. The world-wide decline in agriculture has moreover carried the mass of black farmers, despite heroic endeavor among the few, down to the level of landless tenants and peons.

The World War and its wild aftermath seemed for a moment to open a new door; 2,000,000 black workers rushed North to work in iron and steel, make automobiles and pack meat, build houses and do the heavy toil in factories. They met first the closed trade union which excluded them from the best-paid jobs and pushed them into the low-wage gutter, denied them homes and mobbed them. Then they met the depression.

Since 1929 Negro workers, like white workers, have lost their jobs, have had mortgages foreclosed on their farms and homes, have used up their small savings. But, in the case of the Negro worker, everything has been worse in larger or smaller degree; the loss has been greater and more permanent. Technological displacement, which began before the depression, has been accelerated, while unemployment and falling wages struck black men sooner, went to lower levels and will last longer.

Negro public schools in the rural South have often disappeared, while Southern city schools are crowded to suffocation. The Booker Washington High School in Atlanta, built for 1,000 pupils, has 3,000 attending in double daily sessions. Above all, Federal and State relief holds out little promise for the Negro. It is but human that the unemployed white man and the starving white child should be relieved first by local authorities who regard them as fellow-men, but often regard Negroes as subhuman. While the white worker has sometimes been given more than relief and been helped to his feet, the black worker has often been pauperized by being just kept from starvation. There are some plans for national rehabilitation and the rebuilding of the whole industrial system. Such plans should provide for the Negro's future relations to American industry and culture, but those provisions the country is not only unprepared to make but refuses to consider.

In the Tennessee Valley beneath the Norris Dam, where do Negroes come in? And what shall be their industrial place? In the attempt to rebuild agriculture the Southern landholder will in all probability be put on his feet, but the black tenant has been pushed to the edge of despair. In the matter of housing, no comprehensive scheme for Negro homes has been thought out and only two or three local projects planned. Nor can broad plans be made until the nation or the community decides where it wants or will permit Negroes to live. Negroes are largely excluded from subsistence homesteads because Negroes protested against segregation, and whites, anxious for cheap local labor, also protested.

The colored people of America are coming to face the fact quite calmly that most white Americans do not like them, and are planning neither for their survival, nor for their definite future if it involves free, self-assertive modern manhood. This does not mean all Americans. A saving few are worried about the Negro problem; a still larger group are not illdisposed, but they fear prevailing public opinion. The great mass of Americans are, however, merely representatives of average humanity. They muddle along with their own affairs and scarcely can be expected to take seriously the affairs of strangers or people whom they partly fear and partly despise.

For many years it was the theory of most Negro leaders that this attitude was the insensibility of ignorance and inexperience, that white America did not know of or realize the continuing plight of the Negro. Accordingly, for the last two decades, we have striven by book and periodical, by speech and appeal, by various dramatic methods of agitation, to put the essential facts before the American people. Today there can be no doubt that Americans know the facts; and yet they remain for the most part indifferent and unmoved.

The main weakness of the Negro's position is that since emancipation he has never had an adequate economic foundation. Thaddeus Stevens recognized this and sought to transform the emancipated freedmen into peasant proprietors. If he had succeeded, he would have changed the economic history of the United States and perhaps saved the American farmer from his present plight. But to furnish 50,000,000 acres of good land to the Negroes would have cost more money than the North was willing to pay, and was regarded by the South as highway robbery.

The whole attempt to furnish land and capital for the freedmen fell through, and no comprehensive economic plan was advanced until the advent of Booker T. Washington. He had a vision of building a new economic foundation for Negroes by incorporating them into white industry. He wanted to make them skilled workers by industrial education and expected small capitalists to rise out of their ranks. Unfortunately, he assumed that the economic development of America in the twentieth century would resemble that of the nineteenth century, with free industrial opportunity, cheap land and unlimited resources under the control of small competitive capitalists. He lived to see industry more and more concentrated, land monopoly extended and industrial technique changed by wide introduction of machinery.

As a result, technology advanced more rapidly than Hampton or Tuskegee could adjust their curricula. The chance of an artisan's becoming a capitalist grew slimmer, even for white Americans, while the whole relation of labor to capital became less a matter of technical skill than of basic organization and aim.

Those of us who in that day opposed Booker Washington's plans did not foresee exactly the kind of change that was coming, but we were convinced that the Negro could succeed in industry and in life only if he had intelligent leadership and far-reaching ideals. The object of education, we declared, was not "to make men artisans but to make artisans men." The Negroes in America needed leadership so that, when change and crisis came, they could guide themselves to safety.

The educated group among American Negroes is still small, but it is large enough to begin planning for preservation through economic advancement. The first definite movement of this younger group was toward direct alliance of the

Negro with the labor movement. But white labor today as in the past refuses to respond to these overtures.

For a hundred years, beginning in the Thirties and Forties of the nineteenth century, the white laborers of Ohio, Pennsylvania and New York beat, murdered and drove away fellow-workers because they were black and had to work for what they could get. Seventy years ago in New York, the centre of the new American labor movement, white laborers hanged black ones to lamp posts instead of helping to free them from the worst of modern slavery. In Chicago and St. Louis, New Orleans and San Francisco, black men still carry the scars of the bitter hatred of white laborers for them. Today it is white labor that keeps Negroes out of decent low-cost housing, that confines the protection of the best unions to "white" men, that often will not sit in the same hall with black folk who already have joined the labor movement. White labor has to hate scabs; but it hates black scabs not because they are scabs but because they are black. It mobs white scabs to force them into labor fellowship. It mobs black scabs to starve and kill them. In the present fight of the American Federation of Labor against company unions it is attacking the only unions that Negroes can join.

Thus the Negro's fight to enter organized industry has made little headway. No Negro, no matter what his ability, can be a member of any of the railway unions. He cannot be an engineer, fireman, conductor, switchman, brakeman or yardman. If he organizes separately, he may, as in the case of the Negro Firemen's Union, be assaulted and even killed by white firemen. As in the case of the Pullman Porters' Union, he may receive empty recognition without any voice or collective help. The older group of Negro leaders recognize this and simply say it is a matter of continued striving to break down these barriers.

Such facts are, however, slowly forcing Negro thought into new channels. The interests of labor are considered rather than those of capital. No greater welcome is expected from the labor monopolist who mans armies and navies to keep Chinese, Japanese and Negroes in their places than from the captains of industry who spend large sums of money to make laborers think that the most worthless white man is better than any colored man. The Negro must prove his necessity to the labor movement and that it is a disastrous error to leave him out of the foundation of the new industrial State. He must settle beyond cavil the question of economic efficiency as a worker, a manager and controller of capital.

The dilemma of these younger thinkers gives men like James Weldon Johnson a chance to insist that the older methods are still the best; that we can survive only by being integrated into the nation, and that we must consequently fight segregation now and always and force our way by appeal, agitation and law. This group, however, does not seem to recognize the fundamental economic bases of social growth and the changes that face American industry. Greater democratic control of production and distribution is bound to replace existing autocratic and monopolistic methods.

In this broader and more intelligent democracy we can hope for progressive softening of the asperities and anomalies of race prejudice, but we cannot hope for its early and complete disappearance. Above all, the doubt, deep-planted in the American mind, as to the Negro's ability and efficiency as worker, artisan and administrator will fade but slowly. Thus, with increased democratic control of industry and capital, the place of the Negro will be increasingly a matter of human choice, of willingness to recognize ability across the barriers of race, of putting fit Negroes in places of power and authority by public opinion. At present, on the railroads, in manufacturing, in the telephone, telegraph and radio business, and in the larger divisions of trade, it is only under exceptional circumstances that any Negro, no matter what his ability, gets an opportunity for position and power. Only in those lines where individual enterprise still counts, as in some of the professions, in a few of the trades, in a few branches of retail business and in artistic careers, can the Negro expect a narrow opening.

Negroes and other colored folk, nevertheless, exist in larger and growing numbers. Slavery, prostitution to white men, theft of their labor and goods, have not killed them and cannot kill them. They are growing in intelligence and dissatisfaction. They occupy strategic positions, within nations and beside nations, amid valuable raw material and on the highways of future expansion. They will survive, but on what terms and conditions? On this point a new school of Negro thought is arising. It believes in the ultimate uniting of mankind and in a unified American nation, with economic classes and racial barriers leveled, but it believes this is an ideal and is to be realized only by such intensified class and race consciousness as will bring irresistible force rather than mere humanitarian appeals to bear on the motives and actions of men.

The peculiar position of Negroes in America offers an opportunity. Negroes today cast probably 2,000,000 votes in a total of 40,000,000 and their vote will increase. This gives them, particularly in Northern cities, and at critical times, a chance to hold a very considerable balance of power, and the mere threat of this being used intelligently and with determination may often mean much. The consuming power of 2,800,000 Negro families has recently been estimated at $166,000,000 a month—a tremendous power when intelligently directed. Their man power as laborers probably equals that of Mexico or Yugoslavia. Their illiteracy is much lower than that of Spain or Italy. Their estimated per capita wealth about equals that of Japan.

For a nation with this start in culture and efficiency to sit down and await the salvation of a white God is idiotic. With the use of their political power, their power as consumers, and their brain power, added to that chance of personal appeal which proximity and neighborhood always give to human beings, Negroes can develop in the United States an economic nation within a nation, able to work through inner cooperation, to found its own institutions, to educate its genius, and at the same time, without mob violence or extremes of race hatred, to keep in helpful touch and cooperate with the mass of the nation. This has happened more often than most people realize, in the case of groups not so obviously separated from the mass of people as are American Negroes. It must happen in our case, or there is no hope for the Negro in America.

Any movement toward such a program is today hindered by the absurd Negro philosophy of Scatter, Suppress, Wait, Escape. There are even many of our educated young leaders who think that because the Negro problem is not in evidence where there are few or no Negroes, this indicates a way out! They think that the problem of race can be settled by ignoring it and suppressing all reference to it. They think that we have only to wait in silence for the white people to settle the problem for us; and finally and predominantly, they think that the problem of 12,000,000 Negro people, mostly poor, ignorant workers, is going to be settled by having their more educated and wealthy classes gradually and continually escape from their race into the mass of the American people, leaving the rest to sink, suffer and die.

Proponents of this program claim, with much reason, that the plight of the masses is the fault of the emerging classes. For the slavery and exploitation that reduced Negroes to their present level or at any rate hindered them from rising, the white world is to blame. Since the age-long process of raising a group is through the escape of its upper class into welcome fellowship with risen peoples, the Negro intelligentsia would submerge itself if it bent its back to the task of lifting the mass of people. There is logic in this answer, but futile logic.

If the leading Negro classes cannot assume and bear the uplift of their own proletariat, they are doomed for all time. It is not a case of ethics; it is a plain case of necessity. The method by which this may be done is, first, for the American Negro to achieve a new economic solidarity.

There exists today a chance for the Negroes to organize a cooperative State within their own group. By letting Negro farmers feed Negro artisans, and Negro technicians guide Negro home industries, and Negro thinkers plan this integration of cooperation, while Negro artists dramatize and beautify the struggle, economic independence can be achieved. To doubt that this is possible is to doubt the essential humanity and the quality of brains of the American Negro.

No sooner is this proposed than a great fear sweeps over older Negroes. They cry "No segregation"—no further yielding to prejudice and race separation. Yet any planning for the benefit of American Negroes on the part of a Negro intelligentsia is going to involve organized and deliberate self-segregation. There are plenty of people in the United States who would be only too willing to use such a plan as a way to increase existing legal and customary segregation between the races. This threat which many Negroes see is no mere mirage. What of it? It must be faced.

If the economic and cultural salvation of the American Negro calls for an increase in segregation and prejudice, then that must come. American Negroes must plan for their economic future and the social survival of their fellows in the firm belief that this means in a real sense the survival of colored folk in the world and the building of a full humanity instead of a petty white tyranny. Control of their own education, which is the logical and inevitable end of separate schools, would not be an unmixed ill; it might prove a supreme good. Negro schools once meant poor schools. They need not today; they must not tomorrow. Separate Negro sections will increase race antagonism, but they will also increase economic cooperation, organized self-defense and necessary self-confidence.

The immediate reaction of most white and colored people to this suggestion will be that the thing cannot be done without extreme results. Negro thinkers have from time to time emphasized the fact that no nation within a nation can be built because of the attitude of the dominant majority, and because all legal and police power is out of Negro hands, and because large-scale industries, like steel and utilities, are organized on a national basis. White folk, on the other hand, simply say that, granting certain obvious exceptions, the American Negro has not the ability to engineer so delicate a social operation calling for such self-restraint, careful organization and sagacious leadership.

In reply, it may be said that this matter of a nation within a nation has already been partially accomplished in the organization of the Negro church, the Negro school and the Negro retail business, and, despite all the justly due criticism, the result has been astonishing. The great majority of American Negroes are divided not only for religious but for a large number of social purposes into self-supporting economic units, self-governed, self-directed. The greatest difficulty is that these organizations have no logical and reasonable standards and do not attract the finest, most vigorous and best educated Negroes. When all these things are taken into consideration it becomes clearer to more and more American Negroes that, through voluntary and increased segregation, by careful autonomy and planned economic organization, they may build so strong and efficient a unit that 12,000,000 men can no longer be refused fellowship and equality in the United States.

From *Current History*, June, 1935, Vol. 42, No. 3, pp. 265–70

Postscript
The Negro and Democracy (1924)

The Negro is making America and the world acknowledge democracy as feasible and desirable for all white folk, for only in this way do they see any possibility of defending their world-wide fear of the yellow, brown and black folk.

In a peculiar way, then, the Negro in the United States has emancipated democracy, reconstructed the threatened edifice of Freedom and been a sort of eternal test of the sincerity of our democratic ideals. As a Negro minister, J. W. C. Pennington, said in London and Glasgow before the Civil War: "The colored population of the United States has no destiny separate from that of the nation in which they form an integral part. Our destiny is bound up with that of America. Her ship is ours; her pilot is ours; her storms are ours; her calms are ours. If she breaks upon a rock we break with her. If we, born in America, cannot live upon the same soil upon terms of equality with the descendants of Scotchmen, Englishmen, Irishmen, Frenchmen, Germans, Hungarians, Greeks and Poles, then the fundamental theory of America fails and falls to the ground."

This is still true and it puts the American Negro in a peculiar strategic position with regard to the race problems of the whole world. What do we mean by democracy? Do we mean democracy of the white races and the subjection of the colored races? Or do we mean the gradual working forward to a time when all men will have a voice in government and industry and will be intelligent enough to express the voice?

It is this latter thesis for which the American Negro stands and has stood, and more than any other element in the modern world it has slowly but continuously forced America toward that point and is still forcing. It must be remembered that it was the late Booker T. Washington who planned the beginning of an industrial democracy in the South based on education, and that in our day the National Association for the Advancement of Colored People, nine-tenths of whose members are Negroes, is the one persistent agency in the United States which is voicing a demand for democracy unlimited by race, sex or religion. American Negroes have even crossed the waters and held three Pan-African Congresses to arouse black men through the world to work for modern democratic development. Thus the emancipation of the Negro slave in America becomes through his own determined efforts simply one step toward the emancipation of all men.

From "The Reconstruction of Freedom" in *The Gift of Black Folk*, 1924, pp. 257–58

III. *Afro-American History, Literature and Art*

Prescript
The Propaganda of History (1935)

ONE READS THE truer deeper facts of Reconstruction with a great despair. It is at once so simple and human, and yet so futile. There is no villain, no idiot, no saint. There are just men; men who crave ease and power, men who know want and hunger, men who have crawled. They all dream and strive with ecstasy of fear and strain effort, balked of hope and hate. Yet the rich world is wide enough for all, wants all. So slight a gesture, a word, might set the strife in order, not with full content, but with growing dawn of fulfillment. Instead roars the crash of hell; and after its whirlwind a teacher sits in academic halls, learned in the tradition of its elms and its elders. He looks into the upturned face of youth and in him youth sees the gowned shape of wisdom and hears the voice of God. Cynically he sneers at "chinks" and "niggers." He says that the nation "has changed its views in regard to the political relation of races and has at last virtually accepted the ideas of the South upon the subject. The white men of the South need now have no further fear that the Republican party, or the Republican Administrations, will ever again give themselves over to the vain imagination of the political equality of men."

Immediately in Africa, a black back runs red with the blood of the lash; in India, a brown girl is raped; in China, a coolie starves; in Alabama, seven darkies are more than lynched; while in London, the white limbs of a prostitute are hung with jewels and silk. Flames of jealous murder sweep the earth, while brains of little children smear the hills.

This is education in the Nineteen Hundred and Thirty-fifth year of the Christ; this is modern and exact social science; this is the university course in "History 12" set down by the Senatus academicus; ad quos hae literae pervenerint; Salutem Domino sempeternam!

From *Black Reconstruction*, 1935, p. 728

The Negro in Literature and Art (1913)

The Negro is primarily an artist. The usual way of putting this is to speak disdainfully of his sensuous nature. This means that the only race which has held at bay the life destroying forces of the tropics, has gained therefrom in some slight compensation a sense of beauty, particularly for sound and color, which characterizes the race. The Negro blood which flowed in the veins of many of the mightiest of the Pharaohs accounts for much of Egyptian art, and indeed, Egyptian civilization owes much in its origins to the development of the large strain of Negro blood which manifested itself in every grade of Egyptian society.

Semitic civilization also had its Negroid influences, and these continually turn toward art as in the case of Nosseyeb, one of the five great poets of Damascus under Ommiades. It was therefore not to be wondered at that in modern days one of the greatest of modern literatures, the Russian, should have been founded by Pushkin, the grandson of a full blooded Negro, and that among the painters of Spain was a mulatto slave, Gomez. Back of all this development by way of contact comes the artistic sense of the indigenous Negro as shown in the stone figures of Sherbro, the bronzes of Binen, the marvelous hand-work in iron and other metals which has characterized the Negro race so long that archaeologists today, with less and less hesitation, are ascribing the discovery of the welding of iron to the Negro race.

To America, the Negro could bring only his music, but

that was quite enough. The only real American music is that of the Negro American, except the meagre contribution of the Indian. Negro music divides itself into many parts; the older African wails and chants, the distinctively Afro-American folk song set to religious words and Calvinistic symbolism and the newer music which the slaves adapted from surrounding themes. To this may be added the American music built on Negro themes such as "Suwanee River," "John Brown's Body," "Old Black Joe," etc. In our day Negro artists like Johnson and Will Marion Cook have taken up this music and begun a newer and most important development, using the syncopated measure popularly known as "rag time," but destined in the minds of musical students to a greater career in the future.

The expression in words of the tragic experiences of the Negro race is to be found in various places. First, of course, there are those, like Harriet Beecher Stowe, who wrote from without the race. Then there are the black men like Es Sadi who wrote the Epic of the Sudan in Arabic, that great history of the fall of the greatest of Negro empires, the Songhay. In America the literary expression of Negroes has had a regular development. As early as the eighteenth century, and even before the Revolutionary War, the first voices of the Negro authors were heard in the United States.

Phillis Wheatley, the black poetess, was the early pioneer, her first poems appearing in 1773, and other editions in 1774 and 1793. Her earliest poem was in memory of George Whitefield. She was followed by the Negro, Olaudah Equiano—known by his English name of Gustavus Vassa—whose autobiography of 350 pages, published in 1787, was the beginning of that long series of personal appeals of which Booker T. Washington's *Up from Slavery* is the latest. Benjamin Banneker's almanac represented the first scientific work of American Negroes, and began to be issued in 1792.

Coming now to the first decades of the nineteenth century we find some essays on freedom by the African Society of Boston, and an apology for the new Negro church formed in Philadelphia. Paul Cuffe, disgusted with America, wrote an early account of Sierra Leone, while the celebrated Lemuel

Haynes, ignoring the race question, dipped deep into the New England theological controversy about 1815. In 1829 came the first full-voiced, almost hysterical, protest against slavery and the color line in David Walker's *Appeal* which aroused Southern legislatures to action. This was followed by the earliest Negro conventions which issued interesting minutes and a strong appeal against disfranchisement in Pennsylvania.

In 1840 some strong writers began to appear. Henry Highland Garnet and J. W. C. Pennington preached powerful sermons and gave some attention to Negro history in their pamphlets; R. B. Lewis made a more elaborate attempt at Negro history. Whitfield's poems appeared in 1846, and William Wells Brown began a career of writing which lasted from 1847 until after the war. In 1845 Douglass' autobiography made its first appearance, destined to run through endless editions up until the last in 1893. Moreover, it was in 1841 that the first Negro magazine appeared in America, edited by George Hogarth and published by the A. M. E. Church.

In the fifties William Wells Brown published his *Three Years in Europe*, James Whitfield published further poems, and a new poet in the person of Frances E. W. Harper, a woman of no little ability who died lately; Martin R. Delaney and William Nell wrote further of Negro history, Nell especially making valuable contributions to the history of the Negro soldiers. Three interesting biographies were added in this decade to the growing number: Josiah Henson, Samuel G. Ward and Samuel Northrop; while Catto, leaving general history, came down to the better known history of the Negro Church.

In the sixties slave narratives multiplied like that of Linda Brent, while two studies of Africa based on actual visits were made by Robert Campbell and Dr. Alexander Crummell; William Douglass and Bishop Daniel Payne continued the history of the Negro Church, while William Wells Brown carried forward his work in general history. In this decade, too, Bishop Tanner began his work in Negro theology.

Most of the Negro talent in the seventies were taken up in

politics; the older men like Bishop Wayman wrote of their experiences; William Wells Brown wrote the *Rising Sun*, and Sojourner Truth added her story to the slave narratives. A new poet arose in the person of A. A. Whitman, while James M. Trotter was the first to take literary note of the musical ability of the race. Indeed this section might have been begun by some reference to the music and folklore of the race; the music contained much primitive poetry and the folklore was one of the great contributions to American civilization.

In the eighties there are signs of unrest and different conflicting streams of thought. On the one hand the rapid growth of the Negro Church is shown by the writers on church subjects like Moore and Wayman. The historical spirit was especially strong. Still wrote of the *Underground Railroad*; Simmons issued his interesting biographical dictionary, and the greatest historian of the race appeared when George W. Williams issued his two-volume history of the *Negro Race in America*. The political turmoil was reflected in Langston's *Freedom and Citizenship*, and Fortune's *Black and White*, and Straker's *New South*, and found its bitterest argument in Turner's pamphlets; but with all this went other new thought; a black man published his *First Greek Lessons*, Bishop Payne issued his *Treatise on Domestic Education*, and Stewart studied in Liberia.

In the nineties came histories, essays, novels and poems, together with biographies and social studies. The history was represented by Payne's *History of the A. M. E. Church*, Hood's *History of the A. M. E. Zion Church*; general history of the older type by R. L. Perry's *Cushite* and the newer type in Johnson's history, while one of the secret societies found their historian in Brooks; Crogman's essays appeared and Archibald Grimke's biographies. The race question was discussed in Frank Grimke's published sermons, while social studies were made by Penn, Wright, Mossell, Crummell, Majors and others. Most notable, however, was the rise of the Negro novelist and poet with national recognition; Frances Harper was still writing and Griggs began his race novels, but both of these spoke primarily to the Negro race; on the other hand, Chesnutt's six novels and Dunbar's inimitable works spoke to the whole nation.

Since 1900 the stream of Negro writing has continued, Dunbar has found a worthy successor in the less-known but more carefully cultured Braithwaite; Booker T. Washington has given us his biography and *Story of the Negro*; Kelly Miller's trenchant essays have appeared in book form; Sinclair's *Aftermath of Slavery* has attracted attention, as have the studies made by Atlanta University. The forward movement in Negro music is represented by J. W. and F. J. Work in one direction and Rosamond Johnson, Harry Burleigh and Will Marion Cook in another.

On the whole, the literary output of the American Negro has been both large and creditable, although, of course, comparatively little known; few great names have appeared and only here and there work that could be called first class, but this is not a peculiarity of Negro literature.

The time has not yet come for the great development of American Negro literature. The economic stress is too great and the racial persecution too bitter to allow the leisure and poise for which literature calls. On the other hand, never in the world has a richer mass of material been accumulated by a people than that which Negroes possess today and are becoming conscious of. Slowly but surely they are developing artists of technique who will be able to use this material. The nation does not notice this for everything touching the Negro is banned by magazines and publishers unless it takes the form of caricature or bitter attack, or is so thoroughly innocuous as to have no literary flavor.

Outside of literature the American Negro has distinguished himself in other lines of art. One need only mention Henry O. Tanner, whose pictures hang in the great galleries of the world, including Luxembourg. There are a score of others less known colored painters including Bannister, Harper, Scott and Brown. To these may be added the actors headed by Ira Aldridge, who played in Covent Garden, was decorated by the king of Prussia and the Emperor of Russia, and made a member of learned societies.

There have been many colored composers of music. Popular songs like Grandfather's Clock, Listen to the Mocking Bird, Carry Me Back to Old Virginia, etc., were composed by colored men. There were a half dozen composers of ability among New Orleans freedmen and Harry Burleigh, and Cook and Johnson are well known today. There have been sculptors like Edmonia Lewis, singers like Flora Batson, whose color alone kept her from the grand opera stage.

To appraise rightly this body of art one must remember that it represents the work of those artists only whom accident set free; if the artist had a white face his Negro blood did not militate against him in the fight for recognition; if his Negro blood was visible white relatives may have helped him; in a few cases ability was united to indomitable will. But the shrinking, modest, black artist without special encouragement had little or no chance in a world determined to make him a menial. So this sum of accomplishment is but an imperfect indication of what the Negro race is capable of in America and in the world.

From the *Annals of the American Academy of Political and Social Science*, Vol. 49, September, 1913, pp. 233–37

Criteria of Negro Art (1926)

Delivered at the Chicago Conference of the National Association for the Advancement of Colored People, June, 1926.

I do not doubt but there are some in this audience who are a little disturbed at the subject of this meeting, and particularly at the subject I have chosen. Such people are thinking something like this: "How is it that an organization like this, a group of radicals trying to bring new things into the world, a fighting organization which has come up out of the blood and dust of battle, struggling for the right of black men to be ordinary human beings—how is it that an organization of this kind can turn aside to talk about Art? After all, what have we who are slaves and black to do with Art?"

Or perhaps there are others who feel a certain relief and

are saying, "After all it is rather satisfactory after all this talk about rights and fighting to sit and dream of something which leaves a nice taste in the mouth."

Let me tell you that neither of these groups is right. The thing we are talking about tonight is part of the great fight we are carrying on and it represents a forward and an upward look—a pushing onward. You and I have been breasting hills; we have been climbing upward; there has been progress and we can see it day by day looking back along blood-filled paths. But as you go through the valleys and over the foothills, so long as you are climbing, the direction—north, south, east or west—is of less importance. But when gradually the vista widens and you begin to see the world at your feet and the far horizon, then it is time to know more precisely whither you are going and what you really want.

What do we want? What is the thing we are after? As it was phrased last night it had a certain truth: We want to be Americans, full-fledged Americans, with all the rights of other American citizens. But is that all? Do we want simply to be Americans? Once in a while through all of us there flashes some clairvoyance, some clear idea, of what America really is. We who are dark can see America in a way that white Americans can not. And seeing our country thus, are we satisfied with its present goals and ideals?

In the high school where I studied we learned most of Scott's "Lady of the Lake" by heart. In after life once it was my privilege to see the lake. It was Sunday. It was quiet. You could glimpse the deer wandering in unbroken forests; you could hear the soft ripple of romance on the waters. Around me fell the cadence of that poetry of my youth. I fell asleep full of the enchantment of the Scottish border. A new day broke and with it came a sudden rush of excursionists. They were mostly Americans and they were loud and strident. They poured upon the little pleasure boat—men with their hats a little on one side and drooping cigars in the wet corners of their mouths; women who shared their conversation with the world. They all tried to get everywhere first. They pushed other people out of the way. They made all sorts of incoherent noises and gestures so that the quiet home folk and the visitors from other lands silently and half-wonder-ingly gave way before them. They struck a note not evil but wrong. They carried, perhaps, a sense of strength and accom-plishment, but their hearts had no conception of the beauty which pervaded this holy place.

If you tonight suddenly should become full-fledged Ameri-cans; if your color faded, or the color line here in Chicago was miraculously forgotten; suppose, too, you became at the same time rich and powerful; what is it that you would want? What would you immediately seek? Would you buy the most powerful of motor cars and outrace Cook County? Would you buy the most elaborate estate on the North Shore? Would you be a Rotarian or a Lion or a What-not of the very last degree? Would you wear the most striking clothes, give the richest dinners and buy the longest press notices?

Even as you visualize such ideals you know in your hearts that these are not the things you really want. You realize this sooner than the average white American because, pushed aside as we have been in America, there has come to us not only a certain distaste for the tawdry and flamboyant but a vision of what the world could be if it were really a beautiful world; if we had the true spirit; if we had the Seeing Eye, the Cunning Hand, the Feeling Heart; if we had, to be sure, not perfect happiness, but plenty of good hard work, the inevita-ble suffering that always comes with life; sacrifice and wait-ing, all that—but, nevertheless, lived in a world where men know, where men create, where they realize themselves and where they enjoy life. It is that sort of a world we want to create for ourselves and for all America.

After all, who shall describe Beauty? What is it? I remem-ber tonight four beautiful things: The Cathedral at Cologne, a forest in stone, set in light and changing shadow, echoing with sunlight and solemn song; a village of the Veys in West Africa, a little thing of mauve and purple, quiet, lying content and shining in the sun; a black and velvet room where on a throne rests, in old and yellowing marble, the broken curves of the Venus of Milo; a single phrase of music in the South-ern South—utter melody, haunting and appealing, suddenly arising out of night and eternity, beneath the moon.

Such is Beauty. Its variety is infinite, its possibility is endless. In normal life all may have it and have it yet again. The world is full of it; and yet today the mass of human beings are choked away from it, and their lives distorted and made ugly. This is not only wrong, it is silly. Who shall right this well-nigh universal failing? Who shall let this world be beautiful? Who shall restore to men the glory of sunsets and the peace of quiet sleep?

We black folk may help for we have within us as a race new stirrings; stirrings of the beginning of a new appreciation of joy, of a new desire to create, of a new will to be; as though in this morning of group life we had awakened from some sleep that at once dimly mourns the past and dreams a splendid future; and there has come the conviction that the Youth that is here today, the Negro Youth, is a different kind of Youth, because in some new way it bears this mighty prophecy on its breast, with a new realization of itself, with new determination for all mankind.

What has this Beauty to do with the world? What has Beauty to do with Truth and Goodness—with the facts of the world and the right actions of men? "Nothing," the artists rush to answer. They may be right. I am but an humble disciple of art and cannot presume to say. I am one who tells the truth and exposes evil and seeks with Beauty and for Beauty to set the world right. That somehow, somewhere eternal and perfect Beauty sits above Truth and Right I can conceive, but here and now and in the world in which I work they are for me unseparated and inseparable.

This is brought to us peculiarly when as artists we face our own past as a people. There has come to us—and it has come especially through the man we are going to honor tonight*— a realization of that past, of which for long years we have been ashamed, for which we have apologized. We thought nothing could come out of that past which we wanted to remember; which we wanted to hand down to our children. Suddenly, this same past is taking on form, color and reality, and in a half shamefaced way we are beginning to be proud

* Dr. Carter G. Woodson, who was awarded the Spingarn Medal on this occasion.

of it. We are remembering that the romance of the world did not die and lie forgotten in the Middle Age; that if you want romance to deal with you you must have it here and now and in your own hands.

I once knew a man and woman. They had two children, a daughter who was white and a daughter who was brown; the daughter who was white married a white man; and when her wedding was preparing the daughter who was brown prepared to go and celebrate. But the mother said, "No!" and the brown daughter went into her room and turned on the gas and died. Do you want Greek tragedy swifter than that?

Or again, here is a little Southern town and you are in the public square. On one side of the square is the office of a colored lawyer and on all the other sides are men who do not like colored lawyers. A white woman goes into the black man's office and points to the white-filled square and says, "I want five hundred dollars now and if I do not get it I am going to scream."

Have you heard the story of the conquest of German East Africa? Listen to the untold tale: There were 40,000 black men and 4,000 white men who talked German. There were 20,000 black men and 12,000 white men who talked English. There were 10,000 black men and 400 white men who talked French. In Africa then where the Mountains of the Moon raised their white and snow-capped heads into the mouth of the tropic sun, where Nile and Congo rise and the Great Lakes swim, these men fought; they struggled on mountain, hill and valley, in river, lake and swamp, until in masses they sickened, crawled and died; until the 4,000 white Germans had become mostly bleached bones; until nearly all the 12,000 white Englishmen had returned to South Africa, and the 400 Frenchmen to Belgium and Heaven; all except a mere handful of the white men died; but thousands of black men from East, West and South Africa, from Nigeria and the Valley of the Nile, and from the West Indies still struggled, fought and died. For four years they fought and won and lost German East Africa; and all you hear about it is that England and Belgium conquered German Africa for the allies!

Such is the true and stirring stuff of which Romance is

born and from this stuff come the stirrings of men who are beginning to remember that this kind of material is theirs; and this vital life of their own kind is beckoning them on.

The question comes next as to the interpretation of these new stirrings, of this new spirit: Of what is the colored artist capable? We had had on the part of both colored and white people singular unanimity of judgment in the past. Colored people have said: "This work must be inferior because it is done by colored people." But today there is coming to both the realization that the work of the black man is not always inferior. Interesting stories come to us. A professor in the University of Chicago read to a class that had studied literature a passage of poetry and asked them to guess the author. They guessed a goodly company from Shelley and Robert Browning down to Tennyson and Masefield. The author was Countee Cullen. Or again the English critic John Drinkwater went down to a Southern seminary, one of the sort which "finishes" young white women of the South. The students sat with their wooden faces while he tried to get some response out of them. Finally he said, "Name me some of your Southern poets." They hesitated. He said finally, "I'll start out with your best: Paul Laurence Dunbar"!

With the growing recognition of Negro artists in spite of the severe handicaps, one comforting thing is occurring to both white and black. They are whispering, "Here is a way out. Here is the real solution of the color problem. The recognition accorded Cullen, Hughes, Fauset, White and others shows there is no real color line. Keep quiet! Don't complain! Work! All will be well!"

I will not say that already this chorus amounts to a conspiracy. Perhaps I am naturally too suspicious. But I will say that there are today a surprising number of white people who are getting great satisfaction out of these younger Negro writers because they think it is going to stop agitation of the Negro question. They say, "What is the use of your fighting and complaining; do the great thing and the reward is there." And many colored people are all too eager to follow this advice; especially those who are weary of the eternal struggle along the color line, who are afraid to fight and to whom the money of philanthropists and the alluring publicity are subtle and deadly bribes. They say, "What is the use of fighting? Why not show simply what we deserve and let the reward come to us?"

And it is right here that the National Association for the Advancement of Colored People comes upon the field, comes with its great call to a new battle, a new fight and new things to fight before the old things are wholly won; and to say that the Beauty of Truth and Freedom which shall some day be our heritage and the heritage of all civilized men is not in our hands yet and that we ourselves must not fail to realize.

There is in New York tonight a black woman molding clay by herself in a little bare room, because there is not a single school of sculpture in New York where she is welcome. Surely there are doors she might burst through, but when God makes a sculptor He does not always make the pushing sort of person who beats his way through doors thrust in his face. This girl is working her hands off to get out of this country so that she can get some sort of training.

There was Richard Brown. If he had been white he would have been alive today instead of dead of neglect. Many helped him when he asked but he was not the kind of boy that always asks. He was simply one who made colors sing.

There is a colored woman in Chicago who is a great musician. She thought she would like to study at Fontainebleau this summer where Walter Damrosch and a score of leaders of Art have an American School of music. But the application blank of this school says: "I am a white American and I apply for admission to the school."

We can go on the stage; we can be just as funny as white Americans wish us to be; we can play all the sordid parts that America likes to assign to Negroes; but for anything else there is still small place for us.

And so I might go on. But let me sum up with this: Suppose the only Negro who survived some centuries hence was the Negro painted by white Americans in the novels and essays they have written. What would people in a hundred years say of black Americans? Now turn it around. Suppose you were to write a story and put in it the kind of people you

know and like and imagine. You might get it published and
you might not. And the "might not" is still far bigger than the
"might." The white publishers catering to white folk would
say, "It is not interesting"—to white folk, naturally not. They
want Uncle Toms, Topsies, good "darkies" and clowns. I
have in my office a story with all the earmarks of truth. A
young man says that he started out to write and had his
stories accepted. Then he began to write about the things he
knew best about, that is, about his own people. He submitted
a story to a magazine which said, "We are sorry, but we
cannot take it." I sat down and revised my story, changing the
color of the characters and the locale and sent it under an
assumed name with a change of address and it was accepted
by the same magazine that had refused it, the editor promising to take anything else I might send in providing it was
good enough.

We have, to be sure, a few recognized and successful
Negro artists; but they are not all those fit to survive or even
a good minority. They are but the remnants of that ability
and genius among us whom the accidents of education and
opportunity have raised on the tidal waves of chance. We
black folk are not altogether peculiar in this. After all, in the
world at large, it is only the accident, the remnant, that gets
the chance to make the most of itself; but if this is true of the
white world it is infinitely more true of the colored world. It
is not simply the great clear tenor of Roland Hayes that
opened the ears of America. We have had many voices of all
kinds as fine as his and America was and is as deaf as she
was for years to him. Then a foreign land heard Hayes and
put its imprint on him and immediately America with all its
imitative snobbery woke up. We approved Hayes because
London, Paris and Berlin approved him and not simply because he was a great singer.

Thus it is the bounden duty of black America to begin this
great work of the creation of Beauty, of the preservation of
Beauty, of the realization of Beauty, and we must use in this
work all the methods that men have used before. And what
have been the tools of the artist in times gone by? First of all,
he has used the Truth—not for the sake of truth, not as a

scientist seeking truth, but as one upon whom Truth eternally thrusts itself as the highest handmaid of imagination, as the one great vehicle of universal understanding. Again artists have used Goodness—goodness in all its aspects of justice, honor and right—not for the sake of an ethical sanction but as the one true method of gaining sympathy and human interest.

The apostle of Beauty thus becomes the apostle of Truth and Right not by choice but by inner and outer compulsion. Free he is but his freedom is ever bounded by Truth and Justice; and slavery only dogs him when he is denied the right to tell the Truth or recognize an ideal of Justice.

Thus all Art is propaganda and ever must be, despite the wailing of the purists. I stand in utter shamelessness and say that whatever art I have for writing has been used always for propaganda for gaining the right of black folk to love and enjoy. I do not care a damn for any art that is not used for propaganda. But I do care when propaganda is confined to one side while the other is stripped and silent.

In New York we have two plays; "White Cargo" and "Congo." In "White Cargo" there is a fallen woman. She is black. In "Congo" the fallen woman is white. In "White Cargo" the black woman goes down further and further and in "Congo" the white woman begins with degradation but in the end is one of the angels of the Lord.

You know the current magazine story: A young white man goes down to Central America and the most beautiful colored woman there falls in love with him. She crawls across the whole isthmus to get to him. The white man says nobly, "No." He goes back to his white sweetheart in New York.

In such cases, it is not the positive propaganda of people who believe white blood divine, infallible and holy to which I object. It is the denial of a similar right of propaganda to those who believe black blood human, lovable and inspired with new ideals for the world. White artists themselves suffer from this narrowing of their field. They cry for freedom in dealing with Negroes because they have so little freedom in dealing with whites. DuBose Heywood writes "Porgy" and writes beautifully of the black Charleston underworld. But why does he do this? Because he cannot do a similar thing for the white people of Charleston, or they would drum him out of town. The only chance he had to tell the truth of pitiful human degradation was to tell it of colored people. I should not be surprised if Octavius Roy Cohen had approached the Saturday Evening Post and asked permission to write about a different kind of colored folk than the monstrosities he has created; but if he has, the Post has replied, "No. You are getting paid to write about the kind of colored people you are writing about."

In other words, the white public today demands from its artists, literary and pictorial, racial pre-judgment which deliberately distorts Truth and Justice, as far as colored races are concerned, and it will pay for no other.

On the other hand, the young and slowly growing black public still wants its prophets almost equally unfree. We are bound by all sorts of customs that have come down as second-hand soul clothes of white patrons. We are ashamed of sex and we lower our eyes when people will talk of it. Our religion holds us in superstition. Our worst side has been so shamelessly emphasized that we are denying we have or ever had a worst side. In all sorts of ways we are hemmed in and our new young artists have got to fight their way to freedom.

The ultimate judge has got to be you and you have got to build yourselves up into that wide judgment, that catholicity of temper which is going to enable the artist to have his widest chance for freedom. We can afford the Truth. White folk today cannot. As it is now we are handing everything over to a white jury. If a colored man wants to publish a book, he has got to get a white publisher and a white newspaper to say it is great; and then you and I say so. We must come to the place where the work of art when it appears is reviewed and acclaimed by our own free and unfettered judgment. And we are going to have a real and valuable and eternal judgment only as we make ourselves free of mind, proud of body and just of soul to all men.

And then do you know what will be said? It is already saying. Just as soon as true Art emerges; just as soon as the black artist appears, someone touches the race on the shoulder and says, "He did that because he was an American, not because he was a Negro; he was born here; he was trained here; he is not a Negro—what is a Negro anyhow? He is just human; it is the kind of thing you ought to expect."

I do not doubt that the ultimate art coming from black folk is going to be just as beautiful, and beautiful largely in the same ways, as the art that comes from white folk, or yellow, or red; but the point today is that until the art of the black folk compels recognition they will not be rated as human. And when through art they compel recognition then let the world discover if it will that their art is as new as it is old and as old as new.

I had a classmate once who did three beautiful things and died. One of them was a story of a folk who found fire and then went wandering in the gloom of night seeking again the stars they had once known and lost; suddenly out of blackness they looked up and there loomed the heavens; and what was it that they said? They raised a mighty cry: "It is the stars, it is the ancient stars, it is the young and everlasting stars!"

From *The Crisis*, Vol. 32, No. 6, October, 1926, pp. 290–97

The Vision of Phillis the Blessed (1941)
(An Allegory of Negro American Literature in the Eighteenth and Nineteenth Centuries)

> The blessed Damozel leaned out
>   From the gold bar of Heaven:
> Her eyes were deeper than the depth
>   Of waters stilled at even;
> She had three lilies in her hand
>   And the stars in her hair were seven.

I find in these well-known verses of Rossetti, a text upon which to build a brief review of the literature of American Negroes before the twentieth century. In 1754 there was born in West Africa a little black girl who was miraculously lifted across the wide Atlantic and set down as a servant to a pious well-read New England woman.

"I was a poor little outcast and a stranger when she took me in, not only into her house, but I presently became a sharer in her most tender affections. I was treated by her more like her child than her servant."

Phillis was a child of seven when she landed in Boston; old enough to know the beginnings of life; the first patterns of her ancestral culture; she remembered her mother pouring libations before the rising sun; she sensed the contrast between tropical Africa and bleak New England. From portrait and description we know her as frail and slight, with little hands and feet, thin lips, small nose and wide temples. Her skin was darkly brown, velvet and glossy. Her hair, tight-curled, grasped her high round head like a close woven cap of tendrils. Her eyes were large and black—

> Her eyes were deeper than the depth,
> Of waters stilled at even.

Her gift of verse in a foreign tongue and a stilted repressed culture was not great and yet it was there. She sang to the Earl of Dartmouth when the Stamp Act was repealed—

> Should you, my lord, while you peruse my song,
> Wonder from whence my love of freedom sprung;
> Whence flow those wishes for the common good,
> By feeling hearts alone best understood—
> I, young in life, by seeming cruel fate,
> Was snatched from Afric's fancied happy seat.
> What pangs excruciating must molest,
> What sorrows labour in my parents' breast!
> Steeled was that soul, and by no misery moved,
> That from a father seized his babe beloved:
> Such, such my case.

She made a strange and lonesome figure in the America of the day just before the Revolution—calm and correct without, silent. Her deep sense of religion and evangelical patois veiled her more human soul to us as it did to Thomas Jefferson. Yet within must have bloomed and sung a world of Phantasy. It is these imagined visions of Phillis, in the long days of her childhood wonder, her first happiness of young womanhood and the hard long martyrdom of her after years that made her Phillis the Blessed. There was in Phillis just the suggestion—not more—of something fey, wild and elemental, sternly repressed, confined so that the inner soul never burst through, only the transmuted echo—refined (she loved the word), not crude, not brash:

> Before my mortal eyes,
> The lightnings blaze across the vaulted skies,
> And, as the thunder shakes the heav'nly plains,
> A deep felt horror thrills through all my veins.
> When gentler strains demand thy graceful song,
> The length'ning lines moves languishing along.

Was Phillis blessed? Yes! with security and affection, with education beyond her status, by contact with cultured folk. Surely this is the beginning of blessing; and then with sorrow and bereavement, with poverty and hunger, with death and pain. Only Love was lacking—love and its loss. Reverence, affection, friendship—all these were hers; but she was a love-less child, woman and wife. Lacking this miracle, she could never be a Saint—but she was Phillis the Blessed.

Always a certain sense of mystery lurked in the furtherest reaches of Phillis' consciousness—the miracle of her sudden transport to this far land; the hoarse voice of the Visions, the dire deep Visions, thus floated and drifted, loomed and died in her thoughts and dreams. In the only home she knew—and the only friends she had, she was always partly a stranger. Only her phantasy was real, only her dreams were true. She could not help but have visions—prophetic visions—she who in a single childhood had encompassed the ends of earth.

She loved flowers and saw but few: buttercups and daisies, arbutus and violets; less often, a rose. She dimly remembered riots of blooms; purple wisteria, flowering bougainvillea, orange poinciana and crimson poinsettas; but she shrank from these—thither lay riot and revolt and wild desire and hate; and she shrunk within herself—peace, quiet, silence was her way; only she yearned for quiet lilies; and the stars in her hair were seven.

The stars were her friends, her old and trusted friends. They alone knew her tall ghost mother, and sisters; —Were there sisters and brothers? She thought so, but they were dim and vague. But her tall straight mother, she was real. So were the stars. Some stars were gone—a little jeweled cross from the south was lost as she was; others were misplaced. But she knew them and loved them. They were hers. Mornings they sang together.

Looking out from her own singular and narrow corner of the world, Phillis must have had visions of the souls and voices, who, coming after her, continued and fulfilled her promise and tradition—David Walker and his bitter cry; the lilt of love that sang in Armand Lanusse; the busy chronicle of George Williams; the labored tales of Wells Brown; Alberry Whitman trying desperately to sing; and finally the grown and finished figures of Charles Waddell Chesnutt, master of fiction; and Paul Laurence Dunbar, the Song of Songs.

I seem to see her there then one hundred sixty-five years ago, with hands holding the three lilies of her thought; the tall, white lily of her faith—faith despite the world's paradox, which she saw all too well; the tiger lily, gold and black and typifying her inward frightened revolt; and finally the little purple flower of her sorrow.

She leaned out and then as now Heaven was barred with gold. Without lay poverty, darkness and dirt; without crawled crime and disease, while within the angels sang; and far above and beyond gleamed the morning stars; they sang together, and slowly seven came down and nestled in her hair—her stiff and crinkly close-curled hair; so the stars in her hair were seven. And Phillis yearned down from heaven to earth, striving to lift the soul of a people.

The singing of stars and the odor of lilies typified strange new happenings in America. For in the new born nation, a new folk-song was being born in the throats of slaves and the words set to it made a new folk poetry—unformed, unset, peering out here and there amid dross, in sudden beauty, and halting phrase. These words of the Negro Folk song have been seldom studied, but must not be forgot. Phillis did not

hear them, save as vague prophecy of unremembered things. I
set their voices down at hazard with a few dozen phrases.
They are songs which Phillis never knew but always sensed:

Swing Low Sweet Chariot,
Roll, Jordan, roll!
Steal Away, Steal Away Home!
Nobody Knows the Trouble I See,
Dark Midnight Was My Cry;
I Been Listening All the Night Long,
I Couldn't Hear Nobody Pray.
I'm So Glad Trouble Don't Last Always—

Good News, the Chariot's Coming!
I'm Going to Lay Down My Burden!
Go Down Moses Way Down in Egypt Land!
Stand the Storm, It Won't Be Long,
O the Rocks and the Mountains Shall All Flee Away;
The Moon Runs Down in a Purple Stream,
Deep River, I Want to Cross Over Into Camp Ground!
'Tis Me, 'Tis Me, O Lord Standing in the Need of Prayer!

My God! What a Morning When the Stars Begin to Fall;
O the Stars of the Elements Are Falling and the Moon Drips
   Away Into Blood,
I Hope to Shout Glory When the World's On Fire,
Rise and Shine and Give God the Glory,
Ride On, King Jesus!
Listen to the Lambs All A-Crying;
Children We All Shall Be Free!
O the Land I Am Bound For;
I've Heard of a City Called Heaven
I'm Tramping, Tramping, Trying to Make Heaven My
   Home.

You may bury me in the east,
   You may bury me in the west,
I'll lie in the grave and stretch out my arms;
Dust, dust and ashes, fly over my grave;
I got a rainbow round my shoulder!

Sometimes, not often, and more rarely as time flew, Phillis remembered echoes of African fairy legend. They glided ghostly behind her thought, bringing thrills of happiness, which were almost memories, but never quite. One little tale kept up its mystic, vanishing dance:

The rabbit raced by; the elephant, waiting for his dinner beside the ant-hill asked

"Who are you?"

"I am a hare."

"Where are you going?"

"Blind one, haven't you seen all my comrades passing?"

And the rabbit, circling secretly, ran by again and again. The elephant became uneasy, imagining hundreds of rabbits; so at last as the rabbit again ran by, he saw only the far-off wagging of the elephant's tail.

"There he is! There he is!" cried the rabbit, as the elephant rushed out of sight and left the ant-hill for the rabbit's dinner.

From such vague, half-remembered folk-lore, Phillis never knew how the African rabbit came into American literature.

Continuing my allegory, I see the seven stars in Phillis' hair, set like rare jewels in the dense and clinging mass that crowned her womanhood, as points of utter light, upward towards which strove little unborn souls for whom the soul of Phillis strove and yearned. One by one, over years and centuries, they leapt heavenward like thin flames; and over the birth of each, Phillis shivered with appeal and longing; and before her eyes the Visions passed. Men they were, who for one hundred fifty years, in stress and striving, continued the vision of Phillis the Blessed. They not only mirrored her soul but illumined the ages. What they became in later years, she in a very real sense, fore-shadowed and fore-knew.

With her careful training, her yearning for peace, her obedience to authority and conformity with life, she shared the culture of old New England, and was at home in a world into which her natural disposition fitted. Yet withal she saw its incongruities and contradictions. She was painfully aware that her color set her singularly apart, but she seldom mentioned it. She was aware of slavery but said little about it. She came to know poverty and hardship and in seeking love found death and saw her starving children waste away.

The heaven where she stood as a girl, became transformed in her womanhood. Its golden bar was lowered; happiness poured out, poverty and pain rushed in. Yet she never wavered in the high price she placed on her own womanhood or in her conception of the destiny of her people. Ever she yearned downward to her folk, calling to the skies, the thin flames within their souls.

The reason for this lay deeper than timidity or fear. The world of Phillis Wheatley lay around the American Revolution and the beginnings of a new United States. Black folk of that day were full of hope. The national holiday was the day of dark Crispus Attucks' death. After rebuff, black soldiers had been welcomed into the American armies. Slavery practically disappeared in Massachusetts before Phillis died and the wave of manumission swept south. Soon it seemed, all men would be free and equal.

There came change. There came the death of Phillis Wheatley in 1784, pitiful in her desertion, squalor and poverty; and her dying breath almost swept the face of David Walker even as he was born. He must have been a vision of Phillis the Blessed as she died; the nightmare of that bleak winter of tragedy. Walker never saw Phillis; but he heard of her after he came from North Carolina and conducted his second-hand clothing shop on Brattle Street. He knew that between 1784 when Phillis died and he was born, and 1830 the date of his death, the situation of black folk in the United States changed. It was indeed almost revolutionized. Slavery was no longer dying. It was increasingly excused and defended. For black slaves had become the founding stone of the Cotton Kingdom. The culture of America grew harsher and more vulgar; Southern greed and Yankee thrift on wide rich acres of land and with rich natural resources were beginning to assert themselves and dominate the land. America was no longer Sanctuary; it was becoming Wealth and Power.

Restriction and discrimination increasingly surrounded the Negro and the iron entered his soul.

Out of this rose a harsh voice and the voice was David Walker. He shrieked rather than spoke; he stuttered and never sang; yet his reaction to the new-rooted slavery and the growing degradation of the Negro race was so human and natural a reaction, that he must be set down among men who make literature because he so fiercely voiced his day. The thin flame of the soul of Phillis the Blessed became red revolt in David Walker, he whose stilted, hard-born bitterness cried first in the night of the nineteenth-century slavery. David Walker, six feet in height, dark with flying hair, was the voice of revolt; and before Garrison spoke or Douglass pled, he damned slavery to hell in sharp, angry staccato phrase, with italics and capitals, set down in one thin book which scared a whole nation and brought him death. He had neither English nor manners. He had no grace nor comeliness, but he flamed. He said in 1829, "We (coloured people of these United States) are the most degraded, wretched and abject set of beings, that ever lived since the world began, and I pray God, that none like us ever may live until time shall be no more."

He threw the Declaration of Independence in the nation's face. "See your declaration, Americans!!! Do you understand your own language? Hear your language, proclaimed to the world, July 4, 1776, 'We hold these truths to be self evident —that ALL men are CREATED EQUAL!! that they are endowed by their Creator with certain unalienable rights; that among these are life, liberty, and the pursuit of happiness'!!! compare your own language above, extracted from your Declaration of Independence, with your cruelties and murders inflicted . . . on our fathers and on us!"

The South stormed protest and offered rich reward for Walker's silence. But Walker's *Appeal* ran to three editions in seven months. Suddenly he died.

If David Walker was the bitter vision of Phillis' dying breath, it was not the typical vision of her life. That we shall find in the springtime of 1769. She was then a girl of fifteen, timidly straining at her chrysalis; she had begun to study astronomy and Latin. She was essaying poetry and writing of "the happy dead." She dreamed her dream lying on the new-born grass and bashful flowers of a New England spring. Birds sang in the dark branches of the great trees. The song murmured to melody and dance; far away there was gayety and love; the day dream of Phillis became a Vision. She saw New Orleans and heard it as it lived seventy-five years later, in 1769.

It is rather singular that the same movements and forces which were crushing the mass of Negroes, were in one part of the United States far removed from New England, bringing to Negroes and mulattoes the first flowering of literature; and not simply to black America but to white. The free Negroes of Louisiana profited by the slave system despite the pall it laid upon them; they owned slaves and land; some were wealthy land holders; others, well-to-do in professions and as artisans, easily passed into art and literature. They fought bitterly a caste system which bracketed with slaves those who were not slaves, and with Negroes, those who were only in part of Negro descent.

Education and wealth united their tongues to voice both joy and sorrow. They led singing and dancing in Louisiana, France and Spain. In 1840 a group of young Negro writers in New Orleans, secure in income, if not in wealth, and some of them trained in Europe, began to publish their writings, as well as compose music. First came their lovely folk songs like "Pov' piti Lolotte"; and then in 1843 the *Literary Album*, a journal of young folk, amateurs in literature, appeared, written in French. Finally in 1845, under the leadership of Armand Lanusse, there was published the first anthology of Negro verse, and the second of any verse, in America. It was on a literary level far higher than anything produced contemporaneously anywhere else in the land. It was French in language, culture and fashion; and yet, American in content and American Negro. Scrupulously avoiding propaganda and racial consciousness, nevertheless the under-current of its language had to be the American color line and the slave system.

Some of the young men who produced *Les Cenelles*, that

is, "The Holly-Berries," as the anthology was called—rank high in French literature; particularly Camille Thierry; but the leader of the group, Lanusse, was born and educated in Louisiana and was the moving spirit of this literary blossoming. He dedicated the beautifully printed volume "to the fair sex of Louisiana," and said:

> Receive these Holly-Berries,
> From our devoted hearts;
> A modest glance from eyes cast down
> Will pay us more than wide renown.

In the introduction he explained: "One begins to understand that in the position that fate has placed us, a sound education is the shield to blunt the arrows of scorn and calumny aimed at us. It is then with a feeling of pride that we see increasing daily the number of those among us who pursue with firm step, the difficult path of those arts and sciences toward which they are attracted."

Seventeen colored poets contributed to "The Holly-Berries" which contained eighty-two poems and covered two hundred fifteen pages. Nothing in American Negro literature would have as completely answered the dreams and aspirations of Phillis' soul and the rare pattern of her culture, as *Les Cenelles* published fifty-eight years after her death.

In the summer of 1763 Phillis was nineteen, and already the cold New England climate had affected her lungs. Her thoughtful mistress took her to England where almost literally she stood before kings. Phillis became a center of aristocratic flattery and attention and published her first book of poems under high patronage. She was there the first of a series of Negro American visitors and must have been stirred by ambition. Standing in the sumptuous drawing-room of the Countess of Huntingdon, surrounded by well-bred and well-dressed people, she would certainly dream of a day when some of these skins would be black—when it would be natural to see folk of all races mingling in a democracy of culture. Standing thus and dreaming, if Phillis could have looked forward eighty years, she would have seen another visitor of England—a young and handsome, curly-haired brown man.

He was William Wells Brown. Born in 1815, and dying in 1884, he became one of the most prolific of colored writers, pouring forth essays, novels and histories. None of his writings were great but many of them were widely read. His novel *Clotelle* was a bold venture and had for its heroine the mulatto daughter of a president of the United States. There is a charming passage in his *Black Man* where he tells of seeing Alexandre Dumas at the opera:

I had been in Paris a week without seeing Dumas, for my letter of introduction from Louis Blanc, who was then in exile in England, and to M. Eugene Sue, had availed me nothing as regarded a sight of the great colored author. . . . In a double box nearly opposite me, containing a party of six or eight, I noticed a light complexioned mulatto, apparently about fifty years of age—curly hair, full-face, dressed in a black coat, white vest, white kids—who seemed to be the centre of attraction, not only in his own circle, but in others. Those in the pit looked up, those in the gallery looked down, while curtains were drawn aside at other boxes and stalls to get a sight of the colored man. So recently from America, where caste was so injurious to my race, I began to think that it was his wooly head that attracted attention, when I was informed that the mulatto before me was no less a person than Alexandre Dumas. Every move, look and gesture of the celebrated romancer were watched in the closest manner by the audience. Even Mario appeared to feel that his part on the stage was of less importance than that of the colored man in the royal box.

There is a passage in another book, when as a delegate to the great Peace Congress of 1849 held in Paris, Brown was invited to the home of De Tocqueville, Minister of Foreign Affairs, and seated on the sofa by Madame De Tocqueville's side: "I recognised among many of my countrymen, who were gazing at me, the American Consul, Mr. Walsh. My position did not improve his looks."

But I quote from *Clotell*:

The child, however, watched the chaise, and startled her mother by screaming out at the top of her voice, "Papa! papa!" and clapped her little hands for joy. The mother turned in haste to look at the strangers, and her eyes encountered those of Henry's pale and dejected countenance. Gertrude's eyes were on the child. The swiftness with which Henry drove by could not hide from his wife the striking resemblance of the child to himself. The young wife had heard the child exclaim "Papa! papa!" and she immediately saw by the quivering of his lips and the agitation depicted in his countenance, that all was not right.

"Who is the woman? And why did the child call you papa?" she inquired, with a trembling voice.

Once in a dim and stately Boston library, I can imagine Phillis Wheatley, shrinking from curious eyes, might find herself in an alcove and scanning the volumes she would be startled to see two, strangely almost impossibly, lettered— gold on green. She took a volume down reverently. She saw a steel engraving of the close-cropped hair and strong mulatto face of George Washington Williams. She remembered George Washington. She saw him again with all his aides in military glory as he bent above her dark little hand. She had written to him:

> Where high unfurl'd the ensign waves in air.
> Shall I to Washington their praise recite?
> Enough thou knowest them in the field of fight.
> Thee first in place and honours—we demand
> The grace and glory of thy martial band.
> Fam'd for thy valour, for thy virtues more,
> Hear every tongue thy guardian aid implore!

Washington replied, "However undeserving I may be of such encomium and panegyric, the style and manner exhibit a striking proof of your poetical talents." That was in 1776; but this book, *History of the Negro Race*, was begun in 1876, one hundred years later! Phillis started as she saw its date of publication, one hundred years after her own death. The darkness of sleep fell about her.

George Washington Williams, the first of American Negro historians, was different in thought and kind from Phillis Wheatley. Any vision which Phillis had of him would have been blurred and uncertain. He was a quick, positive, systematic American. I remember seeing him once at the home of a cousin; a rather short man, light brown, with an air of tireless efficiency. This was shown by his monumental history of the Negro race in America. He tells the story of its inception:

> I was requested to deliver an oration on the Fourth of July, 1876, at Avondale, Ohio. It being the one hundredth birthday of the American Republic, I determined to prepare an oration on the American Negro. I at once began an investigation of the records of the nation to secure material for the oration. I was surprised and delighted to find that the historical memorials of the Negro were so abundant and so creditable to him. . . . I became convinced that a history of the Colored people in America was required because of the amply historically trustworthy material at hand; because the Colored people themselves had been the most vexatious problem in North America, from the time of its discovery down to the present day. . . . The single reason that there was no history of the Negro race would have been sufficient reason for writing one. . . . In the preparation of this work I have consulted over twelve thousand volumes—about one thousand of which are referred to in the footnotes—and thousands of pamphlets.

All the while, in these days of Phillis' dreaming, there were ever prophetic whisperings that were hardly voices—never Visions, yet discernible; Jupiter Hammond and George Horton, who put down earnest broken words; Frances Harper, who almost sang; William Nell, who foreran George Williams; and Gustavus Vassa, who started the stream of slave narratives which rose to a flood of protest, plea and threat. The trumpet calls of Douglass and Ringold Ward and the sermons of Crummell rolled back across the years; but they were tuned above the ears of Phillis; they were not literature, they were Life.

From 1774 to 1780, waves of disaster overwhelmed Phillis Wheatley. From the height of favor and restored health at the British Court, she heard of sickness at home and refusing to wait for presentation to George III in person, she hurried back to the death of both kind foster parents. Homeless and aghast, she lived a space alone and with members of the Wheatley family, and then married.

While Phillis never saw among British aristocracy anyone resembling William Wells Brown, when she came back to America, she did become acquainted with the rather unusual figure of John Peters. Little is known of him, and he has been variously and usually rather disparagingly judged. Yet from the scattered facts, the picture of this man is clear. He was one of those atypical men who in the face of public opinion rose above his station and stubbornly clung there in the face of the winds of adversity, perhaps despite his own shortcomings. He was a free colored man who opened a grocery store in Court Street, who dabbled both in medicine and in law, and made a fair living, almost a fortune, for his day. He carried himself as a gentleman of his time: he was handsome and well set-up; he wore a wig and carried a cane; he spoke and wrote with fluency. But when misfortune came, when with dozens of his whiter neighbors he sank beneath the ruin of war and lost his business and his income, he did not surrender; he would not become a servant nor a day laborer. He clung desperately to his role of gentleman and went to jail for debt rather than dig ditches. The world, white and black, snarled and jibed at him.

Coming back from England with the picture of English gentlemen in her mind's eye, with the far off vision of what black folk might become even in a white world, Phillis met and was dazzled by John Peters. They were married in 1778 and with his encouragement she planned to publish another volume of poems dedicated to Benjamin Franklin. But before it appeared, misfortune overtook them. The war ruined Peters. They moved out into the country. Two children were born and died. In 1784, Peters was in jail and Phillis laboring as a servant. A third child and Phillis herself died that year.

The brooding of Phillis in those awful days brought out all the contradiction, the clash of religious submission against the self-assertion of revolt. She sang:

But here I sit, and mourn a grov'ling mind,
That fain would mount, and ride upon the wind.
Not you, my friend, these plaintive strains become,
Not you, whose bosom is the Muses home;
When they from tow'ring Helicon retire,
They fan in you the bright immortal fire,
But I less happy, cannot raise the song,
The fault'ring music dies upon my tongue.

This friend of poets to whom she sang, sang in turn to a soul not yet born; he was not yet alive; he was not yet struggling with the uprush of song within him. He came to earth seventy-five years later than the day when Phillis, sitting beside the sea, heard it crash and roar against New England rock. Even so the hills and skies of Kentucky struggled in the childhood and youth of Alberry Whitman. This unhappy singer saw poverty like that of Phillis. He became a poor preacher, but above all a poet. He sang because he must; because the repressed flood of song born in Phillis and living again in Lanusse, now raged in him for utterance.

The scene had vastly changed since the day of David Walker. Negroes had begun to find themselves and to act in their own defense. They had fought the good fight of employment, from the decades when Irish mobs of competing laborers beat them to death in Cincinnati and New York, to the reign of the celebrated guild of Philadelphia caterers who founded and introduced a new vocation and a new source of income between 1840 and 1870. Negroes had met in convention, they had published newspapers, they had produced public advocates like Frederick Douglass. They had produced in Whitman, a preacher in the African Methodist Church, an agent seeking to raise funds for the new colored university at Wilberforce, a young man who tried desperately to rise above a limited training, amid the examples of mediocre expression current in America, and enter the stream of real literature.

Perhaps he did not quite succeed. Certainly he never became popular. He died prematurely at the age of fifty in Atlanta, and only through his daughters on the vaudeville stage could his family make a living.

But Alberry Whitman had a real gift of song and his long

narrative poems still deserve attention. Stanzas like this, live:

> The tall forests swim in a crimson sea,
> Out of whose bright depths rising silently,
> Great Golden spires shoot into the skies,
> Among the isles of cloudland high, that rise,
> Float, scatter, burst, drift off, and slowly fade,
> Deep in the twilight, shade succeeding shade.

Out of winters of war and disaster, rolled the spring of 1784, the last Spring of Phillis Wheatley. Boston lay still freezing beneath a blanket of soiled snow. Phillis looked out of her attic window on black and staggering buildings, through broken panes and fog. Within was cold and hunger. On a pallet her last child lay dying, moaning and rolling her little head. All others were gone—family, husband, friends. Phillis leaned against the wall back of the bed, fronting the window. Her body was wracked with pain, the child became a gasp. The falling snow without grew whiter and thicker, until it seemed to take the form of Death, Phillis whispered

O happy Death!

The child died. And it was as if Death took Phillis up into his mighty arms where she lay black and frail with star-shine in her uncurbed hair, with crimson drops on her lips. Her great black eyes were straining upwards:

> Her eyes were deeper than the depth
> Of waters stilled at even.

They grew softer as she glimpsed the starlit heavens above the storm. She saw the white heat of Sirius and remembered her vision of the Bitter Cry; she heard again the Songs of the Lilt of Love, which were the blue stars of Orion's belt; her vision of the Labored Tale came back in red Arcturus, and she read again the Annals in the multi-colored Swan. Crimson Antares was surely the song that broke in Whitman's throat. She sighed and closed her weary eyes, but felt the lightening of the world. Morning was breaking in the east and above it blazed the morning star.

"Am I dead" she asked.
Death murmured "You shall never die."
"Whose are these stars" she asked.
"They are your children; they are seven."
She shook her head with infinite weariness.
"My children and my dreams are dead."
"The stars are your children; your dreams are immortal."
"What is this last light of morning?"

There loomed behind the fading wraith of Death, the vast black figure of Time, earth-wide and heaven-high. And Death and Time together said:

"In very truth, Charles Chesnutt is child of the tradition and aspiration of Phillis the Blessed. What matter if they lived a century apart?"

Charles Waddell Chesnutt was a white man with Negro blood; a lawyer and court stenographer, born in North Carolina and living most of his life as a distinguished citizen of Cleveland, Ohio. He was born one hundred years after the birth of Phillis. He was first among us to sense the dramatic possibilities of the life of Negroes and mulattoes in America since the Civil War. Chesnutt knew the American public from close social intermingling and intercourse with them, and finally he was master of a clear, trained English style. The result was that his venture in romance, first published in the *Atlantic Monthly*, soon became a series of volumes, treating nearly every phase of current interracial relations. I need not bring notice of these books to your attention. Surely you know them: *The House Behind the Cedars, The Conjure Woman, The Wife of His Youth, The Colonel's Dream.* Perhaps I might pause for a moment to recall one thrilling picture in *The Marrow of Tradition.*

The colored Janet is facing her white sister, who hitherto has ignored her but now begs Janet's husband, a skilled physician, to save her child, speaks:

"Listen!" she cried, dashing her tears aside. "I have but one word for you—one last word—and then I hope never to see your face again! My mother died of want, and I was brought up by the hand of charity. Now, when I have married a man who can supply my needs, you offer me back the money which you and your friends have robbed me of! You imagined that the shame of being a Negro swallowed up every other ignominy—and in your eyes I am a Negro, though I am your sister, and you are white, and people have taken me for you on the streets—and you, therefore, left me nameless all my life! Now, when an honest man has given me a name of which I can be proud, you offer me the one of which you robbed me, and of which I can make no use. For twenty-five years I, poor, despicable fool, would have kissed your feet for a word, a nod, a smile. Now, when this tardy recognition comes, for which I have waited so long, it is tainted with fraud and crime and blood, and I must pay for it with my child's life!"

"And I must forfeit that of mine, it seems, for withholding it so long," sobbed the other, as, tottering, she turned to go. "It is but just."

"Stay—do not go yet!" commanded Janet imperiously, her pride still keeping back her tears. "I have not done. I throw you back your father's name, your father's wealth, your sisterly recognition. I want none of them—they are bought too dear! ah, God, they are bought too dear! But that you may know that a woman may be foully wronged, and yet may have a heart to feel, even for one who has injured her, you may have your child's life, if my husband can save it! Will," she said, throwing open the door into the next room, "go with her!"

So Phillis died in the thirtieth year of her youth, and never saw the seventh star which was the Song of Songs. She lay stark and stiff, thin as a skeleton, worn to a shadow, her little dark hands crossed on her flat chest, clasping three lilies. Her crinkled hair formed a dim halo about her head. Yet it was even as the crone said, who shrouded her in white: she did not die; she rose again and lived incarnate in Paul Laurence Dunbar. Again that soul of song lived in a thin, black body and behind eyes

> Deeper than the depth
> Of waters stilled at even.

Again there was the same timid sensitiveness, the same restraint; the same inborn culture. Both souls vainly sought love—she silently and sorrow-bound, he whipt of the furies;

Phillis died choking to sing; in Dunbar the gift of song was surer, stronger, deeper.

Paul Laurence Dunbar, one hundred years after Phillis' death, became one of the great American poets. As William Dean Howells said in an oft quoted passage,

> Paul Dunbar was the only man of pure African blood and of American civilization to feel the Negro life aesthetically and express it lyrically. It seemed to me that this had come to its most modern consciousness in him, and that his brilliant and unique achievement was to have studied the American Negro objectively, and to have presented him as he found him to be, with humor, with sympathy, and yet with what the reader must instinctively feel to be entire truthfulness. I said that a race which had come to this effect in any member of it, had attained civilization in him, and I permitted myself the imaginative prophecy that the hostilities and the prejudices which had so long constrained his race were destined to vanish in the arts; that these were to be the final proof God had made of one blood all nations of men.

Dunbar poems are household words in America: "li'l gal," "Little Brown Baby," "When de Co'n pone's hot," "O Mother Race," and "When Malindy sings":

> She jes' spreads huh mouf and hollahs,
> "Come to Jesus," twell you hyeah
> Sinnahs' tremblin' steps and voices,
> Timid-lak a-drawin' neah;
> Den she tu'ns to "Rock of Ages,"
> Simply to de cross she clings,
> An' you fin' yo' teahs a-drappin;
> When Malindy sings.

In one stanza he wrote his own epitaph

> O Earth, O Sky, O Ocean, both surpassing,
> O heart of mine, O soul that dreads the dark!
> Is there no hope for me: Is there no way
> That I may sight and check that speeding bark
> Which out of sight and sound is passing, passing?

And so the story ends and the phantasy is finished. The seven stars have lived and died, if stars ever die; while the tradition of Phillis the Blessed sinks with odor of lilies below the horizon, as her memory rises; Last night and each night:

> The blessed Damozel leaned out
> From the gold bar of Heaven:
> Her eyes were deeper than the depth
> Of waters stilled at even;
> She had three lilies in her hand
> And the stars in her hair were seven.

From the *Fisk News*, Vol. 14, No. 7, May, 1941, pp. 10–15

The Lie of History as It Is Taught Today (1960) (The Civil War: The War to Preserve Slavery)

One hundred years ago next year this nation began a war more horrible than most wars, and all wars stink. From 1861 to 1865 Americans fought Americans, North fought South, brothers fought brothers. All trampled on the faces of four million black folk cowering beneath their feet in mud and blood. Some Americans hated slavery but were unwilling to fight. They would let the "erring sisters depart in peace," with their elegant luxury, cringing service and home-grown concubines. Free Negroes and their white friends organized the escape of slaves and fugitive slaves became a main cause of the war. One man, John Brown, fought slavery with his bare fists and was crucified three years before the flash of Sumter.

So the nation reeled into murder, hate, hurt and destruction until they killed 493,273 human beings in battle, left a million more in pain, and nearly bankrupted the whole nation. "We are not fighting slavery," cried the North. "We are fighting for independence," cried the South. "We are not fighting with Negroes," insisted the North as it returned black fugitives. "Negroes do not want to be free," jeered the South; Negroes whispered: "Let us fight for freedom." The Northerners hated the struggle and nearly all who could bought immunity, while some laborers rioted and hanged Negroes to lamp posts. Most workers refused to volunteer and thousands of soldiers deserted from the ranks.

The South yelled and rushed to war, ran the Northerners home again and again ranted and blustered and tried to frighten victory out of impossible odds, while their soldiers deserted in increasing droves.

Louder and louder rose voices in the North: "Free the slaves!" It was the only real reason for war. Lincoln was firm: "I am not fighting to free slaves but only for Union— union to planting, manufacture and trade." Still voices arose led by Frederick Douglass: "Arm the slaves." Lincoln said: "It would be giving arms to the enemy."

The Northern armies began to use the slaves as servants, stevedores and spies; already the Southerners were using the slaves to guard their families and to raise food and clothes for themselves as they fought the fight for slavery. The world looked in amazement on this new free democracy as it staggered, killed and destroyed, both sides appealing for help.

Slowly in the gloom thousands of black slaves began silently to move from plantation to the camps of the Northern armies. Slowly the nation joined the cry of black and white abolitionists: "Free the slaves!" And the bleeding trenches added: "Arm them. The slaves are already armed with muscles if not with guns. They will feed the slave power unless we use them." Black regiments appeared in Kansas, South Carolina and Louisiana. Finally Lincoln saw the truth and dared to change his mind. He offered compensated emancipation and colonization of blacks abroad: The South refused. The war reached bloody stalemate and the nation trembled. Volunteers ceased to offer and corpses clogged the rivers of Virginia. Lee started North and Lincoln threatened. "Surrender or I abolish slavery," he cried in September, 1862, beneath the smoke of Antietam. He armed eventually two hundred thousand slaves and a million awaited his call.

The Negroes fought like the damned, two hundred thousand of them; led by two hundred black officers and subalterns, they tore into a hundred and more battles and left seventy thousand dead and dying on the fields. They served in every arm of service and in every area of struggle. They were slaughtered at Fort Wagner to hold Carolina. They committed suicide at Port Hudson so that the Father of Waters should flow "unvexed to the sea." They were buried in the Crater to help Grant capture Richmond, the capitol of the Confederacy, and a black regiment led Abraham Lincoln through the city singing,

> John Brown's body lies a moldering in the grave
> But his soul goes marching on . . .

The South cursed them and treated them as outlaws; Forest murdered and burned them at Fort Pillow. But Lincoln testified that without these black soldiers and the hundreds of thousands of Negro laborers, guards, informers and spies we could not have won the war. On January 1, 1863, Lincoln declared the slaves in rebel territory "then, thenceforward and forever free." The South saw hell in the blazing heavens and with one last gasp tried themselves openly to arm the slaves. They failed and Lee surrendered.

Such was the sordid tale of the war which has been called the "Rebellion," the "Civil War" and the "War Between the States," but whose real name was the "War to Preserve Slavery." That was the only name which made sense to those who fought the war and those who supported it. It sang in their songs and chanted in their poetry:

> In the beauty of the lilies
> Christ was born across the sea.
> As he died to make men holy,
> Let us die to make men free . . .

Then we turned from the abolition of slavery to our muttons: to making money. Some Americans stepped forward with alms and teachers for the black freed men. Some rushed South to make money with cheap labor and high cotton. But most of the nation tried to forget the Negro. He was free, what more did he want? He asked for a Freedmen's Bureau and got a small one paid for mainly with the unclaimed bounties of dead black soldiers. Philanthropists gave him a bank and cheated him out of most of his savings when it failed. Votes? Nonsense, unless planters demand a lower tariff, payment for the Confederate debt and compensation for freed slaves.

We refused to let the horrible mistake of war teach our children anything. We gave it less and less space in our textbooks, until today slavery gets a paragraph and the Civil War a page.

Moreover, the whole cause and meaning of the war is distorted in 10,000 books which falsify the real story. Now in weighty tome, gaudy magazine and television the war was merely an unfortunate misunderstanding. It seems nobody wanted slavery and the South, having had it forced upon her, was about to abolish it but for senseless, impatient agitation. All of our history from the Missouri Compromise through the Compromise of 1850 to the secession of South Carolina is being thus rewritten and the Negro painted as a contented slave, a lazy freedman, a thieving voter and today as happily integrated into American life.

Thereupon with no guidance from the past the nation marched on with officers strutting, bands playing and flags flying to secure colonial empire and new cheap slave labor and land monopoly in Asia, Africa and the islands of the seas. We fought two World Wars killing nearly 500,000 American youth, and added 50,000 more dead by "police action" in Korea. In all we destroyed more wealth than we have since been able to count. We are now wasting $40 billion a year for more wars and we owe $284 billion for past wars. In sixty years we have spent only $14 billion for education.

So now comes the time to celebrate the War to Preserve Slavery. The South, which for a century has insisted that theirs was a just war fought with the highest motives by the noblest of men, is pouring forth books and pamphlets to prove this. This all Southern white children have been taught to believe until it is to most of them a matter of absolute and indisputable truth. Historians, North and South, have spread the story and artists have depicted it, so that most Southern states next year will celebrate as a triumph in human effort this despicable struggle to keep black Americans in slavery.

The North, on the other hand, sees little reason to remember or celebrate this war. It would prefer to forget it, but most Northern states will stage some sort of celebration to recall the keeping of this nation united for producing more millionaires than any other people and for proving what philanthropists we are. We gave and are still giving alms to Negroes.

The South will preen itself. What a courageous folk, lynching singlehanded since the Civil War 5,000 helpless Negroes and disfranchising millions. Virginia will lead the rejoicing with a $1,750,000 centennial budget and Mississippi is following with $500,000. Arkansas will join in with Faubus, and Georgia will sing the Jubilee, but not with "Marching Through Georgia." Colored citizens will be asked to attest how loyally they protected old master's family while he fought for slavery.

The whole United States will stage a mighty pageant to cost at first $200,000 and millions later. Big Business, including the Stock Exchange and travel bureaus, will play a major part, but the emancipation of slaves will be ignored. So says the head of the Centennial committee, a nice old white gentleman with a black mammy who serves under an army general, called deservedly the Third Ulysses S. Grant.

Listen America! Hear that we will not celebrate the freeing of four million slaves! O dark Potomac where looms the gloom of the Lincoln Memorial. Father Abraham, unlimber those great limbs; let the bronze blaze with blood and the eyes of sorrow again see. Stand and summon out of the past the woman whose eyes saw "the glory of the coming of the Lord"; the Seer who said: "For what avail the plough or sail or land or life if freedom fail?" The abolitionist who cried: "I will not retreat a single inch and I will be heard!" Arouse Phillips and Sumner, Stevens and Birney and the whole legion who hated slavery and let them march to Capitol Hill. Warn them again, that this nation must have a "new birth of freedom" even if "all the wealth piled up by the bondsmen's two hundred and fifty years of unrequitted toil shall be sunk" and if "every drop of blood drawn by the lash, be paid by another drawn by the sword." As was said three thousand years ago, so still it must be said that "the judgments of the Lord are true and righteous altogether."

This is but the raving of an old man who has long dreamed

that American Negroes could be men and look white America in the face without blinking. Not only dreamed but saw in 1913 the Negroes of six states celebrate the Jubilee of Emancipation without apology. Here in New York we inaugurated an abolition celebration securing a state appropriation of $10,000 and a Negro Board of Control. We spent the money honestly and effectively and centered it on recalling the part which Negroes played in the war. We pictured the progress of American Negroes and the forgotten history of their motherland, Africa. For a week beginning October 21, 1913, in the 11th Regiment Armory, Ninth Avenue and 62nd Street, 30,000 persons attended the celebration and 350 actors took part. Few who saw ever forgot the Egyptian Temple, the Migration of the Bantu and the March of the Black Soldiers. Three times later in Washington, Philadelphia and Los Angeles the pageant was repeated. James Weldon Johnson and I went further and planned for 1918 a Jubilee of the 14th Amendment, but the First World War killed that dream.

Today no Negro leader who holds a good government appointment, or is favored of the great benevolent foundations or has a job in Big Business, or is financed by the State Department to travel abroad, will dare dream of celebrating in any way the role which Negroes played in the Civil War. It would be "racist" for an "integrated" Negro American to recall the Emancipation of black slaves in the United States. And any Negro school or college would risk its income if it staged a celebration.

Possibly the main moral of all this is the failure of history as it is taught today even to attempt to tell the exact truth or learn it. Rather, so many historians conceive it their duty to teach as truth what they or those who pay their salaries believe ought to have been true. Thus we train generations of men who do not know the past, or believe a false picture of the past, to have no trustworthy guide for living and to stumble doggedly on, through mistake after mistake, to fatal ends. Our history becomes "lies agreed upon" and stark ignorance guides our future.

From the *National Guardian*, February 15, 1960

Postscript
What Have You Read? (1936)

I have bought this year [1936] in all, 25 new books. This is rather more than my usual stint, but I am catching up with my professional reading and completing my library in certain directions. Moreover, I am trying to make good the resolution that I adopted several years ago, to be quit of the public library habit. I am convinced that nothing has cheapened American intellectual life more than this habit. It has stopped the buying of books, which means that publishers can only afford to issue thrillers, unless they take long chances. The ordinary, serious reader does not pretend to buy books. He says to an author, as people have repeatedly said to me: "I am going to read your book just as soon as I can get it from the library." And the very moment, the person in question was wearing two octavo volumes on her head, which wasn't worth it.

Du Bois' Column "Forum of Fact and Opinion" in the *Pittsburgh Courier*, August 22, 1936

On Discussion (1936)

One of the disturbing things about Negroes is the lack of discussion. Domineering assertion and loud talk, we have in common with all ignorant people, but the habit of listening carefully, silently and intelligently to prepared and distinctly stated arguments on opposite sides of a question, with careful thought and follow-up reading; this we lack, and without it there can be no real education, no learning, no effective democracy. We have been ruined by "eloquent" sermons and speeches; smart, funny, emotional appeals without facts and without careful preparation, and with no opportunity to ask questions or require explanations. We "enjoy" sermons and speeches. This is sheer damnation. You should listen, question, ponder and remember, if you are to be more than a phonograph or microphone.

Du Bois' Column "Forum of Fact and Opinion" in the *Pittsburgh Courier*, August 22, 1936

A Negro Book-of-the-Year Club (1936)

Nearly 10 years ago when the Book-of-the-Month Club idea began to spread, several of us tried to sponsor the possibility of launching a Negro Book-of-the-Month Club. We went over the matter very carefully with publishers and those who are expert in these lines, and concluded that we could not expect from the colored public sums large enough to make the Club go, and beyond that, we were not at all certain that every month there would be a book we would feel like recommending. Since then, similar difficulties have arisen concerning the Du Bois prize. In the years in which it has been offered, it has only been awarded once because it seemed to us that no volume quite reached the standard which we had tried to get.

I do think, however, that each year there is published a book by a Negro author, or a book on a subject in which Negroes are interested, written by a sympathetic white author which Negroes should buy. We ought to induce 1,000 or even 2,000 Negroes to buy such a book simply by calling it to their attention, and by stressing the fact that it ought to be bought.

This would involve a judgment by a jury whose names should carry conviction. I propose, therefore, that we begin next year and select a jury of 12 or 15 outstanding colored men and by means of correspondence and some other methods which involve little cost, try to see if we could not get 1,000 people to pledge themselves to a selected book, either by paying in installments, or in a lump sum. In succeeding years, other books could be chosen, not necessarily by the same jury, but by a group of people who knew and could vouch for the particular book in question.

. . . . The cost of such an enterprise ought to be nominal. A few hundred post cards could go out, followed later by a letter, asking for five or 10 names of persons who ought to be interested, and then to those 1,000 people, we could send the Book-of-the-Year Club proposal.

With this beginning, I should like to go on in succeeding years, trying to make the selection as catholic and authentic as possible, so as to eliminate any idea of personal advertising. The main point is, if Negroes are going to find publishers who are willing to take the risk of publishing their thoughts, the publishers must be assured of a sale. Any publisher who can see a sale of 1,000 books will be willing to publish almost any book. A Negro Book-of-the-Year Club with 1,000 subscribers would, therefore, insure the publication of a large number of worthwhile books.

From Du Bois' Column "Forum of Fact and Opinion" in the *Pittsburgh Courier,* August 15, 1936

IV. Race Pride—"Black Awareness"

Prescript
On Blackness (1928)

"M. BEN ALI SUGGESTS," said the Princess, "that even you are not black, Mr. Towns."

"My grandfather was, and my soul is. Black blood with us in America is a matter of spirit and not simply of flesh."

From *The Dark Princess*, 1928

Credo (1920)

I believe in God, who made of one blood all nations that on earth do dwell. I believe that all men, black and brown and white, are brothers, varying through time and opportunity, in form and gift and feature, but differing in no essential particular, and alike in soul and the possibility of infinite development.

Especially do I believe in the Negro Race: in the beauty of its genius, the sweetness of its soul, and its strength in that meekness which shall yet inherit this turbulent earth.

I believe in Pride of race and lineage and self: in pride of self so deep as to scorn injustice to other selves; in pride of lineage so great as to despise no man's father; in pride of race so chivalrous as neither to offer bastardy to the weak nor beg wedlock of the strong, knowing that men may be brothers in Christ, even though they be not brothers-in-law.

I believe in Service—humble, reverent service, from the blackening of boots to the whitening of souls; for Work is Heaven, Idleness Hell, and Wage is the "Well done!" of the Master, who summoned all them that labor and are heavy laden, making no distinction between the black, sweating cotton hands of Georgia and the first families of Virginia, since all distinction not based on deed is devilish and not divine.

I believe in the Devil and his angels, who wantonly work to narrow the opportunity of struggling human beings, especially if they be black; who spit in the faces of the fallen, strike them that cannot strike again, believe the worst and work to prove it, hating the image which their Maker stamped on a brother's soul.

I believe in the Prince of Peace. I believe that War is Murder. I believe that armies and navies are at bottom the tinsel and braggadocio of oppression and wrong, and I believe that the wicked conquest of weaker and darker nations by nations whiter and stronger but fore-shadows the death of that strength.

I believe in liberty for all men: the space to stretch their arms and their souls, the right to breathe and the right to vote, the freedom to choose their friends, enjoy the sunshine, and ride on the railroads, uncursed by color; thinking, dreaming, working as they will in a kingdom of beauty and love.

I believe in the training of children, black even as white; the leading out of little souls into the green pastures and beside the still waters, not for pelf or peace, but for life lit by some large vision of beauty and goodness and truth; lest we forget, and the sons of the fathers, like Esau, for mere meat barter their birthright in a mighty nation.

Finally, I believe in Patience—patience with the weakness of the Weak and the strength of the Strong, the prejudice of the Ignorant and the ignorance of the Blind; patience with the tardy triumph of Joy and the mad chastening of Sorrow —patience with God!

From *Darkwater: Voices from Within the Veil,* 1920, pp. 3–4

On Being Black (1920)

My friend, who is pale and positive, said to me yesterday,
as the tired sun was nodding:
"You are too sensitive."
I admit, I am—sensitive. I am artificial. I cringe or am
bumptious or immobile. I am intellectually dishonest, art-
blind, and I lack humor.
"Why don't you stop all this?" she retorted triumphantly.
You will not let us.
"There you go again. You know that I—"
Wait! I answer. Wait!
I arise at seven. The milkman has neglected me. He pays
little attention to colored districts. My white neighbor glares
elaborately. I walk softly, lest I disturb him. The children jeer
as I pass to work. The women in the street car withdraw their
skirts or prefer to stand. The Police is truculent. The elevator
man hates to serve Negroes. My job is insecure because the
white union wants it and does not want me. I try to lunch,
but no place near will serve me. I go forty blocks to Marshall's, but the Committee of Fourteen closes Marshall's; they
say white women frequent it.
"Do all eating places discriminate?"
No, but how shall I know which do not—except—
I hurry home through crowds. They mutter or get angry. I
go to a mass-meeting. They stare. I go to church. "We don't
admit 'niggers!' "
Or perhaps I leave the beaten track. I seek new work. "Our
employees would not work with you; our customers would
object."
I ask to help in social uplift.
"Why—er—we will write you."
I enter the free field of science. Every laboratory door is
closed and no endowments are available.
I seek the universal mistress, Art; the studio door is locked.
I write literature. "We cannot publish stories of colored
folk of that type." It's the only type I know.
This is my life. It makes me Idiotic. It gives me artificial

problems. I hesitate, I rush, I waver. In fine—I am sensitive!
My pale friend looks at me with disbelief and curling
tongue.

"Do you mean to sit there and tell me that this is what
happens to you each day?"

Certainly not, I answer low.

"Then you only fear it will happen?"

I fear!

"Well, haven't you the courage to rise above a—almost
craven fear?"

Quite—quite craven is my fear, I admit; but the terrible
thing is—these things do happen!

"But you just said—"

They do happen. Not all each day—surely not. But now
and then—now seldom, now, sudden; now after a week, now
in a chain of awful minutes; not everywhere, but anywhere—
in Boston, in Atlanta. That's the hell of it. Imagine spending
your life looking for insults or for hiding places from them—
shrinking (instinctively and despite desperate bolstering of
courage) from blows that are not always but ever; not each
day, but each week, each month, each year. Just, perhaps, as
you have choked back the craven fear and cried, "I am and
will be the master of my—"

"No more tickets downstairs; here's one to the smoking
gallery."

You hesitate. You beat back your suspicions. After all, a
cigarette with Charlie Chaplin—then a white man pushes
by—

"Three in the orchestra."

"Yes, sir." And in he goes.

Suddenly your heart chills. You turn yourself away toward
the golden twinkle of the purple night and hesitate again.
What's the use? Why not always yield—always take what's
offered—always bow to force, whether of cannon or dislike?
Then the great fear surges in your soul, the real fear—the
fear beside which other fears are vain imaginings; the fear
lest right there and then you are losing your own soul; that
you are losing your own soul and the soul of a people; that
millions of unborn children, black and gold and mauve, are

being there and then despoiled by you because you are a coward and dare not fight!

Suddenly that silly orchestra seat and the cavorting of a comedian with funny feet become matters of life, death, and immortality; you grasp the pillars of the universe and strain as you sway back to that befrilled ticket girl. You grip your soul for riot and murder. You choke and sputter, and she seeing that you are about to make a "fuss" obeys her orders and throws the tickets at you in contempt. Then you slink to your seat and crouch in the darkness before the film, with every tissue burning! The miserable wave of reaction engulfs you. To think of compelling puppies to take your hard-earned money; fattening hogs to hate you and yours; forcing your way among cheap and tawdry idiots—God! What a night of pleasure! . . .

Why do not those who are scarred in the world's battle and hurt by its hardness travel to these places of beauty and drown themselves in the utter joy of life? I asked this once sitting in a Southern home. Outside the spring of a Georgia February was luring gold to the bushes and languor to the soft air. Around me sat color in human flesh—brown that crimsoned readily; dim soft-yellow that escaped description; cream-like duskiness that shadowed to rich tints of autumn leaves. And yet a suggested journey in the world brought no response.

"I should think you would like to travel," said the white one.

But no, the thought of a journey seemed to depress them.

Did you ever see a "Jim-Crow" waiting-room? There are always exceptions, as at Greensboro—but usually there is no heat in the winter and no air in summer; with undisturbed loafers and train hands and broken disreputable settees; to buy a ticket is torture; you stand and stand and wait and wait until every white person at the "other window" is waited on. Then the tired agent yells across, because all the tickets and money are over there—

"What d'ye want? What? Where?"

The agent browbeats and contradicts you, hurries and confuses the ignorant, gives many persons the wrong change, compels some to purchase their tickets on the train at a higher price, and sends you and me out on the platform, burning with indignation and hatred!

The "Jim-Crow" car is up next the baggage car and engine. It stops out beyond the covering in the rain or sun or dust. Usually there is no step to help you climb on and often the car is a smoker cut in two and you must pass through the white smokers or else they pass through your part, with swagger and noise and stares. Your compartment is a half or a quarter or an eighth of the oldest car in service on the road. Unless it happens to be a through express, the plush is caked with dirt, the floor is grimy, and the windows dirty. An impertinent white newsboy occupies two seats at the end of the car and importunes you to the point of rage to buy cheap candy, Coca-Cola, and worthless, if not vulgar books. He yells and swaggers, while a continued stream of white men saunters back and forth from the smoker to buy and hear. The white train crew from the baggage car uses the "Jim-Crow" to lounge in and perform their toilet. The conductor appropriates two seats for himself and his papers and yells gruffly for your tickets before the train has scarcely started. It is best not to ask him for information even in the gentlest tones. His information is for white persons chiefly. It is difficult to get lunch or clean water. Lunch rooms either don't serve niggers or serve them at some dirty and ill-attended hole in the wall. As for toilet rooms—don't! If you have to change cars, be wary of junctions which are usually without accommodation and filled with quarrelsome white persons who hate a "darky dressed up." You are apt to have the company of a sheriff and a couple of meek or sullen black prisoners on part of your way and dirty colored section hands will pour in toward night and drive you to the smallest corner.

"No," said the little lady in the corner (she looked like an ivory cameo and her dress flowed on her like a caress), "we don't travel much."

Pessimism is cowardice. The man who cannot frankly acknowledge the "Jim-Crow" car as a fact and yet live and hope is simply afraid either of himself or of the world. There is not in the world a more disgraceful denial of human brotherhood than the "Jim-Crow" car of the southern United States; but, too, just as true, there is nothing more beautiful in the universe than sunset and moonlight on Montego Bay in far Jamaica. And both things are true and both belong to this our world, and neither can be denied. . . .

High in the tower, where I sit above the loud complaining of the human sea, I know many souls that toss and whirl and pass, but none there are that intrigue me more than the Souls of White Folk.

Of them I am singularly clairvoyant. I see in and through them. I view them from unusual points of vantage. Not as a foreigner do I come, for I am native, not foreign, bone of their thought and flesh of their language. Mine is not the knowledge of the traveler or the colonial composite of dear memories, words and wonder. Nor yet is my knowledge that which servants have of masters, or mass of class, or capitalist of artisan. Rather I see these souls undressed and from the back and side. I see the working of their entrails. I know their thoughts and they know that I know. This knowledge makes them now embarrassed, now furious! They deny my right to live and be and call me misbirth! My word is to them mere bitterness and my soul, pessimism. And yet as they preach and strut and shout and threaten, crouching as they clutch at rags of facts and fancies to hide their nakedness, they go twisting, flying by my tired eyes and I see them stripped— ugly, human.

The discovery of personal whiteness among the world's peoples is a very modern thing—a nineteenth and twentieth century matter, indeed. The ancient world would have laughed at such a distinction. The Middle Age regarded skin color with mild curiosity; and even up into the eighteenth century we were hammering our national manikins into one, great, Universal Man, with fine frenzy which ignored color and race even more than birth. Today we have changed all that, and the world in a sudden, emotional conversion has discovered that it is white and by that token, wonderful! . . .

As we saw the dead dimly through rifts of battle-smoke and heard faintly the cursings and accusations of blood brothers, we darker men said: This is not Europe gone mad; this is not aberration nor insanity; this *is* Europe; this seeming Terrible is the real soul of white culture—back of all culture—stripped and visible today. This is where the world has arrived—these dark and awful depths and not the shining and ineffable heights of which it boasted. Here is whither the might and energy of modern humanity has really gone.

But may not the world cry back at us and ask: "What better thing have you to show? What have you done or would do better than this if you had today the world rule? Paint with all riot of hateful colors the thin skin of European culture—is it not better than any culture that arose in Africa or Asia?"

It is. Of this there is no doubt and never has been; but why is it better? Is it better because Europeans are better, nobler, greater, and more gifted than other folk? It is not. Europe has never produced and never will in our day bring forth a single human soul who cannot be matched and over-matched in every line of human endeavor by Asia and Africa. Run the gamut, if you will, and let us have the Europeans who in sober truth over-match Nefertari, Mohammed, Rameses and Askia, Confucius, Buddha, and Jesus Christ. If we could scan the calendar of thousands of lesser men, in like comparison, the result would be the same; but we cannot do this because of the deliberately educated ignorance of white schools by which they remember Napoleon and forget Sonni Ali.

Why, then, is Europe great? Because of the foundations which the mighty past have furnished her to build upon: the iron trade of ancient, black Africa, the religion and empire building of yellow Asia, the art and science of the "dago" Mediterranean shore, east, south, and west, as well as north. And where she has builded securely upon this great past and learned from it she has gone forward to greater and more splendid human triumph; but where she has ignored this past and forgotten and sneered at it, she has shown the cloven hoof of poor, crucified humanity—she has played, like other empires gone, the world fool!

From the *New Republic*, February 18, 1920; also in *Dark-water: Voices from Within the Veil*, 1920, pp. 29–52 and 221–30

Race Pride (1920)

Our friends are hard—very hard—to please. Only yesterday they were preaching "Race Pride."

"Go to!" they said, "and be *proud* of your race."

If we hesitated or sought to explain—"Away," they yelled; "Ashamed-of-Yourself and Want-to-be-White!"

Of course, the Amazing Major is still at it, but do you notice that others say less—because they see that bull-headed worship of any "race" as such, may lead and does lead to curious complications?

For instance: Today Negroes, Indians, Chinese, and other groups, are gaining new faith in themselves; they are discovering that the current theories and stories of "backward" peoples are largely lies and assumptions; that human genius and possibility are not limited by color, race, or blood. What is this new self-consciousness leading to? Inevitably and directly to distrust and hatred of whites; to demands for self-government, separation, driving out of foreigners: "Asia for the Asiatics," "Africa for the Africans," and "Negro officers for Negro troops!"

No sooner do whites see this unawaited development than they point out in dismay the inevitable consequences: "You lose our tutelage," "You spurn our knowledge," "You need our wealth and technique." They point out how fine is the world role of Elder Brother.

Very well. Some of the darker brethren are convinced. They draw near in friendship; they seek to enter schools and churches; they would mingle in industry—when lo! "Get out," yells the White World—"You're not our brothers and never will be"—"Go away, herd by yourselves"—"Eternal Segregation in the Lord!"

Can you wonder, Sirs, that we are a bit puzzled by all this and that we are asking gently, but more and more insistently, Choose one or the other horn of the dilemma:

1. Leave the black and yellow world alone. Get out of Asia, Africa, and the Isles. Give us our states and towns and sections and let us rule them undisturbed. Absolutely segregate the races and sections of the world.
OR—
2. Let the world meet as men with men. Give utter justice to all. Extend Democracy to all and treat all men according to their individual desert. Let it be possible for whites to rise to the highest positions in China and Uganda and blacks to the highest honors in England and Texas.

Here is the choice. Which will you have, my masters?

From *The Crisis*, Vol. 19, January, 1920

New Creed for American Negroes (1935)

1. We American Negroes are threatened today with lack of opportunity to work according to Gifts and training and lack of income sufficient to support healthy families according to standards demanded by modern culture.
2. In industry, we are a labor reservoir, fitfully employed and paid a wage below subsistence; in agriculture, we are largely disfranchised peons; in public education, we tend to be disinherited illiterates; in higher education, we are the parasites of reluctant and hesitant philanthropy.
3. In the current reorganization of industry, there is no adequate effort to secure us a place in industry, or to open opportunity for Negro ability, or to give us security in age or employment.
4. Not by the development of upper classes anxious to exploit the workers, nor by the escape of individual genius into the white world, can we effect the salvation of our group in America. And the salvation of this group carries with it the emancipation not only of the darker races of men who make the vast majority of mankind, but of all men of all races. We,

therefore, propose this: BASIC AMERICAN NEGRO CREED. (BANC)

(a) As American Negroes, we believe in the unity of racial effort, so far as this is necessary for self-defense and self-expression, leading ultimately to the goal of a united humanity and the abolition of all racial distinctions.

(b) We repudiate all artificial and hate-engendering deification of race separation as such; but just as sternly, we repudiate an enervating philosophy of Negro escape into an artificially privileged white race which has long sought to enslave, exploit and tyrannize over all mankind.

(c) We believe that the Talented Tenth among American Negroes, fitted by education and character to think and do, should find primary employment in determining by study and measurement the present field and demand for racial action and the method by which the masses be guided along this path.

(d) We believe that the problems which now call for such racial planning are Employment, Education and Health; these three: but the greatest of these is Employment.

(e) We believe that the labor force and intelligence of 12 million people is more than sufficient to supply their own wants and make their advancement secure. Therefore, we believe that, if carefully and intelligently planned, a cooperative Negro industrial system in America can be established in the midst of and in conjunction with the surrounding industrial organization and in intelligent accord with that reconstruction of the economic basis of the nation which must sooner or later be accomplished.

(f) We believe that Negro workers should join the labor movement and affiliate with such trade unions as welcome them and treat them fairly. We believe that workers' councils organized by Negroes for interracial understanding should strive to fight race prejudice in the working class.

(g) We believe in the ultimate triumph of some form of socialism the world over; that is, state ownership and control of the means of production and equality of income.

(h) We do not believe in lynching as a cure for crime; nor in war as a necessary defense of culture; nor in violence as the only path to economic revolution. Whatever may have been true in other times and places, we believe that today in America we can abolish poverty by reason and the intelligent use of the ballot, and above all by that dynamic discipline of soul and sacrifice of comfort which, revolution or no revolution, must ever be the real path to economic justice and world peace.

(i) We conceive this matter of work and equality of adequate Income is not the end of our effort, but the beginning of the rise of the Negro race in this land and the world over, in power, learning and accomplishment.

(j) We believe in the use of our vote for equalizing wealth through taxation, for vesting the ultimate power of the state in the hands of the workers; and as an integral part of the working class, we demand our proportionate share in administration and public expenditure.

(k) This is and is designed to be a program of racial effort and this narrow goal is forced upon us today by the unyielding determination of the mass of the white race to enslave, exploit and insult Negroes; but to this vision of work, organization and service, we welcome all men of all colors so long as their subscription to this basic creed is sincere and is proven by their deeds.

From the *National Baptist Voice*, October 5, 1935; also in *Dusk of Dawn*, 1940, pp. 319–22

Postscript
Race Pride: Comments (1960)

We are not doing as much as we can about schools. Some of us do not care enough whether our children study or not. Some children come home and there is no place for them to study. . . .

We should see ourselves as ourselves not through the eyes of the white world. We buy the same books the white man buys. The publishers pay attention to what the white man buys.

We should make it so they depend on what the colored man buys. . . .

We are progressing in a good many ways. We are carrying on more endeavors. We are getting better jobs. We are going slowly. Look back fifty years, you can see the progress.

But there has been a division of the colored people into classes. This splits them so that they are no longer the single body. They are different sets of people with different interests, no longer banded together in a single whole as 50 years ago.

From "Comments on Negroes in 1960" in the *Afro-American Weekly*, Magazine Section, February 27, 1960

V. Segregation Versus Integration— Race Solidarity and Economic Cooperation

Prescript
On the Duty of Whites (1899)

THERE IS A TENDENCY on the part of many white people to approach the Negro question from the side which just now is of least pressing importance, namely, that of the social intermingling of races. The old query: Would you want your sister to marry a Nigger? still stands as a grim sentinel to stop much rational discussion. And yet few white women have been pained by the addresses of black suitors, and those who have, easily got rid of them. The whole question is little less than foolish; perhaps a century from to-day we may find ourselves seriously discussing such questions of social policy, but it is certain that just as long as one group deems it a serious mesalliance to marry with another just so long few marriages will take place, and it will need neither law nor argument to guide human choice in such a matter. Certainly the masses of whites would hardly acknowledge that an active propaganda of repression was necessary to ward off intermarriage. Natural pride of race, strong on one side and growing on the other, may be trusted to ward off such mingling as might in this stage of development prove disastrous to both races. All this therefore is a question of the far-off future.

To-day, however, we must face the fact that a natural repugnance to close intermingling with unfortunate ex-slaves has descended to a discrimination that very seriously hinders them from being anything better. It is right and proper to object to ignorance and consequently to ignorant men; but if by our actions we have been responsible for their ignorance and are still actively engaged in keeping them ignorant, the argument loses its moral force. So with the Negroes; men have a right to object to a race so poor and ignorant and inefficient as the mass of Negroes; but if their policy in the past is parent of much of this condition, and if to-day by shutting black boys and girls out of most avenues of decent employment they are increasing pauperism and vice, then they must hold themselves largely responsible for the deplorable results.

There is no doubt that in Philadelphia the centre and kernel of the Negro Problem so far as white people are concerned is the narrow opportunities afforded Negroes for earning a decent living. Such discrimination is morally wrong, politically dangerous, industrially wasteful, and socially silly. It is the duty of white people to stop it, and to do so primarily for their own sakes. Industrial freedom of opportunity has by long experience been proven to be generally best for all. Moreover the cost of crime and pauperism, the growth of slums, and the pernicious influences of idleness and lewdness, cost the public far more than would the hurt to the feelings of a carpenter to work beside a black man, or a shopgirl to stand beside a darker mate. This does not contemplate the wholesale replacing of white workmen for Negroes out of sympathy or philanthropy; it does mean that talent should be rewarded, and aptness used in commerce and industry whether its owner be black or white; that the same incentive to good, honest, effective work be placed before a black office boy as before a white one—before a black porter as before a white one; and unless this is done the city has no right to complain that black boys lose interest in work and drift into idleness and crime. Probably a change in public opinion on this point to-morrow would not make very much difference in the positions occupied by Negroes in the city: some few would be promoted, some few would get new places—the mass would remain as they are; but it would make one vast difference: it would inspire the young to try harder, it would stimulate the idle and discouraged and it would take away from this race the omnipresent excuse for failure: prejudice. Such a moral change would work a revolution in the criminal rate during the next ten years. Even a Negro bootblack could black boots better if he knew he was a menial not because he was a Negro but because he was best fitted for that work.

We need then a radical change in public opinion on this point; it will not and ought not to come suddenly, but instead of thoughtless acquiescence in the continual and steadily encroaching exclusion of Negroes from work in the city, the leaders of industry and opinion ought to be trying here and there to open up new opportunities and give new chances to bright colored boys. The policy of the city to-day simply drives out the best class of young people whom its schools have educated and social opportunities trained, and filled their places with idle and vicious immigrants. It is a paradox of the times that young men and women from some of the best Negro families of the city—families born and reared here and schooled in the best traditions of this municipality—have actually had to go to the South to get work, if they want to be aught but chambermaids and bootblacks. Not that such work may not be honorable and useful, but that it is as wrong to make scullions of engineers as it is to make engineers of scullions. Such a situation is a disgrace to the city—a disgrace to its Christianity, to its spirit of justice, to its common sense; what can be the end of such a policy but increased crime and increased excuse for crime? Increased poverty and more reason to be poor? Increased political serfdom of the mass of black voters to the bosses and rascals who divide the spoils? Surely here lies the first duty of a civilized city.

Secondly, in their efforts for the uplifting of the Negro the people of Philadelphia must recognize the existence of the better class of Negroes and must gain their active aid and co-operation by generous and polite conduct. Social sympathy must exist between what is best in both races and there must no longer be the feeling that the Negro who makes the best of himself is of least account to the city of Philadelphia, while the vagabond is to be helped and pitied. This better class of

Negro does not want help or pity, but it does want a generous recognition of its difficulties, and a broad sympathy with the problem of life as it presents itself to them. It is composed of men and women educated and in many cases cultured; with proper co-operation they could be a vast power in the city, and the only power that could successfully cope with many phases of the Negro problems. But their active aid cannot be gained for purely selfish motives, or kept by churlish and ungentle manners; and above all they object to being patronized.

Again, the white people of the city must remember that much of the sorrow and bitterness that surrounds the life of the American Negro comes from the unconscious prejudice and half-conscious actions of men and women who do not intend to wound or annoy. One is not compelled to discuss the Negro question with every Negro one meets or to tell him of a father who was connected with the Underground Railroad; one is not compelled to stare at the solitary black face in the audience as though it were not human; it is not necessary to sneer, or to be unkind or boorish, if the Negroes in the room or on the street are not all the best behaved or have not the most elegant manners; it is hardly necessary to strike from the dwindling list of one's boyhood and girlhood acquaintances or school-day friends all those who happen to have Negro blood, simply because one has not the courage now to greet them on the street. The little decencies of daily intercourse can go on, the courtesies of life be exchanged even across the color line without any danger to the supremacy of the Anglo-Saxon or the social ambition of the Negro. Without doubt social differences are facts not fancies and cannot lightly be swept aside; but they hardly need to be looked upon as excuses for downright meanness and incivility.

A polite and sympathetic attitude toward these striving thousands; a delicate avoidance of that which wounds and embitters them; a generous granting of opportunity to them; a seconding of their efforts, and a desire to reward honest success—all this, added to proper striving on their part, will go far even in our day toward making all men, white and black, realize what the great founder of the city meant, when he named it the City of Brotherly Love.

From *The Philadelphia Negro: A Social Study*, 1899, pp. 393–97

On Segregation (1934)

I have read with interest the various criticisms on my recent discussions of segregation. Those like that of Mr. Pierce of Cleveland, do not impress me. I am not worried about being inconsistent. What worries me is the Truth. I am talking about conditions in 1934 and not in 1910. I do not care what I said in 1910 or 1810 or in B.C. 700. . . .

Many persons have interpreted my reassertion of our current attitude toward segregation as a counsel of despair. We can't win, therefore, give up and accept the inevitable. Never and nonsense. Our business in this world is to fight and fight again, and never to yield. But after all, one must fight with his brains, if he has any. He gathers strength to fight. He gathers knowledge, and he raises children who are proud to fight and who know what they are fighting about. And above all, they learn that what they are fighting for is the opportunity and the chance to know and associate with black folk. They are not fighting to escape themselves. They are fighting to say to the world: the opportunity of knowing Negroes is worth so much to us and is so appreciated, that we want you to know them too.

Negroes are not extraordinary human beings. They are just like other human beings, with all their foibles and ignorance and mistakes. But they are human beings, and human nature is always worth knowing, and withal splendid in its manifestations. Therefore, we are fighting to keep open the avenues of human contact; but in the meantime, we are taking even, advantage of what opportunities of contact that are already open to us, and among those opportunities which are open, and which are splendid and inspiring, is the opportunity of Negroes to work together in the twentieth century for the uplift and development of the Negro race. It is no counsel of despair to emphasize and hail the opportunity for such work.

THE ANTI-SEGREGATION CAMPAIGN

The assumptions of the anti-segregation campaign have been all wrong. This is not our fault, but it is our misfortune. When I went to Atlanta to teach in 1897, and to study the Negro Problem, I said, confidently, that the basic problem is our racial ignorance and lack of culture. That once Negroes know civilization, and whites know Negroes, then the problem is solved. This proposition is still true, but the solution is much further away than my youth dreamed. Negroes are still ignorant, but the disconcerting thing is that white people on the whole are just as much opposed to Negroes of education and culture, as to any other kind, and perhaps more so. Not all whites, to be sure, but the overwhelming majority.

Our main method, then, falls flat. We stop training ability. We lose our manners. We swallow our pride, and beg for things. We agitate and get angry. And with all that we face the blank fact: Negroes are not wanted; neither as scholars nor as business men; neither as clerks nor as artisans; neither as artists nor as writers. What can we do about it? We cannot use force. We cannot enforce law, even if we get them on statute books. So long as overwhelming public sanction justifies and defends color segregation, we are helpless and without remedy. We are segregated. We are cast back upon ourselves, to an Island Within; "To your tents, Oh Israel!"

Surely then, in this period of frustration and disappointment, we must turn from negation to affirmation, from the ever-lasting "No" to the ever-lasting "Yes." Instead of sitting, sapped of all initiative and independence; instead of drowning our originality in imitation of mediocre white folk; instead of being afraid of ourselves and cultivating the art of skulking to escape the Color Line; we have got to renounce a program that always involves humiliating self-stultifying scrambling to crawl somewhere where we are not wanted; where we crouch panting like a whipped dog. We have got to stop this and

learn that on such a program they cannot build manhood.
No, by God, stand erect in a mud-puddle and tell the white
world to go to hell, rather than lick boots in a parlor.

Affirm, as you have a right to affirm, that the Negro race is
one of the great human races, inferior to none in its accomplishment and in its ability. Different, it is true, and for most
of the difference, let us reverently thank God. And this race,
with its vantage grounds in modern days, can go forward of
its own will, of its own power, and of its own initiative. It is
led by the twelve million American Negroes of average modern intelligence; three or four million educated African Negroes are their full equals and several million Negroes in the
West Indies and South America. This body of at least twenty-
five million modern men are not called upon to commit suicide because somebody doesn't like their complexion or their
hair. It is their opportunity and their day to stand up and
make themselves heard and felt in the modern world.

Indeed, there is nothing else we can do. If you have passed
your resolution, "No segregation, never and Nowhere," what
are you going to do about it? Let me tell you what you are
going to do. You are going back to continue to make your
living in a "Jim-Crow" school; you are going to dwell in a
segregated section of the city; you are going to pastor a "Jim-
Crow" church; you are going to occupy political office because of a "Jim-Crow" political organization that stands back
of you and forces you into office. All these things and a
thousand others you are going to do because you have got
to.

If you are going to do this, why not say so? What are
you afraid of? Do you believe in the Negro race or do you
not? If you do not, naturally, you are justified in keeping still.
But if you do believe in the extraordinary accomplishment of
the Negro Church and the Negro College, the Negro School
and the Negro Newspaper, then say so, and say so plainly,
not only for the sake of those who have given their lives to
make these things worthwhile, but for those young people
whom you are teaching, by that negative attitude, that there
is nothing that they can do, nobody that they can emulate,

and no field worthwhile working in. Think of what Negro art and literature have yet to accomplish if they can only be free and untrammeled by the necessity of pleasing white folk! Think of the splendid moral appeal you can make to a million children tomorrow if once you can get them to see the possibilities of the American Negro today and now, whether he is segregated or not, or in spite of all possible segregation.

PROTEST

Some people seem to think that the fight against segregation consists merely of one damned protest after another. That the technique is to Protest and wail and protest again, and to keep this thing up until the gates of public opinion are open and the walls of segregation fall down.

The difficulty with this program is that it is physically and psychologically impossible. It would be stopped by cold and hunger and strained voices, and it is an undignified and impossible attitude and method to maintain indefinitely. Let us, therefore, remember that this program must be modified by adding to it a positive side. Make the protest and keep on making it, systematically and thoughtfully. Perhaps now and then even hysterically and theatrically; but at the same time go to work to prepare methods and institutions which will supply those things and those opportunities which we lack because of segregation. Stage boycotts which will put Negro clerks in the stores which exploit Negro neighborhoods. Build a 15th Street Presbyterian Church, when the First Presbyterian would rather love Jesus without your presence.

Establish and elaborate a Washington system of public schools comparable to any set of public schools in the nation; and when you have done this, and as you are doing it, and while in the process you are saving your voice and your temper, say softly to the world: see what a precious fool you are. Here are stores as efficiently clerked as any where you trade. Here is a church better than most of yours. Here is a set of schools where you should be proud to send your children.

THE CONSERVATION OF RACES

The Second Occasional Papers published by the American Negro Academy was "The Conservation of Races" by W. E. B. Du Bois, and was published in 1897. On page 11 I read with interest this bit:

Here, then, is the dilemma, and it is a puzzling one, I admit. No Negro who has given earnest thought to the situation of his people in America has failed, at some time in life, to find himself at these cross-roads; has failed to ask himself at some time: What after all, am I? Am I an American or am I a Negro? Can I be both? Or is it my duty to cease to be a Negro as soon as possible and be an American? If I strive to be a Negro, am I not perpetuating the very cleft that threatens and separates Black and White America? Is not my only possible practical aim the subduction of all that is Negro in me to the American? Does my black blood place upon me any more obligation to assert my nationality than German, or Irish or Italian blood would?

It is such incessant self-questioning and the hesitation that arises from it, that is making the present period a time of vacillation and contradiction for the American Negro: combined race action is stifled, race responsibility is shirked, race enterprises languish, and the best blood, the best talent, the best energy of the Negro people cannot be marshalled to do the bidding of the race. They stand back to make room for every rascal and demagogue who chooses to cloak his selfish deviltry under the veil of race pride. Is this right? Is it rational? Is it good policy? Have we in America a distinct mission as a race—a distinct sphere of action and opportunity for race development, or is self-obliteration the highest end to which Negro blood dare aspire?

On the whole, I am rather pleased to find myself still so much in sympathy with myself.

METHOD OF ATTACK

When an army moves to attack, there are two methods which it may pursue. The older method includes brilliant forays with bugles and loud fanfare of trumpets, with waving swords, and shining uniforms. In Coryn's "The Black Eagle," which tells the story of Bertrand Guesclin, one sees that kind of fighting power in the fourteenth century. It was thrilling, but messy, and on the whole rather ineffective.

The modern method of fighting is not nearly so spectacular. It is preceded by careful, very careful planning. Soldiers are clad in drab rather dirty khaki. Officers are not riding out in front and using their swords; they sit in the rear and use their brains. The whole army digs in and stays hidden. The advance is slow, calculated forward mass movement. Now going forward, now advancing in the center, now running around the flank. Often retreating to positions that can be better defended. And the whole thing depending upon G. H. Q.; that is, the thought and knowledge and calculations of the great general staff. This is not nearly as spectacular as the older method of fighting, but it is much more effective, and against the enemy of present days, it is the only effective way. It is common sense based on modern technique.

And this is the kind of method which we must use to solve the Negro problem and to win our fight against segregation. There are times when a brilliant display of eloquence and picketing and other theatrical and spectacular things are not only excusable but may actually gain ground. But in practically all cases, this is true simply because of the careful thought and planning that has gone before. And it is waste of time and effort to think that the spectacular demonstration is the real battle.

The real battle is a matter of study and thought; of the building of loyalties; of the long training of men; of the inculcation of racial and national ideals. It is not a publicity stunt. It is a life.

From "Postscript" (Editorials), *The Crisis* (W. E. B. Du Bois, Editor), April and June, 1934

Where Do We Go from Here? (1933) *(A Lecture on Negroes' Economic Plight)*

An Address Delivered at The Rosenwald Economic Conference In Washington, D.C., May, 1933.

The real question that I am to suggest an answer for is, "Where do we go from here?" We are looking for guide posts and we are coming to realize that we have got to choose more or less new roads.

In the past we had a fairly clear program worked out: First, we assumed a reasonably stable world, going on at a uniform rate of progress, toward well-defined goals. Our particular problem was to find our place and part in this world, and that seemed to be primarily a matter of exertion and effort on our part in certain clearly defined lines. We have got to demonstrate our ability to be modern men, and we have got to deserve the respect and consideration of the world.

We have found the main wall of race prejudice impenetrable. I say this with deliberation for I am no counsellor of despair. Like the Negro who was arguing about liquor and said:

"I am temperance, but I ain't no fanatic"; so I am an optimist, but I've got eyes.

FAILED TO BECOME FULL CITIZENS

We have done a great deal without doubt; in spite of a bad and incomplete school system, we have learned in large measure to read and write. Our progress in art and literature, in science, even in business, has been notable. Our determined opening of labor opportunities is astounding. Conferences like this show vast interracial advance over a comparatively short period. I have known the Negro problem to be seriously discussed in America by conferences made up entirely of white people.

We have all seen in many places promising meetings of minds between colored and white people. At the same time, as I have said, in our main objectives of becoming recognized American citizens, judged by character and not color, we have failed, and the failure is of such a significant sort that it calls for careful thinking and thoughtful planning for our future, lest our failure be final and complete.

OLD CRY, "YOU ARE NOT READY"

To instance but one part of our failure, there is no doubt about the native ability that has been shown by members of the Negro race in the United States. I sat night before last spellbound by two voices. Had they been in white bodies you know their destiny. As it is, you know equally well. Magazine articles no longer decry or belittle Negro genius. They do not even call it an illustrative exception.

At the same time, when we come forward and ask for corresponding justice, the reply is much more discouraging than it used to be. Formerly men could say, "You cannot vote; you cannot be admitted to civil rights; you cannot enter here and there, but after all, it is because of your lack of training. You are not ready for it."

But today there are unnumbered cases to which no such answer can be given. May I cite one of a thousand cases?

QUAKER SCHOOLS DRAW LINES

Recently three young boys applied for admission to various Friends' Schools. The Quakers are among the finest of Americans. Their reputation over a long series of years is something of which the nation and the world is proud. And too, these boys were from the finest of families; they had had exceptional training and there was unusual need and reason that they have further good schooling. They were handsome, well bred, charming.

They have not been able to find in the United States a single Quaker school that would receive them, and the excuse has been simply and boldly the fact that they had Negro grandfathers.

EARNING A LIVING

But our greatest failure is in ability to earn a decent living. Whatever we have lacked of accomplishment has come from the plain fact that the average income of the Negro family since emancipation has been below the standard which civilization today requires.

There has been an effort to tell us in various papers read here that we are after all no worse off than whites in the various aspects of the depression. The very sincerity and pervasiveness of this desire to encourage us is eloquent, but this emphasis does not change our all too definite knowledge.

IT SPELLS HELL

One per cent makes little difference to a statistician, but it spells hell to man on the edge of starvation. As a people we are on the narrow ridge of decent economic survival and we know it. We are the surplus laborer without security of job or certainty of public relief. We are the professional and business man with no adequate clientele.

Every time I hear the Negro farmer discussed, I get mad. I want to throw things. I know that he faces the difficulties of all farmers today, but I know, too, that he faces more than that. He faces mob law, no schools, no vote, crop lien, usury and cheating.

When a man discusses the Negro farmer and neglects or forgets to mention these facts I cannot believe in his sincerity. Of course, Negro farmers are stupid, slow and afraid—all the cream of swift intelligence, initiative and courage has run or crawled away or lies murdered to fertilize southern soil.

FOREIGN WAVE CLIMBS OVER US

We have seen wave after wave of the poor and ignorant and unskilled come into America, climb over our bent and broken backs and achieve success, honor and wealth and thumb their noses in our faces.

Look at the Irish, the Italians, the Russian and Polish Jews, Greeks and the people from the Balkans. I am not jealous of them. I do not even blame them in the environment of race hatred in which they unwittingly come.

I simply say that America will not let us succeed. We have done more for this land than any of its recent immigrants. They have succeeded. We are still at the bottom and the blow of this depression falls on us with more crushing force than any element in this nation—statistics to the contrary notwithstanding.

There is no point in meeting this fact with modest self-blame. We are human with human faults and failures. But no group in the modern world has accomplished as much with as little and gained so limited and grudging a reward.

WARNING AGAINST OPTIMISM

This is no counsel of despair. It is a warning against the optimism of the fool.

Now, it may be said, in the face of this, that failure is natural to human beings and particularly to great groups of human beings; that we have in the United States an exceptional situation; that it would have been nothing unusual if the American slave in two or three generations had shown no appreciable advance or recognition, and that therefore the *next steps* before us consist in renewed efforts at training our ability and deserving the world's recognition and that of the American nation.

MATTER OF PSYCHOLOGY

There are two answers to this—one is a matter of psychology. Our nerves are a bit frayed with the unusual efforts that we have put forward. It is going to be difficult with the present generation of young black people, to prove to them that they ought to try to get the good opinion and the recognition of their white fellows.

They are asking, "After all, who are these people who require of us so much more than they require of others, and whence came their right and assumption of world ownership? But that is a minor matter.

FACING REVOLUTION

The other matter, and the matter of greatest import, is that instead of our facing today a stable world, moving at a uniform rate of progress toward well-defined goals, we are facing revolution. I trust you will not be as scared by this word as you were Thursday night. I am not discussing a coming revolution, I am trying to impress the fact upon you that you are

already in the midst of a revolution; you are already in the
midst of war; that there has been no war of modern times
that has taken so great a sacrifice of human life and human
spirit as the extraordinary period through which we are passing today.

REAL REVOLUTION WITHIN

Some people envisage revolution chiefly as a matter of
blood and guns and the more visible methods of force. But
that, after all, is merely the temporary and outward manifes-
tation. Real revolution is within. That comes before or after
the explosion—is a matter of long suffering and deprivation,
the death of courage and the bitter triumph of despair. This is
the inevitable prelude to decisive and enormous change, and
that is the thing that is on us now.

We are not called upon then to discuss whether we want
revolution or not. We have got it. Our problem is how we are
coming out of it. I would be very glad indeed if the matter
were as simple as the presiding officer of Thursday night
indicated; that we are not on the brink of anything but simply
preparing to mount solid steps in plain view. I am afraid that
down in the mud in which most of us are wallowing, it is not
a matter of steps. We have trees and cliffs to climb. We have
swamps to wade through and forests to penetrate.

STAND ON ONE SIDE

But that is all aside; because this matter of world depression and revolutionary changes in social life and industry is
not primarily the problem of the American Negro, and just
because it is not our problem, we have plain proof of the
thing that I said before, namely, that we are not in reality a
part of this nation.

We stand, even in its greatest crisis, at one side, only partially connected with its remedies, but dumb victims of its
difficulties, and by just that token because we are outside the
main current of the country, we have got most carefully to
ask ourselves what we are going to do to protect our past and
to insure our future.

SEPARATE NEGRO STATE

I was exceedingly interested the other night when Mr. Gandy (President John Gandy of Virginia State College) suggested a separate Negro state. It is arresting to see how often this old solution drifts back again and again to the American Negro. I remember what the Negroes of Newport said to the Negroes of Philadelphia back at the end of the eighteenth century, when the same thing had been suggested.

If we were living in the seventeenth century, there is no doubt but what Mr. Gandy's suggestion would be the next natural step: that we should say to the American people, "We have tried to be reasonable, decent citizens, and to meet all of the difficult requirements that have been put upon us, and we have been unable to satisfy you. Now we are going off to be by ourselves and to seek to satisfy ourselves."

Today, however, the very fact that such a solution is suggested makes it evident how far many of our best minds are from realizing just the situation in this world. The organized industry of the world today, the organized finance and commerce, the empire of concentrated capital, will not let any group of people escape.

LIBERIA

I have been studying the extraordinary developments in Liberia under the domination of the National City Bank and the Firestone interests. Liberia, born of slavery, started without capital. She tried to borrow $500,000 in 1870. She got $100,000 and had to pay practically the whole $500,000, and all she got out of it was a small rubber forest.

She tried in our day to borrow five million dollars of the Firestone interests in return for this rubber forest and other rubber land, and today she is paying nearly 75 per cent of her total income simply as service charges and white men's salaries on this debt. She is financially ruined and almost politically defunct unless the American Negro vote can stop the power of the Firestones.

HAITI

In the same way in Haiti every claim or shadow of a claim against that state has been capitalized at its peak and the state saddled with a debt far beyond its power to pay, with the United States army and navy to enforce its demands.

If the 12,000,000 Negroes in the United States should leave this country and find space where they could settle with reasonable resources for development, unless they had their own capital and skill, materials and machines, and unless the present world slaving to capital monopoly is first overthrown, they would find themselves under the power of the banking interests of this or some other country backed by military tyranny and unable to make any direct appeal to the sovereign rulers of any land.

NEGROES WILL MIGRATE

I admit freely the difficulties of the frying pan, but I am not attracted to the fire. When that fire is out, I expect mass emigration of American Negroes unless vital change comes to America.

We must then recognize the facts of the case. We are the victims of a caste system in the United States whose main lines we have been unable to break. We are at the beginning of a vast change in the organization of industry· here and in the world, and the question is, what part are we going to take during this change and how are we going to prepare for a place in the world that comes after?

PRIVATE PROFITS TO STOP

It is rather curious that those very people who put special stress upon spiritual values do not usually, when it comes to practical reform, take any account of the inner spirit of man.

The economic change that is coming into the world has got to take account of it. Primarily what is happening, and what must be accomplished whether it takes place next year or a dozen years hence, is that we are going to stop the organization of work for private profit and substitute therefore work for public welfare.

And the essential thing about this change is not new law or a Fascist regime but it is a change of spirit. The average man must give up the idea that the chief end of an American is to be a millionaire. Now this is a tremendous change. Only the other day a friend of mine was talking to a young banker. The banker said:

THE BANKER SAYS

"My opinion is that now is the time when the foundations of the great fortunes of the future are going to be laid."

In other words, in a day when we are suffering all the disaster that has come from this founding of great private fortunes, with its war and waste, its cheating and lying, its murder of men and women and children and death of ambition and beauty, the idea of this young man was that just as soon as we get over this crisis, we were going right back to doing the same thing again and yet again, and indeed unless we suffer a spiritual revolution by which men are going to envisage small incomes and limited resources and endless work for the larger goals of life, unless we have this, nothing can save civilization either for white people or black.

GREATEST REASON FOR PRIDE

Now it happens that the colored people in the United States are the group that has gone least forward on this program of the exploitation of the many for the benefit of the few. It has not been our fault. Rather we have been blamed and blamed ourselves for this lack of "economic progress," as it is called. We are rather ashamed that we have not developed more millionaires and more big businesses.

But I venture to say that at some future day this will be our greatest reason for pride; because, after all, we have had the temptation and we have made terrific effort; we have tried just as far as possible to divide the American Negro into economic classes, with the professional and investing classes at the top, and the mass of partially unlettered laborers at the bottom; and it has only been the impenetrability of American prejudice that has made our advance in these lines so small.

COMMUNIST WEDGE

The task that I have recently been setting myself is to blunt the wedge which the Communist party is driving into our group because of these very tendencies, and I do this, not because of any enmity or fear or essential disagreement with the Communists. If I were in Russia, I should be an enthusiastic Communist.

If the Communist party in the United States had the leadership and the knowledge which our situation calls for, I certainly should join it; but it is today ignorant of fact and history and the American scene and is trying to over-emphasize the truth that the natural leaders of the colored people, the educated and trained classes, have had goals and interests different from the mass of Negroes.

There is a partial truth in this, and a partial falsehood. American race prejudice has so pounded the mass of Negroes together that they have not separated into such economic classes; but on the other hand they undoubtedly have had the ideology and if they had been free we would have had within our race the same exploiting set-up that we see around about us.

Now, however, in the tremendous change which sooner or later is bound to come in the world, we have a chance to be the first to make the change and make it with the least internal catastrophe, and our only reason for fear is that at this crucial moment we be robbed of our intelligent leadership.

LESSON TO LEARN

Before our leaders can essay this new task they have a vast lesson to learn. As has been charged here, in the most courageous address of the conference, we have been timid and conservative, we have sought peace at any price; we have placated philanthropy and kowtowed humbly to the rich.

Today our turning to saner and more manly methods does not involve throwing bricks or calling names. It does involve an inner readjustment of ideals. We must rid ourselves of the persistent idea that the advance of mankind consists of the scaling off of layers who become incorporated with the world's upper and ruling classes, leaving always dead and inert below the ignorant and unenlightened mass of men.

Our professional classes are not aristocrats and our masters —they are and must be the most efficient of our servants and thinkers whose legitimate reward is the advancement of the great mass of American Negroes and with them the uplift of all men.

CONCEPTION OF BIGNESS

We, even before America, must slough off the preconception of bigness, growth and eternal success. This world makes progress in little things, in contractions and failures as well as tremendous surpluses and increased prices and wild expansion.

We must face revolution calmly and sanely. No revolution destroys the past. The past must be foundation of any future. Our huge and intricate and marvelously ingenious industrial organization must be saved for any future reorganized state. We shall need machines and capital, engineers, and captains of industry. Russia proves this. But the object, the end, the reward, the measure of success—there is the kernel and meat of the problem and the judgment of success and failure of revolution.

TOO MUCH EVERTHING

I think we have all been secretly astonished at the peculiar problems suggested here. Too much coal, too much cotton, less ingenuity, less land, for people who are cold and naked, who work too hard and too long and get nothing for it.

What kind of fantastic world are we visioning? Nonsense,

there is no such world; it is mirage. We want more coal, more cunning machines, more cotton, more everything, but for all men and not for private monopoly. If this is not to be done, we are lost, black and white, in one world-wide disaster.

NO PROFIT IDEA

For us then revolutionary change calls for the following steps:

1. The no-profit idea. That is the idea of carrying on business not for private profit but for service; the pay being not the surplus value which is made out of the hiring of labor or the monopoly of machines or the theft of raw material but a reasonable and even meagre salary scale.

Such change, as I said before, has got to be spiritual. Just as long as we have within the Negro race and any race, young men of education and power who believe that they ought to have the right to spend $100,000 a year, just so long we are facing toward those same seas of disaster upon which already the world has met shipwreck.

PRIMARILY SERVICE

2. Our work has got to be primarily service. I know that this word has been overworked, but let me give a concrete example of what I mean.

We have among American Negroes 1,230 lawyers. On the other hand, in every state in the United States when the average Negro is arrested the chances are that he is going to be started on a criminal career simply because he has no proper legal defense. Our jails are filled with black folk who are simply monuments to miscarried justice. The N.A.A.C.P. has done some legal defense work; but it had to be in exceptional cases, to establish some great principle of law. We have not had, and we could not expect to have, the money necessary for carrying on complete legal defense on the scale it ought to be.

Every single city, every single county in the United States

where there are any number of Negroes ought to have Negro lawyers of ability working on small and regular salary, not to aid the rich to break the law or help the poor to beat it, but standing ready to defend black people who need defense in simple human rights.

25,000 CHURCHES

Moreover, we have a part of the machinery to do this. We have 25,000 ministers and churches, twice as many in proportion as the whites, and the real criticism of the church which I and others have voiced from time to time is not a criticism of belief. It is not my business what anybody believes so long as it is sincere. I may not share his belief or comprehend his mentality, but I respect it.

My criticism is not one of organization because some Negro churches are marvelous organizations, but it is a criticism of the effective work for which they are organized.

There is no reason in the world why every one of the 25,000 Negro churches should not furnish the salary for one lawyer to defend Negroes who need it, even if once in a while they cannot pay the minister's salary.

The same kind of socialized medicine, dentistry and nursing, could be widely and extensively used.

A THOUGHT OF MARRIAGE

In the third place, we have got to take thought concerning the Negro family for sheer physical survival of our best. As it is today, we are making no plans for marriage of our children at the age when they ought to be married; we are not keeping in mind that the marriage of young people is as much a matter of careful planning and forethought as any other object of civilized life. We have thousands of marriageable men and marriageable women kept from mating because of a public opinion in their own group that calls for a standard of living we cannot and ought not to afford. The resulting repressions and complexes are disastrous.

THE MATTER OF WORK

But finally and above all, key to all the rest, there comes the matter of work. Here it is extraordinary how the patterns of the present set-up of business have completely captured our imagination. *Practically this conference has come to the conclusion that we have got to make obeisance to Big Business and ask it please to allow us to be exploited on the same terms that good white people are; on the contrary I am firmly convinced that in the methods and objectives of big industry there is absolutely no hope for the American Negro.*

I don't care what the steel trust has done for us, or what the food trust may do or what the coal trust will do. In truth, they all are using us as tools to make fortunes which no human being has a right to possess and which works for the damnation of his soul and the starvation of our bodies.

BIG INDUSTRY OFFERS BLANK WALL

We have no right to exist for such a purpose. The American Negro will only be admitted to organized industry as his labor returns a profit and a bigger profit than white labor does, and upon the wage thus received no civilization or culture can possibly be built. As long, therefore, as big industry is dominated by these ideas, we are facing something worse than a blank wall.

WHAT CAN GOVERNMENT DO?

On the other hand, what can the Government do for us? We are turning to the Government today like babies crying for mother's milk. And yet this is not the effort of intelligent masters of democratic method bent on making an efficient instrument do its work. It is rather the despair and debacle of laissez-faire.

The impasse of government today lies in the fact that it has no intelligent democracy upon which it can depend. We are turning to dictators because of the stupidity and ignorance of the average voter, white, black or yellow.

DICTATORS

If we give Mr. Roosevelt the right to meddle with the dollar, if we give Herr Hitler the right to expel the Jew, if we give to Mussolini the right to think for Italians, we do this because we know nothing ourselves. We are as a nation ignorant of the function and meaning of money, and we are looking around helplessly to see if anybody else knows.

This is not, as some assume, the failure of democracy—it is the failure of education, of justice and of truth. We have lied so long about money and business, we do not know now where truth is.

DEMOCRACY IS KILLED

Democratic government without intelligence back of it simply cannot function and therefore if we expect that the American government is going to rescue the Negro worker when he and his fellow white workers are disfranchised because of their lack of experience and intelligence, we are again hoping against hope. *The present dictatorship of industry in America has killed Democracy as definitely as any dictatorship in Europe or in South America.*

THE CONSUMER

Now, what is the alternative? The alternative, as I have said many times, and as I am going to continue to say, is to look for rescue to the intelligent consumer. The consumer in America is made almost ham-strung because his thought is dominated by extraordinary stupid patterns. It is assumed for instance, that the man who does not buy everything at the cheapest price is an idiot. I have known women to spend ten cents in wear and tear of shoes in order to save ten cents on the price of cabbage.

I have known Negroes to put a good colored grocer, giving two colored clerks work, out of business in order to support a chain store which wouldn't hire a colored dog, and they saved

15 cents on the week's grocery bill. When the consumer learns that buying is a bargain in which he is becoming a partner in industry; that it is not the matter of buying the cheapest thing, but of paying the fair price, then things begin.

MERCY OF ADVERTISERS

Or again, we are today at the mercy of advertising and display, a plain waste of money, for which we pay with our hard earned cash. Most of our essential trade could be done in a back room of a fifth floor flat, without a plate glass window or nickel plated counter. But we do not seem to think so. We have been taught differently.

Or again, we have been told here of the havoc that machines have wrought and it has seemed as though some of the speakers had no conception of any escape from that dilemma. Here comes the machine—out go 400 workers. It must happen in the name of progress.

COOPERATIVE GROUPS

But why must it happen? Who gets the saving that is made from the use of the machine? Who lets him get it but the man who buys what the machine makes? And must the machine be monopolized? We are on the threshold of a day when the house, industry and the privately owned machine or the machine owned by a small cooperative group can come into its own, if we have the requisite sense. The Muscle Shoals development is going to make it possible to have village after village of people supporting themselves by house industry, supplying their own wants, buying of themselves, more and more independent of factory and trust.

Professor Murchison weeps over the plight of the poor mill owner: I am unmoved. My tears are for the people who wear his dresses. There ought to be village after village of colored people at Muscle Shoals building an independent self-supporting economy.

USE OF THE BALLOTS

Again we are not at all clear as to how we are going to use the votes that we have for our economic uplift. We have used them for certain changes—in law, for putting in office people who have spoken pleasantly before election and sometimes after, but we have not used our vote for certain clear things which we might accomplish and which go to the foundation and undermining of our industrial dictatorship—enforced publicity of all ownership of property, the right to name the thieves who loot savings banks and gamble with others' money, in fine the right to make clear the wretched methods of so much of present business activity. We could use our vote continually to refuse to give monopolistic privileges like patents to certain kinds of business which increase the tremendous tyranny of industry.

12,000,000 MUST FEED THEMSELVES

All this is a part that the consumer can play and a voluntary part. And finally, he can cooperate not only in consumption, but in manufacture. I know how much this proposition is criticized, but I say again, as I have said before, by intelligent planning and self-denying ordinance, 12 million black people in the U.S.A. can work themselves and feed themselves, can pay themselves and organize their own industry unless they are incurably stupid.

For a great mass of people to sit up and actually starve to death in the midst of plenty is to prove not only to the world but to themselves that they are going to be of no real use in the ultimate reorganization of industry.

In other words, I propose as the next step which the American Negro can give to the world a new and unique gift. We have tried song and laughter and with rare good humor a bit condescending the world has received it; we have given the world work, hard, backbreaking labor and the world has let black John Henry die breaking his heart to beat the machine.

It is now our business to give the world an example of intelligent cooperation so that when the new industrial commonwealth comes we can go into it as an experienced people and not again be left on the outside as mere beggars.

Because as has been said here in the reorganization of industry which the world is bound to see, there is no guarantee that race prejudice will be eliminated unless there is adequate reason.

THE RUSSIAN JEW

In Russia the Jew was the ideologist of revolution, the born foe of religious superstition and the first citizen of the international. Of course, anti-semitism died suddenly. So in America, if leading the way as intelligent cooperating consumers, we rid ourselves of the ideas of a price system and become pioneer servants of the common good, we can enter the new city as men and not as mules.

And the thing that I want finally to impress upon this audience is that new industrial commonwealth is coming. You can be scared about it if you want to, you can shudder when Russia and Communism are mentioned, but the reorganization of industry in this world for the benefit of those that work and not of those that buy and sell is certain.

It may not come next year, it may not come in the next decade, but if there is any foundation to our belief in human intelligence, it has got to come.

From the *Baltimore Afro-American*, May 20, 1933

The Present Economic Problem of the American Negro (*1935*)

Delivered at the Sixty-fifth Annual Session of the National Baptist Convention, New York City, September, 1935.

The present economic situation in the world is one of the most difficult which man has faced in modern times, and it is no wonder that most people are grievously puzzled and unable to judge what is right or wise under the circumstances. It is not difficult to see why this is true. The facts concerning work and wages, capital and profit, income and expenditure, production and distribution are exceedingly complicated. Few experts understand them in their entirety and yet all of us, whether expert or not, whether worker or capitalist, must not only take part in the economic life of the nation, but indeed the part he takes forms so large and important a group of his activities that it has often been said that man is an economic animal and that his work and wage must be more important to him than anything else because of sheer necessity of his physical existence.

These are reasons for increased and more careful study of work and industry and wages and perhaps the one great good which has come out of the depression is the fact that so many people that took the surrounding economic organization as for granted, today have been compelled to study it, to read about it, and to take some action concerning it.

The main outlines of our present situation can be briefly and simply stated.

THE TRAGEDY OF 1914

In 1914, the world organized itself for mass murder. It proceeded to kill millions of human beings, maim other millions and to destroy a vast amount of property. It disorganized international relations and national industry, and then, from 1918 to the present day, it tried to get back to normalcy. But when you have broken up an organization, disrupted a household or bankrupted a city, you are suddenly fronted with the problem: what is normalcy? It is natural to think of normal conditions as those which preceded the catastrophe and that has been what the world has been doing for the most part in its effort to recover from the effects of the World War, and to become just as it was before the war. But the difficulty is that the world before the war in many vital respects was not a satisfactory world and it was especially unsatisfactory in its arrangement of work and wages, profits and industry, the production and the distribution of wealth.

Dissatisfaction with industrial conditions had long been expressed. When the new capitalism arose in the Eighteenth Century, it was criticized by a group of men who came to be called Socialists and afterward by a new body of doctrine denominated "Communism." But the new order of industry which began with the African slave trade and accompanied and caused the vast development of America, the British Empire and the French and German nations, was too successful to be changed by criticism. And the whole system developed until the catastrophe of the World War. What, now, was this system and what was the criticism against it? The final law of existence is, that if men will have food, they must work for it. There are, of course, variations of this law. The men who eat the food may not be necessarily those who do the work which produces it. The father may work for the children, the young may work for the old, the weak may work for the powerful. But the necessity of work in order that men may enjoy the satisfactions of life is an inexorable law.

In earlier and simpler days, this was arranged with a considerable approach to justice, although not with exact justice. On the West Coast of Africa there still exist the great clans or aggregations of families. The father or grandfather, or the eldest surviving son or nephew is chief of the clan. In a general way, assisted by the advice of the older people, he directs the work of the tribe; divides the land; sees that the members of the tribe able to work do their work properly and punishes them if they do not. The resulting crops are divided, not necessarily according to the amount of work that the man does or the efficiency of it, but according to the needs of the members of the tribe. The old people and the children get their share and there is always some discrimination in the shares given away, according to the esteem in which different members of the tribe are held. And yet, certain things are always true: There are no people unemployed who can work; there are no people who are forced to starve; there is no one who cannot have land to work upon. And there is abundant

leisure and for the most part a singularly happy life except
for disease and those accidents like drought and hurricane
and war from without which the tribe is not able to foresee or
to withstand.

THE USE OF CAPITAL

Into this situation there come certain changes as the tribe
grows in size and as its demands for goods and services vary.
The greatest and most significant change is what we call the
use of capital; that is, the preparation of goods, not for eating
and wearing and enjoying, but to be used in further preparation of other goods. There is always some capital in a primitive tribe. Some of the seed of the corn is not eaten, but saved
for further harvest, some of the iron is fashioned not for
spear-heads, but for knives with which furniture can be
made. As the amount and usefulness of this capital increases,
the whole situation in the tribe is changed.

In a modern nation, consider for a moment the goods used
as capital; that is, as agencies which produce other goods and
services. Most of our buildings, all of our railroads, all of our
multitudinous machines and engines, most of our ships and
airplanes, all of our factories and stores and offices, most of
our raw material, wheat, cotton, iron, steel, stone; indeed, the
great bulk of the valuable and important things about us are
not for direct use and enjoyment, but indirectly used to produce the things which we eat and wear and use directly. And
think of the time consumed in making these goods. The appearance of this kind of goods which we call capital immediately brings changes in the idea of property. Property, first, is
a simple concept. A man makes his own arrows; his own
fishing rods; his own clothes. They belong to him because he
made them. On the other hand, he does not make the land
upon which he works; and the primitive machines which he
employs are usually made by several men working together.
The land, therefore, is never conceived of as private property
in a primitive tribe. The machines are looked upon as belonging to the community; while the individual tools and weapons
are conceived of as belonging to the individual. When, now,

the capital goods, the goods which are designed to make other goods, the tools and machines grow in number, to whom do they belong? This question was never settled in early industrial life or in later developments by decisions of abstract justice and right and considerations of the best interests of the community.

In such developments as accompanied the rise and fall of Rome, the descent of the barbarians, the wars and counterwars which marked the growth of European nations, chance, power and cunning influenced the result. So that when we come to modern times, we find that not by design or purpose, not according to religion or ethics, but as a matter of fact, difficult or even impossible to explain; the land belonged to a few people; the machines and materials were monopolized by the rich and the mass of the workers without land and without capital, sold their toil for wages which were seldom above the amount necessary for their existence and reproduction. A great deal of bitter charge and invective have been brought against the rich and powerful who thus monopolize wealth. But this is not entirely fair. Most of the wealthy gained their power and resources by heritage, by opportunity, by hard work and especially by the public opinion of their times which encouraged and praised this acquisition of power.

Nevertheless, the excuses which then and now may be very properly made for capitalists and rich people do not at all alter the fact that the plight of the mass of workers is simply impossible and must be changed. Demands for such a change came in the Eighteenth and especially in the early Nineteenth Centuries. They were chiefly philanthropic demands, that is, they were appeals on the part of persons who knew the plight of the poor and who were sensitive to human welfare and who said: this sort of industry is not civilization; it is not in accordance with religion and it must be changed. But the difficulty was that here was a pattern set and hardened by the authority of hundreds of years. Most people, for instance, looked upon private ownership of land as a natural and God-given thing. There are plenty of people today who still have that idea. They have no conception of the fact that during most of the years in which man has been civilized, private ownership of land was not only uncommon, but unthought of. Indeed, very largely, inconceivable. The source of the present ownership and monopoly of machines and raw materials is hard to extricate from a complicated industrial history.

There are those who insist that all property and all capital is theft and if we mean by theft the taking of goods for ourselves which others have produced, then it is true that property is theft; but we must remember that law, gospel and custom for a thousand years has called that sort of accumulation of property not only justifiable but as right and indispensable to the proper carrying on of industry. Today, therefore, we need not waste our time as to the past history and ethics of capital and industry, but we must, on the other hand, ask today; why is it that in a world where it is possible to raise enough food and manufacture enough clothing and build enough housing for the accommodation of all men, and in addition to this, give them services which will educate and amuse and develop them, when all this is undoubtedly possible and made possible by the reasonable amount of toil of the mass of men who can work, why is it, in spite of this that millions upon millions of workers can find no more to do, while other millions who do work cannot get for their toil enough to sustain them and clothing and housing sufficient to protect them? And children and old people and the sick are faced with starvation. This is not merely a philosophy of envy. It need not lead to hatred and bloodshed, but it must lead to reform or civilization cannot go on.

EFFORTS TO SOLVE PROBLEMS

The whole world is facing problems of this sort and European countries especially have been trying to settle them. The methods of settlement have been different. In the case of Russia, we have seen a vast attempt in which the nation has taken over ownership of all land and nearly all capital and is seeking to give employment to the workers at wages which will furnish them a decent standard of life; and above all, is trying to do this in the interests of the working class and not in the interest of an aristocracy of owners of land and capital. This experiment has only begun. It has had so far unusual success and it is not too much to say that the masses of the world are anxiously looking to Russia to see how far it will be able to go. On the other hand, in Germany and Italy, the state has assumed partial control, although not actual ownership of land and capital, and tried by the concentrated power of the state to direct employment and wages and limit profits so as to carry on successful industry. These so-called Fascist experiments have aroused in the countries affected, a great deal of apparent enthusiasm and loyalty, but because of the suppression of news and facts, it is impossible for outsiders to know just how successful they really are and there is a well-grounded suspicion that the experiments cannot last, because these states are still conducted for the rich and not for the poor. On the other hand, in France and England, the state, while not assuming control, either of land or capital, has through its power of taxation and other general powers, tried to rearrange to some degree the re-distribution of wealth. It has tried to raise wages and to do away with unemployment; it has distributed large sums in charity, to alleviate poverty and unemployment, and it has limited the profits of the owners of land and wealth. The results here are better than in the Fascist countries, but they are still not satisfactory. The criticism is made that the reason that the results are not satisfactory is because the state has not gone far enough in re-distributing wealth and raising wages; while the answer is that vast changes of this sort must be accomplished slowly and experimentally and that there is no guaranty that what Russia has attempted could be successfully carried through in France or England.

THE AMERICAN SCENE

Let us turn now from past history and foreign countries, to the United States. In the United States, we long had an idea that here was a country not subjected to the difficulties which beset Europe. In the first place, while there was private ownership of land, there was so much free public land that for a long time we boasted that any man could become a land-holder. The accumulation of wealth by capitalists was great, but for many years almost any thrifty American could accumulate some capital and become at least a small capitalist. Indeed, the American doctrine went so far as to assume, if it did not actually say, that any man who was poor was lazy and any man who was rich deserved his wealth because of his industry and brains. Two facts challenged this situation. First, the Negro slave and freedman; and secondly, the situation after the World War. The Negro slave was emancipated without land and capital and had no real opportunity to get either. He was forced, therefore, to become a landless peasant and worker employed at the lowest wage. And this competition inevitably tended to depress the wages of white laborers, especially of the new immigrant. Then, again, after the World War, it became evident that the methods by which we accumulated wealth, not only did not mean that wealth was distributed to the mass of workers, but on the contrary, it tended more and more to be monopolized in the hands of a comparatively small group of people, until by 1929, the property and investments of this group of owners called for profits and interest charges which industry simply could not stand. Or in other words we produced enormously for people who could not buy and we had that extraordinary panic from which we have not today recovered. Suddenly, then we find ourselves in the plight of all modern nations and we have got to decide how in the United States we can see that the goods which we are able to make and the services which we can render, are distributed among the mass of people so that all can live decently; and on the other hand, that the abundance of work which always needs to be done shall be done and done efficiently by intelligent, healthy and willing labor.

THE NEW DEAL

The New Deal attempted to face this problem, and without going into detail, let me try to make it clear just what the New Deal sought to do. It tried to say to the American people; the object of industry, the object of organized industrial life, is to increase general welfare, and if by any and all means we increase this general welfare, we will have solved the problem of industry. That brought President Roosevelt and his advisers face to face with methods of increasing this general welfare and they chose the methods of increasing the profits of those who own land and capital.

Now it was this very profit and the concentration of its ownership and power of government that lay in this ownership that was the cause of the world panic. The New Deal had therefore to attempt to curb profit by increasing wages and multiplying employment, and these two lines of effort were certainly to a large extent contradictory. If you are going to increase the returns to capital, it is going to be difficult at the same time to increase the returns to labor. If the object of industry is general welfare, then the object of industry cannot be at the same time increased profit. And it is upon the rocks of these contradictions that the New Deal went partially to pieces. It did not altogether fail and its greatest success lay in the fact that it implanted in the public mind the idea of general welfare as the object of industry; the idea that the state and the nation were interested not primarily in protecting the land and capital, but in seeing that the mass of workers got a decent income and a fair chance to earn it. If the New Deal accomplished nothing more than this, it would deserve well of the nation.

THE POOR LANDLESS SLAVE

Now let us leave these general considerations and go back to this poor and landless slave who was emancipated and thrust into this situation. The Negro tried during Reconstruction Times to accumulate capital; but he did more than that. He realized that he was a representative of the working classes and through the Reconstruction Legislatures he attempted repeatedly to legislate for the general welfare of the workers for land, education and protection.

I have expanded and emphasized this thesis in my recent book, "Black Reconstruction," which despite its size and price, I hope many of you will read. The same principle of the primary interest of the worker in the state which Russia is emphasizing today, was emphasized by the black legislators of South Carolina, Mississippi and Louisiana, and the reason that they did not and could not go further in this line was because of their lack of intelligent leadership; a necessary and explicable lack in a mass of former slaves.

The result was that in 1876 the land monopolists and the owners of capital, North and South, united to displace these representatives of black and white labor and instituted governments in the Southern States which helped carry out in the nation tremendous and unlimited development of capitalistic enterprise.

THE NEGRO UNDER THE NEW DEAL

The place of the Negro under the New Deal and what will it be under the development which is following those efforts? Under the New Deal, Negro labor received recognition, and the Negro was envisaged in practically all of the plans adopted. But the main benefit that came to him was small, because of divided councils within his own ranks, and because of race prejudice in the ranks of employers and white laborers. That makes it important that we should very carefully take council among ourselves because in the future developments that are coming, we must not contradict ourselves, neutralize our own efforts and stand in our own way. When, for instance, the subsistence homesteads were proposed by the New Deal, I strongly advocated them. They included methods of furnishing employed workers with gardens in which they and their families could help out their income by raising food and materials. It was, of course, a temporary make-shift, but was a valuable one and it could have been of great help to numbers of workers. No sooner, however, was it proposed to establish such homesteads for Negroes than large numbers of Negro leaders and organizations opposed the whole thing because it involved segregation. Of course, it involved segregation, but when you have to choose between segregation and starvation, you are a fool not to choose food for your children. But this does, of course, bring up important questions of principles. Negroes have passed through many stages of social planning to help their industrial condition. There was a time when because of slavery nothing but bloody revolt seemed to be the answer. And this answer was made by Denmark Vesey and Nat Turner and Toussaint L'Ouverture. After them came the plan of the fugitive slave; of escaping from slavery into a free country and becoming there a free laborer. That, perhaps, did more than any single thing eventually to overthrow the slave system. Then, as free laborers, came the plan of uniting with the white laborers. It is the fashion today of some young and very earnest but also very ignorant leaders to assume that the Negro has never tried to be a part of a white labor movement. This is ridiculous. He made every effort before the Civil War.

He joined the labor unions when he could, but usually was absolutely excluded. When emancipation came, he tried to join the National Labor Union, but they would not have him, and he finally formed his own National Labor Union and spread the organization over a large part of the United States. Later, he went in large numbers into the Knights of Labor, but when the Knights of Labor was succeeded by the American Federation of Labor, the Negro was faced by tactics before which he was helpless. The general Federation blandly invited him to join and the powerful unions which composed it for the most part refused to admit him. The result was he was excluded from the labor movement. His next effort and a perfectly natural one, was alliance with the capitalistic employers; and attempt to train himself by industrial education so as to become a skilled artisan and to solicit employment from employers on the plea that he could do the work as well as anybody else. His only real weapon, of course, under such circumstances, was his willingness if necessary to work for a lower wage and not to strike or join the Federal Labor Movement. This movement failed because of the power of the white unions and the comparative indifference of employers when it came to the real interests of black workers. Meantime, there grew up among Negroes an economic theory which we may perhaps call "Separatism." The idea was that the mass of the workers was going to get along as it could, but that trained and exceptional men, artisans, business men and professional men, could by individual effort make their way into American industry and social life; that they would be recognized according to their individual desert; that they would accumulate wealth and receive social and political recognition, and that in this way the elite of American Negroes would become a part of the governing classes of America, and by abolishing the Color Line against themselves, automatically abolish it for the masses of workers. This theory has seldom been openly and plainly announced, but it has been for years the real thought of large numbers of Negroes.

A BEAUTIFUL THEORY BUT—

Gradually, however the more careful thinkers among us have seen that this was breaking down. In the first place, the organized resistance of American prejudice to any interpenetration of social and industrial organization by black men, no matter what their effort and ability, has been much stronger than most of us thought. Exceptions have occurred to be sure, but on the whole, it has been increasingly difficult and to a large extent impossible, for a Negro in genuine white enterprises to become a capitalist or technician, a manufacturer or producer, a member of the government with real executive power, or a manager and man of power in any line.

Exceptions have occurred, but the group resistance has been such that there remain exceptions and we are forced today more to turn toward segregated or united action. We resent this. I have been called by those who resent it as an advocate of segregation and as changing the basic principles upon which my life work has been based. This is, of course, nonsense. The change, of which there was one, has come in that hardening American attitude which refuses ever more strongly today than yesterday to recognize ability under a dark skin and the subsequent absolute necessity of those who are of Negro descent to stand together in united action for their economic emancipation. What now must this action involve? There are four alternatives offered us: Communism, Socialism, Technocracy and the Doctrine of the Elite.

COMMUNISM

Communism is the natural thought of one of the greatest philosophers of modern times, Karl Marx; a man of unselfish devotion to the working class; a Jew who was crucified all over Europe for his radicalism, a trained University graduate who was not a worker and not a member of the proletariat, but who espoused the cause of the mass, more successfully than, almost any prophet of the nineteenth century. The doctrine of Karl Marx was: That the wealth which the working masses produce and which is supplied by nature, has been and is being dishonestly taken from them by the forced sale of their labor at less than its real value; this reduces the laborer to poverty while the surplus value of their work thus exploited goes to increase the wealth and power of the employing class. That the only cure for this that the working class unite and by forceful revolution seize the land, the tools and the machines, and conduct the state for the benefit of the workers. And Marx went further to say that the method which this was going to be done was an inevitable development which would come by the forces of nature of its own evolution and could not in the long run be stopped or turned aside.

Of the essential truth and justice beneath the Marxian doctrine there can be no doubt. The goods and services produced by the working classes are today distributed with gross injustice and the central problem of our day is to stop this injustice. On the other hand, the Marxian idea that the development by which this reform was coming about is inevitable and must follow the beaten path which he laid down, is undoubtedly not true and simply a result of his academic training in Hegelianism. For revolution is a horribly costly thing. No people who think in terms of the World War can dare to emphasize it. I doubt if Marx himself, if he were alive today, would stress it as he did in 1848. Even in the case of

Russia, the conditions were so different and that state so backward as compared with most modern states, that correlation is impossible. But the real difficulty with the Marxian state is the question as to who is to re-build after the tearing down; and the greatness of Lenin and those people who are leading Russia lies in the fact that they did not hesitate for a moment in revising the Marxian doctrine and providing a dictatorship to lead a proletariat, unable to lead itself; that is, a small set of trained people have gripped and held the power in the Russian state. And yet so far are carrying on for the undoubted benefit of the mass. Here, then, lies the crux of the problem. How are you going to get the proper leadership for a reform, whether the reform is violent, as it was in Russia, or whether it is gradual and philanthropic as in case of England, France and the United States?

The real problem is the problem of these guiding few. Socialism is the Reformist program which tries by any possible method to lift the condition and increase the power of the working masses by equalizing the income; and it works usually through the intelligentsia; by means of people who are not workers, but thinkers and planners, and who try like Fourier and Owen to change the state by reform and not by revolution. To this have lately been added two other sections of thought: Veblen has stressed the fact that the technician, the man who can best take it, is the one who can best take over the control of the state and make it most just and efficient. But of course the difficulty here is to find technocrats who not only have the technical knowledge and efficiency, but also the will to carry on this state for the benefit of the mass of workers; and finally, there comes the somewhat cynical Pareto who insists that always and everywhere, the elite, the people of real knowledge and ability, are going to rule the state, and for the most part they are going to rule it for their own interests and it becomes our problem to say how far this elite can be induced through a spirit of service and sacrifice to carry on the state or to lead the group, not for their own interests, but for the interests of the mass of men.

The suggestion which I have continually made is that in our peculiar position we cannot choose any one of these four main paths, but must make selected choice which suits our condition and which can be carried through to success by brains and unselfish devotion. This selection would take from Communism its fine Democratic idea of a state conducted in the interests of the working class and by such members of the working class as become intelligent and technically efficient. And with Communism, we would stress the fact that the economic organization of any age or group is the fundamental thing out of which its civilization must necessarily grow. We can turn to Socialism and take from Socialism its program of reform, including old-age pensions, minimum wage, the abolition of child labor and the gradual socialization of wealth so that the state would eventually own both land and capital. But we cannot stop here, for the difficulty with us, even more than with the mass of the whites, is that our labor classes have neither the education, the technique, or the experience to carry through difficult plans of this sort, and therefore, we must have the training and cooperation of men who understand the technique of modern industry, and we must seek to raise a Talented Tenth among us who would become the intelligent leaders and directors of our masses. We must guard against the difficulty that such a Talented Tenth may easily think of itself as the object of its own efforts, and think of the masses of Negroes as existing for the aggrandizement of the few. Our tendency toward this must be strongly repressed. The educated and talented must look upon themselves as the servants to do the work for the great mass of the uneducated and inexperienced.

THE NEGATIVE PROGRAM

So much for our positive program. As for the negative: We cannot for a moment contemplate joining a party of revolutionists. If we should attempt it, we will become the shock troops and the victims of the whole movement. All the race prejudice in the United States, based on color, would be turned on Communism carried on by colored people. Moreover, revolution is not an end; it is a means. And as I have said before, it does not seem to me or to many persons as an inevitable thing. It may come, but it should never come by our hand or by our advocacy. On the other hand, we should stand for the great ideals roughly comprehended under the name of "Socialism," that is, for the idea that the state should be carried on not for the benefit of the few, of the educated, of the rich, or of the well-born, but of the great mass of men out of whom it is possible in the future to evolve as fine human beings as there have been evolved out of aristocracy. Thirdly, we must evolve among American Negroes the technicians and technocrats; the people who know modern methods of development and can do them and we have got to do it by united efforts on our part, by segregated labor institutions which attempt production, manufacture, organization, literature, and all the means of civilization in order to take part in modern industry. But when I have advocated methods of this sort and have pointed out that we have the men who can do this; that we could unite in cooperative enterprise and settlements and church organizations in order to carry this through, many of the younger leaders have objected and have said: The college bred man, the graduated men of knowledge, are not interested in the mass of the people; they want to be an elite; they want to be the spoiled darlings for whom the whole race exists. Their income, their comfort and their wellbeing are the sole object of their existence. My answer to this is: That I know only too well that a large number of the thousands of educated colored men whom we have poured out in the last years are persons of this sort; that the old ideas of the early graduates for service and knighthood have paled and disappeared; that the young colored man, the young business man, and the young professional man have conceived a curious and fearful selfishness which may easily be the damnation of the Negro race; but I nevertheless hope and believe that out from this group we can evolve a larger and larger number who are going to use their ability and their opportunity for the raising of their masses of the black race and for their leadership in a new industrial organization. Unless this can be done, we are lost.

For advance, the masses must have leadership. Their leadership must be trained leadership. If our trained men will not

assume this unselfishly, not for themselves but for the best
interests of the workers of the Negro race, we can do nothing; but on the other hand, if they will do this, then we have
one of the greatest opportunities of the modern world; and it
seems to me that the business of the Church is to see to it
first, that the ideals of these trained young people become
what they should be. You can only do this as you yourselves
become an organization of efficient and unselfish men against
whom the finger of complaint and guilt and dishonesty cannot be pointed. Churches must form not simply organizations
for worship and amusement, but must furnish houses, employment; must be centers for manufacture, for production,
for social organization of all sorts, and thus become units and
centers of a new life and a new people. Crowded on Sunday,
why can it not furnish good cheap food Monday? If it can
make clothes for the sick why not for the well? Why should
the Church fear economic activity which does honest work
and pays decent wages?

There is only one reason: That is our preconception that
while Religion is unselfish to make better men, business and
industry must be selfish and aim to cheat. There is no such
real distinction and that is the lesson of the depression.

From the *National Baptist Voice*, October, 1935

The Negro and Socialism (1958)

The United States, which would like to be regarded as a
democracy devoted to peace, finds itself today making the
greatest preparations for war of any nation on earth and
holding elections where citizens have no opportunity to vote
for the policies which they prefer.

What are the causes of this contradictory situation? First,
we know that our main reason in preparing for war is the fact
that slowly but surely socialism has spread over the world
and become a workable form of government. Today for the
first time in history the majority of mankind live under socialist regimes, either complete socialism as in the Soviet Union
and China, or partial socialism as in India and Scandinavia.

Most Americans profess to believe that this spread of socialism is mainly the result of a conspiracy led by the Soviet Union and abetted by a section of American citizens. For fear of this group, we have curtailed democratic government, limited civil liberties, and planned war on a gigantic scale.

The spread of socialism in the last one hundred years is unquestionably a fact. It stemmed from growing protest against that tremendous expansion of business enterprise which followed the French revolution. This private initiative and economic anarchy resulted in the factory system, which stemmed from the American slave trade, the sugar empire and the cotton kingdom. All this was concurrent with such suffering and degradation among the laboring masses that by the end of the nineteenth century there was hardly a man of thought and feeling, scarcely a scientist nor an artist, who did not believe that socialism must eventually supplant unbridled private capitalism, or civilization would die.

All over the earth since the Civil War in America, socialism has grown and spread and become more and more definite. It has emerged from dream and doctrinaire fantasy such as characterized Fourier and St. Simon into the rounded doctrine of Karl Marx and finally into the socialist states of Lenin and Mao Tse-tung. In all this struggling advance lay the central idea that men must work for a living, but that the results of their work must not mainly be to support privileged persons and concentrate power in the hands of the owners of wealth; that the welfare of the mass of people should be the main object of government.

To ensure this end the conviction grew that government must increasingly be controlled by the governed; that the mass of people, increasing in intelligence, with incomes sufficient to live a good and healthy life, should control all government and that they would be able to do this by the spread of science and scientific technique, access to truth, the use of reason, and freedom of thought and of creative impulse in art and literature.

The difficulty of accomplishing this lay in the current culture patterns—in repressive religious dogmas, and in the long inculcated belief that nothing better than private ownership and control of capital could be planned, with human nature as it is.

Democratic control, therefore, while it increased, tended to be narrowly political rather than economic. It had to do with the selection of officials rather than with work and income. Discovery of new natural forces and of increased use of machines with intricate industrial techniques tended to put land, labor, and the ownership of capital and wealth into control of the few who were fortunate or aggressive or unscrupulous and to emphasize a belief that, while the mass of citizens might share in government by electing officials to administer law, and legislators might make laws in certain areas of government, the people could not control industry or limit income.

As science increased its mastery of nature and as industry began to use world trade to expand markets, an entirely new problem of government arose. Industry realized that, unless industrial organization largely controlled government, it could not control land and labor, monopolize materials, set prices in the world market, and regulate credit and currency. For this purpose new and integrated world industry arose called "Big Business"—a misleading misnomer. Its significance lay not simply in its size. It was not just little shops grown larger. It was an organized super-government of mankind in matters of work and wages, directed with science and skill for the private profit of individuals. It could not be controlled by popular vote unless that vote was intelligent, experienced, and cast by persons essentially equal in income and power. The overwhelming majority of mankind was still ignorant, sick and poverty stricken.

Repeated and varying devices for keeping and increasing democratic control over industry and wealth were regularly rendered useless by the superior training and moral unscrupulousness of the owners of wealth, as against the ignorance and inexperience of the voters. Bribery of the poorer voters; threats and even violence; fear of the future and organized conspiracy of the interested few against the unorganized many; lying and deftly spread propaganda used race hate, religious dogma and differing family and class interests to ruin democracy. In our own day we have seen that the income tax, designed to place the burden of government expense on property owners in ratio to income, actually lays the heaviest weight of taxation on the low income classes, while the rich individuals and corporations escape with the least proportion of taxes.

When the American farmers and workers revolted against the beginnings of the British colonial system and set out to establish a republic of free and equal citizens, it seemed to most thinking people that a new era in the development of western civilization had begun. Here, beyond the privilege of titled Europe, beyond the deep-seated conditioning of the masses to hereditary inequality and subservience to luxury and display, was to arise a nation of equal men. That equality was to be based on economic opportunity which, as Karl Marx later preached, was the only real equality.

But unfortunately while the United States proclaimed, it never adopted complete equality. First, it prolonged the European recognition of property as more significant than manhood. Then it discovered that theft of land from the Indians was not murder but a method of progress. Next, America reduced the African labor, which rising British commerce had forced on her, to slave status and gained thereby such fabulous income from tobacco, sugar and cotton that Europe became the center of triumphant private capitalism, and the United States its handmaid to furnish free land and cheap labor.

This nation had to fight a Civil War to prevent all American labor from becoming half enslaved. Thus from 1620 when the Puritans landed until 1865 when slavery was abolished, there was no complete democracy in the United States. This was not only because a large part of the laboring class was enslaved, but also because white labor was in competition with slaves and thus itself not really free.

In the late nineteenth and twentieth centuries, while socialism advanced in the leading European nations and in North America, in most of the world European monopoly of wealth and technique—strengthened by theories of the natural inferiority of most human beings—led to the assumed right of western Europe to rule the world for the benefit and amusement of white people. This theory of world domination was hidden behind the rise of the western working classes, and helped keep democracy and social progress from eastern Europe, Asia, and Africa; from Central and South America, and the islands of the seven seas.

In western Europe a labor movement and popular education kept forcing increasing numbers of the workers and of the middle classes into a larger share of economic power. But on the other hand, the mass of colored labor, and white labor in backward Latin and Slavic lands, were reduced to subordinate social status so that increased profit from their land and labor helped to maintain the high profits and high wages of industry in western Europe and North America. Also it was easy there to hire white soldiers to keep "niggers," "chinks," and "dagoes," and "hunkies" in their places. This was the essence of colonial imperialism. It was industry organized on a world scale, and holding most of mankind in such economic subjection as would return the largest profit to the owners of wealth.

Meantime, the new effort to achieve socialism, fathered by Karl Marx and his successors, increased. It declared that even before the mass of workers were intelligent and experienced enough themselves to conduct modern industry, industrial guidance might be furnished them by a dictatorship of their own intelligent and devoted leaders. As knowledge and efficiency increased, democracy would spread among the masses and they would become capable of conducting a modern welfare state. This social program the world governed by owners of capital regarded as impossible without the dictatorship falling out of their well-meaning hands and into the hands of demogogues. Every sort of force was employed to stop even the attempt to set up such states. Yet the first World War, caused by rivalry over the ownership of colonies, resulted in the effort to start a complete socialist state in Russia; and after the second World War, arising from the same cause as the first, a similar attempt was made in China.

Despite wide and repeated opposition, which used every despicable and criminal method possible, both of these states have become so successful and strong that their overthrow by outside force or inner revolt does not today seem at all likely. Also and meantime, in all leading countries, socialistic legislation steadily increased. It did not creep. It advanced with powerful strides.

This development has emphasized the fight between beleaguered private capitalism and advancing socialism, the Communists pointing out the unnecessary lag of socialization in western lands and the capitalists accusing communism of undemocratic dictatorship.

In order to fight socialism super Big Business, as contrasted with ordinary small business enterprise, had to become itself socialism in reverse. If public welfare instead of private profit became its object, if public officials supplanted private owners, socialistic government would be in control of industry. However, those Americans who hope that the welfare state will thus be realized under a system of private capital are today having the carpet pulled from beneath their feet by the recession of democracy in the United States. This has come about by the repudiation of socialism by organized labor and the consequent refusal of the labor vote to follow even the goals of the New Deal. This surrender of labor has been led by the new industrial South, with favorable climate, cheap labor, and half that labor disfranchised and most of it unorganized. The mass of Southerners do not vote. In the Congressional District where the black boy Till was murdered, there live 400,000 Negroes and 300,000 whites. Yet only 7,000 voters went to the polls to elect the present Congressman. The disfranchisement of the black half of the labor vote in the South keeps Negroes poor, sick, and ignorant. But it also hurts white labor by making democratic government unworkable so long as the South has from three to ten times the voting power of the North and West.

Because of this systematic and illegal disfranchisement, a majority of American voters can often be outvoted by a minority. Laws like the McCarran and Smith Acts can become illegal statutes, because a minority of voters can prevail

over a majority. Figures to prove this are easy to adduce, but
I only mention now the fact that former Senator Lehman of
New York represented the vote of 5 million citizens who
went to the polls, while Senator Eastland of Mississippi represented less than 150 thousand voters. Yet Eastland was far
more powerful than Lehman.

This loss of democratic control of the government of our
nation can be even more clearly demonstrated. There was no
effective candidate for the Presidency in the last national
election who stood pledged for peace, disarmament, abolition
of the draft, lower taxes, recognition of the right of the Soviet
Union and China to have the government which they choose
and for stopping our effort to force other nations to do as we
want them to do. Not only did we have no chance to decide
our foreign policy, but we were equally helpless in deciding
our course in domestic affairs. Our system of education is
falling to pieces. We need teachers and school houses by the
millions, but we cannot have them if we continue making
weapons at the present rate and setting our youth to learn
death and destruction instead of building, healing, and teaching.

Is this curtailment of democracy the result of knowledge
and discussion? On the contrary, knowledge and discussion
are today so far curtailed that most men do not even attempt
to express their opinions, lest they be accused of treason and
conspiracy.

Why is this?

At the very time when the colonial peoples were trying
desperately to have food and freedom, powerful Americans
became obsessed by the ambition to have North America
replace Britain as the empire upon which the sun never dared
set. They demanded high profits and high wages even if the
rest of the world starved. In order to restore world rule of
organized industry, shaken by war and depression, the United
States prefers preparation for universal and continuous world
war, until a colonial imperialism in some form is restored
under our leadership.

To this program most of the people of the United States
have submitted. How was such submission brought about?

Such a national policy found unexpected support in our long encouraged prejudice against people with black or colored skins and against all groups of foreign-born who were not of Anglo-Saxon descent. This provincial point of view, repudiated by science and religion, still remains in America a living and powerful motive guiding our lives and likes. This support of the colonial system by American race prejudice has resulted in our present program of war. How was this accomplished? How have the majority of American people been convinced that preparation for war, suspension of civil liberties and curtailment of democracy are our best paths to progress?

America is an intelligent nation, despite large illiterate groups and the lack of an integrated background of culture. We still have large numbers of the poor and sick, but our average income is far higher than that of most nations. This nation wants to do right, as evidenced by a plethora of churches and a wide and loud profession of religion. If any country is ready for increase of democracy, it is the United States. Yet we are preparing our sons for war, because we actually have been induced to believe that the Soviet Union is behind a world-wide criminal conspiracy to destroy the United States and that socialism is the result. The statement is so fantastic that most foreign peoples cannot conceive how it can be true that we really accept this fairy tale.

To restore our lost opportunity to make huge profit on private investment in Russia, the Balkans, and particularly in China, Big Business has restricted and guided public access to truth. It has dominated news gathering, monopolized the press and limited publishing. By fear of losing employment, by secret police and high pay to informers, often confessed liars; by control of education and limitation of radio and television and censorship of the drama—by all these methods and others, the public opinion of the nation has been forced into one iron channel of disaster.

In order to let the nation return to normal sanity we must realize that socialism is not a crime nor a conspiracy, but the path of progress toward which the feet of all mankind are set. Some of the greatest intellectual leaders of our era have been advocates of socialism: Charles Kingsley, Leo Tolstoi, Edward Bellamy, William Morris, Henry George, Robert Owen, Bernard Shaw, Sidney and Beatrice Webb, Kier Hardie, H. G. Wells, Harold Laski. The footsteps of the long oppressed and staggering masses are not always straight and sure, but their mistakes can never cause the misery and distress which the factory system caused in Europe, colonial imperialism caused in Asia and Africa, and which slavery, lynching, disfranchisement, and Jim-Crow legislation have caused in the United States.

Our way out of this impasse is straight and clear and as old as the struggle of freedom for the mind of man: Americans must face the facts at all costs. Walking with determination through a morass of deliberate distortion, we must insist on the right to know the truth, to discuss it and to listen to its interpretation by men of intelligence and honesty; we must restore to all citizens their civil rights and the right to vote, no matter whether they are Negroes, Communists, or naturalized foreign-born. We must insist that our foreign policy as well as our domestic problems and especially our problem of industry, be subjects on which we shall have the right to vote.

Meantime, we are prisoners of propaganda. The people of the United States have become completely sold to that method of conducting industry which has been so powerful and triumphant in the world for two centuries that Americans regard it as the only normal way of life. We regard the making of things and their purchase and sale for private profit as the chief end of living. We look on painting and poetry as harmless play. We regard literature as valuable only as handmaiden to industry. We teach Business as a science when it is only an art of legal theft. We regard advertising as a profession even when it teaches the best way to lie. We consider the unselfish sacrifice of one to the progress of all as wasted effort. Wealth is the height of human ambition even when we have no idea of how to spend it, except to make more wealth or to waste it in harmful or useless ostentation. We want high profits and high wages even if most of the world starves.

Putting aside questions of right, and suspecting all our neighbors of being as selfish as we are, we have adopted a creed of wholesale selfishness. We believe that, if all people work for their own selfish advantage, the whole world will be the best of possible worlds. This is the rat race upon which we are set, and we are suspicious and afraid of folk who oppose this program and plead for the old kindliness, the new use of power and machine for the good of the unfortunate and the welfare of the world of very race and color. We can and do give charity abundantly, particularly when we are giving away money or things which we cannot ourselves use. We give to beggars but we hate the beggars who recoil from begging. This is what stands back of our murderous war preparation as well as back of our endless itch to be rich. At any cost, or in any way, this is our reason for living, gambling on radio, on stock exchange or on race track is our way of life.

The power of wealth and private industry extends itself over education, literature and art and we live in fear, with a deliberately low standard of culture, lest democracy displace monopoly of wealth in the control of the state.

One of the devastating effects of our current education on our youth is the training of them by military officials. They are indoctrinated by propaganda against socialism, by ridicule for their attachment to their mothers, and with disrespect for all women. They learn to kill and destroy, and force as a social method of progress is extolled. Small wonder that what we call "juvenile delinquency" increases among us.

One of the contradictions of our day is our argument about the distribution of property and the relative size of incomes, at a time when secrecy as to the truth about these matters is a matter of official compulsion, and most carefully guarded on the ground that a man's income is his private business and the ownership of property concerns the owner primarily. These propositions are false and ridiculous. The distribution of income is a public affair since it is increasingly the result of public function. Property is a matter of state control, permitted to rest in private hands only so long as it is of public benefit that it should so rest. For any reasonable thought or action concerning property, there should come first open information as to its ownership. Without that, no science or ethic of wealth is possible. We can only guess madly and conclude erroneously. Taking the meager guess-work of the United States census, as some approximation of the truth: it is clear that the poor are still with us in this rich land.

There are nearly 40 per cent of our families who receive less than $2,000 a year and over six million of our 46½ million families receive less than $500. In addition to this there is a psychological poverty, in some ways more frighten-ing than actual lack of income: there is the great number of artisans, white collar workers and professional men who could live plainly on their incomes but who skimp and bor-row and gamble, and sometimes steal to "keep up with the Joneses"; who drive a car and spend too little on food and medicine; who buy fur coats and crowd into one room. American culture is made uneasy and insane by the millions among us who expect in some way to get flamboyantly rich and cannot be satisfied with that simple life which all experi-ence teaches is the finest and best.

Especially must American Negroes, awaking from their present fear and lethargy, reassert that leadership in the American world of culture which Phillis Wheatley began in the eighteenth century, Frederick Douglass led in the nine-teenth, and James Weldon Johnson and Carter Woodson ad-vanced in the twentieth. American Negroes must study social-ism, its rise in Europe and Asia, and its peculiar suitability for the emancipation of Africa. They must realize that no system of reform offers the American Negro such real eman-cipation as socialism. The capitalism which so long ruled Europe and North America was founded on Negro slavery in America, and that slavery will never completely disappear so long as private capitalism continues to survive.

The fight to preserve segregation along the color line in the United States only helps to drive the American Negro much faster into the arms of socialism. The movement of the whole nation toward the welfare state, and away from the concept of private profit as the only object of industry, is bound to show itself sooner or later in the whole nation. But if the Negro tenth of the nation is forced ahead by color discrimination, the socialization of the nation will come that much sooner. Consider the situation: there are today about 16 million Americans of admitted Negro descent. They are by reason of this descent subjected to public insult, loss of opportunity to work according to ability or to receive wages level with white workers; most of these people are disfranchised and segregated in education, travel, civil rights and public recreation. Ten million of these Negroes are poor, receiving less than $50 a week per family. Half of them cannot read and write. They live mostly in the rural districts and small towns of the former slave states, whence their efforts to escape are hindered by law, mob violence, and scarcity of places of refuge which welcome or give them work or places to live.

Above this depressed 10 million are 4 million Negroes who are economically insecure and on the edge of poverty. They work as laborers and servants in the towns and cities. They can read and write, but among them are a class of criminals. Next come 1½ million middle class Negroes living in cities. They have education and property and are engaged in semi-skilled work and white collar jobs. Many are trained in the better paid work of personal service, some are teachers and ministers of religion. Out of this group have come the leading intelligentsia. At the economic apex of this middle economic group are a half million Negroes who are well-to-do, receiving at least $10,000 a year. They are professional and business men, civil servants and public entertainers. They have good, sometimes elaborate homes, motor cars and servants. They live mostly in the larger cities.

When discussing American Negroes, one must distinguish among these classes. Southerners raving about the degradation of Negroes are usually talking about their disfranchised and exploited serfs. Negroes talking of their progress are usually referring to their bourgeoisie. But the Negro intelligentsia must ask how it happens that in free, rich America so many Negroes must be poor, sick and ignorant while in Communist Russia, peasants who were emancipated at nearly the same time as Negroes, live without poverty, with universal education and with national attack on disease? Why is it that the Chinese coolie, who recently was as low as the Negro slave, is today a man in his own country, with the bloodsucking whites driven out? Every effort is made in America to suppress this line of thought among Negroes; but as thought in America regains its lost freedom, as democracy begins to replace plutocracy, the social thought of the nation will find increasing support from Negroes.

Even before such freedom comes, the segregated Negro group will increasingly be forced toward socialistic methods to solve their inner problems. They will unite in boycotts as in Montgomery, Alabama; they will turn to consumers' co-operation; a new Negro literature must soon burst out of prison bonds and will find in socialism practically its only voice. Negro schools and colleges, so long as students are excluded from public education, will become centers of thought where the Soviet Union and China cannot escape intelligent discussion.

The modern rise of Africans in the twentieth century to self-expression and organized demand for autonomy and freedom was due in a large part to the Pan-African movement started by American Negroes. Today every part of Africa has a national congress fighting for the ends which the Pan-American movement started in 1919. Further leadership of Africa by black America has been stopped—but too late. Already the Africans have their own leaders, and these leaders like Nkrumah and Aziwiki are quite aware of the Soviet Union and China and are building their new nations on socialist lines.

Moreover as the mass of the colored peoples of the world move toward socialism in Asia and Africa, it is inevitable that they influence American Negroes. I had long hoped that American Negroes would lead this procession because of their chances for education. But "philanthropy," disguised in bribes, and "religion" cloaked in hypocrisy, strangled Negro education and stilled the voices of prophets. The yellow, brown and black thinkers of Asia have forged ahead. But nevertheless the black folk of America will hear their voices and, what is more compelling, will see their outstanding success. On March 6, 1957, when ancient Ghana was reborn in West Africa, American Negroes realized how far toward socialism this group of black folk had gone. Soon, too, socialism in the black Sudan, in East Africa, in the Belgian Congo and South Africa will place the Black world in the train of Soviet Russia, China, and India and tear loose from the allegiance, which American Negroes try now to profess, to the dictatorship of wealth in the United States.

One thing and one alone keeps socialism from growing even more rapidly than it is—that is the fear of war and especially of attack by the Soviet Union and China. Most of our vast national income is spent for preparation for such war and we have but small funds left for education, health and water development and control which we so sorely need. The frantic and continual cultivation of the national fear goes on just as the danger of war decreases. The class structure of our nation grows tremendously at the very time that our propagandists are fiercely denying it. We have a privileged class of men with more income than they can possibly spend and more power than they can hire brains to use. In the guise of idle rich, with trained executives and with a vast and useless military organization throwing away the taxes piled on the workers, this ruling clique outrivals the aristocracy of George III or Louis XIV. We have a middle class of white collar workers, technicians, artisans, professional men and teachers able to live in comfort so long as they restrict their thought and planning, and deceive themselves in thinking they will sometime join the "independently" rich.

Our last presidential election was a farce. We had no chance to vote for the questions in which we were really interested: Peace, Disarmament, the Draft, unfair taxation, race bias, education, social medicine, and flood control. On the contrary we had before us one ticket under two names and the nominees shadowboxed with the false fanfare and advertisement for the same policies, with infinitesimal shades of difference and with spurious earnestness. Small wonder that half of the American voters stayed home.

Thus it is clear today that the salvation of American Negroes lies in socialism. They should support all measures and men who favor the welfare state; they should vote for government ownership of capital and industry; they should favor strict regulation of corporations or their public ownership; they should vote to prevent monopoly from controlling the press and the publishing of opinions. They should favor public ownership and control of water, electric, and atomic power; they should stand for a clean ballot, the encouragement of third parties, independent candidates, and the elimination of graft and gambling on television and even in churches.

The question of the method by which the socialist state can be achieved must be worked out by experiment and reason and not by dogma. Whether or not methods which were right and clear in Russia and China fit our circumstances is for our intelligence to decide. The atom bomb has revolutionized our thought. Peace is not only preferable today, it is increasingly inevitable. Passive resistance is not the end of action, but the beginning. The Negro church which stops discrimination against bus riders must next see how those riders can earn a decent living and not remain helplessly exploited by those who own busses and make Jim-Crow laws. This may well be a difficult program, but it is the only one.

"The Negro and Socialism" from *Toward a Socialist America —A Symposium of Essays by Fifteen Contemporary American Socialists*, edited by Helen Alfred, 1958, pp. 179–191.

Postscript
On the Duty of Negroes (1899)

That the Negro race has an appalling work of social reform before it need hardly be said. Simply because the ancestors of the present white inhabitants of America went out of their way barbarously to mistreat and enslave the ancestors of the present black inhabitants, gives those blacks no right to ask that the civilization and morality of the land be seriously menaced for their benefit. Men have a right to demand that the members of a civilized community be civilized; that the fabric of human culture, so laboriously woven, be not wantonly or ignorantly destroyed. Consequently a nation may rightly demand, even of a people it has consciously and intentionally wronged, not indeed complete civilization in thirty or one hundred years, but at least every effort and sacrifice possible on their part toward making themselves fit members of the community within a reasonable length of time; that thus they may early become a source of strength and help instead of a national burden. Modern society has too many problems of its own, too much proper anxiety as to its own ability to survive under its present organization, for it lightly to shoulder all the burdens of a less advanced people, and it can rightly demand that as far as possible and as rapidly as possible the Negro bend his energy to the solving of his own social problems—contributing to his poor, paying his share of the taxes and supporting the schools and public administration. For the accomplishment of this the Negro has a right to demand freedom for self-development, and no more aid from without than is really helpful for furthering that development. Such aid must of necessity be considerable; it must furnish schools and reformatories, and relief and preventive agencies; but the bulk of the work of raising the Negro must be done by the Negro himself, and the greatest help for him will be not to hinder and curtail and discourage his efforts. Against prejudice, injustice and wrong the Negro ought to protest energetically and continuously, but he must never forget that he protests because those things hinder his own efforts, and those efforts are the key to his future.

And those efforts must be mighty and comprehensive, persistent, well-aimed and tireless; satisfied with no partial success, lulled to sleep by no colorless victories; and, above all, guided by no low selfish ideals; at the same time they must be tempered by common sense and rational expectation. In Philadelphia those efforts should first be directed toward a lessening of Negro crime; no doubt the amount of crime imputed to the race is exaggerated, no doubt features of the Negro's environment over which he has no control, excuse much that is committed; but beyond all this the amount of crime that can without doubt rightly be laid at the door of the Philadelphia Negro is large and is a menace to a civilized people. Efforts to stop this crime must commence in the Negro homes; they must cease to be, as they often are, breeders of idleness and extravagance and complaint. Work, continuous and intensive; work, although it be menial and poorly rewarded; work, though done in the travail of soul and sweat of brow, must be impressed upon Negro children as the road to salvation, that a child must feel it a greater disgrace to be idle than to do the humblest labor. The homely virtues of honesty, truth and chastity must be instilled in the cradle, and although it is hard to teach self-respect to a people whose million fellow citizens half-despise them, yet it must be taught as the surest road to gain the respect of others.

It is right and proper that Negro boys and girls should desire to rise as high in the world as their ability and just desert entitle them. They should be ever encouraged and urged to do so, although they should be taught also that idleness and crime are beneath and not above the lowest work. It should be the continual object of Negroes to open up better industrial chances for their sons and daughters. Their success here must of course rest largely with the white people, but not entirely. Proper cooperation among forty or fifty thousand colored people ought to open many chances of employment for their sons and daughters in trades, stores and shops, associations and industrial enterprises.

Further, some rational means of amusement should be furnished young folk. Prayer meetings and church socials have their place, but they cannot compete in attractiveness with the dance halls and gambling dens of the city. There is a legitimate demand for amusement on the part of the young which may be made a means of education, improvement and recreation. A harmless and beautiful amusement like dancing might with proper effort be rescued from its low and unhealthful associations and made a means of health and recreation. The billard table is no more wedded to the saloon than to the church if good people did not drive it there. If the Negro homes and churches cannot amuse their young people, and if no other efforts are made to satisfy this want, then we cannot complain if the saloons and clubs and bawdy-houses send these children to crime, disease and death.

There is a vast amount of preventive and rescue work which the Negroes themselves might do: keeping young girls off the street at night, stopping the escorting of unchaperoned young ladies to church and elsewhere, showing the dangers of the lodging system, urging the buying of homes and removal from crowded and tainted neighborhoods, giving lectures and tracts on health and habits, exposing the dangers of gambling and policy-playing, and inculcating respect for women. Day-nurseries and sewing-schools, mothers' meetings, the parks and airing places, all these things are little known or appreciated among the masses of Negroes, and their attention should be directed to them.

The spending of money is a matter to which Negroes need to give especial attention. Money is wasted to-day in dress, furniture, elaborate entertainments, costly church edifices, and "insurance" schemes, which ought to go toward buying homes, educating children, giving simple healthful amusement to the young, and accumulating something in the savings bank against a "rainy day." A crusade for the savings bank as against the "insurance" society ought to be started in the Seventh Ward without delay.

Although directly after the war there was great and remarkable enthusiasm for education, there is no doubt but that this enthusiasm has fallen off, and there is to-day much neglect of children among the Negroes, and failure to send them regularly to school. This should be looked into by the Negroes themselves and every effort made to induce full regular attendance.

Above all, the better class of Negroes should recognize their duty toward the masses. They should not forget that the spirit of the twentieth century is to be the turning of the high toward the lowly, the bending of Humanity to all that is human; the recognition that in the slums of modern society lie the answers to most of our puzzling problems of organization and life, and that only as we solve those problems is our culture assured and our progress certain. This the Negro is far from recognizing for himself; his social evolution in cities like Philadelphia is approaching the mediaeval stage when the centrifugal forces of repulsion between social classes are becoming more powerful than those of attraction. So hard has been the rise of the better class of Negroes that they fear to fall if now they stoop to lend a hand to their fellows. This feeling is intensified by the blindness of those outsiders who persist even now in confounding the good and bad, the risen and the fallen in one mass. Nevertheless the Negro must learn the lesson that other nations learned so laboriously and imperfectly, that his better classes have their chief excuse for being in the work they may do toward uplifting the rabble. This is especially true in a city like Philadelphia which has so distinct and creditable a Negro aristocracy; that they do something already to grapple with these social problems of their race is true, but they do not yet do nearly as much as they must do, nor do they clearly recognize their responsibility.

Finally, the Negroes must cultivate a spirit of calm, patient persistence in their attitude toward their fellow citizens rather than of loud intemperate complaint. A man may be wrong, and know he is wrong, and yet some finesse must be used in telling him of it. The white people of Philadelphia are perfectly conscious that their Negro citizens are not treated fairly in all respects, but it will not improve matters to call names or impute unworthy motives to all men. Social reforms move slowly and yet when Right is reinforced by calm but persistent Progress we somehow all feel that in the end it must triumph.

From *The Philadelphia Negro: A Social Study*, 1899, pp. 389–93

PART TWO

Africa

I. African Culture—Colonialism—Rise to Freedom—Independence and Unity of the Continent

Prescript
Africa's Mighty Past (1940)

GREAT AS HAS been the human advance in the last one thousand years, it is, so far as native human ability, so far as intellectual gift and moral courage are concerned, nothing as compared with any one of ten and more millenniums before, far back in the forests of tropical Africa and in hot India, where black and brown humanity first fought climate and disease and bugs and beasts; where man dared simply to live and propagate himself. There was the hardest and greatest struggle in all the human world. If in sheer exhaustion or in desperate self-defense during this last moment of civilization he has rested, half inert and blinded with the sweat of his effort, it is only the silly onlooker who sees but the passing moment of time, who can think of him as sub-human and inferior.

From *Dusk of Dawn*, 1940, pp. 150–51

The Rape of Africa—Trade in Men (1939)

Such is the story of the Rape of Ethiopia—a sordid, pitiful, cruel tale. Raphael painted, Luther preached, Corneille wrote, and Milton sang, and thru it all for four hundred years, the dark captives wound to the sea amid the bleaching bones of the dead; for four hundred years the sharks followed the scurrying ships; for four hundred years America was strewn with the living and dying millions of a transplanted race; for four hundred years Ethiopia stretched forth her hand to God. . . . These were not days of decadence, but a period that gave the world Shakespeare, Martin Luther, Raphael, Haroun-al-Raschid and Abraham Lincoln. It was the day of the greatest expansion of two of the world's most pretentious religions, and beginnings of modern organization of industry. In the midst of this advance and uplift, this slave trade and slavery spread more human misery, inculcated more disrespect for and neglect of humanity, a greater callousness to suffering, and more petty, cruel, human hatred than can be calculated. We may excuse and palliate it, and write history so as to let men forget it; it remains a most inexcusable blot on modern history.

From *Black Folk—Then and Now*, 1939, pp. 135–44

What Is Civilization?—Africa's Answer (1925)

Three things Africa has given the world, and they form the essence of African culture: Beginnings, the village unit, and Art in sculpture and music.

Long before the last two thousand years, which we call the years of modern civilization, lay the beginnings of human culture. For ten thousand years—perhaps fifty thousand years and more—mankind struggled with the first steps of advance; struggled and wavered, forged forward, retreated, fell, and rose again. This was a period fateful for all mankind —for all culture. It was far more tremendous in its ultimate significance than anything that has happened since.

It was during these years that the black race, in its own land, Africa, and in all the paths by which it wended its way thither, seems always to have been first. Wherever one sees the first faint steps of human culture, the first successful fight against wild beasts, the striving against weather and disease, there one sees black men. To be sure, they were not the only beginners, but they seem to have been the successful and persistent ones. Thus Africa appears as the Father of mankind, and the people who eventually settled there, wherever they have wandered before or since—along the Ganges, the Euphrates, and the Nile, in Cyprus and about the Mediterranean shores—form the largest and often the only group of human beings successfully advancing from animal savagery toward primitive civilization. The ancient world looked upon them continually as creators of human culture and rang with their tributes. Hammurabi, the law giver of Babylonia, is called "to go forth like the sun over the Black race." The Greeks sent Zeus and Poseidon to feast annually with the "Blameless Blacks," and the Roman historians tell us that the Blacks "conceive themselves to be of greater antiquity than any other nation. They suppose themselves also to be the inventors of divine worship, of festivals, of solemn assemblies, of sacrifices, and every religious practice. They affirm that the Egyptians are one of their colonies."

Out of many things that these beginnings emphasize we may select one: the discovery of the use of iron. Probably the properties of iron have been discovered in the world many times and in many places, but it seems likely that while Europe was still in its stone age and while neither Egypt nor Western Asia nor ancient China knew iron, the black Africans had invented the art of smelting. It was a moment big with promise for the uplift of the human race. No effective industry, no sure defense was possible for mankind with laboriously chipped stone tools. Copper and bronze made great advance over stone, but only hard iron founded modern industry; and this marvelous discovery was made by African Negroes.

The second thing that came out of the early strife of black folk was the village unit. I shall never forget my first glimpse of an African village. The night before, we had ridden the bar in the moonlight with the curious singing of lithe black boys. Above on the great headland twinkled Monrovia; below lay the black and silent forests beside a sombre sea. But this morning down by the sea and down by the forests suddenly we walked out into a little town. It was a town of the Vais. It was a thing of clay, colored cream and purple; clean, quiet, small, with perhaps a dozen or more homes. Authority was here and religion, industry and trade, education and art. It was not a complete thing from a modern point of view. It had little or no machinery; it lay almost defenseless against surrounding malaria. Of news service with the greater world, there was none. Though its whole inner being had been changed and in some respects upset by the new surrounding and invading economy, this little village was a mighty thing; it had come down from a mighty past. Its beginning stretched back in time thousands and thousands of years; it gathered to itself traditions and customs springing almost from the birth of the world. In space alone it stretched back along a path leading from the low thunder of the sea on the black West Coast to the great central plateau of Africa with forest, lake, and sand, two hundred miles away. Perhaps the great successive movements of this vast continent, so veiled to-day in mystery, had brought it even further seaward from the regions of the Mountains of the Moon, past Ethiopia and Nubia, Melle and Songhay, Haussaland and Benin, those shadowy empires of the past. Perhaps even this little village here once knew Atlantis itself, and Greece and Phoenicia.

No matter whence the African village came and how it is to-day distorted and changed, and has been in the past glorified and degraded, it is a singularly persistent and eternal thing. Again and again this village with its conical huts, its central fire, its grassy streets, its fields of grain and fruit, and its cattle has been reborn in Africa and has spread itself over the endless miles of the continent. Even the African city as it rose time and time again was a city of villages. Ancient Jenne, whence comes our modern word Guinea, "had seven thousand villages so near to one another that the chief of Jenne had no need of messengers," but cried his messages from gate to gate and village to village until within a few moments they had gone a hundred miles to Lake Dibo.

We know the village unit the world over and among all people, but among most folk the village early lost itself in some larger unit, and civilization became a matter of city and state and nation. But the African village, because of geography and climate, because perhaps of some curious inner tenacity and strength of tradition, persisted and did on a small scale what the world has continually attempted on a wider scale and never satisfactorily accomplished. The African village socialized the individual completely, and yet because the village was small this socialization did not submerge and kill individuality. When the city socializes the modern man he becomes mechanical, and cities tend to be all alike. When the nation attempts to socialize the modern man the result is ofen a soulless Leviathan. The African village attempted a small part of the task of the modern city and state, and accomplished that part more successfully. It lost thereby breadth and power, it failed to integrate into a larger permanent imperialism. It never succumbed wholly to a militarism of its own but for that very reason it tasted slavery of every sort to others. But it was and is and perhaps will long be in its limited way a perfect human thing.

In the African village were bred religion, industry, government, education, and art, and these were bred as integral interrelated things. The primitive religion of Africa as developed by the African village underlies the religions of the world. Egyptian religion was in its beginning and later development of purely Negro character, and mulatto Egyptian priests on the stones of Egypt continually receive their symbols of authority from the black priests of Ethiopia. The Negro religion thus developed had something about it that was grim and terrible, and for that very reason it powerfully expressed the feelings of the first fighters in the world. The fire and desert, water and jungle of Africa, the beast and bird and serpent, the devil of disease with his flies and insects and worms and the infinitesimal germs that creep in the skin and veins and marrow of men—all these are personified by the African Fetish. Fetish is a primitive philosophy of life. It is a spiritual explanation of physical evil and it explains by making all things spirit, both the good and the bad, and by seeking spiritual cure for physical ill.

The religion of the black man spread among all the Mediterranean races. Shango, god of the West Coast, hurler of thunderbolts and lord of the storms, render of trees and slayer of men, cruel and savage and yet beneficent, was prototype of Zeus and Jupiter and Thor.

The African villagers from early days wove cloth, baked earthenware, manufactured instruments and arms, baskets and shoes, soap and glass. They worked in iron, copper, brass, bronze, gold, silver, bone, and ivory. They built in fibre, wood, and stone. They developed an original division of industry, a division first by families and clans, so that even the militarized Zulus are to this day divided according to Industrial designation like "the men of iron" and "sons of corn cleaners." Beyond that, division of industry appeared among the villages so that they were grouped according to their reciprocal activities and became complements one to another. One village specialized in fishing, another in wine, another in metals, and still another in trade—importing from without. Sometimes the division was even more delicate: One Congo village carves elephant tusks, another makes a particular style of hat, and others swords, copper rings, wood carvings, and burnt clay pitchers.

Out of this industry developed the African market-place which knit the continent together with paths and trade centres, from the Gulf of Guinea to Zanzibar and from Walfish Bay to Lake Chad, long before the modern coming of Europe. The trade of African villages early reached the world —Egypt, Persia, and India, Cyprus, Greece, and Rome, Byzantium, Spain and Italy.

What the village system lacked in breadth and vision it gained in depth and personal knowledge. There was no monopoly, no poverty, no prostitution, and the only privilege was the definite, regulated, and usually limited privilege of the chief and head men, given in return for public service and revocable for failure. This primal village life has to-day largely disintegrated before the white invader, before machine goods and imperial compulsion, but it played its part in the world and was a rare contribution to civilization.

For stubbornly clinging to this fine and narrow village type of government and association, Africa has paid with dispersion and slavery. Dispersion came because the Village could not corral and hold its strongly developed individualities as could the state and empire. So that from days before the dawn of history down to our era a stream of black men have passed out of black Africa and into the world and profoundly influenced Civilization by their genius. There was Nefertari, the black queen of Egypt who drove out the Hyksos and was as Flinders Petrie says, "the most venerated figure of Egyptian history"; there was the black Mutemua, mother of the great Amen-hote III who built the temple at Luxor and whose direct descendant was the royal princess who by marriage made Tut-ankh-amen, Pharoah of Egypt. As the late Professor Chamberlain wrote: "Besides these marked individual instances, there is the fact that the Egyptian race itself in general had a considerable element of Negro blood, and one of the prime reasons why no civilization of the type of that of the Nile arose in other parts of the continent, if such a thing were possible, was that Egypt acted as a sort of channel by which the genius of Negroland was drafted off into the service of the Mediterranean and Asiatic culture."

The second and more terrible way in which Africa paid for her individualistic village culture was by the slave trade; Christian Europe traded in human beings for four hundred years. The slave trade alone cost Africa in dead and stolen nearly one hundred million souls. And yet people to-day ask the cause of the stagnation of culture in that land since 1600!

Nevertheless for all this there was compensation, and this compensation was African art. The sense of beauty is the last and best gift of Africa to the world and the true essence of the black man's soul. African art is the offspring of the climate and the Negro soul. The sunshine of central Africa cloaks you like a golden blanket; it hangs heavy about your shoulders; it envelops you; it smothers you in a soft but mighty embrace. The rain of Africa is a consuming flood, a river pouring out of heaven, without banks or current. In Africa the swift, the energetic are the dead. In Africa the "lazy" survive and live. This African laziness is several things;

it is shelter from the penetrating rain; it is defense from malaria. And it brings with it leisure and dreams and human intercourse.

Deep in the forest fastness and by the banks of low, vast rivers; in the deep tense quiet of the endless jungle, the human soul whispered its folk tales, carved its pictures, sang its rhythmic songs, and danced and danced. The languages of Africa grew and developed for their unique work, "so simple and clear in their phonology, so logical in their syntax." From these has descended one of the richest masses of oral tradition of poetry and folk lore which the world knows. To this was early added the art of sculpture.

We have long known of the African artist. Traces of his work have been found in prehistoric Europe, in parts of Asia, and of course in Egypt. Later rich centres of African art were brought to European knowledge on the African western coast. It was long customary to think of this art first as imitation, secondly as inexpressibly crude and funny; but to-day more recent interpretations show that the primitive art of Africa is one of the greatest expressions of the human soul in all time, "that black men invented fire," that they spread their ideas of art among their white neighbors, and that their earliest expressions had an originality and fidelity of purpose that the primitive world never surpassed.

Finally, out of Africa and out of the soul of black folk came music and rhythm. The African not only sang beautiful melodies but he invented part singing, and his instinct for rhythm developed syncopation. He early made musical instruments, and especially did he make the drum a living and speaking thing. His songs, "rich as is their weave of rhythm and polyphony are not the only music of the African, but through other instruments of his own invention the black man achieves the independence of human voice that presupposes a conception of music as an art, demanding an understanding of tone qualities and again a sense for the structural building of rhythmic and melodic balances of sound."

What is African music? Have you heard the tom-tom in O'Neill's "Emperor Jones"? Below this ecstacy of Fear runs that rhythmic obligato—low, sombre, fateful, tremendous;

full of deep expression and infinite meaning; have you dancing in your soul and have you heard a Negro orchestra playing Jazz? Your head may revolt, your ancient conventions scream in protest, but your heart and body leap to rhythm. It is a new and mighty art which Africa gave America and America is giving the world. It has circled the world, it has set hundreds of millions of feet a-dancing—it is a "new" and "American" art which has already influenced all music and is destined to do more. Or again, have you heard the Sorrow Song?

Once upon a time—I was a youth of eighteen—I taught school in the hills of Tennessee. I was new to section and people, and of a soft and dark lovely night, I went out under the stars. And there rolling down across the valley came music. It was the Voice of Angels upon the Hills of God. It was the sorrow of riven souls suddenly articulate; it was the tears of slaves, the sobs of raped daughters, the quiver of murdered bodies, the defiance of deathless hope. I shivered and ran. I hurried along the stony creek, and up hard hills, and through the gray twinkling village. And ever as I ran the music, the terrible, beautiful music swept nearer. It became more human, louder, pulsating with life and vigor and yet more poignantly sweet.

There was a building set upon a hill—a dim dilapidated thing, half furnished with bench and board and a far-flung door and window. There within swayed and danced a people mad with song. It was the demoniac possession of infinite music. Wild arms waved in the air, wild feet beat out the time, wild faces, dark, sweat-creased, stared up to God and wild and wilder words cut the night:—

Stand the Storm, It Won't Be Long, We'll Anchor By and By!
Oh, the Stars of the Elements Are Falling and the Moon Drips
Away Into Blood—!
Roll, Jordan, Roll!

Oh, it was bizarre—the people were black and dirty and funny but I stood and wept, and when, in a flash of silence, a woman leaped into the air and shrieked as the dying shriek I sat down cold with terror and hot with new ecstasy.

Again and yesterday I sat in old St. George's, New York, and heard a whole service intoned to the music set by a Negro composer, built on Negro music and sung by a white choir. The audience within was spellbound, and without, a thousand friends of Harry Burleigh clamored for admittance in vain.

And finally, last Christmas, I looked out of my window. The moonlight drifted down on palm and mango. Strange blossoms spread their scent on the soft hot breeze. I could hear the dull roar of the Atlantic beyond Cape Mesurado. I could hear music, songs that rose and rolled nearer. Words half English, half Vai, tunes that were once gospel hymns, but Africa had taken them, Africa had given them rhythm and syncopation; high soared the soprano obligato, low rolled the strong big voices of men. It was the strangest combination, re-weaving, new-birthing of an old thing, I had ever heard. Such is the gift of music which Africa is still giving the world.

The essence of African culture then lies in its initial strife which began all culture; in its development of the village unit in religion, industry, and government; and finally in its art— its realization of beauty in folk lore, sculpture, and music. All this Africa has given the modern world together with its suffering and its woe.

The Forum, Vol. 73, No. 2, February, 1925, pp. 179–88

Africa and the French Revolution (1961)

If you should penetrate the campus of an American Ivy League college and challenging a Senior, ask what, in his opinion, was the influence of Africa on the French Revolution, he would answer in surprise if not pity, "None." If, after due apology, you should venture to approach his teacher of "historiography," provided such sacrilege were possible, you would be told that between African slavery in America and the greatest revolution of Europe, there was of course some connection, since they both took place on the same earth; but nothing causal, nothing of real importance, since Africans have no history.

Nevertheless, it is a perfectly defensible thesis of scientific history that Africans and African slavery in the West Indies were the main causes and influences of the American Revolution and of the French Revolution. And when, after long controversy and civil war, Negro slavery and serfdom were not suppressed, the United States turned from democracy to plutocracy and opened the path to colonial imperialism and made wide the way for the final world Revolutions in the twentieth century.

Let us now look at the story. Columbus had a Negro pilot, and in the sixteenth century his son Diago was governor of the island of San Domingo and his slaves staged a revolt in 1522. A few years later Vasquez d'Allyon tried to settle in Virginia but his slaves revolted. From the sixteenth century on, the revolt of the black workers stolen in Africa and transported to America continued. This was proven by the fright of the planters shown by the increased severity of the laws; at the same time, their desire to pretend that the slave system for blacks was perfect and was not resented.

Early in the sixteenth century the Maroons appeared all over the West Indies. This was the name given to runaway slaves who took refuge in the mountains of Cuba, Haiti, Jamaica and Central America. They formed their own governments and even built cities. They fought with the Spanish, the British and the French; they made treaties which the Whites broke.

Meantime, by the middle of the seventeenth century Cromwell had seized Jamaica and the French had started sugar planting on their islands. White indentured servants were imported into the West Indies and the African slave trade increased. Between 1700 and 1776, 600,000 blacks were imported to the West Indies, Central and South America. French commerce quadrupled between 1714 and 1789. Dutch slaves revolted and gained their independence, and in Haiti a succession of black rulers in this land of mountains carried on continuous governmental organization which lasted through the eighteenth century and still exists.

San Domingo was an island of mountains rising in places 6,000 feet above sea level. The San Domingo planters and the British and French bourgeoisie were the new owners of some of the richest property in the world. Of these three the most important in 1790 were the planters of San Domingo. The island was beautiful. The climate was favorable, and crops grew the year round. The planters lived luxuriously, and spent their vacations or old age in Paris. In France they formed a powerful political force as their counterparts did in England. French women from the gutter as well as the middle class came to the colony. French aristocracy came to rebuild their shattered fortunes. They took Negro concubines. Colonial cities were centers of dirt, gambling and debauchery. In 1789, of 7,000 mulatto women in San Domingo, 5,000 were either prostitutes or mistresses. Failures from all countries flocked to San Domingo. No white person was a servant or did any work that he could get a Negro to do for him. The owners lived in barbaric luxury and the island produced more sugar, coffee, chocolate, indigo, timber and spices than all the rest of the West Indies put together. As early as 1685 Louis XIV had issued a Code Noir which made wives and children of Frenchmen free. By the beginning of the eighteenth century mulattoes began to accumulate property and educate their children in France. Their children began to return by 1763 and tried as freemen to take part in public affairs.

Meantime, the British were profiting by the slave trade and building up their mercantile system of colonial trade.

The French regarded the colonies as existing for the profit of France. Colonies must buy all manufactured goods from France and could sell their produce only to France. The goods must be transported in French ships. Sugar must be refined in France. In 1664 France gave the rights of trade with San Domingo to a private company. The colonists refused and the governor had to ease restrictions. This happened again in 1722. There was another insurrection, the governor was imprisoned and the privileges of the company modified. The colonies thought of separating from France. Long before 1789 the French bourgeoisie was the most powerful force in France and the slave trade in the colonies, the basis of its power. The fortunes created at Bordeaux and at Nantes by the slave trade gave the bourgeoisie the pride that demanded "liberty." In 1666, 108 ships went from Nantes to Africa with 37,430 slaves valued at 37 million dollars and giving the owners from 15 to 20 per cent on their money. In 1700 Nantes was sending 50 ships a year to the West Indies with food, clothing and machinery. Nearly all the industries developed in France were based on the slave trade with America. Bordeaux grew rich by 1750 with 16 factories refining sugar. San Domingo was the special center of the Marseilles trade. A dozen other great towns refined sugar. Hides and cotton came from the West Indies. Two to six million Frenchmen depended for their livelihood upon colonial slave trade. In 1789 San Domingo received in its ports more ships than Marseilles. France used for the San Domingo trade 750 vessels employing 24,000 soldiers. In 1774 the colonies owed France 200 million and by 1789 between 3 and 5 million. The British envied San Domingo with alarm after the independence of America. San Domingo doubled its production between 1783 and 1789.

The British slave trade became an increasing source of profit and their monopoly of colonial trade a matter of increasing importance. When, therefore, the American colonists tried to extricate themselves from British power they struck first at the slave trade. Already the Negro workers were beginning to take part in the struggle. Crispus Attucks led a mob in Boston and Daniel Webster said that the severance of America from the British empire dated from his death. The day of his death was a national American holiday for nearly a quarter of a century.

In 1776 Jefferson emphasized the slave trade as America's grievance against Great Britain. The American Revolution stopped the trade. In 1774, the Second Article of the Continental Association said: "that we will neither import nor purchase slaves imported after the first day of December next, after which we will wholly discontinue the slave trade." This all agreed would stop slavery. As the war progressed Negroes took part. General Nathaniel Green writes: "The natural state of the country appears to me to consist more in the blacks than in the whites." American Negroes fought for freedom, perhaps a larger proportion of them than among whites. In the early battles of the revolutionary war Negro soldiers fought side by side with the whites. It was feared that their presence might encourage slaves in the South to accept the offer of freedom given by the British governor, Dunmore, of Virginia, and for a while Washington was induced to refuse colored enlistments. But this he soon gave up. Negroes fought throughout the revolutionary war, mostly on the side of the Americans, but some on the side of the British. And Negro slavery was certainly one of the strongest arguments for the American Revolution. After America gained its freedom in 1783 it was felt in France and America that slavery in America was at an end.

The French Revolution has been written so largely from the white point of view that the part which the blacks played in this drama has been either forgotten or unknown.

A revolution is a transfer of power from the top aristocracy of a nation to lower and lower classes. Very often all the work and demand of an aristocracy is interpreted as transfer of power to the masses of people. This is usually untrue. Magna Carta was not a democratic movement. It was a successful attempt of the higher British aristocracy to wrest power from the King. The writ of habeas corpus did not mean that the working masses escaped unjust imprisonment; it was for the benefit of the rich middle class. And so in France the fall of the Bastille was a victory for unjustly treated aristocrats.

The freedom which France demanded in 1787 was freedom to build their current prosperity on the products of slave labor supported by a slave trade from Africa. Profits from this source were at their highest and French migrants were rushing to San Domingo to get rich. About this time the colored bastards whom the Code Noir had declared to be free and Negroes who had either earned or bought their freedom began to demand French citizenship, and French theorists and dreamers backed them as Friends.

In 1788, France exported to French San Domingo 21 million dollars in flour, wine, and manufactures, with 580 vessels in this trade and 98 in the African trade, and 29,500 slaves were brought to San Domingo from Africa.

In 1789, the West Indian colony of San Domingo supplied two-thirds of the overseas trade to France and was the greatest individual market for the European slave trade. It was an integral part of the economic life of the age, the pride of France, and the envy of every imperialist nation. The whole structure rested on the labor of the half million black slaves.

San Domingo was now incomparably the finest colony in the world and its possibilities were limitless. But without slaves San Domingo was doomed. The British colonies had enough slaves from all their trade and the British bourgeoisie who had no other West Indian interests set up a howl for the abolition of the slave trade. The rising British industrial bourgeoisie turned toward free trade and the exploitation of India and called the West Indies, "sterile rocks."

Adam Smith and Arthur Young condemned slave labor. India, after the loss of America, became a source of sugar. The production of cotton in India doubled in a few years. Indian free labor cost only a penny a day. There were hoards of gold, silver and jewels.

In 1786 Wilberforce began the anti-slave trade campaign. Pitts egged him on. Liberals in France, including the great names of the revolution, formed a society, The Friends of the Negro, aimed at the abolition of slavery.

In the Estates General which met in 1789 the French aristocracy gave up many of their rights and formed the Constituent Assembly under the domination of the upper middle class. They for three years made this bourgeoisie equal in power to the former aristocrats. Thus equality which came in France was equality for the property owners and not for the working, starving masses. For a year the mass of workers began to put forward their demands in the Legislative Assembly and then finally for three years came real revolution. The monarchy was abolished. A Committee of Public Safety was established and pure democracy which allowed the masses to vote was proposed but not ratified. The King was killed and the parties fought for power. A reign of terror ensued which by 1794 was killing 354 people a month until suddenly came Thermidor. Robespierre himself was killed. The power of the Paris Commune with its extreme democracy was stopped. Babeuf, the serf, was executed. But the people were starving and there must be a change. In which direction would the change go, to a further devolution of power to the workers—Certainly not, said the respectable people. They turned to Bonaparte who had just married the granddaughter of a Negro and finished an Italian campaign. They brought him back from his wild Egyptian venture and the coup d'état of the 18th Brumaire which ended in the empire. This is the story we are told and Africa touches it nowhere, save that we say that the terror in France was copied in Haiti and that Napoleon gave Louisiana to America.

This is not the complete story. Let us go over the details again: when the revolution broke out in France in 1787 San Domingo was the source of the greatest accumulation of wealth. San Domingo had more than three-quarter million slaves, the cities of France were flourishing with the slave trade. The French who were gaining equality with the former aristocrats were basing this equality on the profits of the slave trade and on crops grown by black slaves. From the very beginning two parties appeared in France: the moral philosophers and the social theorists, demanding freedom of the slaves. On the other hand, the planters demanded recognition as citizens and the exclusion of the poor whites and mulattoes.

The planters supported the monarchy against the revolution. The poor whites supported the revolution against the King but opposed the mulattoes. The mulattoes sought alliance with either or both groups of whites. In 1789 the mulattoes sent Raymond and Oge to Paris with 6 million pounds in gold and a promise of this and one-fifth of the property which the mulattoes owned in San Domingo to pay the French public debt. The delegates were received by the Constituent Assembly, and the Assembly thus recognized the citizenship of free Negroes. The planters were opposed as were also the manufacturers and merchants of the great French cities. The Constituent Assembly voted by large majority not to interfere with the internal government of the colonies and refused to abolish the slave trade. But on March 18, 1790, the Amis des Noirs secured a vote declaring free Negroes citizens. Planters in Martinique, Guadaloupe and San Domingo all decreed that the law recognizing the right to vote applied only to white persons. The planters and poor whites fought each other, but both were against the Negroes.

The planters of San Domingo by secret manipulation placed six of their number in the Constituent Assembly. When representatives of the free Negroes and mulattoes appeared in Paris to demand hearing they were received and backed by the organization called the Friends of Negroes. The Declaration of the Rights of Man was adopted.

Oge returned to America with British money, landing secretly in north San Domingo. He collected 300 men. He was attacked and took refuge in the Spanish part of the island; the governor surrendered him. Oge and Chavannes were sentenced while alive to have their arms, legs and spines broken and then be exposed to the sun. This was done in the presence of the northern provincial assembly gathered in state.

War started between the planters and the free Negroes. The planters, reinforced by poor whites from France pouring in to make money from slavery, numbered 40,000. The free Negroes and mulattoes were about 26,000. And, despite the supporting votes of the National Convention, the war was going against them.

Then the unexpected happened. The bolder slaves had formed bands of Maroons in the mountains and before 1700 became dangerous. Over 1,000 Maroons are reported in 1720, 3,000 in 1751. By 1750 their greatest chief was Macandel. He planned a rebellion but was captured and burned alive. The planters were determined that nothing would interfere with their methods and the slave system. A half-million black Africans long self-trained in the mountains of Haiti on August 22, 1791, in a midnight thunderstorm, attacked. Thiers tells us: "In an instant twelve hundred coffee and two hundred sugar plantations were in flames; the buildings, the machinery, the farmhouses, were reduced to ashes; and unfortunate proprietors were hunted down, murdered or thrown into the flames, by the infuriated Negroes. The horrors of a servile war universally appeared. The unchained African signalized his ingenuity by discovery of new methods and unheard-of modes of torture."

They killed, raped and murdered. They destroyed property. The smoke of the fires blotted out the sun for days. The richest colony of France lay in ruins. The world shuddered. The slave-holders were frightened to death. But only gradually on slow sailing ships, loaded with lies, did the truth about what was happening reach France. Only after months did it realize that the foundations of its wealth and prosperity had disappeared. It was this and not any demands from the masses of French workers or of European philanthropists that turned the reaction of Thermidor into a reality and in time brought the counter-revolution of the 18th Brumaire.

The Terror did not spread from France to Haiti in 1793. Already in 1791 it came to France from Haiti. It was Africa in America and Africans led by Toussaint L'Ouverture who struck the French Revolution after it had given freedom to property-holders, and faced it with chaos. They plunged into anarchy, tempered by murder, until the reaction of Thermidor restored property to power.

The revolt was all the more startling because while it had been in the fears and imagination of the colonists for two hundred years, it was always undreamed of as an actual occurrence. There had been numberless revolts, which had spread terror to whites all over the West Indies, Central America and the mainland of the United States; but once they were quickly suppressed, their details and facts minimized, the records destroyed and the memory forgotten.

In San Domingo itself the dangers of slave revolts were not unknown. For years runaway slaves had hidden in the mountains, especially in the northeastern part of the island. There were serious slave revolts in 1679, 1691 and 1718, and in the middle of the eighteenth century a Negro, Macandel, carried out systematic poisoning which created a panic.

In Europe the organization of the lowest classes of workers and servants, peasants and laborers to gain political power and property was rare and cannot be compared to the corresponding organizations of African slaves in the West Indies and South America. Many European revolts which are pictured as risings of the masses are nothing of the sort. The Protest revolution had no sympathy with the peasants and Martin Luther kicked them in the teeth when they revolted. There were revolts of the suffering masses in Hungary, France and England but they were small compared with the concerted, long-continued rebellion of the black Maroons. While the blacks of San Domingo were in wild rebellion France faced two paths: one was that of Babeuf who came up from the bottom of modern class organization, the servant class; he saw the masses starving, he felt their misery and he sang the dirge of the dying. He struggled for a commune of the workers; equality not of property owners but of those who gave property its value. He prayed and struggled for his Paris commune, but the mounting power of the property owners pushed and beat him back until he died. He died on the scaffold in 1796 but he rose from the dead in 1848 and again in 1871; in 1917 in Russia; in 1939 in China and in 1961 in Cuba.

France repudiating Babeuf, in its unconscious frenzy, took refuge in the reaction of Thermidor, after abolishing monarchy, killing the King and murdering their leaders. Thermidor was the rule of the property-holders displacing the aristocrats. But in San Domingo horror faced Toussaint and his rebels. Toussaint revered the King, his Chieftain; he believed in discipline and authority. He deserted impious France and led his legions to the service of Charles IV of Spain. Slowly he and his successors in after years developed his ancient tribal communalism in San Domingo. Beyond these political provisions, he turned attention toward the economic; the island was divided into districts with inspectors who were to see that the freedmen returned to their work. A fifth part of the produce of each estate was to go to the workers. Commercial arrangements were made with the United States and England. He immediately issued a manifesto to all Negroes and mulattoes. "I am Toussaint L'Ouverture; my name is perhaps known to you. I have undertaken to avenge your wrongs. It is my desire that liberty and equality shall reign in

San Domingo! I am striving to this end. Come and unite with us, brothers, and fight with us for the same cause."

Through the prowess of Toussaint, the Spanish pushed the French farther and farther back and in a short time secured possession of nearly the whole north of the island and part of the south. The French commission found itself in a tight place and tried to extricate itself in June, 1793, by offering to free all slaves who would enroll in the army. In August they went even further and proclaimed universal emancipation in San Domingo, and this action was confirmed by the French National Convention, February 4, 1794.

The first proclamation had no influence upon Toussaint. As a Spanish general, he refused to recognize the authority of the French. But when the English invaded San Domingo, the aspect of things changed. They landed in September and soon had captured that city with its heavy artillery and two million dollars' worth of shipping in its harbor. Toussaint knew the British as slave traders, and he now suspected that Spain wanted vengeance on France rather than freedom for the slaves. When, therefore, the French government affirmed universal emancipation early in 1794, he returned to French allegiance to the open delight of the commission. They said, "Remember that distinctions of color are no more!"

The blacks under Toussaint now proceeded to restore San Domingo to France. The mere magic of his name did much without fighting. In April Toussaint left the Spanish army; in May the French Flag was flying at Gonaives. From now on Toussaint was known as L'Ouverture, the Savior. Gradually the whole northern part of the island was in his possession. As Sonthonax wrote in his diary, "These Negroes perform miracles of bravery."

In after years, the successors of Toussaint, Dessalines and Christophe developed communalism and made the Haitian state independent and owner of its land and crops; but the surrounding world whirled away: it monopolized wealth in private hands, organized military power in their hand and France, the United States and Britain forced Haiti to become the victim of their stooge who rules Haiti today. Still high in its mountains roll the tom-toms of ancient Africa and its dreams.

People who achieved equality in the French Revolution had neither liberty nor brotherhood for the black slaves of Haiti who were dying for the glory of France. For two years a National Convention was in control, which abolished the monarchy and vainly planned an equalitarian democracy. They tried to free the slaves, their own reaction could not survive slavery and live.

Meantime, separated by a vast ocean, with news traveling by slow sailing vessels, and couriers loaded with lies, France and San Domingo led for a long period almost separate lives, neither knowing exactly what was occurring in the other. The French commissioners representing the state arrived in San Domingo. They joined the mulattoes and free Negroes and revoked the abolition of the slavery of the blacks. Toussaint, leader of the blacks, went over to the Spaniards and the French planters appealed to the British.

The governor of the colony helplessly called on the revolting Negroes to surrender. In answer Toussaint wrote: "Sir —We have never thought of failing in the duty and respect which we owe to the representative of the person of the King, nor even to any of his servants whatever; we have proof of the fact in our hands; but do you, who are a just man as well as a general, pay us a visit; behold this land which we have watered with our sweat or rather, with our blood—those edifices which we have raised, and that in the hope of a just reward! Have we obtained it? The King—the whole world— has bewailed our lot, and broken our chains; while on our part, we, humble victims, were ready for anything, not wishing to abandon our masters. What do we say? We are mistaken; those, who next to God, should have proved our fathers, have been tyrants, monsters unworthy of the fruits of our labours: and do you, brave general, desire that as sheep we should throw ourselves into the jaws of the wolf? No! it is too late. God, who fights for the innocent is our guide; he will never abandon us. Accordingly, this is our motto—*Death or Victory!*"

Thus while the slaves arranged themselves with the King as symbolic head of the state, the new colonial assembly August 24, 1791, instead of appealing to France, begged protection, especially for their property, from England: "Fire lays waste our possessions, the hands of our Negroes in arms are already dyed with the blood of our brethren. Very prompt assistance is necessary to save the wreck of our fortunes—already half destroyed; and confined within the towns, we look for your aid."

The British after five years were sick of their attempt to conquer Haiti. By September 30, 1796, out of the whole number of white troops, British and foreign, who had landed in Haiti since 1795, at least 15,000 men, only 3,000 were left alive. April 22, 1798, the British Commander Maitland evacuated all towns in Haiti except Mole St. Nicholas. He had only a thousand troops alive.

The brilliant success of Toussaint not only aroused the envy of the mulattoes, but the suspicion of France. The commissioner, Sonthonax,* who had returned from San Domingo, reported to the new government in the Director in France, the facts concerning Toussaint, and they thought it best to send a governor who would curb his power. Hedouville, the new governor, arrived April 20, 1798, and proposed to take charge of the negotiations with the English; but Maitland, the English commander, was only too glad to affront France by dealing directly and exclusively with Toussaint and to attempt to gain for England by flattery and bribery what he could not take by force. After five years of fighting, the loss of thirty thousand men and the expenditure of one hundred million dollars, he offered to surrender.

On October 1, 1798, Toussaint entered Mole St. Nicholas as conqueror. The white troops saluted him. He was dined in the public square, on a silver service which was afterwards presented to him in the name of the King of England. A treaty was signed by which the English gave up the island,

*The Frenchman, Sonthonax, was a true representative of the revolution. "With the blacks his name was already a talisman, and in an insurrection which took place in the revolutionary center, Port-de-Paix, where whites were massacred, the laborers had risen to cries, 'long live Sonthonax.' " *The Black Jacobins,* C. R. L. James, Chap. 8, p. 146.

recognized Haiti as independent, and entered into a commercial agreement. Then they tried secretly to induce Toussaint to declare himself King, but he refused.

Paris between March 1793 and July 1794 passed through one of the supreme epochs of political history. In these few months of their nearest approach to power the masses did not forget the blacks. They felt toward them as brothers, and the old slave-owners whom they knew to be supporters of the counter-revolution, they hated as if Frenchmen themselves had suffered under the whip. There were many so moved by the sufferings of the slaves that they had long ceased to drink coffee, thinking of it as drenched with blood and sweat of men turned into brutes.

This was the France to which, in January 1794, three deputies sent by San Domingo to the Convention arrived. Bellay, a Negro slave, who had purchased his freedom, Mills, a mulatto, and Dufay, a white man. On February 3rd they attended their first session. What happened there was quite unpremeditated.

The Chairman of the Committee on Decrees addressed the Convention, "Citizens, your Committee on Decrees has verified the credentials of the deputies from San Domingo. It finds them in order, and I move that they be admitted to their places in the Convention." Comboulas rose. "Since 1789 the aristocracy of birth and the aristocracy of religion have been destroyed; but the aristocracy of the skin still remains. That too is now at its last gap, and equality has been consecrated. A black man, a yellow man, are about to join this Convention in the name of the free citizens of San Domingo." The three deputies of San Domingo entered the hall. The black face of Bellay and the yellow face of Mills excited long and repeated bursts of applause.

Lacroix (of Eure-et-Loire) followed. "The Assembly has been anxious to have within it some of those men of colour who have suffered oppression for so many years. Today it has two of them. I demand that their introduction be marked by the President's fraternal embrace."

Next day, Bellay, the Negro, delivered a long and fiery oration, pledging the blacks to the cause of the revolution and asking the Convention to declare slavery abolished. It was fitting that a Negro and ex-slave should make the speech which introduced one of the most important legislative acts ever passed by any political assembly. No one spoke after Bellay. Instead Levasseur (of Sarthe) moved: "When drawing up the constitution of the French people we paid no attention to the unhappy Negroes. Posterity will bear us a great reproach for that. Let us repair the wrong—let us proclaim the liberty of the Negroes. Mr. President, do not suffer the Convention to dishonor itself by discussion." The Assembly rose in acclamation. The two deputies of color appeared on the tribune and embraced while the applause rolled round the hall from members and visitors. Lacroix led the Mulatto and the Negro to the President who gave them the presidential kiss, when the applause started again.

Cambon, a deputy, drew the attention of the House to an incident which had taken place among the spectators.

"A citizeness of colour who regularly attends the sittings of the Convention has just felt so keen a joy at seeing us give liberty to all her brethren that she has fainted (applause). I demand that this act be recorded in the minutes, and that this citizeness be admitted to the sitting and receive at least this much recognition of her civic virtues." The motion was carried and the woman walked to the front bench of the amphitheatre and sat to the left of the President, drying her tears amidst another burst of cheering.

Lacroix, who had spoken the day before, then proposed the draft of the decree. "I demand that the Minister of Marine be instructed to despatch at once advices to the Colonies to give them the happy news of their freedom, and I propose the following decree: The national Convention declares slavery abolished in all the colonies. In consequence it declares that all men, without distinction of colour, domiciled in the colonies, are French citizens, and enjoy all the rights assured under the Constitution."

During this time, the leaders of French industry continued their protests outside the National Convention.

"There is no longer any ship-building in our ports, still less any construction of boats. The manufactories are deserted and the shops even closed. Thus, thanks to your sublime decrees, every day is a holiday for the workers. We can count more than three hundred thousand in our different towns who have no other occupation than, arms folded, to talk about the news of the day, of the Rights of Man, and of the Constitution."

On June 5th, the day after the celebration of the King's birthday and the capture of Port-au-Prince, the English commanders at St. Kitts heard that seven French ships had escaped the British fleet and landed at Guadeloupe. In command was Victor Hugues, a Mulatto, "One of the great personalities of the French revolution to whom nothing was impossible," taken from his post as public prosecutor in Rochefort and sent to the West Indies. Hugues brought only 1,500 men, but he brought also the Convention's message to the blacks. There was no black army in the Windward islands as in San Domingo. He had to make one out of raw slaves. But he gave them the revolutionary message and dressed them in the colors of the Republic. The black army fell on the victorious British, began to drive them out of the French colonies, then carried the war into the British islands.

Toussaint got the news of the decree sometime in May. The fate of the French in San Domingo was hanging by a thread, but now that the decree of Sonthonax was ratified in France, Toussaint did not hesitate a moment but at once told Laveaux that he was willing to join him. Laveaux, overjoyed, accepted the offer and agreed to make him a Brigadier-General, and Toussaint responded with a vigor and audacity that left all San Domingo gasping. He sent to the destitute Laveaux some good ammunition from the Spanish stores. Then he persuaded those of his followers who were with him to change over, and all agreed—French soldiers, ex-slaves of the rank-and-file and all of his officers, blacks and white royalists who had deserted the Republic to join him. "His demeanour at Mass was so devout that D'Hermona watching him communicate one day commented that God if he came to earth could not visit a purer spirit than Toussaint L'Ouverture."

The Directory which ruled from 1794 to 1799 turned to

Napoleon who hated blacks. Nevertheless, he married the granddaughter of a Negro, Josephine, who was a leader of current French society. On the other hand, he dismissed General Dumas from his army solely because of his color. Napoleon was rising to prominence. He conducted a brilliant campaign in Italy and then from the foot of the Pyramids looked toward India, but the British blocked him until unemployment in England brought the Peace of Amiens.

The French planters appealed to Napoleon. He took their side, saying: "the liberty of the blacks is an insult to Europe." But Toussaint was powerful. Napoleon had to flatter and cajole him. After consultation with French bankers, Napoleon planned an American empire based on African slavery. He lured Toussaint to France and killed him. He gathered a vast army under his brother-in-law, Leclerc, who sailed for San Domingo in 1801. He took five squadrons with 80 vessels and 21,000 troops. The Africans and the fever conquered this army and left Dessalines and Christophe, successors of Toussaint, masters of Haiti.

Napoleon was unable to start colonial imperialism in America. That was accomplished in later years when American democracy restored African slavery in the cotton kingdom.

But the world hailed Toussaint, he was one of the great men of his time. He made an extraordinary impression upon those who knew him personally or studied his life, whether they were friends or enemies. Auguste Comte included him with Washington, Plato, Buddha and Charlemagne as worthy to replace all the calendar saints. Morvins, biographer of Napoleon, calls him "a man of genius." Beauchamp refers to him as "one of the most extraordinary men of a period when so many extraordinary men appeared on the scene." Lamartine wrote a drama with Toussaint as his hero. Harriet Martineau wrote a novel on his life. Whittier wrote about him. Sir Spencer St. John, consular agent in Haiti, called him "one grand figure of a cruel war." Rainsford, a British officer, refers to him as "that only great man." Chateaubriand charges that Bonaparte not only murdered, but imitated him.

A French planter said, "God in his terrestrial Globe did not commune with a purer spirit." Wendell Phillips said, "You think me a fanatic, for you read history, not with your eyes, but with your prejudices. But fifty years hence, when Truth gets a hearing, the Muse of history will put Phocion for the Greek, Brutus for the Roman, Hampden for England, LaFayette for France; choose Washington as the bright consummate flower of our earliest civilization; and then, dipping her pen in the sunlight, will write in the clear blue, above them all, the name of the soldier, the statesman, the martyr, Toussaint L'Ouverture." Wordsworth sang:

> There's not a breathing of the common wind
> That will forget thee: thou hast great allies;
> Thy friends are exultations, agonies,
> And love, and Man's unconquerable mind.

In 1802 and 1803 nearly forty thousand French soldiers died of war and fever. Leclerc himself died in November, 1803. Rochambeau succeeded to his command and was promised soldiers by Napoleon; but already in May, 1803, Great Britain started new war with France and communication between France and San Domingo was impossible. The black insurgents held the land; the British held the sea. In November, 1803, Rochambeau surrendered and white authority died in San Domingo forever.

The effect of all this was far-reaching. Napoleon gave up his dream of American empire and sold Louisiana for a song. As DeWit Talmadge said: "Thus, all of Montana and the Dakotas, and most of Colorado and Minnesota, all of Washington and Oregon States, came to us as the indirect work of a despised Negro. Praise, if you will, the work of a Robert Livingstone or a Jefferson, but today let us not forget our debt to Toussaint L'Ouverture, who was indirectly the means of America's expansion by the Louisiana Purchase of 1803."

From *Freedomways*: A Quarterly Review of the Negro Freedom Movement, Vol. 1, No. 2, Summer, 1961, pp. 136–51

Realities in Africa (1943)

In modern times two great world movements have hinged on the relation of Africa to the other continents: the African slave trade, which transferred perhaps ten million laborers from Africa to America and played a major role in the establishment of capitalism in England and Europe based on sugar and cotton; and the partitioning of Africa after the Franco-Prussian War which, with the Berlin Conference of 1884, brought colonial imperialism to flower.

The primary reality of imperialism in Africa today is economic. Since 1884 there has been invested in that continent a sum larger than the total gold reserve of the British Empire and France in 1939. Due to this investment there were exported annually from Africa, just before the present war, seven hundred million dollars' worth of products. And this valuation of African exports is abnormally low, since in a market controlled by the manufacturers the labor cost is depressed so as to yield high profit; the potential value of African raw materials runs into the billions.

These, then, are the two facts to keep in mind in our discussions of the future of Africa—that in the nineteenth century the African trade in men changed to a trade in raw materials; and that henceforth the political domination which insured monopoly of raw materials to the various contending empires was predicated on the exploitation of African labor inside the continent. The integration of Africa into the world economic organization since the Industrial Revolution has been of far greater significance than social scientists like to admit. A quite natural reticence regarding the immense extent of the slave trade fostered the tendency to treat that question as an incidental moral lapse which was overshadowed and atoned for by the abolitionist crusade of 1800–1860. But an understanding of the economic background is basic to the correct interpretation of the twentieth century and its two world wars.

In the eighteenth century England became the great slave-trading nation of the world and made America a land of chattel slavery. But in the nineteenth century England appears as the emancipator, who stopped the slave trade at great cost, abolished slavery in her own territories and stimulated the reaction against Negro slavery throughout the world. How do these attitudes harmonize? The rise of liberal and philanthropic thought in the latter part of the eighteenth century accounts, of course, for no little of the growth of opposition to slavery and the slave trade; but it accounts for only a part of it. Other and dominant factors were the diminishing returns of the African slave trade itself, the bankruptcy of the West Indian sugar economy through the Haitian revolution, the interference of Napoleon and the competition of Spain. Without this pressure of economic forces, Parliament would not have yielded so easily to the abolition crusade. Moreover, new fields of investment and profit were being opened to Englishmen by the consolidation of the empire in India and by the acquisition of new spheres of influence in China and elsewhere. In Africa, British rule was actually strengthened by the anti-slavery crusade, for new territory was annexed and controlled under the aegis of emancipation. It would not be right to question for a moment the sincerity of Sharpe, Wilberforce, Buxton and their followers. But the moral force they represented would have met with greater resistance had it not been working along lines favorable to English investment and colonial profit.

There followed a brief but interesting period of readjustment. For a while after the triumph of the abolition movement the idea was fairly widespread in England that Africa was to be allowed its own development so long as trade was free. Sierra Leone, the British Negro settlement, was promised eventual autonomy; and when Napier overthrew Theodore of Ethiopia in 1868, he withdrew without even attempting permanent control or annexation. But soon the investing countries realized that strong political control in African and Asiatic colonies would result in such a monopoly of labor and raw material as to insure magnificent profits. The slave trade and slavery would not only be unnecessary; they were actually a handicap to profitable investment.

The process of strengthening control over the people of

Africa was therefore developed in the name of stopping the slave trade and abolishing slavery. For a while, English philanthropy and English imperialism seemed to have found one of those pre-established harmonies in economic life upon which Bentham and the Physiocrats had loved to expatiate. Increased trade and stable government in Africa were going to be the best way of civilizing the natives and lifting them toward self-government. Philanthropy, guided by men like Livingstone, envisaged the raising of the status of black labor in Africa as not only compatible with industrial profit, but practically synonymous with it. It was equally clear that unless there was political domination of these colonies to insure virtual monopoly of material and labor, the colonial investment there would not be secure. The almost complete investtion of Africa followed, settling in the hands of England a vast colonial empire and yielding to France and to Germany less valuable but nevertheless large imperial domains.

A technique of domination was gradually developed. Physical force backed by superior firearms was used in the Sudan. In South Africa, economic pressure was applied by land monopoly, supplemented by a head tax which meant compulsory labor. A caste system of Negroes subordinated to whites was widely instituted, but to some extent modified by cultural segregation, sometimes called "Indirect Rule," by which the cultural integrity of African tribes was within limits permitted for local government, but their economic activities guided by the interests of investment in the hands of the governing country. Just as European peasants did not get a cent of compensation for the three and a half million acres of common land taken from them between 1801 and 1831, so in the Union of South Africa the natives who formed eighty percent of the population came to possess only eight percent of the land. In Kenya 3,000,000 natives are confined today to 50,000 square miles of the poorest land; the best land has been given to Europeans, often at a nominal price, in estates so large that they can only be cultivated by hired labor. Again and again forced labor has been legalized in Kenya; and it is legal today. Labor in the mines of South Africa was long removed only a step from serfdom, and labor conditions there now allow a native wage of $15 a month. In the Belgian Congo and French Equatorial Africa there has been a sordid history of cruelty, extermination and exploitation. We must not blink the fact that in the past it has been profitable to a mother country to possess colonies. One sometimes hears that colonies represent a sort of philanthropic enterprise. The colonial system is commended for whatever education and social services it has given to the natives and is not blamed if these social services have been miserably inadequate as compared to the need. The fact is that so far as government investment is concerned, the money which Great Britain, France, Portugal and Germany *as governments* have invested in Africa has yielded small returns in taxes and revenues. But this governmental investment and its concomitant political control have been the basis upon which private investors have built their private empires, being thus furnished free capital by home taxation; and while the mass of people in the mother country have been taxed and often heavily for this governmental gift abroad, the private capitalist who has invested in the colonies has reaped not only interest from his own investment but returns from investments which he did not make and which are protected by armies and navies which he only partially supported. Immense sums have been derived from raw material and labor whose price has been depressed to a minimum while the resulting goods processed in the mother country are sold at monopoly prices. The profits have not been evenly distributed at home; but the net return to the white races for their investment in colored labor and raw material in Africa has been immense. That, very briefly, is the fundamental fact of the situation which confronts us in Africa today.

II

For convenience we refer to "Africa" in a word. But we should remember that there is no one "Africa." There is in the continent of Africa no unity of physical characteristics, of cultural development, of historical experience, or of racial identity.

We may distinguish today at least eleven "Africas." There is North Africa—though Libya and Algeria are in large degree a part of southern Europe. There is French West Africa, a vast and loosely integrated region, in one small part of which an educational and cultural development of the natives is in evidence and where there has been some economic progress. There is Egypt, which is still a political and economic satellite in the British Empire; but from Egypt the Anglo-Egyptian Sudan has been cut off and presents a different economy and faces a different destiny. To the south lies Ethiopia, whose long and tragic history foreshadowed the present war. Turning westward again, we have French Equatorial Africa, an economic echo of the Belgian Congo, the seat in the past of terrible exploitation and in the present of a new arming of blacks for European wars.

Then there is British West Africa. It consists of four colonies and demonstrates the most advanced possibilities of the Negro race in Africa; even here those possibilities are held in check by the limited application of democratic methods and by carefully organized exploitation. There is the Belgian Congo, whose astonishing history is known to all. There is British East Africa, consisting of Uganda, Kenya, and the former German colony of Tanganyika. There is Portuguese Africa, almost split in two by British territory and dependent mainly upon British economic organization. Finally, there are South Africa and the Rhodesias, where 3,000,000 white people are holding 10,000,000 darker folk in economic serfdom. This is preeminently the land of gold, jewels and metals.

Current world opinion makes little distinction among these groups. Berbers of North Africa are usually classed as "white" peoples; Abyssinians are now and then declared not to be Negroes; but on the whole, all Africans, save recent white European immigrants and their offspring, are classed among the peoples of the earth who are inferior in status and in kind.

This decree of inferiority is not based on scientific study— indeed the careful anthropological and social study of Africa has only just begun. Again we must come back to dollars, pounds, marks and francs. The judgment on Africa was rendered on economic grounds (although, of course, pseudo-scientific dogma were adduced to bolster it). Liberal thought and violent revolution in the eighteenth and early nineteenth centuries shook the foundations of a social hierarchy in Europe based on unchangeable class distinctions. But in the nineteenth and early twentieth centuries the Color Line was drawn as at least a partial substitute for this stratification. Granting that all white men were born free and equal, was it not manifest—ostensibly after Gobineau and Darwin, but in reality after James Watt, Eli Whitney, Warren Hastings and Cecil Rhodes—that Africans and Asiatics were born slaves, serfs or inferiors? The real necessity of this fantastic rationalization was supplied by the demands of modern colonial imperialism. The process of exploitation that culminated in the British, French and German empires before the First World War turned out to be an investment whose vast returns depended on cheap labor, under strict colonial control, without too much interference from mawkish philanthropy.

Philanthropy has fought stout battles for a liberalization of imperialistic rule in the past. The focus of these battles has usually been the question of education of the peoples of Africa; it was the difference of opinion on this issue which awoke philanthropy from its dream of foreordained harmony between the cohorts of Christianity and business. The painful question inevitably arose: to what degree should native people be allowed an education, in view of the fact that educated men do not make cheap and docile laborers? Sharp disputes took place between missionaries and administrative officials over the missionaries' plans for schools and for training of skilled artisans, civil servants, and professional men such as physicians. In some cases, at least, the insistence of the missionaries was so great that government was forced to yield.

The cultural possibilities of the African native are undeniable. It is admitted even in South Africa today that the native is not being kept out of skilled labor because he is incapable. And his capacity for political self-rule is shown by the success of the native states of the West Coast, the Bunga of the Transkei and other such experiments. Missionaries, travellers, and now many government agents agree that it would be possible to place centers of education in Africa which would in a few generations train an intelligentsia capable eventually of taking fairly complete charge of the social development of the continent. There are beginnings of such centers today at Fort Hare, South Africa; Achimota and Fourah Bay, West Africa; and Makerere, Uganda.

Cutting across this whole question comes the issue of the use of Negroes in war. The Civil War in the United States was fought with the help of 200,000 black troops with a growing possibility of enlisting a majority of the slaves; and their use made further slavery unthinkable. The First World War was fought with the help of black troops which France brought to Europe to ward off annihilation; the blacks of French West Africa were armed on a large scale and became an effective fighting force in Europe. Europe protested—the English in South Africa as well as the Germans in Europe. If armed natives were going to be used in European disputes, would not native colonial revolt be only a matter of years? Today the Free French are not only using black troops but using them under a black governor of French Equatorial Africa, while Senegalese troops of French West Africa and colored troops of North Africa are used in increasing numbers.

Unless the question of racial status is frankly and intelligently faced it will become a problem not simply of Africa but of the world. More than the welfare of the blacks is involved. As long as there is in the world a reservoir of cheap labor that can raise the necessary raw materials, and as long as arrangements can be made to transport these raw materials to manufacturing countries, this body of cheap labor will compete directly or indirectly with European labor and will be often substituted for European labor. This situation will increase the power of investors and employers over the political organization of the state, leading to agitation and revolt within the state on the part of the laboring classes and to wars between states which are competing for domination over these sources of profit. And if the fiction of inferiority is maintained, there will be added to all this the revolt of the suppressed races themselves, who, because of their low wages, are the basic cause of the whole situation.

The World War of 1914–1918 was caused in part by the German demand for a larger share in the domination over labor and the exploitation of raw materials in Asia and Africa. An important aspect of the World War of 1939 is the competition for the profit of Asiatic labor and materials— competition in part between European countries, in part between those countries and Japan. Submerged labor is revolting in the East Indies, Burma and India itself. It would be a grave mistake to think that Africans are not asking the same questions that Asiatics are: "Is it a white man's war?"

The social development of Africa for the welfare of the Africans, with educated Africans in charge of the program, would certainly interfere with the private profits of foreign investment and would ultimately change the entire relationship of Africa to the modern world. Is the development of Africa for the welfare of Africans the aim? Or is the aim a world dominated by Anglo-Saxons, or at least by the stock of white Europe? If the aim is to keep Africa in subjection just as long as possible, will it not plant the seeds of future hatreds and more war?

III

One would think that Africa, so important in world trade and world industrial organization and containing at least 125,000,000 people, would be carefully considered today in any plan for post-war reconstruction. This does not seem to be the case. When we examine the plans which have been published we find either no mention of Africa or only vague references. In President Roosevelt's "four freedoms" speech in January 1941, he did not seem to be thinking of Africa when he mentioned freedom of speech, freedom from want and freedom from fear. When Pope Pius XII spoke in June 1941 on "Peace and the Changing Social Order" his only phrase which could have referred to Africa was "the more favorable distribution of men on the earth's surface." The British Christian leaders in May 1941 made ten proposals for a lasting peace. The tenth reference was to the resources of the earth which "should be used as God's gifts to the whole human race." The American Friends Service in June 1941 similarly asked that all nations be assured "equitable access to markets." That refers to Africa—but it is an ominous reference. The eight points of the Atlantic Charter were so obviously aimed at European and North American conditions that Winston Churchill frankly affirmed this to be the case, although he was afterward contradicted by President Roosevelt. The proposals which have been made by publicists like Clarence Streit and Henry Luce imply a domination of the world by English-speaking peoples, with only passing consideration of black folk. Only in the recent report on "The Atlantic Charter and Africa from an American Standpoint," by the Committee on Africa, the War, and Peace Aims is a more realistic attitude toward Africa manifest. The Committee insists "That Africa today should be the subject of intelligent study in this country for many reasons, but especially because it is the ancestral home of one-tenth of our population, and that it is a continent of vast possibilities and difficult problems, and of vital concern to the United Nations in the present war . . . that Africa still represents the largest undeveloped area in the world, with mineral deposits, agricultural land, waterpower, forest and wildlife, resources of importance, all of which are decreasing in value because of careless or reckless use or exploitation; and that these resources need development for its own defense and welfare."

The largest undeveloped area in the world! Is that phrase, spoken frankly by a body particularly conscious of African problems, the clue to the reticence of the other post-war statements on the subject of Africa? I do not mean to be unduly pessimistic; but realism demands that we face the fact that after this war the United Nations will be almost irresistibly tempted to consider Africa from an industrial and commercial point of view as a means of helping pay war costs and reestablishing prosperity.

The memorable phrase of the First World War, the German demand for "a place in the sun," meant that Germany demanded metals, vegetable oils, fibres and foods from Africa on equal terms with England, either by pooling or preferably by dividing up Africa's land, labor and resources afresh. To return to such a plan after a generation of indecision, after another ghastly war, and in a period bursting with the components of still another and vaster war, would be blindness indeed. Yet this is precisely what many have in mind. If the rivalry of dominant European nations for colonial profit can be composed by a more equitable distribution of raw materials and labor, they say, then peace will be assured in the world. When they say nothing about the aspirations of the peoples of Africa themselves, what they are actually saying is that peace will be assured if we will all merely return to the eighteenth century.

IV

The first National Congress of British West Africa met in Accra, capital of the Gold Coast Colony, in mid-March, 1920. The Congress, composed of delegates from Nigeria, the Gold Coast, Sierra Leone and Gambia, drafted a memorial to His Majesty the King which is a worthy and remarkable document:

In presenting the case for the franchise for the different colonies composing British West Africa, namely, the Gambia, Sierra Leone, the Gold Coast and Nigeria, it is important to remember that each of these colonies is at present governed under the Crown Colony System. By that is meant that the power of selecting members for the legislative councils is in the Governor of each colony and not dependable upon the will of the people through an elective system. In the demand for the franchise by the people of British West Africa, it is not to be supposed that they are asking to be allowed to copy a foreign institution. On the contrary, it is important to notice that the principle of electing representatives to local councils and bodies is inherent in all the systems of British West Africa. According to African institutions every member of a community belongs to a given family with its duly accredited head, who represents that family in the village council, naturally composed of the heads of the several families. Similarly in a district council the different representatives of each village or town would be appointed by the different villages and towns, and so with the Provincial Council until, by the same process, we arrive at the Supreme Council, namely, the State Council, presided over by the Paramount Chief. . . .

The Congress presses for the appointment of duly qualified and experienced legal men to judicial appointments in British West Africa no matter how high the emolument might be. It also presses for the appointment of African barristers of experience, many of whom as jurists and legislative councillors are found along the West Coast, to appointments on judicial bench as well as other judicial appointments. The Congress contends that there are African legal men of experience capable of holding any judicial office in British West Africa. It may be mentioned that in Sierra Leone years ago the late Hon. Sir Samuel Lewis, Knight, C.M.G., an African, held the appointment of Acting Chief Justice; the late Mr. J. Renner Maxwell of Oxford University, an African, held the office of Chief Magistrate of the Gambia, which was equivalent then to the office of Chief Justice; that His Honor the late Mr. Justice Francis Smith, an African, was the Senior Puisne Judge of the Gold Coast, and on several occasions held appointment of Acting Chief Justice; that the late James A. McCarthy, an African, was for many years the Queen's Advocate of Sierra Leone, which was then equivalent to the post of Attorney General, and on many occasions acted as Chief Justice of that Colony. Subsequently he became the Solicitor General of the Gold Coast, and acted as Puisne Judge on several occasions in that Colony. Further, the late Sir Conrad Reeves, an African, was Chief Justice of Jamaica for many years. Therefore it is no new thing to suggest that worthy Africans should be admitted to the highest judicial offices in the judicial service of British West Africa. It is worthy of note that so renowned is the forensic ability of the African legal practitioner, generally a barrister of one of the Inns of Court in London, that they usually control all the practice in British West Africa and the percentage of European practitioners is hardly three.

It must be remembered that this clear and concise demand for elementary democratic rights among the black people of British West Africa was drafted by native-born Africans of Negro descent. In response to it an elective element was admitted to the governors' councils in four colonies. The governor retained the selection of a majority of the council. Any legislation which he wished was guaranteed passage. In these same councils, in all the colonies, sat men representing business and industry directly, that is, voting in the name of and for foreign investors. They still do.

It should be noted also that many of the preferments listed by the Congress came in that period when, under the triumph of philanthropy, England was hesitating between a policy of slavery and colonial autonomy. Soon, as we have seen, the die was cast.

Beside this document, now, place a statement made in 1923 by the white settlers of Kenya. It is the voice of triumphant commercialism, formulating a racial philosophy for the modern world:

It has been shown that the Black Race possesses initiative but lacks constructive powers, characteristics which justify Lugard's judgment that for the native African "the era of complete independence is not yet visible on the horizon of time." The controlling powers may, therefore, aim at advancing the black race as far along the road of progress as its capacity allows, without misgivings that the success of their endeavors will lead to a demand for their withdrawal, entailing loss of prestige and trade. The development of British territories in Africa opens up a vista of commercial expansion so endless that calculated description is difficult. The bare facts are that the area of these territories is 4,000,000 square miles, as compared with India's 1,900,000; that India's overseas trade is about 350,000,000 lbs., and British Africa's (excluding Egypt) is about 292,000,000 lbs.; that the non-self-governing territories, whose total area is 2,628,498 square miles, already produce an overseas trade of 76,500,000 lbs., although their development can hardly be said to have begun; that the average fertility and mineral wealth of their soil are at least equal to those of any other great land mass; that they hold an intelligent fast-breeding native population of about 60 millions, waiting for guidance to engage in the production of the raw materials of industry and foodstuffs; and that white settlement cooperating with the native populations does stimulate production many hundreds of times, and does bring about a demand for manufactured articles out of all proportion to its numerical strength.

Here, then, is the African question: European profit—or Negro development? There is no denying that the training of an African intelligentsia implies most difficult problems—the problem of preserving rather than destroying the native cultural patterns and all the problems that come with inexperienced social leadership. The point is that the decision in these matters must not be left to those interested primarily in financial gain, or to white people alone. If there is to be real Negro development there must be created some organ of international trusteeship and the native intelligence of Africa must be represented on the guiding boards. Can we expect Europe and America to approach this question in a way that promises a solution? We could not expect it under ordinary circumstances; but the circumstances today are not ordinary.

If I were to try to state summarily the objectives of postwar planning for Africa, looking forward to the achievement of the world peace which we all so deeply feel must follow this world war, I would say first that it is necessary to renounce the assumption that there are a few large groups of mankind called races, with hereditary differences shown by color, hair and measurements of the bony skeleton which fix forever their relations to each other and indicate the possibilities of their individual members. There is no proof that persons and groups in Africa are not as capable of useful lives and effective progress as people in Europe and America.

I would say, second, that we must repudiate the more or less conscious feeling, widespread among the white peoples of the world, that other folk exist not for themselves, but for their uses to Europe; that white Europe and America have the right to invade the territory of colored peoples, to force them to work and to interfere at will with their cultural patterns, while demanding for whites themselves a preferred status and seriously and arbitrarily restricting the contacts of colored folk with other and higher culture. The most dangerous excuse for this situation is the relation between European capital and colored labor involving high profit, low wages and cheap raw material. It places the strong motive of private profit in the foreground of our inter-racial relations, while the greater objects of cultural understanding and moral uplift are pushed into the background.

I would say, third, that it must be agreed that in Africa the land and the natural resources belong primarily to the native inhabitants. The necessary capital for the development of Africa's resources should be gradually and increasingly raised from savings of the African natives which a higher wage and a just incidence of taxation would make possible. I would say, fourth, that a systematic effort must be begun to train an educated class among the natives, and that class must be allowed to express its opinions and those opinions be given due weight. And I would say, finally, that political control must be taken away from commercial and business interests owned and conducted in the foreign nations which dominate the continent, and this control be vested provisionally in an international mandates commission.

These, in simplest form, are the proposals for the future which correspond to the present realities in Africa.

From *Foreign Affairs*: An American Quarterly Review, Vol. 21, No. 4, July, 1943

Pan-Africanism: A Mission in My Life (1955)

Naturally there has always been among American Negroes a great interest in Africa. In the eighteenth century this took the form of a desire to return to Africa, and from this arose the present state of Liberia. This movement died down when American Negroes realized that they were not Africans and were not regarded as Africans by the current African tribes. Moreover, the continued American propaganda against Africa and the black race resulted in widespread distaste among American Negroes for being regarded as Africans. They even objected widely to the use of the word "Negro."

Africa has come to the place where action has succeeded talk. The West Coast already sees freedom in the offing; South Africa is writhing; the Sudan is approaching autonomy; Kenya is struggling in blood. Belgium is appeasing the intelligentsia with a start in higher education in the Congo. The Rhodesians are striking and Tanganyika is calling out. If a Sixth Pan-African Congress meets in Africa in 1956, what may we not be able to report there?

However, as the educated element increased there came a new interest in Africa, exhibited by various Negro church organizations, and finally at the time of the first world war there came suggestions that American participation in this war should lead to a recognition of the rights of African people as against the imperial powers.

President Wilson was approached on the subject and a memorandum was directed to the Peace Congress of Versailles. To implement this the NAACP in sending me to Paris after the Armistice to inquire into the treatment of Negro troops, also permitted me to attempt to call a Pan-African Congress. This was an effort to bring together leaders of the various groups of Negroes in Africa and in America for consolidation and planning for the future.

I had difficulty in calling such a Congress because martial law was still in force in France and the white Americans representing the United States there had little sympathy with my ideas. I was in consultation with Colonel House, who was President's Wilson's spokesman, and with others, but could accomplish nothing. Finally, however, I secured the sympathy and cooperation of Blaise Diagne, who was Colonial Under-Secretary in the cabinet of Clemenceau and who had been instrumental in bringing to France the 700,000 Africans who as shock troops saved the nation.

Diagne secured the consent of Clemenceau to our holding a Pan-African Congress, but we then encountered the opposition of most of the countries in the world to allowing delegates to attend. Few could come from Africa, passports were refused to American Negroes and English whites. The Congress therefore, which met in 1919, was confined to those representatives of African groups who happened to be stationed in Paris for various reasons. This Congress represented Africa partially. Of the fifty-seven delegates from fifteen countries, nine were from African countries with twelve delegates. Of the remaining delegates, sixteen were from the United States and twenty-one from the West Indies.

The Congress specifically asked that the German colonies be turned over to an international organization instead of being handled by the various colonial powers. Out of this idea came the Mandates Commission. The *New York Herald* of February 1919 said: "There is nothing unreasonable in the program drafted at the Pan-African Congress which was held in Paris last week. It calls upon the Allied and Associated Powers to draw up an international code of law for the protection of the nations of Africa and to create, as a section of the League of Nations, a permanent bureau to insure observance of such laws and thus further the racial, political and economic interests of the natives."

The National Association for the Advancement of Colored People did not adopt the "Pan-African" movement on its official program, but it allowed me on my own initiative to promote the effort. With a number of colleagues we went to work in 1921 to assemble a more authentic Pan-African Congress and movement. We corresponded with Negroes in all parts of Africa and in other parts of the world and finally arranged for a congress to meet in London, Brussels, and Paris in August and September. Of the one hundred and thirteen delegates to this Congress, forty-one were from Africa, thirty-five from the United States, twenty-four represented Negroes living in Europe, and seven were from the West Indies.

The London meetings of the Congress of 1921 were preceded by a conference with the International Department of the English Labour party, where the question of the relation of white and colored labor was discussed. Beatrice Webb, Leonard Woolf, Mr. Gillies, Norman Leyes, and others were present. Otlet and LaFontaine, the Belgian leaders of Internationalism, welcomed the Congress warmly to Belgium.

Resolutions passed without dissent at the meeting in London contained a statement concerning Belgium, criticizing her colonial regime, although giving her credit for plans of reform for the future. This aroused bitter opposition in Brussels, and an attempt was made to substitute an innocuous statement concerning goodwill and investigation, which Diagne of France, as the presiding officer, supported. At the Paris meeting the original London resolutions, with some minor correction, were adopted. They said in part:

To the world: The absolute equality of races, physical, political and social is the founding stone of world and human advancement. No one denies great differences of gift, capacity and attainment among individuals of all races, but the voice of Science, Religion and practical Politics is one in denying the God-appointed existence of super-races or of races naturally and inevitably and eternally inferior.

The Second Pan-African Congress sent me with a committee to interview the officials of the League of Nations in Geneva. I talked with Rappard who headed the Mandates Commission; I saw the first meeting of the Assembly, and I had an interesting interview with Albert Thomas, head of the International Labor Office. Working with Bellegarde of Haiti, a member of the Assembly, we brought the status of Africa to the attention of the League. The League published our petition as an official document, saying in part:

The Second Pan-African Congress wishes to suggest that the spirit of the world moves toward self-government as the ultimate aim of all men and nations and consequently the mandated areas, being peopled as they are so largely by black folk, have a right to ask that a man of Negro descent, properly fitted in character and training, be appointed a member of the Mandates Commission so soon as a vacancy occurs.

We sought to have these meetings result in a permanent organization. A secretariat was set up in Paris and functioned for a couple of years, but was not successful. The third Pan-African Congress was called for 1923, but postponed. We persevered and finally without proper preparation met in London and Lisbon late in the year. The London session was small. It was addressed by Harold Laski and Lord Olivier and attended by H. G. Wells; Ramsay MacDonald was kept from attending only by the pending election, but wrote: "Anything I can do to advance the cause of your people on your recommendation, I shall always do gladly."

The meeting of an adjourned session of this Congress in Lisbon the same year was more successful. Eleven countries were represented there, including Portuguese Africa. The resolutions declared:

The great association of Portuguese Negroes with headquarters at Lisbon, which is called the Liga Africana, is an actual federation of all the indigenous associations scattered throughout the five provinces of Portuguese Africa and represents several million individuals . . . This Liga Africana which functions at Lisbon, in the very heart of Portugal so to speak, has a commission from all the other native organizations and knows how to express to the government in no ambiguous terms but in dignified manner all that should be said to avoid injustice or to bring about the repeal of harsh laws. That is why the Liga Africana of Lisbon is the director of the Portuguese African movement; but only in the good sense of the word, without making any appeal to violence and without leaving constitutional limits.

I planned a Fourth Pan-African Congress in the West Indies in 1925. My idea was to charter a ship and sail down the Caribbean, stopping for meetings in Jamaica, Haiti, Cuba and the French islands. But here I reckoned without my steamship lines. At first the French Line replied that they could "easily manage the trip," but eventually no accommodations could be found on any line except at the prohibitive price of fifty thousand dollars. I suspect that colonial powers spiked this plan.

Two years later, in 1927, American Negro women revived the Congress idea, and a Fourth Pan-African Congress was held in New York. Thirteen countries were represented, but direct African participation lagged. There were two hundred and eight delegates from twenty-two American states and ten foreign countries. Africa was sparsely represented by representatives from the Gold Coast, Sierra Leone, Liberia and Nigeria. Chief Amoah III of the Gold Coast, and anthropologists like Herskovits, then at Columbia, and Mensching of Germany, and John Vandercook were on the program.

In 1929 we made a desperate effort to hold a Fifth Pan-African Congress on the continent of Africa itself; we selected Tunis because of its accessibility. Elaborate preparations were begun. It looked as though at last the movement was going to be geographically African. But two insuperable difficulties intervened: first, the French government very politely but firmly informed us that the Congress could take place in any French city, but not in French Africa; and second, there came the Great Depression.

The Pan-African idea died apparently until twenty years afterwards, in the midst of World War II, when it leaped to life again in an unexpected manner. At the Trade Union Conference in London in 1944 to plan for world organization of labor, representatives from black labor appeared from the Gold Coast, Libya, British Guiana, Ethiopia and Sierra Leone. Among these, aided by colored persons resident in London, Lancashire, Liverpool, and Manchester, there came a spontaneous call for the assembling of another Pan-African Congress in 1945 when the world federation of Trade Unions would hold their meeting in Paris. This proved not feasible, and the meeting place was changed to London. Here again we met difficulty in securing meeting places and hotel accommodation. However a group of Negroes in Manchester invited us and made all accommodations.

The Fifth Pan-African Congress, therefore, met from 15 to 21 October 1945 in Manchester, England, with some two hundred delegates representing East and South Africa and the West Indies. Its significance lay in the fact that it took a step towards a broader movement and a real effort of the peoples of Africa and the descendants of Africa the world over to start a great march towards democracy for black folk.

At this meeting Africa was for the first time adequately represented. From the Gold Coast came Nkrumah, now Prime Minister of the first African British Dominion. With him was Ashie-Nikoi of the cocoa farmers cooperative. From Kenya was Jomo Kenyatta; from Sierra Leone the trade union leader, Wallace Johnson; from Nigeria, Chief Coker; from the West Indies came a number of trade union leaders; from South Africa the writer, Peter Abrahams, acted as publicity director, while George Padmore was general director.

It was interesting to learn that from the original Pan-African Congress the idea had spread so that nearly every African province now had its national congress, beginning historically with the great congress of West Africa held in 1920 just after the First Pan-African Congress in Paris. There are now national congresses in South Africa, Rhodesia, Nyasaland, Tanganyika and Angola.

The following reports from the Fifth Pan-African Congress are of interest. I thus painted the general scene:

In a great square Hall in Manchester in the midst of that England of the Economic Revolution where the slave trade first brought Capitalism to Europe, there met yesterday and today the Fifth Pan-African Congress.

As I entered the Hall there were about 100 Black men present. They represented many parts of Africa: the Gambia, that oldest and smallest of English West African colonies that numbered 200,000 Negroes; Sierra Leone with 2 million, the Gold Coast with half a million and so to Nigeria with more than 20 million. They were mostly young men and full of enthusiasm and a certain exuberant determination. Around the walls were slogans "Africa, arise, the long night is over"; "Africa for the Africans"; Down with the Color Bar"; and the slogans reached out—"Freedom for all subject Peoples"; "Oppressed Peoples of the Earth Unite"; "Down with Anti-Semitism"; and some specific demands like "Ethiopia wants outlet to the Sea"; "Arabs and Jews Unite against British Imperialism."

There were at the morning session, Tuesday, 7 speakers. One from the Gold Coast, educated in America, Nkrumah. He demanded absolute independence and a federation of West African Republics. Nikoi followed, Chairman of the West African Delegation to the Colonial Office. He spoke with force and rhythmic eloquence, charging Great Britain with the beginnings of slavery and speaking as a representative of that Aborigines' Protection Society which obtained from Queen Victoria the dictum, "I had rather have your loyalty than your land." He was fierce in his demand: "Down with Imperialism! No Dominian Status—I want to be Free." He represents 300,000 farmers of the Gold Coast, the upper class farmers who raised the greatest crop of Cocoa in the world. He complained of the new Colonial Secretary of Labor Government who refused to remove economic controls. He said that the West African Produce Control monopolises the natural products and fixes prices for a mass of people whose average income is 20 dollars a year.

Then came Annan, a worker delegate from the Gold Coast

Railway Employees Union. He told how in 1944 they had celebrated on the Gold Coast the Centenary of the Bond; that original
effort at Black Democracy in West Africa, and a century after
that Bond the issue on the Gold Coast is poverty—grinding poverty. He reminded his hearers that the workers must be able to
live in order to vote, that the Gold Coast needed industrial development and that sacrifices were necessary if their demands were
to be granted. They must be willing to live with the dockers and
miners. There is imperialism among us Negroes, ourselves, and
we must remember that we can expect no more from a British
Labor Government than from a Tory Government.

Coker, Delegate of the Nigeria Trade Union Congress, was
more measured in his demands. He, too, represents the Cocoa
Farmers, but he stressed certain remedies like cooperation and
planning, and believed that India's Gandhi had the remedy in
non-violence.

Then came perhaps the best known man in West Africa, Wallace Johnson, Delegate of the Sierra Leone Trade Union Congress
and of the Moslem League. He represents 10,000 organized workers and 25,000 unorganized workers, and in order to establish
these Unions he has spent 5 years in British West African prisons.
Trade unionism in Africa, he said, was developed against and in
spite of the Law, and they had a much harder time than unionism
in Britain. He drew violent applause from the audience. "I have
brought," he said, "a monster document to the Labor Government.
In 150 years Britain, in my country, has made five per cent of
the population literate and today instead of sending prepared
students to England they cater to reaction and complacency." He
instanced the fact that in Sierra Leone, ginger, bringing 25 pounds
a ton in the open market before the War, had to be sold to the
merchants for 11 pounds a ton, and after the fall of Singapore
when the price rose to 144 pounds a ton, the Black merchants
got only 30 pounds.

Downs-Thomas of Gambia spoke for the oldest West African
colony and demanded the abolition of Crown Colony Government.
"How," he said, "can 40 different colonies in all stages of development be ruled by the Colonial Office?"

Perhaps the best and most philosophical speech was made by
H. O. Davis of the Nigerian Youth Movement. He said that the
long range program was independence for Nigeria, but the short
range program had to meet internal hindrances like poverty, ig-

norance and disease and the fact that the Negroes were unarmed; that the external hindrance was the British Government itself which would never willingly give up the colonies. The leaders must go down to the masses, and he agreed with the West African States Union that it is idiotic to think of the colonies as liabilities. If they were they never would be kept by the Imperial Government. Atrocities are not confined to the German and Japanese prisons. They were all too common in the English prisons before the War and British Democracy was not for export.

Later speakers were

Mr. Kenyatta who covered the six territories Somaliland, Kenya, Uganda, Tanganyika, Nyasaland and the Rhodesias. He gave an outline of the conditions under which the native peoples lived before the advent of the Europeans. A picture of happy and contented peoples enjoying the common use of the land with an agricultural, pastoral and hunting economy. He contrasted that picture with present-day conditions with a landless native people of 14 millions, and a small minority of white Europeans forcing the Natives to work at slave rates under appalling conditions. Mr. Kenyatta detailed the conditions obtaining in the territories upon which he was reporting, varying only in detail, and all displaying the characteristic pattern of imperialistic capitalism that Mr. Kenyatta condemned. He called for political independence for East Africa, and an end to racial discrimination.

Mr. George Padmore spoke on Southern Rhodesia, where there was a population of 50,000 Europeans and two million Africans; before bills concerning Black people could be made law, they must have sanction of the Colonial Office. The land had been taken from the Africans and given to Europeans, and the Natives were then forced to work upon the farms and tobacco plantations at low wages. The Europeans wanted the three states to come together so that the laws now prevailing in Southern Rhodesia would be extended. Of Northern Rhodesia Mr. Padmore told of London and American controlled copper mines where the wages paid to colored workers amounted to 1s 6d a day. White miners got one pound per day. Profits of the mining companies over the last sixty years averaged 10,000,000 pounds and out of this there had been paid only about 1,500,000 pounds in wages. Profits and income tax are paid to the Exchequer in London, the mining companies being registered in London, and taxes are paid to the country in which they are registered. Mr. Padmore spoke of the increasingly progressive element among the younger colored people and called on the Congress to give all support for the aspirations and demands of the peoples of East African territories. Mr. Ken Hill, representative of Jamaica BWI Trade Union Council, brought greetings and messages of solidarity to the people of Africa. He paid tribute to the work of Marcus Garvey. Mr. Hill said his people were tired of special promises and declarations and were now demanding self-government and an end to Crown Colony rule. He complained of absentee investors of Insurance companies and so-called Government Savings Banks whose profits were exported abroad while poverty and unemployment remained in the islands. He warned that trouble would arise unless fair treatment was given to members of the armed forces. "If our people are good enough to fight for the empire," he said, "then they are good enough to be thought of as civilized human beings when they are demobilized and to enjoy the fruits of a lasting peace."

A final report of the Congress said:

The Fifth Pan-African Congress meeting in Manchester with 200 delegates representing 60 nations and groups of African descent finished their work today and will adjourn with a Mass Meeting tomorrow at Chorlton Town Hall. On Thursday and Friday complaints and appeals were heard from Ethiopia and the West Indies. Ethiopia demands the return of Eritrea and Somaliland and ports of the sea. She charges that England is occupying and proposing to keep some of the best grain lands of Ethiopia. The delegates from the West Indies, that former Empire of sugar by sugar for sugar, complained of poverty and neglect with land monopoly and low wages in the face of 100 per cent increase in the cost of living. The situation brought revolutionary strikes and riots in 1937, led by Butler, Bustanmente and Payne, who were promptly thrown in jail. Reforms followed. Something approaching Home Rule has been granted in Jamaica and other places, but insufficient reforms in various islands. Later a black professor from Londonderry reported on French Africa and its rising Nationalism.

This was the final resolution:

The 200 Delegates of the Fifth Pan-African Congress believe in peace. How could they do otherwise when for centuries they have been victims of violence and slavery? Yet if the world is still determined to rule mankind by force, then Africans as a last resort may have to appeal to force, in order to achieve freedom, even if force destroys them and the world.

We are determined to be free; we want education, the right to earn a decent living; the right to express our thoughts and emotions and to adopt and create forms of beauty. Without all this, we die even if we live.

We demand for Black Africa autonomy and independence so far and no further than it is possible in this "One World" for groups and peoples to rule themselves subject to inevitable World Unity and Federation.

We are not ashamed to have been an age-long patient people; we are willing even now, to sacrifice and strive to correct our all too human faults; but we are unwilling longer to starve while doing the world's drudgery, in order to support by our poverty and ignorance a false aristocracy and a discredited imperialism. We condemn monopoly of capital and rule of private wealth and industry for private profit alone. We welcome economic democracy; wherefore, we are going to make the world listen to the facts of our conditions. For their betterment we are going to fight in all and every way we can.

Since this Manchester meeting the world has moved far and fast; to War and Hate in an Atomic Age; with the world split into two and armaments reaching fantastic heights. In Asia and Africa, however, the trend is forward and upward: the great Chinese people have become independent of Western colonial domination; the United States of Indonesia have thrown off the domination of the Dutch; Indo-China is in part free. Africa has come to the place where action has succeeded talk. The West Coast already sees freedom in the offing; South Africa is writhing; the Sudan is approaching autonomy; Kenya is struggling in blood. Belgium is appeasing the intelligentsia with a start in higher education in the Congo. The Rhodesians are striking and Tanganyika is calling out. If a Sixth Pan-African Congress meets in Africa in 1956, what may we not be able to report there?

From "Africa in the Modern World," a Symposium, in *United Asia*, April, 1955

The Future of All Africa Lies in Socialism (1958)

Dr. Du Bois' Message to the All-African People's Conference, Accra, 1958.

FELLOW AFRICANS: About 1735, my great-great grandfather was kidnaped on this coast of West Africa and taken by the Dutch to the colony of New York in America, where he was sold in slavery. About the same time a French Huguenot, Jacques Du Bois, migrated from France to America and his great-grandson, born in the West Indies and with Negro blood, married the great-great granddaughter of my black ancestor. I am the son of this couple, born in 1868, hence my French name and my African loyalty.

As a boy I knew little of Africa save legends and some music in my family. The books which we studied in the public school had almost no information about Africa, save of Egypt, which we were told was not Negroid. I heard of few great men of Negro blood, but I built up in my mind a dream of what Negroes would do in the future, even though they had no past.

Then happened a series of events: In the last decade of the nineteenth century, I studied two years in Europe, and often heard Africa mentioned with respect. Then, as a teacher in America I had a few African students. Later at Atlanta University a visiting professor, Franz Boas, addressed the students and told them of the history of the Black Sudan. I was utterly amazed and began to study Africa for myself. I attended the Paris Exposition in 1900, and met with West Indians in London in a Pan-African Conference. This movement died, but in 1911 I attended a Races Congress in Lon-

Note: Dr. Du Bois was enroute to Accra to attend the Conference and deliver his message in person, but on reaching Moscow, doctors counseled him against making the journey in Africa's hottest season. He acceded to the doctors' advice to spend some time in a rest home in Moscow. His message to the Conference was read by his wife, Shirley Graham.

don which tried to bring together representatives from all the races of the world. I met distinguished Africans and was thrilled. However, World War killed this movement.

We held a small meeting in 1919 in Paris. After peace was declared, in 1921, we called a much larger Pan-African Congress in London, Paris and Brussels. The two hundred delegates at this congress aroused the fury of the colonial powers and all our efforts for third, fourth and fifth congresses were only partially successful because of their opposition. We tried in vain to convene a congress in Africa itself.

The great depression of the thirties then stopped our efforts for fifteen years. Finally in 1945 black trade union delegates to the Paris meeting of trade unions called for another Pan-African Congress. This George Padmore organized and, at his request, I came from America to attend the meeting at Manchester, England. Here I met Kwame Nkrumah, Jomo Kenyatta, Johnson of Liberia and a dozen other young leaders.

The program of Pan-Africa as I have outlined it was not a plan of action, but of periodical conferences and free discussion. And this was a necessary preliminary to any future plan of united or separate action. However, in the resolutions adopted by the successive Congresses were many statements urging united action, particularly in the matter of race discrimination. Also, there were other men and movements urging specific work.

World financial depression interfered with all these efforts and suspended the Pan-African Congresses until the meeting in Manchester, 1945. Then it was reborn and the meeting now in Accra is the sixth effort to bring this great movement before the world and to translate its experience into action.

My only role in this meeting is one of advice from one who has lived long, who has studied Africa and has seen the modern world.

In this great crisis of the world's history, when standing on the highest peaks of human accomplishment we look forward to Peace and backward to War, when we look up to Heaven and down to Hell, let us mince no words. We face triumph or tragedy without alternative.

Africa, ancient Africa, has been called by the world and

has lifted up her hands! Africa has no choice between private capitalism and socialism. The whole world, including capitalist countries, is moving toward socialism, inevitably, inexorably. You can choose between blocs of military alliance, you can choose between groups of political union; you cannot choose between socialism and private capitalism because private capitalism is doomed!

But what is socialism? It is a disciplined economy and political organization in which the first duty of a citizen is to serve the state; and the state is not a selected aristocracy, or a group of self-seeking oligarchs who have seized wealth and power. No! The mass of workers with hand and brain are the ones whose collective destiny is the chief object of all effort.

Gradually, every state is coming to this concept of its aim. The great Communist states like the Soviet Union and China have surrendered completely to this idea. The Scandinavian states have yielded partially; Britain has yielded in some respects, France in part, and even the U.S. adopted the New Deal which was largely socialism; though today further American socialism is held at bay by 60 great groups of corporations who control individual capitalists and the trade union leaders.

On the other hand, the African tribe, whence all of you sprung, was communistic in its very beginnings. No tribesman was free. All were servants of the tribe of whom the chief was father and voice.

When now, with a certain suddenness, Africa is whirled by the bitter struggle of dying private capitalism into the last great battle-ground of its death throes, you are being tempted to adopt at least a passing private capitalism as a step to some partial socialism. This would be a grave mistake.

For 400 years Europe and North America have built their civilization and comfort on theft of colored labor and the land and materials which rightfully belong to these colonial peoples.

The dominant exploiting nations are willing to yield more to the demands of the mass of men than were their fathers. But their yielding takes the form of sharing the loot—not of stopping the looting. It takes the form of stopping socialism by force and not of surrendering the fatal mistakes of private capitalism. Either capital belongs to all or power is denied all.

Here then, my brothers, you face your great decision: Will you for temporary advantage—for automobiles, refrigerators and Paris gowns—spend your income in paying interest on borrowed funds; or will you sacrifice your present comfort and the chance to shine before your neighbors, in order to educate your children, develop such industry as best serves the great mass of people and make your country strong in ability, self-support and self-defense? Such union of effort for strength calls for sacrifice and self-denial, while the capital offered you at high price by the colonial powers like France, Britain, Holland, Belgium and the U.S., will prolong fatal colonial imperialism, from which you have suffered slavery, serfdom and colonialism.

You are not helpless. You are the buyers and to continue existence as sellers of capital, these great nations, former owners of the world must sell or face bankruptcy. You are not compelled to buy all they offer now. You can wait. You can starve a while longer rather than sell your great heritage for a mess of Western capitalist pottage. You can not only beat down the price of capital as offered by the united monopolized Western private capitalists, but at last today you can compare their offers with those of socialist countries like the Soviet Union and China, which with infinite sacrifice and pouring out of blood and tears, are at last able to offer weak nations needed capital on better terms than the West.

The supply which socialist nations can at present spare is small as compared with that of the bloated monopolies of the West, but it is large and rapidly growing. Its acceptance involves no bonds which a free Africa may not safely assume. It certainly does not involve slavery and colonial control which the West has demanded and still demands. Today she offers a compromise, but one of which you must be aware:

She offers to let some of your smarter and less scrupulous leaders become fellow capitalists with the white exploiters if in turn they induce the nation's masses to pay the awful cost.

This has happened in the West Indies and in South America. This may happen in the Middle East and Eastern Asia. Strive against it with every fibre of your bodies and souls. A body of local private capitalists, even if they are black, can never free Africa; they will simply sell it into new slavery to old masters overseas.

As I have said, this calls for sacrifice. Great Goethe sang, "Entbehren sollst du, sollst entbehren"—"Thou shalt forego, shalt do without." If Africa unites, it will be because each part, each nation, each tribe gives up a part of its heritage for the good of the whole. That is what union means; that is what Pan-Africa means: When the child is born into the tribe the price of his growing up is giving a part of his freedom to the tribe. This he soon learns or dies. When the tribe becomes a union of tribes, the individual tribe surrenders some part of its freedom to the paramount tribe.

When the nation arises, the constituent tribes, clans and groups must each yield power and some freedom to the demands of the nation or the nation dies before it is born. Your local tribal, much loved languages must yield to the few world tongues which serve the largest numbers of people and promote understanding and world literature.

This is the great dilemma which faces Africans today, faces one and all: Give up individual rights for the needs of Mother Africa; give up tribal independence for the needs of the nation.

Forget nothing, but set everything in its rightful place: the glory of the six Ashanti Wars against Britain; the wisdom of the Fanti Confederation; the growth of Nigeria; the song of the Songhay and Hausa; the rebellion of the Mahdi and the hands of Ethiopia; the greatness of Basuto and the fighting of Chaka; the revenge of Mutessi, and many other happenings and men; but above all—Africa, Mother of Men.

Your nearest friends and neighbors are the colored people of China and India, the rest of Asia, the Middle East and the sea isles, once close bound to the heart of Africa and now long severed by the greed of Europe. Your bond is not mere color of skin but the deeper experience of wage slavery and contempt. So too, your bond with the white world is closest

to those who support and defend China and help India and
not those who exploit the Middle East and South America.

Awake, awake, put on thy strength, O Zion! Reject the
weakness of missionaries who teach neither love nor brotherhood, but chiefly the virtues of private profit from capital,
stolen from your land and labor. Africa, awake! Put on the
beautiful robes of Pan-African socialism.

You have nothing to lose but your chains! You have a
continent to regain! You have freedom and human dignity
to attain!

From *National Guardian*, December 22, 1958

Postscript
Young Africa (1950)

What young Africa must learn and deeply understand is
that if socialism is good for Britain and most of the present
world, as every wise man knows it is, it is also good for
Africa, and that is true no matter what is taught by British
Tories or in reactionary American schools. In Africa, as nowhere else in the world, lies the opportunity to build an
African socialism which can teach the world; on land historically held in common ownership; on labor organized in the
past for social ends and not for private profit, and on education long conducted by the family and clan for the progress
of the state and not mainly for the development of profitable
industry. What is needed—and all that is needed—is science
and technique to the group economy by men of unselfish
determination and clear foresight.

From an address before the National Convention of the Phi
Beta Sigma Fraternity, 1950, quoted in *Freedomways*
(Du Bois Memorial Issue), 1965, p. 46

Friends of Africa (1958)

[Africa] your nearest friends and neighbors are the colored people of China and India, the rest of Asia, the Middle East and the sea isles, once close bound to the heart of Africa and now long severed by the greed of Europe. Your bond is not mere color of skin but the deeper experience of wage slavery and contempt. So too, your bond with the white world is closest to those who support and defend China and help India and not those who exploit the Middle East and South America.

Awake, awake, put on thy strength, O Zion! Reject the weakness of missionaries who teach neither love nor brotherhood, but chiefly the virtue of private profit from capital, stolen from your land and labor. Africa, awake! Put on the beautiful robes of Pan-African socialism.

You have nothing to lose but your chains! You have a continent to regain! You have freedom and human dignity to attain!

From Message to the Accra Conference, 1958

PART THREE

The Darker Races

I. The World of Color—
"The Third World Concept"

Prescript
The Colored Majority of Mankind (1938)

MOST MEN in this world are colored. A Faith in humanity, therefore, a belief in the gradual growth and perfectibility of men must, if honest, be primarily a belief in colored men.

Quoted in "W. E. B. Du Bois As a Prophet" by Truman Nelson, *Freedomways* (Du Bois Memorial Issue), 1965, p. 53

The Dark Workers of the World (1939)

. . . one cannot forget the reciprocal influence of labor and its treatment in Africa on labor in Europe and America, and one must ask how far democratic government is going to be possible in a world supported to a larger and larger degree by products from a continent like Africa, and governed by the industrial caste which owns Africa. There is here a paradox and a danger that must not be overlooked.

It seems clear today that the masses of men within and without civilization are depressed, ignorant and poor chiefly because they have never had a chance; because they have lacked inspiring contacts; because the results of their labor have been taken from them; because the opportunity to know the facts of human life has never been presented to them, and because disease and crime have been made easier than health and reason.

For centuries the world has sought to rationalize this condition and pretend that civilized nations and cultured classes are the result of inherent and hereditary gifts rather than climate, geography and happy accident. This explanation, which for years was supported by the phenomenal onrush of European culture, is today, because that the decline and fall of this hegemony, less widely believed; and whatever mankind has accomplished through the ages and in many modern regions of the world is beginning to be looked upon as forecast and promise of what the great majority of human beings can do, with wider and deeper success, if mere political democracy is allowed to widen into industrial democracy of culture and art.

The possibility of this has long been foreseen and emphasized by the socialists, culminating in the magnificent and apostolic fervor of Karl Marx and the communists; but it is hindered and may be fatally hindered today by the relations of white Europe to darker Asia and darkest Africa; by the persistent determination in spite of the logic of facts and the teaching of science, to keep the majority of people in slavish subjection to the white race; not simply to clothe and feed them and administer to their comfort, but to submerge them with such useless and harmful luxury that the effort of their rich to get richer is making civilization desperately poor.

Poverty is unnecessary and the clear result of greed and muddle. It spawns physical weakness, ignorance and dishonesty. There was a time when poverty was due mainly to scarcity, but today it is due to monopoly founded on our industrial organization. This strangle hold must be broken. It can be broken not so much by violence and revolution, which is only the outward distortion of an inner fact, but by the ancient cardinal virtues: individual prudence, courage, temperance, and justice, and the more modern faith, hope and love. Already the working of these virtues has increased health, intelligence, and honesty despite poverty; and further increase is only thwarted by the blind and insane will to mass murder which is the dying spasm of that decadent exploitation of human labor as a commodity, born of the Negro slave trade; and this attitude is today strengthened and justified by persistent disbelief in the ability and desert of the vast majority of men. The proletariat of the world consists not simply of white European and American workers but overwhelmingly of the dark workers of Asia, Africa, the islands of the sea, and South and Central America. These are the ones who are supporting a superstructure of wealth, luxury, and extravagance. It is the rise of these people that is the rise of the world. The problem of the twentieth century is the problem of the Color Line.

From *Black Folk—Then and Now*, 1939, pp. 382–83

The Color Line Belts the World (1906)

We have a way in America of wanting to be "rid" of Problems. It is not so much a desire to reach the best and largest solution as it is to clean the board and start a new game. For instance, most Americans are simply tired and impatient over our most sinister social problem, the Negro. They do not want to solve it, they do not want to understand it, they want simply to be done with it and hear the last of it. Of all possible attitudes this is the most dangerous, because it fails to realize the most significant fact of the opening century, viz.; The Negro Problem in America is but a local phase of a world problem. "The problem of the twentieth century is the problem of the Color Line." Many smile incredulously at such a proposition, but let us see.

The tendency of the great nations of the day is territorial, political, and economic expansion, but in every case this has brought them in contact with darker peoples, so that we have to-day England, France, Holland, Belgium, Italy, Portugal, and the United States in close contact with brown and black peoples, and Russia and Austria in contact with the yellow. The older idea was that the whites would eventually displace the native races and inherit their lands, but this idea has been rudely shaken in the increase of American Negroes, the experience of the English in Africa, India, and the West Indies, and the development of South America. The policy of expansion, then, simply means world problems of the Color Line.

The color question enters into European imperial politics and floods our continents from Alaska to Patagonia.

This is not all. Since 732, when Charles Martel beat back the Saracens at Tours, the white races have had the hegemony of civilization—so far so that "white" and "civilized" have become synonymous in everyday speech; and men have forgotten where civilization started. For the first time in a thousand years a great white nation has measured arms with a colored nation and has been found wanting. The Russo-Japanese War has marked an epoch. The magic of the word "white" is already broken, and the Color Line in civilization has been crossed in modern times as it was in the great past. The awakening of the yellow races is certain. That the awakening of the brown and black races will follow in time, no unprejudiced student of history can doubt. Shall the awakening of these sleepy millions be in accordance with, and aided by, the great ideals of white civilization, or in spite of them and against them? This is the problem of the Color Line. Force and Fear have hitherto marked the white attitude toward darker races; shall this continue or be replaced by Freedom and Friendship?

In *Collier*, October 20, 1906

Will the Church Remove the Color Line? (1931)

Will the church of tomorrow solve the problem of the Color Line? The problem of the Color Line, particularly in America, is well known. It is the question of the treatment and place in society and in the state of the descendants of African slaves who were freed by the civil war. Not only are these persons, numbering some twelve millions or more, more or less physically distinct from the nation because of color and race, but also they are otherwise segregated because slavery made them poor, kept them ignorant and plunged them into such sickness and crime as poverty and ignorance always cause. For these and other reasons they form in the United States an inferior social caste.

This is the problem of the Color Line as it presents itself in the United States. But, of course, the Color Line extends beyond our own country. The majority of the people of the world are colored and belong to races more or less distinct from the white people of Europe and North America. Because, however, of imperial aggression and industrial exploitation, most of these colored peoples are under the political or commercial domination of white Europe and America, and their consequent problems of self-government, social status, and work and wages present the greatest difficulties the world over.

SCIENTIFIC POSTULATES

In addition to all this, various scientific questions have been involved. The attitude of science towards colored races has greatly changed in the last four centuries, but there arose in the nineteenth century a question that persists in the minds of large numbers of white people today, as to how far the earth is inhabited by nations and races essentially equal in their gifts and power of accomplishment, or how far the world is a hierarchy headed by the white peoples, with other groups graduating down by grades of color to smaller and smaller brain power, ability and character.

What now should be the relation of the great racial groups of the world? Shall they live together as brothers? Shall they organize and regard each other as potential or actual enemies? Or shall their relation be that of rulers and ruled, with the races that are now dominated held in subjection, either by physical force or by their own submission to what they come to realize or are forced to admit is the greater power, or greater ability, or greater desert of the white race?

Here, then, is the problem of the Color Line and it is not only the most pressing social question of the modern world; it is an ethical question that confronts every religion and every conscience.

This paper is a frank attempt to express my firm belief that the Christian church will do nothing conclusive or effective; that it will not settle these problems; that on the contrary it will as long as possible and whenever possible avoid them; that in this, as in nearly every great modern moral controversy, it will be found consistently on the wrong side and that when, by the blood and tears of radicals and fanatics of the despised and rejected largely outside the church, some settlement of these problems is found, the church will be among the first to claim full and original credit for the result.

THE CHURCH AND SLAVERY

The proof of this to me lies chiefly in the history of the Christian church and Negro slavery in America. Unfortunately, the editor of The Christian Century has not space for me to go into this matter in detail, and perhaps many of us would rather forget it; and yet we cannot forget that under the aegis and protection of the religion of the Prince of Peace —of a religion which was meant for the lowly and unfortunate—there arose in America one of the most stupendous institutions of human slavery that the world has seen. The Christian church sponsored and defended this institution, despite occasional protest and effort at amelioration here and there. The Catholic church approved of and defended slavery; the Episcopal church defended and protected slavery; the Puritans and Congregationalists recognized and upheld slavery; the Methodists and Baptists stood staunchly behind it; the Quakers gave their consent to it. Indeed, there was not a single branch of the Christian church that did not in the end become part of an impregnable bulwark defending the trade in human beings and the holding of them as chattel slaves. There must have been between 1619 and 1863 in the United States alone ten million sermons preached from the text, "Servants, obey your masters, for this is well pleasing in the sight of the Lord"! Then, finally, when the conscience of mankind began to revolt and abolition became a dream, a propaganda, a political scheme, what was the attitude of the church?

GARRISON'S TESTIMONY

The only Christian body that gave the abolitionists aid and countenance was the Quakers, who, toward the end of the eighteenth century, and in the beginning of the nineteenth, gradually took a stand against slavery and began to agitate for emancipation.

William Lloyd Garrison, reviewing the attitude of the Christian church as a whole, said in the Liberator in 1835: "It is a fact, indisputable and shameful, that the Christianity of the nineteenth century, in this country, is preached and professed by those who hold their brethren in bondage as brute beasts! And so entirely polluted has the church become, that it has not moral power enough to excommunicate a member who is guilty of man-stealing! Whether it be Unitarian or orthodox, Baptist or Methodist, Universalist or Episcopal, Roman Catholic or Christian, it is full of innocent blood—it is the stronghold of slavery—it recognizes as members those who grind the faces of the poor, and usurp over the helpless the prerogatives of the Almighty! At the South, slaves and slaveholders, the masters and their victims, the spoilers and the spoiled, make up the Christian church! The churches of the north partake of the guilt of oppression, inasmuch as they are in full communion with those at the South."

Frederick Douglass added in 1845: "I can see no reason, but the most deceitful one, for calling the religion of this land Christianity."

AFTER EMANCIPATION

After emancipation and in those pregnant twenty years from 1863 to 1883, years whose history has not yet been completely weighed nor written, the world, moral and economic, accepted the fact of free Negroes in America. What attitude should be taken toward these new freedmen and citizens? The church, which had been busy with nursing and relief of the wounded, became involved in schemes for education of refugees, almost before it knew it. The extension of the New England ideal of universal education to black folk was an easy and momentous step. Nevertheless, only part of the church accepted it. The Catholics and the Episcopalians did practically nothing. The southern white Methodists and Baptists naturally took no part. The Presbyterians took but a small part.

The New England Congregationalists, followed by the Northern Methodists and Baptists, stepped forward eagerly and inaugurated what has sometimes been called the ninth crusade, the crusade for Negro education. It was a splendid movement, and has had tremendous results, and it was perhaps the one great effort of any considerable part of the Christians in America in behalf of the Negroes.

RISE OF COLOR CASTE

But after an effort extending over about thirty years, reaction set in, even in the Congregational church. The effort of the south to disfranchise the Negro and to establish a color caste received sympathy in the north for economic reasons and because of the new industrial imperialism which was sweeping the world. Many began to express a fear lest the Negro became "over-educated" and too ambitious, and America began to face frankly the problem as to just what it wanted the American Negro to be. Was he to be trained as a free citizen, economically and socially equal to other Americans, or was he to be trained as a servile caste, the recipient of charity and good will, but a full-fledged member of American democracy?

Thus, the new color caste idea arose in the country and swept over the churches. The Christian church began openly to join those who decried political equality on the part of Negroes, who discountenanced social intercourse between black and white, and who believed that Negroes should be satisfied with humble service and low wages.

What finally has been the attitude of the Christian church toward Negro caste from reconstruction down until this day?

While the church has hesitated and made numbers of explanations and excuses, it is fair to say that the white Christian church has accepted the program of caste for Negroes. The Congregational church stood by its ideals longest, but gradually the contributions for Negro education fell off and the interest in the Negro dwindled. Catholics were forced to face the problem of proselyting among Negroes by the gift of Catherine Drexel. But the work was handicapped by the fact that in 150 years the Catholic church had ordained but seven Negro priests and most of the schools and seminaries refuse, even today, to admit Negro students. It began the new proselyting by giving charity to the very poor and ignorant, and as these entered the church, they hastened to segregate in separate congregations under white priests, who usually had not the faintest conception of the problems of these black folk.

AFRICAN MISSIONS

The Methodist church, south, got rid of Negroes absolutely and formed a new Negro church. The Northern Methodist church segregated them into separate conferences, and several times they invited all of them to join the Negro Methodists. Today, the Negro membership of the Methodist Episcopal church is almost entirely a separate institution, although it is still represented in the general conference. The Baptists have no national unity and are separated individually into colored and white churches, which more and more have no common meeting ground, although there is some cooperation in education and missionary work. The Episcopal church is divided, with very few exceptions, into colored and white congregations, and for its colored congregations it has ordained black bishops.

Thus, gradually the Christian church has lessened its support of Negro education; has seldom taken any stand against lynching and mob violence; against discrimination, or even against laws which in most states of the union class all Negro women and prostitutes together, so far as legal marriage with whites is concerned.

The Christian church thus acquiesced in a new and strict drawing of the color line, not only in political and civil life, but even in church work. Nothing illustrates this better than the attitude of white churches today toward Christian missions in Africa. Remember, that the whole argument of the church for centuries in support of Negro slavery was that this was God's method of redeeming heathen Africa. For a long time this was interpreted as meaning that a few slaves were to be converted to Christianity; then, as gradually voluntary emancipation freed more of the slaves, these slaves were to return to Africa and be the efficient and logical means of converting the Africans.

NEGROES AND MISSIONS

Numbers of American Negroes today would be willing to work in Africa. What does the Christian church say to this? Out of 158 African missionaries in 1928, the Protestant Episcopal church had 1 American Negro; the Presbyterian 2 out of 88; the Northern Baptists 1 out of 20; the Methodist Episcopal church 5 out of 91; the American board 4 out of 97. Of 793 other missionaries to Africa sent out by American missionary societies, including the United Presbyterians, the United Missionary society, the United Brethren-in-Christ, the Southern Baptists, the African Inland mission, the Friends, the Women's general mission society of the United Presbyterian church, the Lutherans, and the Sudan Interior mission, there is not a single American Negro!

What is the reason for this? As a matter of fact, missionary societies of the United States started out, for the most part, with the obvious policy of sending Negroes to convert Africa. Then they found out that this involved social equality between white and black missionaries; the paying of Negro missionaries on the same scale as white missionaries, and their promotion and treatment as civilized beings. With few exceptions, American white Christianity could not stand this, and they consequently changed their policy.

LESS DISCRIMINATION OUTSIDE CHURCH

Here, then, we may well pause and let the matter stand, with this summing up of the situation: the Christian church in this country, on the whole, instead of exhibiting itself as a unifying human force, moving toward the brotherhood of men, regardless of lines of color, condition or caste, has shown less unity than almost any other human institution. In education, we have a great deal of separation by color and race; nevertheless, throughout most of the country, and in the case of the majority of its inhabitants, white and colored children attend the same school, and to some extent, white and colored teachers teach regardless of race, as in New York city. In labor and general economic organization, there is widespread separation by race in the United States. Nevertheless, both white and black labor is employed in the United States side by side in many of the great industries. In literature and art, and to some extent in science, there is a great deal less discrimination by race than there is in Christianity. Even in matters of amusement and public enjoyment, colored people more often attend the same parks, the same theater and the same movie house and enjoy equal treatment in the same institutions for public entertainment, than they attend the same church.

Thus, the record of the church, so far as the Negro is concerned, has been almost complete acquiescence in caste, until today there is in the United States no organization that is so completely split along the color line as the Christian church—the very organization that according to its tenets and beliefs should be no respecter of persons and should draw no line between white and black, "Jew or Gentile, barbarian, Scythian, bond or free."

TOO MUCH TO HOPE

Looking these facts squarely in the face, what can we say as to the possibility of the church in the future settling the problem of the color line and leading the world toward treating Negroes and colored peoples as men and brothers? If we conceive the church as a social organization of well-meaning but average human beings, we can only hope that while they will not lead public opinion toward world brotherhood, yet as they see the light and the trend, they will be willing, slowly but surely, to follow, and just as they came to recognize the freedom of the slave, they will in time come to conceive the essential equality of all men. But it is too much to imagine that an organization will oppose wealth and power and withstand respectable conservatism by choosing the right first and adhering at any social cost to the choice which its principles and conscience dictate.

This conception of the church is violently repudiated by all but the most advanced and radical religionists. The church, as a whole, insists on a divine mission and divine guidance and the indisputable possession of the truth. Is there anything in the record of the church in America in regard to the Negro to prove this? There is not. If the treatment of the Negro by the Christian church is called "divine," this is an attack on the conception of God more blasphemous than any which the church has always been so ready and eager to punish.

WHAT OF THE FUTURE?

Thus, judging from the past, I see no reason to think that the attitude of the Christian church toward problems of race and caste is going to be anything different from its attitude in the past. It is mainly a social organization, pathetically timid and human; it is going to stand on the side of wealth and power; it is going to espouse any cause which is sufficiently popular, with eagerness; it is, on the other hand, often going to transgress its own fine ethical statements and be deaf to its own Christ in unpopular and weak causes. And then when human brotherhood is a fact and the color line is remembered only as a fatal aberration and disease of the twentieth century, the Christian church, if it still survives, is going to take the same attitude which it took after emancipation in 1863: from a thousand pulpits it will thunder the triumph of

Christianity and the way in which the Lord has led his people.

From *The Christian Century*: Journal of Religion, Vol. 68, No. 49, December 9, 1931, pp. 1554–56. Copyright 1931 Christian Century Foundation. Reprinted by permission.

The Vast Miracle of China Today (1959)

A Report on a Ten-Week Visit to the People's Republic of China

I have traveled widely on this earth since my first trip to Europe 67 years ago. Save South America and India, I have seen most of the civilized world and much of its backward regions. Many leading nations I have visited repeatedly. But I have never seen a nation which so amazed and touched me as China in 1959.

I have seen more impressive buildings but no more pleasing architecture; I have seen greater display of wealth, and more massive power; I have seen better equipped railways and boats and vastly more showy automobiles; but I have never seen a nation where human nature was so abreast of scientific knowledge; where daily life of everyday people was so outstripping mechanical power and love of life so triumphing over human greed and envy and selfishness as I see in China today.

It is not a matter of mere numbers and size; of wealth and power; of beauty and style. It is a sense of human nature free of its most hurtful and terrible meannesses and of a people full of joy and faith and marching on in a unison unexampled in Holland, Belgium, Britain and France; and simply inconceivable in the United States.

A typical, ignorant American put it this way in Moscow: "But how do you make it go without niggers?" In China he would have said: "But see them work": dragging, hauling, lifting, pulling—and yet smiling at each other, greeting neighbors who ride by in autos, helping strangers even if they are "niggers"; seeking knowledge, following leaders and believing in themselves and certain destiny. Whence comes this miracle of human nature, which I never saw before or believed possible?

I was ten weeks in China. There they celebrated my 91st birthday with a thoughtfulness and sincerity that would simply be impossible in America even among my own colored people. Ministers of state were there, writers and artists, actors and professional men; singers and children playing fairy tales. Anna Louise Strong came looking happy, busy and secure. There was a whole table of other Americans, exiled for daring to visit China; integrated for their skills and loyalty.

I have traveled 5,000 miles, by railway, boat, plane and auto. I saw all the great cities: Peking, Shanghai, Hankow and its sisters; Canton, Chungking, Chengtu, Kunming and Nanking. I rode its vast rivers tearing through mighty gorges; passed through its villages and sat in its communes. I visited its schools and colleges, lectured and broadcast to the world. I visited its minority groups. I was on the borders of Tibet when the revolt occurred. I spent four hours with Mao Tse-tung and dined twice with Chou En-lai, the tireless Prime Minister of this nation of 680 million souls.

The people of the land I saw: the workers, the factory hands, the farmers and laborers, scrubwomen and servants. I went to theaters and restaurants, sat in the homes of the high and the low; and always I saw happy people; people with faith that needs no church nor priest and laughs gaily when the Monkey King fools the hosts of Heaven and overthrows the angels.

In all my wandering, I never felt the touch or breath of insult or even dislike—I who for 90 years in America scarcely ever saw a day without some expression of hate for "niggers."

What is the secret of China in the second half of the twentieth century? It is that the vast majority of a billion human beings have been convinced that human nature in some of its darkest recesses can be changed, if change is necessary. China knows, as no other people know, to what depths human meanness can go.

I used to weep for American Negroes, as I saw through what indignities and repressions and cruelties they had passed; but as I have read Chinese history in these last months and had it explained to me stripped of Anglo-Saxon lies, I know that no depths of Negro slavery have plumbed such abysses as the Chinese have seen for 2,000 years and more.

They have seen starvation and murder: rape and prostitution; sale and slavery of children; and religion cloaked in opium and gin, for converting the "Heathen." This oppression and contempt came not only from Tartars, Mongolians, British, French, Germans and Americans, but from Chinese themselves: Mandarins and warlords, capitalists and murdering thieves like Chiang Kai-shek; Kuomintang socialists and intellectuals educated abroad.

Despite all this, China lives, and has been transformed and marches on. She is not ignored by the United States. She ignores the United States and leaps forward. What did it? What furnished the motive power and how was it applied?

First it was the belief in himself and in his people by a man like Sun Yat-sen. He plunged on, blind and unaided, repulsed by Britain and America, but welcomed by Russia. Then efforts toward socialism, which wobbled forward, erred and lost, and at last was bribed by America and Britain and betrayed by Chiang Kai-shek, with its leaders murdered and its aims misunderstood, when not deliberately lied about.

Then came the Long March from feudalism, past capitalism and socialism to communism in our day. Mao Tse-tung, Chou En-lai, Chu Teh and a half dozen others undertook to lead a nation by example, by starving and fighting; by infinite patience and above all by making a nation believe that the people and not merely the elite—the workers in factory, street, and field—composed the real nation. Others have said this often, but no nation has tried it like the Soviet Union and China.

And the staggering and bitter effort of the Soviets, beleaguered by all Western civilization, and yet far-seeing enough to help weaker China even before a still weak Russia was safe—on this vast pyramid has arisen the saving nation of this stumbling, murdering, hating world.

In China the people—the laboring people, the people who in most lands are the doormats on which the reigning thieves and murdering rulers walk, leading their painted and jeweled prostitutes—the people walk and boast. These people of the slums and gutters and kitchens are the Chinese nation today. This the Chinese believe and on this belief they toil and sweat and cheer.

They believe this and for the last ten years their belief has been strengthened until today they follow their leaders because these leaders have never deceived them. Their officials are incorruptible, their merchants are honest, their artisans are reliable, their workers who dig and haul and lift do an honest day's work and even work overtime if the state asks it, for they are the State; they are China.

A kindergarten, meeting in the once Forbidden City, was shown the magnificence of this palace and told: "Your fathers built this, but now it is yours; preserve it." And then pointing across the Ten An Men square to the vast building of the new Halls of Assembly, the speaker added: "Your fathers are building new palaces for you; enjoy them and guard them for yourselves and your children. They belong to you!"

China has no rank nor classes; her universities grant no degrees; her government awards no medals. She has no blue book of "society." But she has leaders of learning and genius, scientists of renown, artisans of skill and millions who know and believe this and follow where these men lead. This is the joy of this nation, its high belief and its unfaltering hope.

China is no utopia. Fifth Avenue has better shops where the rich can buy and the whores parade. Detroit has more and better cars. The best American housing outstrips the Chinese and Chinese women are not nearly as well-dressed as the guests of the Waldorf-Astoria. But the Chinese worker is happy.

He has exorcised the Great Fear that haunts the West: the fear of losing his job; the fear of falling sick; the fear of accident; the fear of inability to educate his children; the fear of daring to take a vacation. To guard against such catastrophe Americans skimp and save, cheat and steal, gamble and arm for murder.

The Soviet citizen, the Czech, the Pole, the Hungarian have kicked out the stooges of America and the hoodlums set to exploit the peasants. They and the East Germans no longer fear these disasters; and above all the Chinese sit high above these fears and laugh with joy.

They will not be rich in old age. They will not enjoy sickness but they will be healed. They will not starve as thousands of Chinese did only a generation ago. They fear neither flood nor epidemic. They do not even fear war, as Mao Tse-tung told me. War for China is a "Paper Tiger." China can defend itself and back of China stands the unassailable might of the Soviet Union.

Envy and class hate is disappearing in China. Does your neighbor have better pay and higher position than you? He has this because of greater ability or better education, and more education is open to you and compulsory for your children.

The young married couple do not fear children. The mother has prenatal care. Her wage and job are safe. Nursery and kindergarten take care of the child and it is welcome, not to pampered luxury but to good food, constant medical care and education for his highest ability.

All this is not yet perfect. Here and there it fails, falls short and falters; but it is so often and so widely true, that China believes, lives on realized hope, follows its leaders and sings: "O, Mourner, get up offa your knees." The women of China are free. They wear pants so that they can walk, climb and dig; and climb and dig they do. They are not dressed simply for sex indulgence and beauty parades. They occupy positions from ministers of state to locomotive engineers, lawyers, doctors, clerks and laborers. They are escaping household "drudgery"; they are strong and healthy and beautiful not simply of leg and false bosom but of real brain and brawn.

In Wuhan, I stood in one of the greatest steelworks of the world. A crane which moved a hundred tons loomed above. I said, "My God, Shirley, look up there!" Alone in the engine-room sat a girl with ribboned braids, running the vast machine.

You won't believe this, because you never saw anything like it; and if the State Department has its way, you never will. Let *Life* lie about communes; and the State Department shed crocodile tears over ancestral tombs. Let Hong Kong wire its lies abroad. Let "Divine Slavery" persist in Tibet until China kills it. The truth is there and I saw it.

America makes or can make no article that China is not either making or can make better and cheaper. I saw its export exposition in Canton: a whole building of watches, radios, electric apparatus, cloth in silk and wool and cotton; embroidery, pottery, dishes, shoes, telephone sets. There were five floors of goods which the world needs and is buying in increasing quantities, except the ostrich United States, whose ships rot.

Fifteen times I have crossed the Atlantic and once the Pacific. I have seen the world. But never so vast and glorious a miracle as China.

From the *National Guardian*, June 8, 1959

China and Africa (1959)

By courtesy of the government of the 680 million people of the Chinese Republic, I am permitted on my ninety-first birthday to speak to the people of China and Africa and through them to the world. Hail, then, and farewell, dwelling places of the yellow and black races. Hail human kind!

I speak with no authority: no assumption of age or rank; I hold no position, I have no wealth. One thing alone I own and that is my own soul. Ownership of that I have even while in my own country for near a century I have been nothing but a "nigger." On this basis and this alone I dare speak, I dare advise.

China after long centuries has arisen to her feet and leapt forward. Africa arise, and stand straight, speak and think!

Act! Turn from the West and your slavery and humiliation for the last 500 years and face the rising sun. Behold a people, the most populous nation on this ancient earth which has burst its shackles, not by boasting and strutting, not by lying about its history and its conquests, but by patience and long suffering, by hard, backbreaking labor and with bowed head and blind struggle, moved up and on toward the crimson sky. She aims to "make men holy; to make men free." But what men? Not simply the rich, but not excluding the rich. Not simply the learned, but led by knowledge to the end that no man shall be poor, nor sick, nor ignorant; but that the humblest worker as well as the sons of emperors shall be fed and taught and healed and that there emerge on earth a single unified people, free, well and educated.

You have been told, my Africa: My Africa in Africa and all your children's children overseas; you have been told and the telling so beaten into you by rods and whips, that you believe it yourselves, that this is impossible; that mankind can only rise by walking on men; by cheating them and killing them; that only on a doormat of the despised and dying, the dead and rotten, can a British aristocracy, a French cultural elite or an American millionaire be nurtured and grown. This is a lie. It is an ancient lie spread by church and state, spread by priest and historian, and believed in by fools and cowards, as well as by the down-trodden and the children of despair.

Speak, China, and tell your truth to Africa and the world. What people have been despised as you have? Who more than you have been rejected of men? Recall when lordly Britishers threw the rickshaw money on the ground to avoid touching a filthy hand. Forget not, the time, when in Shanghai no "Chinaman" dared set foot in a park which he paid for. Tell this to Africa, for today Africa stands on new feet, with new eyesight, with new brains and asks: Where am I and why? The Western sirens answer; Britain wheedles; France cajoles; while America, my America, where my ancestors and descendants for eight generations have lived and toiled; America loudest of all, yells and promises freedom. If only Africa allows American investment. Beware Africa, America bargains for your soul. America would have you believe that they freed your grandchildren; that Afro-Americans are full American citizens, treated like equals, paid fair wages as workers, promoted for desert and free to learn and earn and travel across the world. This is not true. Some are near freedom; some approach equality with whites; some have achieved education; but the price for this has too often been slavery of mind, distortion of truth and oppression of our own people. Of 18 million Afro-Americans, 12 million are still second-class citizens of the United States, serfs in farming, low-paid laborers in industry, and repressed members of union labor. Most American Negroes do not vote. Even the rising six million are liable to insult and discrimination at any time.

But this, Africa, relates to your descendants, not to you. Once I thought of you Africans as children, whom we educated Afro-Americans would lead to liberty. I was wrong. We could not even lead ourselves, much less you. Today I see you rising under your own leadership, guided by your own brains.

Africa does not ask alms from China nor from the Soviet Union nor from France, Britain, nor the United States. It asks friendship and sympathy and no nation better than China can offer this to the Dark Continent. Let it be given freely and generously. Let Chinese visit Africa, send their scientists there and their artists and writers. Let Africa send its students to China and its seekers after knowledge. It will not find on earth a richer goal, a more promising mine of information. On the other hand, watch the West. The new British West Indian Federation is not a form of democratic progress but a cunning attempt to reduce these islands to the control of British and American investors. Haiti is dying under rich Haitian investors who with American money are enslaving the peasantry. Cuba is showing what the West Indies, Central and South America are suffering under American Big Business. The American worker himself does not always realize this. He has high wages and many comforts. Rather than lose these, he keeps in office by his vote the servants of industrial exploitation so long as they maintain his wage. His labor leaders represent exploitation and not the fight against the exploitation of labor by private capital. These two sets of exploiters fall out only when one demands too large a share of the loot. This China knows. This Africa must learn. This the American Negro has failed so far to learn. I am frightened by the so-called friends who are flocking to Africa. Negro Americans trying to make money from your toil, white Americans who seek by investment at high interest to bind you in serfdom to business as the Near East is bound and as South America is struggling with. For this America is tempting your leaders, bribing your young scholars, and arming your soldiers. What shall you do?

First, understand! Realize that the great mass of mankind is freeing itself from wage slavery, while private capital in Britain, France, and now in America, is still trying to maintain civilization and comfort for a few on the toil, disease and ignorance of the mass of men. Understand this, and understanding comes from direct knowledge. You know America and France and Britain to your sorrow. Now know the Soviet Union and its allied nations, but particularly know China.

China is flesh of your flesh and blood of your blood. China is colored and knows to what a colored skin in this modern world subjects its owner. But China knows more, much more than this: she knows what to do about it. She can take the insults of the United States and still hold her head high. She can make her own machines or go without machines, when America refuses to sell her American manufacturers even, and throws her workers out of jobs, though it hurts American industry, China does not need American nor British missionaries to teach her religion and scare her with tales of hell. China has been in hell too long, not to believe in a heaven of her own making. This she is doing.

Come to China, Africa, and look around. Invite Africa to come, China, and see what you can teach just by pointing. Yonder old woman is working on the street. But she is happy. She has no fear. Her children are in school and a good school. If she is ill, there is a hospital where she is cared for free of charge. She has a vacation with pay each year. She can die and be buried without taxing her family to make some undertaker rich.

Africa can answer: but some of this we have done; our tribes undertake public service like this. Very well, let your tribes continue and expand this work. What Africa must realize is what China knows: that it is worse than stupid to allow a people's education to be under the control of those who seek not the progress of the people but their use as means of making themselves rich and powerful. It is wrong for the University of London to control the University of Ghana. It is wrong for the Catholic church to direct the education of the black Congolese. It was wrong for Protestant churches supported by British and American wealth to control higher education in China. The Soviet Union is surpassing the world in popular and higher education, because from the beginning it started its own complete educational system.

The essence of the revolution in the Soviet Union and China and in all the "iron curtain" nations, is not the violence that accompanied the change: no more than starvation at Valley Forge was the essence of the American revolution again Britain. The real revolution is the acceptance on the part of the nation of the fact that hereafter the main object of the nation is the welfare of the mass of the people and not of a lucky few.

Government is for the people's progress and not for the comfort of an aristocracy. The object of industry is the welfare of the workers and not the wealth of the owners. The object of civilization is the cultural progress of the mass of workers and not merely of an intellectual elite. And in return for all this, communist lands believe that the cultivation of the mass of people will discover more talent and genius to serve the state than any closed aristocracy ever furnished. This belief the current history of the Soviet Union and China is proving true each day. Therefore don't let the West invest when you can avoid it. Don't buy capital from Britain, France and the United States if you can get it on reasonable terms from the Soviet Union and China. This is not politics; it is common sense. It is learning from experience. It is trusting your friends and watching your enemies.

Refuse to be cajoled or to change your way of life so as to make a few of your fellows rich at the expense of a mass of workers growing poor and sick and remaining without schools so that a few black men can have automobiles.

Africa, here is a real danger which you must avoid or return to the slavery from which you are emerging. All I ask from you is the courage to know; to look about you and see what is happening in this old and tired world; to realize the extent and depth of its rebirth and the promise which glows on yonder hills.

Visit the Soviet Union and visit China. Let your youth learn the Russian and Chinese languages. Stand together in this new world and let the old world perish in its greed or be born again in new hope and promise. Listen to the Hebrew prophet of communism:

Ho! every one that thirsteth; come ye to the waters; come, buy and eat, without money and without price!

Again, China and Africa, hail and farewell!

From *The World and Africa*, enlarged edition, 1965 by International Publishers, pp. 311–16; also in *New World Review*, April, 1959

India's Relation to Negroes and the Color Problem (*1965*)

To most Indians, the problem of American Negroes—of twelve million people swallowed in a great nation, as compared with the more than three hundred millions of India—may seem unimportant. It would be very easy for intelligent Indians to succumb to the wide-spread propaganda that these Negroes have neither brains nor ability to take a decisive part in the modern world. On the other hand, American Negroes have long considered that their destiny lay with the American people; that their object was to become full American citizens and eventually lose themselves in the nation by continued intermingling of blood. But there are many things that have happened and are happening in the modern world to show that both these lines of thought are erroneous. The American

Negroes belong to a group which went through the fire of American slavery and is now a part of the vast American industrial organization; nevertheless, it exists as a representative of two hundred or more million Negroes in Africa, the West Indies and South America. In many respects, although not all, this group may be regarded as the leading intelligentsia of the black race and no matter what its destiny in America, its problem will never be settled until the problem of the relation of the white and colored races is settled throughout the world.

India has also had temptation to stand apart from the darker peoples and seek her affinities among the whites. She has long wished to regard herself as "Aryan" rather than "colored" and to think of herself as much nearer physically and spiritually to Germany and England than to Africa, China or the South Seas. And yet the history of the modern world shows the futility of this thought. European exploitation desires the black slave, the Chinese coolie and the Indian laborer for the same ends and the same purposes, and calls them all "niggers."

If India has her castes, American Negroes have in their own internal color lines the plain shadow of a caste system. For American Negroes have a large infiltration of white blood and the tendency to measure worth by the degree of this mulatto strain.

The problem of the Negroes thus remain a part of the world-wide clash of color. So, too, the problem of the Indians can never be simply a problem of autonomy in the British commonwealth of nations. They must always stand as representatives of the colored races—as the yellow and black peoples as well as the brown—of the majority of mankind, and together with the Negroes they must face the insistent problem of the assumption of the white peoples of Europe that they have a right to dominate the world and especially so to organize it politically and industrially as to make most men slaves and servants.

This attitude on the part of the white world has doubtless softened since the (First) World War. Nevertheless the present desperate attempt of Italy in Ethiopia and the real reasons back of the unexpected opposition on the part of the League of Nations, show that the ideals of the white world have not yet essentially changed. If now the colored peoples —Negroes, Indians, Chinese and Japanese—are going successfully to oppose these assumptions of white Europe, they have got to be sure of their own attitude toward their laboring masses. Otherwise they will substitute for the exploitation of colored by white races, an exploitation of colored races by colored men. If, however, they can follow the newer ideals which look upon labor as the only real and final repository of political power, and conceive that the freeing of the human spirit and real liberty of life will only come when industrial exploitation has ceased and the struggle to live is not confined to a mad fight for food, clothes and shelter; then and only then, can the union of the darker races bring a new and beautiful world, not simply for themselves, but for all men.

From Aptheker's "Du Bois' Unpublished Writings" in *Freedomways* (Memorial Issue), First Quarter, 1965, pp. 115–17

Postscript
The Color Line (1903)

I have seen a land right merry with the sun, where children sing, and rolling hills lie like passioned women wanton with harvest. And there in the King's Highway sat and sits a figure veiled and bowed, by which the traveller's footsteps hasten as they go. On the fainted air broods fear. Three centuries' thought has been the raising and unveiling of that bowed human heart, and now behold a century new for the duty and the deed. The Problem of the Twentieth Century is the Problem of the Color Line.

From "Of the Dawn of Freedom" in *The Souls of Black Folk*, 1903, p. 40

The Modern Labor Problem (*1935*)

Here is the real modern labor problem. Here is the kernel of the problem of Religion and Democracy, of Humanity. Words and futile gestures avail nothing. Out of the exploitation of the dark proletariat comes the Surplus Value filched from human beasts which in cultured lands, the Machine and harnessed Power veil and conceal. The emancipation of man is the emancipation of labor and the emancipation of labor is the freeing of that basic majority of Workers who are yellow, brown and black.

From "The Black Worker" in *Black Reconstruction*, 1935, p. 16

. . . the plight of the white working class throughout the world today is directly traceable to Negro slavery in America, on which modern commerce and industry was founded, and which persisted to threaten free labor until it was partially overthrown in 1863. The resulting color caste founded and retained by capitalism was adopted, forwarded and approved by white labor, and resulted in subordination of colored labor to white profits the world over. Thus the majority of the world's laborers, by the insistence of white labor, became the basis of a system of industry which ruined democracy and showed its perfect fruit in World War and Depression.

From "The White Worker" in *Black Reconstruction*, 1935, p. 30

On Truth (*1961*)

. . . there are no two sides to every question but only one Truth which must be found and followed—or disaster follows. Disaster, therefore, threatens the West for it is still determined to live off the slave labor and stolen materials of the "backward" world forever, and this in spite of the revolt of Asia, South America and Africa.

From the *National Guardian*, 1961

PART FOUR

Youth: Afro-America and Africa

I. The Ideals of Youth—
The Challenge of Truth—Honesty—
Integrity—Courage—Selflessness—
Sacrifice—Work—Knowledge and
Reason—(Commencement Addresses
to Negro Graduates)

Prescript
"The Immortal Child" (1920)

IF A MAN die shall he live again? We do not know. But this we do know, that our children's children live forever and grow and develop toward perfection as they are trained. All human problems, then, center in the Immortal Child and his education is the problem of problems. . . .

A world guilty of this last mightiest war has no right to enjoy or create until it has made the future safe from another Arkansas or Rheims. To this there is but one patent way, proved and inescapable, education, and that not for me or you but for the Immortal Child. All children are the children of all and not of individuals and families and races. The whole generation must be trained and guided and out of it as out of a huge reservoir must be lifted all genius, talent, and intelligence to serve all the world.

From "The Immortal Child" in *Darkwater*, 1920, pp. 193–217

Youth—A Different Kind (1926)

Who shall restore to men the glory of sunsets and the peace of quiet sleep?

We black people may help for we have within us as a race new stirrings; stirrings of the beginning of a new appreciation of Joy, of a new desire to create, of a new will to be; as though in this morning of group life we had awakened from some sleep that at once dimly mourns the past and dreams a splendid future; and there has come the conviction that the Youth that is here today, the Negro Youth, is a different kind of Youth, because in some new way it bears this mighty prophecy on its breast, with a new realization of itself, with new determination for all mankind.

From "Criteria of Negro Art" in *The Crisis*, Vol. 32, No. 6, October, 1926, pp. 290–97

St. Francis of Assisi (1907)

Delivered at the Joint Commencement Exercises of Miner Normal School, M Street High School, and Armstrong Manual Training School, Washington, D.C., June, 1907

We have all been recently talking and thinking of San Francisco, that opulent, busy city which one day faced the shining western waters and next fell into poverty, death and ruin because beneath its feet the earth trembled. And then again in its staggering rise it has been swept by greed and prejudice, and the throes of its new birth. Such strange catastrophe gives the whole world pause; it is not new, it is old, so old, and yet ever and again we need to be reminded that back of the hurrying throbbing life of every city and every

One of the first, if not the first of Dr. Du Bois' commencement addresses, was delivered in 1904, to Negro graduates of a school in Washington, D.C., on the subject "The Joy of Living." Dr. Herbert Aptheker, to whom Dr. Du Bois entrusted much of his writings before leaving for Africa, had this address published, perhaps for the first time, in *Political Affairs: Theoretical Journal of the Communist Party, USA.*, Vol. XLIV, No. 2, February, 1965, pp. 35–44.

My request for permission to include "The Joy of Living" in this collection was refused. Undoubtedly, it will appear in a collection of Dr. Du Bois' writings which it has been said Dr. Aptheker is now compiling for publication. When the reader has access to "The Joy of Living," it should be considered as first, both in time of delivery and in historical setting, of this group of commencement addresses.

Commencement addresses delivered at Johnson C. Smith and Dillard Universities along with other items, were deleted from this collection because of space considerations.

day lie the world-old things—birth and death, joy and sorrow, fraud and fear, human love and human hate—that these
and these alone make life; and with these each life must
deal.

We remember this all the more keenly in the case of San
Francisco because of the magic spell of the city's golden
history and because of the life of the man after whom this
stricken metropolis was named: He stands forth in the
world's annals as one of those saints and prophets who
sought to read life's riddle and tell the world its true unraveling. San Francisco is the Spanish form of the name of St.
Francis of Assisi, and it is to this life and life teaching that I
want to call your attention tonight; the fullness of his young
manhood and his riper years lay in the thirteenth century:
that last great cycle of the Middle Ages, seven hundred long
years ago. It is hard to picture the life of other years and
other centuries, and yet remember that there lived boys and
girls then, throbbing with life as you are, listening and waiting for the call. It was the day of Dante and Philip the Fair;
the day when Venice and Genoa were in the first flush of
their glory, and the German Hansa towns were building their
quaint and beautiful halls. All through the world ran the
thrill of that restless striving and awakening; then it was that
a boy was born in the Italian city of Assisi, in Umbria,
perhaps a hundred miles north of Rome. His father, Pietro
Bernardone, was a rich merchant trading to France, and
while the mother would proudly call the boy John, the father
proudly called him Francis after his rich and beloved France,
and showered his wealth upon him. Wealth then meant even
more than wealth means now, and now it means much.
Think of a handsome, red-blooded boy, born in the beautiful
hills of a beautiful land, surrounded by luxury, pampered by
his parents, and flattered and bowed down to by all his little
world. Accompanied by a crowd of gay young fellows he
spent a glorious, roistering youth, fishing for trout and stur-
geon in the mountain streams, dancing in the merry springtime, drinking the clear white wine in summer, and feasting
in the red autumnal days.

Was not this a glorious life? Suppose that before you tonight stretched this glorious vista of wealth and laughter and gay abandon, would not you be perfectly happy? Probably you would. Probably for a time, life would be simply singing as it was for a time with Francis of Assisi.

After that, however, if you were honest and unselfish, if you opened your clear eyes and looked upon the real world, there would come to you as there came to this gay Italian seven hundred years ago a sense of vague discomfort, of unfilled destiny, of wasted power. There would rise a dim realization of the misery and sorrow of the world on which your strident gayety would fall amost as mockery, as blasphemy. Not that it would seem wrong to be joyful but rather that your joy alone would not suffice; not that it would be wrong to laugh, but that laughter would not cure all of the world's ills, and that the world has ills. Something would be lacking—a great dark void of crying want stretching forth out of the shadowy valley and up the tremulous sides of the great wide hills, crying till souls must listen, even in their laughter, your soul and mine, the soul of Socrates and Jesus Christ, and the soul of St. Francis of Assisi.

This time of listening, of pausing, of sudden assumption of responsibility we call Commencement—the Beginning of Life. To some of you it approaches in this celebration, to others it has come earlier than this, and still to others it will not come till many years have passed with their messages of warning and enlightenment. To St. Francis of Assisi it came just in his budding of manhood, and he paused in astonishment to ask these questions, old and ever new: what am I? And what is this world about me? And this world and I, how shall we live together in laughter and work?

So the youth sat him down in the sunshine and pondered, hearing the shouting of his companions afar, dreaming over the faint echos of music and seeing new meaning in sun and river. What thought came to him? The thought of every awakening young soul. Is life Joy? Yes and No. Yes, because it is right to be happy, and yet, No, because I cannot be happy in a world of misery. Is life Wealth? Yes and No. Yes, because wealth is but that stored and garnered work which ministers to men's wants, and yet, No, because there are human wants and aspirations that no heaped treasure can satisfy. Is life Glory and Fame? Yes and No. Yes, for fame is the right reward of work well done and yet, No, for much of the world's greatest applause is given for work ill done and undone.

So the boy pondered as all boys ponder, not consciously and clearly but subtly and half-doubtingly. When he faced the gift of joy, he threw himself into the mad vortex of delight and then slowly withdrew and looked on the pain and sorrow about him; when he faced the gift of wealth, he tossed away the gold lightly, spending like a prince, wearing his silken hose and velvet doublet, drinking and feasting until he noticed men starving by the roadside. He threw them alms, they seized them and were hungry again, and in their dull eyes he saw a greater, deeper hunger; "Not alms but a friend!" it cried. Then he faced the luring glory of fame; and what was fame in the Middle Ages but War? He donned the warrior's flashing uniform; he heard the martial music swelling on the olive crowned hills of Umbria; he listened to the tramping of a hundred horsemen as they cried, "Long live Assisi, down with Perugia!" Among the singing waters they thundered, drunk with the mad wine of conquest, in that great yellow Italian morning, but at evening they came wandering back. There was blood upon their garments, and the horror of murder in their souls. The damp sharp wind beat mercilessly on the naked misery of a soldier dying in a wayside ditch, and Francis of Assisi paused and undid the chased and silver buckle of his velvet cloak and laid it gently across the wretched man; and then all silently he rode into the night. And that night he turned suddenly, swiftly, as all men turn at the turning points of life, crying, " 'Not by wealth nor by violence but by my spirit,' saith the Lord." And he meant by this that the joy of the world was not to be gained by selfishness, not by force but by the broad bonds of human sympathy. And what was true seven hundred years ago, is it not true tonight?

Quaintly and cheerfully he began his life work. "Poverty shall be my bride," he said. Poverty and beggary would he wed, and wandering human charity would be his first calling. He gathered a little band about him, and thus St. Francis of

Assisi became the little brother of the poor, a beggar and an outcast among men, a listener to birds and little children. Nor does all this sound as strange today as it did in the year of our Lord 1208. We Americans have a certain contempt for the poor and unfortunate, but our attitude toward human misfortune is angelic beside the disdain of the thirteenth century. Then it was only the wealthy and well-born who were people. Beneath the knot of privileged aristocrats festered the mass of neglected despised poor—beggars and unfortunates, poor workingmen, cripples, feebled-minded and insane—all too far below the world, the good rich world, for the world to notice. When Francis turned from his idle playing and spending of wealth and his work of war and faced the bitter misery of the world, when he said, "The greatest evil of Italy is Poverty, and I will make the Lady Poverty my bride," his proud father Pietro threw up his hands in horror and disgust. "Fool," he cried, "to give up wealth, position and fame for a crazy cause; you are no son of mine." But Francis crossed his breast and cried, "Pietro, Pietro Bernardone, until now I have called you father, but henceforth I can truly say with these, 'Our Father who art in heaven,' for he is my wealth and hope." Out in the world then he wandered alone. His friends wagged their heads and laughed, as some friends will, but his mother waited. And then, not suddenly and triumphantly, but slowly, in weary years and sickening strife, after defeat and ridicule, persecution and doubt, came the new deep revelation. Along the dusty Italian roads moved roughclad silent men, gentle of speech, preaching Peace and Patience, tending the wounded, relieving the distressed and reclaiming the erring. It was the first great mediaeval effort at social reform, at organized charity, at the work of the visiting nurse. It was the first great recognition in the Middle Ages of the abject misery of the masses of men, the first listening to the wretched cry of outcast humanity.

The pebble thrown widened in ever circling waves of good until the beggar of 1208 stood at the head of the vast movement which swept the Christian world, dashed its spray on the strongholds of Mohammed, and which has lived even to our day. So St. Francis grew to busy, blameless, gentle life;

the friend of birds and living things, the helper of the poor
and needy; a homeless wanderer, yet standing before kings
and the mighty of the earth, until after less than fifty years of
life he found eternal rest on the vine-clad bosom of the
Apennines, and the marks of the sorrows of God rested on
his hands and heart.

Why have I brought you this old fashioned tale of the life
of a mediaeval saint? Century after century has rolled by
since his dust crumbled and floated in the mists that hover on
the head waters of the Arno and Tiber. The world has
changed its hastening, hurrying, hungry whirl of weal and
woe. Why should we look backward rather than forward for
our guiding star?

I have brought this life back to your memory to fix in your
minds a certain attitude toward wealth and distinction, and
the need and place of human training to emphasize this attitude. The lesson of St. Francis of Assisi is not the renunciation of wealth and the deification of poverty; it is on the
contrary simply this great truth: the work of the world is to
satisfy the world's wants. Now the world wants material
wealth, such as food and clothing and shelter, but this is not
all, nor even the greater part of its need; it wants human
service and human sympathy, it wants knowledge and inspiration, it wants hope and truth and beauty, and so great
are these greater wants, that often their satisfaction demands
in some St. Francis of Assisi an utter renunciation of much
of the material good of the world, that its spiritual starvation
may be satisfied. In the thirteenth century this was peculiarly
true. So poverty stricken was the world in simple human
goodness that it actually needed this more than it needed food
and clothes, and to this end a brave unselfish man addressed
himself. Today, in the twentieth century, the world is rich in
material resources and richer too than ever before in spiritual
content. And, yet, even today we are not so wealthy in
human sympathy that we can turn our attention wholly to
material wealth and neglect the greater wants of the world-
soul. On the countrary, our very excess of material accumulation and deftness of process is additional reason for increased

attention toward making men more intelligent, more unselfish, and more broadly human.

Thus is it not clear that with all the change in time and
circumstances there remain the same old questions of attitude
toward life? What am I? And what is the world? And this
world and I, how shall we laugh and work together?

Ever in this questioning the old human drama is acted
again and again on the hard grey bosom of the earth. Ever
the joyous youth arises in the great dim morning of life and
sees the golden lure of endless joy and wealth beckoning on
the horizon; ever the blood of the growing man hears the wild
trumpet blast of the still voice of wisdom, " 'Not by wealth nor
by violence but by my spirit,' saith the Lord." This was the
history of St. Francis of Assisi, and this will be your history,
my young friends. And for this reason I am asking you to
pause tonight and listen to the old story and learn the life
lesson it contains.

It will be fully easy, let me repeat, to misinterpret such a
history; to tell you that joy has no part in life, that wealth is
merely temptation, that fame is mockery, and that only by
total renunciation can come the real good of living. Yet this
would be wrong; this is untrue, and least of all does the life
of St. Francis teach this contradiction of life. Rather this
life emphasizes the beauty and joy of living, but not simply
for ourselves, rather for all men; his life emphasized the need
and use of work and wealth, but it also emphasizes the fact
that material wealth satisfies only a part of life's want and
that it maybe necessary to sacrifice a part or even the larger
part of material well-being for the advancement of science
and humanity. Indeed at all time human life must be a bal-
ancing of limited means against infinite ends, and while all
these objects are desirable, yet some are more desirable than
others, and the poverty of human energies and resources
forces us always to choose the more weighty and important
and let the others wait. In St. Francis' day this choosing left
him in direst physical poverty. In our day this is not
necessary, and yet the choosing of the greater needs of life
today by an individual and any nation precludes all the
thought of great individual wealth, for material wealth is not

man's sole aim, but rather wealth of mind and soul as well as
of body should be his ambition; and finally the life of St.
Francis shows that true fame, the only fame worth having and
striving for is the "Well done" of the master, who knows the
sweat of the toil and worth of the service.

Such is the lesson which in a thousand places the world is
seeking to teach its children, and this is the true object of the
educational system whose fruition and celebration you and
your friends represent tonight.

Put thus in terse and concrete meaning, what does the
twentieth century demand of youth who, standing at the
threshold of life, wish to do for their world something of
the work that St. Francis did for his? It demands, I take it,
four things: Ambition or Force, Ideal or Object, Renunciation or Unselfishness, Technique or Work.

First of all it demands ambition—the striving within your
soul of every latent power of doing, of all the slumbering fire,
the quickening of muscle and stretching of sinew and the
burning, scintillating flesh of brain, the whole massed might
of this wonderful human machine alert, panting, instinct with
holy zeal to hurl itself into the world's work. That was the
thing with which Francis of Assisi started: the fiery impulse,
the joyous enthusiasm, the unshaken determination to make
life tell for its utmost in spite of the contempt and mocking of
men or the machinations of the devil. This is the spirit that
must animate you, young men and women, as you step forth
in the world. I mean, too, by ambition not mere desire for
success, not the follow up of successful endeavor; any fool
can have that. But I mean grim grit, tenacious bull-dog courage to face defeat and disappointment and still aspire. That
defiant attitude toward the ills of life that Henley sang of
when he cried,

> Out of the night that covers me
> Black as the Pit from pole to pole,
> I thank whatever gods may be
> For my unconquerable soul.
>
> In the fell clutch of circumstance
> I have not winced nor cried aloud.

Under the bludgeonings of chance
My head is bloody, but unbowed. . . .

It matters not how strait the gate,
How charged with punishments the scroll,
I am the master of my fate.
I am the captain of my soul.

This dynamic power is the first demand of modern life, but alone this power is dangerous. It is the bridled charger stamping at the portcullis and chafing his bit; it is the armoured warrior gleaming in the morning sun, twisting and twirling his spear; but at the sight, the world trembles and cries, "Whither, to murder or rescue, to good or bad, to life or death?"

So tremulous with balanced possibilities of good and evil is ambitious youth at this life crisis that many good people at times half cry out against ambition, half preferring lifeless, nerveless, unwakened mediocrity to the stirrings of such infinite power as may, to be sure, knock at the gate of Heaven, and may just as surely rattle the doorposts of Hell. These days are the days when in a few weeks you may begin the greater life, and they are days when you may start in the paths that lead to crime and debauchery and the never ending throng of hearsed dead. This is the reason that in later years we hear so little said to Negro youth of ambition, power, and unconquerable resolve. Men fear you, and some fear lest with the might of power of manhood you may fail, and some, I shame to say, fear lest you may succeed. But I do not fear you because I know you. I know that being but human some of you must needs fail and the very force of your energy must drive you downward, but I know too that most of you will not fail but will triumph with the triumph of ten million.

The great efficient cause of this triumph, when it comes, will be your education. Life is not learned at a leap. This world is too old and complicated to be known by sudden inspiration. For this reason we educate children; for this reason the state seeks to give its future citizens the knowledge of the Tree of Life, lest in the evening they see the flaming of the sword of death.

But what does this education teach or essay to teach? It seeks to teach the other three of the four things mentioned: First. The ideals toward which civilization strives. Second. The good which can today be done. Third. The technical method by which each can help do this work. Or, as I have said, Ideal, that "one far off divine event toward which the whole creation moves"; Renunciation, which but means the choice of the best possible good for all out of the infinite desirable; and finally, Technique, of the best actual method of doing your share. Thus stated, the work of an educational system seems easy and clear, and it would be if the ideal were fixed and unchangeable, the duty of renunciation, clear and undoubted, and the technique of life, always the same. But this is far from true. Life is flux and changes. Ideals rise, expand and grow, and the choice of the better among the good is the most baffling of life's dark problems; and with every changing want, invention and discovery, the technique of industry and work changes.

Thus the educational system has within itself eternal conflict, it can never be final, it can only continually hold clear its vast aim to teach children the greater goals toward which men are striving, to teach them what of these are at present attainable, and then to give to mind and hand such training as shall make them efficient helpers in the world's work of attaining these goods.

In the working out of the details there must ever be thought, controversy, and often dispute.

I doubt not that many of my younger hearers and not a few of the older ones have been sorely puzzled in these later days as to the true aim and method of education, as were Pietro the father and Francis the son seven hundred years ago. On the one hand come those educators and seers crying, "Hitch your wagon to a star"; and on the other hand come the business men and artisans saying, "Learn by doing; earn a living." Now it does not settle the real conflict of thought and aim here expressed by assuming that there are two sides of the same device. There may be and there may not be. Given a St. Francis with holy zeal to relieve the wretchedness of outcast humanity, and it was the essence of wisdom to cry in his ear: learn by doing; succor the first beggar that crosses your path; systematize your work so that your followers may live and earn their living at this work. On the other hand, given Francis, son of Pietro, whose ideal of life was selfishly to display his wealth and fight and carouse, to tell him to learn by doing and earn that sort of living would be to send him to the devil as fast as money could pay the bills. So today, given young black men with the dynamic of ambition and add to this an education which, on the one hand, gives them ideals of human service and manly renunciation, and, on the other, teaches them something of the world's experience and the technique of modern industry, given these things you have a perfect system of training. But given young men and women of your age starting out with the idea that the chief object of living is to gain as much cash and personal applause as can be gotten without serious infraction of the criminal code, to add an ever so thorough a knowledge of the technique of modern industry to such low and perverted ideals is to disgrace the righteous ambition of a people and ruin the hope of the Negro race.

So long as the world consists of the fortunate and the unfortunate, the weaker and the stronger, the rich and the poor, true human service will involve ideal and renunciation. If you really have at heart the good of the world, you simply cannot give your whole time and energy to the selfish seeking of your personal good. If you wish the Negro race to become honest, intelligent, and rich, you cannot make accumulation of wealth for yourself the sole object of your education and life. The object of St. Francis of Assisi was not to make the world poorer by his poverty but richer. No doctrine of universal selfishness will ever reform society and lift men to the highest plane, simply because the world is too full of careless unfortunates and incompetent, vicious souls. While you are confining yourself to the work of selfishly raising yourself, these forces are dragging down a dozen of your neighbors and children. You must be your brother's keeper as well as your own, or your brother will drag you and yours down to his ruin.

The life of St. Francis teaches us, then, that renunciation is the inevitable first payment for healthy social uplift, not renunciation to poverty such as the thirteenth century demanded, for the twentieth century is placing physical poverty in the background, but certainly today among us a renunciation of dreams of great wealth and instead a contentment with humble means, along with deep unselfish devotion to a splendid cause. This is the equipment which is needed today as sadly and pressingly as in any century of the Middle Ages.

On the other hand, the further the world goes on its journey of civilization the greater the need of specialization and technique—men must know how to do the world's work. They must have the specialized skill, the knowledge, and insight to do a practical piece of the labor well. The skilled artisan approaches today the inspired artist, and both in common strive and sweat and toil. For what? For so much a day? No, for the glory of their handicraft, for the good their work does the human beings whose welfare is their own welfare. Their bride is not Poverty but Carpentry or Painting or Weariness or Pain, and their reward is the reward of St. Francis—a better, truer, richer world.

Thus the work of the public school is not on the one hand to fire aimless ambition without sound ideals; not to inspire human hearts with a vision of the true, the good, and the beautiful without pointing the practical way of realizing some of these dreams here and now in their own lives; not to imagine, on the one hand, that Desire and Knowledge alone will lift a race out of poverty and weakness, nor dream, on the other hand, that infinite skill with hammer or hoe will ever lead a man to do that which his native ambition and educated aspiration do not inspire him to do; remembering that in the colored schools particularly that great as is the need of a new race for technical skill and efficiency, there is even greater need for the lifting and training of the racial consciousness in knowledge and inspiration, renunciation and ideal.

I trust then, young men and women, that the years of training which this school has given you with great expenditure of money and human energy have placed you tonight on that great vantage ground where the burning ambition of your youth has been, on the one hand, inspired by ideals as broad and human as those that inspired St. Francis of Assisi, and has, on the other hand, taught you something of the actual technique of living and earning a living. If this is true, then it remains for me only to greet you and cry, God speed.

The careers you enter will be builded of interlaced joy and sorrow, shade and shine; and although shadow-hands from other worlds will join in that building, yet in your own hands will the major part of the making of your lives lie. Build well. Build stubbornly and doggedly, build carefully and painfully with skilled technique, but above all build by some large and worthy plan. Face defeat as cheerfully as triumph. Face success as coolly as defeat. Face everything that comes; and then, not only here tonight but there in the mists of God's great morning, when His darker children bring their hard-won triumphs up from the Gates of Despair and the Valley of the Shadow of Death, lay your laurels not on your own heads but at the feet of those mothers and fathers who have nurtured you and toiled for you and smoothed the way of your life with their own grey hairs and tears—with their own lifeblood.

As it was the great object of St. Francis of Assisi to bring peace and succor to the down-trodden of his day, let it be your highest ambition to be able one day to say to this heart-hurt and weary mother race of ours:

> Thy sun shall not more go down,
> Neither shall thy moon withdraw itself;
> For the Lord shall be thine everlasting light,
> And the days of thy mourning shall be ended.

From *Readings from Negro Authors for Schools and Colleges* by Otelia Cromwell, Lorenzo Dow Turner, and Eva B. Dykes, 1931, pp. 273–84

Education and Work (1930)

APOLOGY

Between the time that I was graduated from college and the day of my first experience at earning a living, there was arising in this land, and more especially within the Negro group, a controversy concerning the type of education which American Negroes needed. You, who are graduating today, have heard but echoes of this controversy and more or less vague theories of its meaning and its outcome. Perhaps it has been explained away to you and interpreted as mere misunderstanding and personal bias. If so, the day of calm review and inquiry is at hand. And I suppose that, of persons living, few can realize better than I just what that controversy meant and what the outcome is. I want then today in the short time allotted me, to state, as plainly as I may, the problem of college and industrial education for American Negroes, as it arose in the past; and then to restate it as it appears to me in its present aspect.

DILEMMA

First of all, let me insist that the former controversy was no mere misunderstanding; there was real difference of opinion, rooted in deep sincerity on every side and fought out with a tenacity and depth of feeling due to its great importance and fateful meaning.

It was, in its larger aspects, a problem such as in all ages human beings of all races and nations have faced; but it was new in 1895 as all Time is new; it was concentered and made vivid and present because of the immediate and pressing question of the education of a vast group of the children of former slaves. It was the ever new and age-young problem of Youth, for there had arisen in the South a Joseph which knew not Pharoah,—a black man who was not born in slavery. What was he to become? Whither was his face set? How should he be trained and educated? His fathers were slaves, for the most part, ignorant and poverty-stricken; emancipated in the main without land, tools, nor capital, —the sport of war, the despair of economists, the grave perplexity of Science. Their children had been born in the midst of controversy, of internecine hatred, and in all the economic dislocation that follows war and civil war. In a peculiar way and under circumstances seldom duplicated, the whole program of popular education became epitomized in the case of these young black folk.

FIRST EFFORTS

Before men thought or greatly cared, in the midst of the very blood and dust of battle, an educational system for the freedmen had been begun; and with a logic that seemed, at first, quite natural. The night school for adults had become the day school for children. The Negro day school had called for normal teaching and the small New England college had been transplanted and perched on hill and river in Raleigh and Atlanta, Nashville and New Orleans, and a half dozen other towns. This new Negro college was conceived of as the very foundation stone of Negro training. But, meantime, any formal education for slaves or the children of slaves not only awakened widespread and deep-seated doubt, fear and hostility in the South, but it posed, for statesmen and thinkers, the whole question as to what the education of Negroes was really aiming at, and indeed, what was the aim of educating any working class. If it was doubtful as to how far the social and economic classes of any modern state could be essentially transformed and changed by popular education, how much more tremendous was the problem of educating a race whose ability to assimilate modern training was in grave question and whose place in the nation and the world, even granted they could be educated, was a matter of baffling social philosophy. Was the nation making an effort to parallel white civilization in the South with a black civilization? Or was it trying to displace the dominant white master class with new black masters or was it seeking the difficult but surely more reasonable and practical effort of furnishing a trained set of free black laborers who might carry on in place of the violently disrupted slave system? Surely, most men said, this economic and industrial problem of the New South was the first—the central, the insistent problem of the day.

TWO SCHOOLS OF THOUGHT

There can be no doubt of the real dilemma that thus faced the nation, the Northern philanthropist and the black man. The argument for the New England college, which at first seemed to need no apology, grew and developed. The matter of man's earning a living, said the college, is and must be important, but surely it can never be so important as the man himself. Thus the economic adaptation of the Negro to the South must in education be subordinated to the great necessity of teaching life and culture. The South, and more especially the Negro, needed and must have trained and educated leadership if civilization was to survive. More than most, here was land and people who needed to learn the meaning of life. They needed the preparation of gifted persons for the profession of teaching, and for other professions which would in time grow. The object of education was not to make men carpenters but to make carpenters men.

On the other hand those practical men who looked at the South after the war said: this is an industrial and business age. We are on the threshold of an economic expansion such as the world never saw before. Whatever human civilization has been or may become, today it is industry. The South because of slavery has lagged behind the world. It must catch up. Its prime necessity after the hate and holocaust of war is a trained reliable laboring class. Assume if you will that Negroes are men with every human capacity, nevertheless, as a flat fact, no rising group of peasants can begin at the top. If poverty and starvation are to be warded off, the children of the freedmen must not be taught to despise the humble work, which the mass of the Negro race must for untold years pursue. The transition period between slavery and freedom is a dangerous and critical one. Fill the heads of these children with Latin and Greek and highfalutin' notions of rights and political power, and hell will be to pay.

On the other hand, in the South, here is land and fertile land, in vast quantities, to be had at nominal prices. Here are employers who must have skilled and faithful labor, and have it now. There is in the near future an industrial development coming which will bring the South abreast with the new economic development of the nation and the world. Freedom must accelerate this development which slavery so long retarded. Here then is no time for a philosophy of economic or class revolution and race hatred. There must be friendship and good will between employer and employee, between black and white. They have common interests, and the matter of their future relations in politics and society, can well be left for future generations and different times to solve. "Cast down your buckets where you are," cried Booker T. Washington; "In all things that are purely social we can be as separate as the fingers, yet one hand in all things essential to mutual progress."

What was needed, then, was that the Negro first should be made the intelligent laborer, the trained farmer, the skilled artisan of the South. Once he had accomplished this step in the economic world and the ladder was set for his climbing, his future would be assured, and assured on an economic foundation which would be immovable. All else in his development, if he proved himself capable of development, even to the highest, would inevitably follow. Let us have, therefore, not colleges but schools to teach the technique of industry and to make men learn by doing.

These were the opposing arguments. They were real arguments. They were set forth by earnest men, white and black, philanthropist and teacher, statesman and seer. The controversy waxed bitter. The disputants came to rival organizations, to severe social pressure, to anger and even to blows. Newspapers were aligned for and against; employment and promotion depended often on a Negro's attitude toward industrial education. The Negro race and their friends were split in twain by the intensity of their feeling and men were

labelled and ear-marked by their allegiance to one school of
thought or to the other.

PRESENT CONDITIONS

Today, all this past; by the majority of the older of my
hearers, it is practically forgotten. By the younger, it appears
merely as a vague legend. Thirty-five years, a full generation
and more, have elapsed. The increase in Negro education by
all measurements has been a little less than marvelous. In
1895, there were not more than 1,000 Negro students of full
college grade in the United States. Today, there are over
19,000 in college and nearly 150,000 in high schools. In
1895, 60 percent of American Negroes, ten years of age or
over, were illiterate. Today, perhaps three-fourths can read
and write. The increase of Negro students in industrial and
land grant colleges has been equally large. The latter have
over 16,000 students and the increasing support of the government of the states; while the great industrial schools, especially Hampton and Tuskegee, are the best endowed institutions for the education of black folk in the world.

WAS THE CONTROVERSY SETTLED?

What then has become of this controversy as to college and
industrial education for Negroes? Has it been duly settled, and
if it has, how has it been settled? Has it been transmuted into
a new program, and if so, what is that program? In other
words, what is the present norm of Negro education, represented at once by Howard University, Fisk and Atlanta on
one hand, and by Hampton Institute, Tuskegee, and the land
grant colleges on the other?

I answer once for all, the problem has not been settled. The
questions raised in those days of controversy still stand in all
their validity and all their pressing insistence on an answer.
They have not been answered. They must be answered, and
the men and women of this audience and like audiences
throughout the land are the ones from whom the world de-

mands final reply. Answers have been offered; and the present status of the problem has enormously changed, for human problems never stand still. But I must insist that the fundamental problem is still here.

WHAT THE COLLEGE HAS DONE

Let us see. The Negro college has done a great work. It has given us leadership and intelligent leadership. Doubtless, without these colleges the American Negro would scarcely have attained his present position. The chief thing that distinguishes the American Negro group from the Negro groups in the West Indies, and in South America, and the mother group in Africa, is the number of men that we have trained in modern education, able to cope with the white world on its own ground and in its own thought, method and language.

On the other hand, there cannot be the slightest doubt but that the Negro college, its teachers, students and graduates, have not yet comprehended the age in which they live: the tremendous organization of industry, commerce, capital, and credit which today forms a super-organization dominating and ruling the universe, subordinating to its ends government, democracy, religion, education and social philosophy; and for the purpose of forcing into the places of power in this organization American black men either to guide or help reform it, either to increase its efficiency or make it a machine to improve our well-being, rather than the merciless mechanism which enslaves us; for this the Negro college has today neither program nor intelligent comprehension.

On the contrary there is no doubt but that college and university training among us has had largely the exact effect that was predicted; it has turned an increasing number of our people not simply away from manual labor and industry, not simply away from business and economic reform, into a few well-paid professions, but it has turned our attention from any disposition to study or solve our economic problem. A disproportionate number of our college-trained students are crowding into teaching and medicine and beginning to swarm into other professions and to form at the threshold of these better-paid jobs, a white-collar proletariat, depending for their support on an economic foundation which does not yet exist.

Moreover, and perhaps for this very reason, the ideals of colored college-bred men have not in the last thirty years been raised an iota. Rather in the main, they have been lowered. The average Negro undergraduate has swallowed hook, line and sinker, the dead bait of the white undergraduate, who, born in an industrial machine, does not have to think, and does not think. Our college man today, is, on the average, a man untouched by real culture. He deliberately surrenders to selfish and even silly ideals, swarming into semi-professional athletics and Greek letter societies, and affecting to despise scholarship and the hard grind of study and research. The greatest meetings of the Negro college year like those of the white college year have become vulgar exhibitions of liquor, extravagance, and fur coats. We have in our colleges a growing mass of stupidity and indifference.

I am not counselling perfection; as desperately human groups, we must expect our share of mediocrity. But as hitherto a thick and thin defender of the college, it seems to me that we are getting into our Negro colleges considerably more than our share of plain fools.

Acquiring as we do in college no guidance to a broad economic comprehension and a sure industrial foundation, and simultaneously a tendency to live beyond our means, and spend for show, we are graduating young men and women with an intense and overwhelming appetite for wealth and no reasonable way of gratifying it, no philosophy for counteracting it.

Trained more and more to enjoy sexual freedom as undergraduates, we refuse as graduates to found and support even moderate families, because we cannot afford them; and we are beginning to sneer at group organization and race leadership as mere futile gestures.

Why is this? What is wrong with our colleges? The method of the modern college has been proven by a hundred centuries of human experience: the imparting of knowledge by the old to the young; the instilling of the conclusions of experience, "line upon line, and precept upon precept." But, of course, with this general and theoretical method must go a definite and detailed object suited to the present age, the present group, the present set of problems. It is not then in its method but in its practical objects that the Negro college has failed. It is handing on knowledge and experience but what knowledge and for what end? Are we to stick to the old habit of wasting time on Latin, Greek, Hebrew and eschatology, or are we to remember that, after all, the object of the Negro college is to place in American life a trained black man who can do what the world today wants done; who can help the world know what it ought to want done and thus by doing the world's work well may invent better work for a better world? This brings us right back to the object of the industrial school.

WHAT THE INDUSTRIAL SCHOOL HAS DONE

Negro industrial training in the United States has accomplishments of which it has a right to be proud; but it too has not solved its problem. Its main accomplishment has been an indirect matter of psychology. It has helped bridge the transition period between Negro slavery and freedom. It has taught thousands of white people in the South to accept Negro education, not simply as a necessary evil, but as a possible social good. It has brought state support to a dozen higher institutions of learning, and to some extent, to a system of public schools. On the other hand, it has tempered and rationalized the inner emancipation of American Negroes. It made the Negro patient when impatience would have killed him. If it has not made working with the hands popular, it has at least removed from it much of the stigma of social degradation. It has made many Negroes seek the friendship of their white fellow citizens, even at the cost of insult and caste. And thus through a wide strip of our country it has brought peace and not a sword.

But this has all been its indirect by-product, rather than its direct teaching. In its direct teaching, the kind of success which it has achieved differs from the success of the college.

In the case of the industrial school, the practical object was absolutely right and still is right: that is, the desire of placing in American life a trained black man who could earn a decent living and make that living the foundation stone of his own culture and of the civilization of his group. This was the avowed object of the industrial school. How much has it done toward this? It has established some skilled farmers and among the mass some better farming methods. It has trained and placed some skilled artisans; it has given great impetus to the domestic arts and household economy; it has encouraged Negro business enterprise. And yet we have but to remember these matters to make it patent to all that the results have been pitifully small compared with the need. Our Negro farm population is decreasing; our Negro artisans are not gaining proportionately in industry and Negro business faces today a baffling crisis. Our success in household arts is due not to our effective teaching so much as to the mediaeval minds of our women who have not yet entered the machine age. Most of them seem still to think that washing clothes, scrubbing steps and paring potatoes were among the Ten Commandments.

Why now has the industrial school with all its partial success, failed absolutely in its main object when that object of training Negroes for remunerative occupation is more imperative today than thirty-five years ago?

The reason is clear: if the college has failed because with the right general method it has lacked definite objects appropriate to the age and race; the industrial school has failed because with a definite object it lacked appropriate method to gain it. In other words, the lack of success of the industrial education of Negroes has come not because of the absence of desperate and devoted effort, but because of changes in the world which the industrial school did not foresee, and, which even if it had foreseen, it could not have prevented, and to which it had not the ability to adapt itself.

It is easy to illustrate this. The industrial school assumed that the technique of industry in 1895, even if not absolutely fixed and permanent, was at least permanent enough for training children into its pursuit and for use as a basis of broader education. Therefore, school work for farming, carpentry, bricklaying, plastering and painting, metal work and blacksmithing, shoemaking, sewing and cooking was introduced and taught. But, meantime, what has happened to these vocations and trades? Machines and new industrial organizations have remade the economic world and ousted these trades either from their old technique or their economic significance. The planing mill does today much of the work of the carpenter and the carpenter is being reduced rapidly to the plane of a mere laborer. The building trades are undergoing all kinds of reconstruction, from the machine-made steel skyscraper, to the cement house cast in molds and the mass-made mail-order bungalow. Painting and masonry still survive, but the machine is after them; while printing and sewing are done increasingly by elaborate machines. Metal is being shaped by stamping mills. Nothing of shoemaking is left for the hands save mending, and in most cases, it is cheaper to buy a new shoe than to have an old one cobbled. When it comes to the farm, a world-wide combination of circumstances is driving the farmer to the wall. Expensive machinery demands increasingly larger capital; excessive taxation of growing land values is eliminating the small owner; monopolized and manipulated markets and carriers make profits of the individual farmer small or nil; and the foreign competition of farms worked by serfs at starvation wages and backed by world-wide aggregations of capital—all this is driving farmers, black and white, from the soil and making the problem of their future existence one of the great problems of the modern world. The industrial school, therefore, found itself in the peculiar position of teaching a technique of industry in certain lines just at the time when that technique was changing into something different, and when the new technique was a matter which the Negro school could not teach. In fact, with the costly machine, with mass production and organized distribution, the teaching of technique becomes increasingly difficult. Any person of average intelligence can take part in the making of a modern automobile, and he is paid, not for his technical training, but for his endurance and steady application.

There were many lines of factory work, like the spinning

and weaving of cotton and wool, which the Negro could have successfully been set to learning, but they involved vast expenditures of capital which no school could control, and organized business at that time decreed that only white folk could work in factories. And that decree still stands. New branches of industry, new techniques are continually opening —like automobile repairing, electrical installments, and engineering—but these call for changing curricula and adjustments puzzling for a school and a set course of study.

In the attempt to put the Negro into business, so that from the inner seats of power by means of capital and credit he could control industry, we have fallen between two stools, this work being apparently neither the program of the college nor of the industrial school. The college treated it with the most approved academic detachment; while the industrial school fatuously assumed as permanent a business organization which began to change with the Nineteenth Century, and bids fair to disappear with the Twentieth. In 1895 we were preaching individual thrift and saving; the small retail store and the partnership for business and the conduct of industry. Today, we are faced by great aggregations of capital and world-wide credit, which monopolize raw material, carriage and manufacture, distribute their products through cartels, mergers and chain stores, and are in process of eliminating the individual trader, the small manufacturer, and the little job. In this new organization of business the colored man meets two difficulties: First, he is not trained to take part in it; and, secondly, if he gets training, he finds it almost impossible to gain a foothold. Schools cannot teach as an art and trade that which is a philosophy, a government of men, an organization of civilization. They can impart a mass of knowledge about it, but this is the duty of the college of liberal arts and not the shop work of the trade school.

Thus the industrial school increasingly faces a blank wall and its astonishing answer today to the puzzle is slowly but surely to transform the industrial school into a college. The most revolutionary development in Negro education for a quarter-century is illustrated by the fact that Hampton today is one of the largest of Negro colleges and that her trade teaching seems bound to disappear within a few years. Tuskegee is a high school and college, with an unsolved program of the future of its trade schools. And the land grant colleges, built to foster agriculture and industry, are becoming just like other colleges. And all this, as I said, is not the fault of the industrial school, it comes from this tremendous transformation of business, capital and industry in the Twentieth Century, which few men clearly foresaw and which only a minority of men or of teachers of men today fully comprehend.

THE LABOR MOVEMENT

In one respect, however, the Negro industrial school was seriously at fault. It set its face toward the employer and the capitalist and the man of wealth. It looked upon the worker as one to be adapted to the demands of those who conducted industry. Both in its general program and in its classroom, it neglected almost entirely the modern labor movement. It had little or nothing to teach concerning the rise of trade unions; their present condition, and their future development. It had no conception of any future democracy in industry. That is, the very vehicle which was to train Negroes for modern industry neglected in its teaching the most important part of modern industrial development: namely, the relation of the worker to modern industry and to the modern state.

The reason for this neglect is clear. The Negro industrial school was the gift of capital and wealth. Organized labor was the enemy of the black man in skilled industry. Organized labor in the United States was and is the chief obstacle to keep black folk from earning a living by its determined policy of excluding them from unions just as long as possible and compelling them to become "scabs" in order to live. The political power of Southern white labor disfranchised Negroes, and helped build a caste system. How was the Negro industrial school easily to recognize, in this Devil of its present degradation, the Angel of its future enlightenment? How natural it was to look to white Capital and not to Labor for the emancipation of the black world—how natural and how yet how insanely futile!

THE UNSOLVED PROBLEM

Here then are the successes and the failures of both Negro college and industrial school and we can clearly see that the problem still stands unsolved: How are we going to place the black American on a sure foundation in the modern state? The modern state is primarily business and industry. Its industrial problems must be settled before its cultural problems can really and successfully be attacked. The world must eat before it can think. The Negro has not found a solid foundation in that state as yet. He is mainly the unskilled laborer; the casual employee; the man hired last and fired first; the man who must subsist upon the lowest wage and consequently share an undue burden of poverty, crime, insanity and ignorance. The only alleviation of his economic position has come from what little the industrial school could teach during the revolution of technique and from what the college took up as part of its mission in vocational training for professions.

For the college had to become a trainer of men for vocations. This is as true of the white college as of the colored college. They both tended to change their college curricula into pre-vocational preparation for a professional career. But the effort of the Negro college here was half-hearted. There persisted the feeling that the college had finished its work when it placed a man of culture in the world, despite the fact that our graduates who are men of culture are exceptional, and if placed in the world without ability to earn a living, what little culture they have does not long survive.

Thus, at the end of the first third of the Twentieth Century, while both college and industrial school can point to something accomplished, neither has reached its main objective, and they are in process of uniting to become one stream of Negro education with their great problem of object and method unsolved. The industrial school has done but little to impart the higher technique of the industrial process or of the business organization and it has done almost nothing toward putting the Negro working man in touch with the great labor movement of the white world.

On the other hand, the Negro college has not succeeded in establishing that great and guiding ideal of group development and leadership, within a dominating and expanding culture, or in establishing the cultural life as the leading motif of the educated Negro. Its vocational work has been confined to the so-called learned professions, with only a scant beginning of the imparting of the higher technique of industry and science.

THE NEW INDUSTRIAL REVOLUTION

The result which I have outlined is not wholly unexpected. Perhaps we can now say that it was impossible fully to avoid this situation. We have a right to congratulate ourselves that we have come to a place of such stability and such intelligence as now to be ready to grapple with our economic problem. The fact of the matter is, we have up to this time been swept on and into the great maelstrom of the white civilization surrounding us. We have been inevitably made part of that vast modern organization of life where social and political control rests in the hands of those few white folk who control wealth, determine credit and divide income. We are in a system of culture where disparity of income is such that respect for labor as labor cannot endure; where the emphasis and outlook is not what a man does but what he is able to get for doing it; where wealth despises work and the object of wealth is to escape work, and where the ideal is power without toil.

So long as a lawyer can look forward to an income of $100,000 a year while a maid servant is well-paid with $1,000, just so long the lawyer is going to be one hundred times more respectable than the servant and the servant is going to be called by her first name. So long as the determination of a person's income is not only beyond democratic control and public knowledge, but is a matter of autocratic power and secret manipulation, just so long the application of logic and ethics to wealth, industry and income is going to be a difficult if not insoluble problem.

In the modern world only one country is making a frontal

attack upon this problem and that is Russia. Other countries are visualizing it and considering it, making some tentative and half-hearted effort but they have not yet attacked the system as a whole, and for the most part they declare the present system inevitable and eternal and incapable of more than minor and stinted improvement.

In the midst of such a world organization we come looking for economic stability and independence. Of course, our situation is baffling and contradictory. And it is made all the more difficult for us because we are by blood and descent and popular opinion an integral part of that vast majority of mankind which is the Victim and not the Beneficiary of present conditions; which is today working at starvation wages and on a level of brute toil and without voice in its own government or education in its ignorance, for the benefit, the enormous profit, and the dazzling luxury of the white rulers of the world.

Here lies the problem and it is the problem of the combined Negro college and vocational school. Without the intellectual leadership of college-bred men, we could not hitherto have held our own in modern American civilization, but must have sunk to the place of the helpless proletariat of the West Indies and of South Africa. But, on the other hand, for what has the college saved us? It has saved us for that very economic defeat which the industrial school was established to ward off and which still stands demanding solution. The industrial school acted as bridge and buffer to lead us out of the bitterness of Reconstruction to the toleration of today. But it did not place our feet upon the sound economic foundation which makes our survival in America or in the modern world certain or probable; and the reason that it did not do this was as much the fault of the college as of the trade school. The industrial school without the college was as helpless yesterday as the college is today helpless without systematic training for modern industry.

Both college and industrial school have made extraordinary and complementary mistakes in their teaching force: the industrial school secured usually as teacher a man of affairs and technical knowledge, without culture or general knowledge. The college took too often as teacher a man of books and brains with no contact with or first-hand knowledge of real every-day life and ordinary human beings, and this was true whether he taught sociology, literature or science. Both types of teacher failed.

THE NEW EDUCATIONAL PROGRAM

What then is the unescapable task of the united college and vocational school? It is without shadow of doubt a new broad and widely efficient vocational guidance and education for men and women of ability, selected by the most careful tests and supported by a broad system of free scholarships. Our educational institutions must graduate to the world men fitted to take their place in real life by their knowledge, spirit, and ability to do what the world wants done. This vocational guidance must have for its object the training of men who can think clearly and function normally as physical beings; who have a knowledge of what human life on earth has been, and what it is now; and a knowledge of the constitution of the known universe. All that, and in addition to that, a training which will enable them to take some definite and intelligent part in the production of goods and in the furnishing of human services and in the democratic distribution of income so as to build civilization, encourage initiative, reward effort and support life. Just as the Negro college course with vision, knowledge and ideal must move toward vocational training, so the industrial courses must ascend from mere hand technique to engineering and industrial planning and the application of scientific and technical knowledge to problems of work and wage.

This higher training and vocational guidance must turn out young men and women who are willing not only to do the work of the world today but to provide for the future world. Here then is the job before us. It is in a sense the same kind of duty that lies before the educated white man but it has an essential and important difference. If we make a place for ourselves in the industrial and business world today, this will be done because of our ability to establish a self-supporting organization sufficiently independent of the white organization to insure its stability and our economic survival and eventual incorporation into world industry. Ours is the double and dynamic function of tuning in with a machine in action so as neither to wreck the machine nor be crushed or maimed by it. Many think this is impossible. But if it is impossible, our future economic survival is impossible.

Let there be no misunderstanding about this, no easy going optimism. We are not going to share modern civilization just by deserving recognition. We are going to force ourselves in by organized far-seeing effort—by out-thinking and out-flanking the owners of the world today who are too drunk with their own arrogance and power successfully to oppose us if we think and learn and do.

It is not the province of this paper to tell in detail just how this problem will be settled. Indeed, I could not tell you if I would. I merely stress the problem and emphasize the possibility of the solution. A generation ago those who doubted our survival said that no alien and separate nation could hope to survive within another nation; that we must be absorbed or perish. Times have changed. Today it is rapidly becoming true that only within some great and all inclusive empire or league can separate nations and groups find freedom and protection and economic scope for development. The small separate nation is becoming increasingly impossible and the League of Nations as well as Briand's proposed League of Europe shout this from the housetops. And just as loudly, the inevitable disintegration of the British Empire shows the impossibility of world embracing centralized autocracy. This means that the possibility of our development and survival is clear, but clear only as brains and devotion and skilled knowledge point the way.

TEACHERS

We need then, first, training as human beings in general knowledge and experience; then technical training to guide and do a specific part of the world's work. The broader training should be the heritage and due of all but today it is curtailed by poverty. The technical training of men must be directed by vocational guidance which finds fitness and ability. Then actual and detailed technical training will be done by a combination of school, laboratory and apprenticeship, according to the nature of the work and the changing technique.

The teachers of such a stream of students must be of a high order. College teachers cannot follow the mediaeval tradition of detached withdrawal from the world. The professor of mathematics in a college has to be more than a counting machine, or proctor of examinations; he must be a living man, acquainted with real human beings, and alive to the relation of his branch of knowledge to the technical problem of living and earning a living. The teacher in a Negro college has got to be something far more than a master of a branch of human knowledge. He has got to be able to impart his knowledge to human beings whose place in the world is today precarious and critical and the possibilities and advancement of that human being in the world where he is to live and earn a living is of just as much importance in the teaching process as the content of the knowledge taught.

The man who teaches blacksmithing must be more than a blacksmith. He must be a man of education and culture, acquainted with the whole present technique and business organization of the modern world, and acquainted too with human beings and their possiblities. Such a man is difficult to procure. Because industrial schools did not have in the past such teachers for their classes and could not get them, their whole program suffered unmerited crticism. The teachers, then, cannot be pedants or dilettantes, they cannot be mere technicians and higher artisans, they have got to be social statesmen and statesmen of high order. The student body of such schools has got to be selected for something more than numbers. We must eliminate those who are here because their parents wish to be rid of them or for the social prestige or for passing the time or for getting as quickly as possible into a position to make money to throw away; and we must concentrate upon young men and women of ability and vision and will.

IDEAL

Today there is but one rivalry between culture and vocation, college training and trade and professional training, and that is the rivalry of Time. Some day every human being will have college training. Today some must stop with the grades, and some with high school, and only a few reach college. It is of the utmost importance, then, and the essential condition of our survival and advance that those chosen for college be our best and not simply our richest or most idle.

But even this growth must be led; it must be guided by Ideals. We have lost something, brothers, wandering in strange lands. We have lost our ideals. We have come to a generation which seeks advance without ideals—discovery without stars. It cannot be done. Certain great landmarks and guiding facts must stand eternally before us; and at the risk of moralizing, I must end by emphasizing this matter of the ideals of Negro students and graduates.

The ideal of *Poverty*. This is the direct antithesis of the present American ideal of Wealth. We cannot all be wealthy. We should not all be wealthy. In an ideal industrial organization no person should have an income which he does not personally need; nor wield a power solely for his own whim. If civilization is to turn out millionaires it will also turn out beggars and prostitutes either at home or among the lesser breeds without the law. A simple healthy life on limited income is the only reasonable ideal of civilized folk.

The ideal of *Work*—not idleness, not dawdling, but hard continuous effort at something worth doing, by a man supremely interested in doing it, who knows how it ought to be done and is willing to take infinite pains doing it.

The ideal of *Knowledge*—not guess work, not mere careless theory; not inherited religious dogma clung to because of fear and inertia and in spite of logic, but critically tested and laboriously gathered fact martialed under scientific law and feeding rather than choking the glorious world of fancy and imagination, of poetry and art, of beauty and deep culture.

Finally, and especially, the ideal of *Sacrifice*. I almost hesitate to mention this—so much sentimental twaddle has been written of it. When I say sacrifice, I mean sacrifice. I mean a real and definite surrender of personal ease and satisfaction. I embellish it with no theological fairy tales of a rewarding God or a milk and honey heaven. I am not trying to scare you into the duty of sacrifice by the fires of a mythical Hell. I am repeating the stark fact of survival of life and culture on this earth:

> *Entbehren sollst du—sollst enthehren.*
> Thou shalt forego, shalt do without.

The insistent problem of human happiness is still with us. We American Negroes are not a happy people. We feel perhaps as never before the sting and bitterness of our struggle. Our little victories won here and there serve but to reveal the shame of our continuing semi-slavery and social caste. We are torn asunder within our own group because of the rasping pressure of the struggle without. We are as a race not simply dissatisfied, we are embodied Dissatisfaction.

To increase abiding satisfaction for the mass of our people, and for all people, someone must sacrifice something of his own happiness. This is a duty only to those who recognize it as a duty. The larger the number ready to sacrifice, the smaller the total sacrifice necessary. No man of education and culture and training, who proposes to face his problem and solve it can hope for entire happiness. It is silly to tell intelligent human beings: Be good and you will be happy. The truth is today, be good, be decent, be honorable and self-sacrificing and you will not always be happy. You will often be desperately unhappy. You may even be crucified, dead and buried, and the third day you will be just as dead as the first. But with the death of your happiness may easily come increased happiness and satisfaction and fulfillment for other people—strangers, unborn babes, uncreated worlds. If this is not sufficient incentive, never try it—remain hogs.

The present census will show that the American Negro of the educated class and even of the middle industrial class is reproducing himself at an even slower rate than the corresponding classes of whites. To raise a small family today is a sacrifice. It is not romance and adventure. It is giving up something of life and pleasure for a future generation.

If, therefore, real sacrifice for others in your life work appeals to you, here it is. Here is the chance to build an industrial organization on a basis of logic and ethics, such as is almost wholly lacking in the modern world. It is a tremendous task, and it is the task equally and at once of Howard and Tuskegee, of Hampton and Fisk, of the college and of the industrial school. Our real schools must become centers of this vast Crusade. With the faculty and the student body girding themselves for this new and greater education, the major part of the responsibility will still fall upon those who have already done their school work; and that means upon the alumni who, like you, have become graduates of an institution of learning. Unless the vision comes to you and comes quickly, of the educational and economic problem before the American Negro, that problem will not be solved. You not only enter, therefore, today the worshipful company of that vast body of men upon whom a great center of learning, with ancient ceremony and colorful trappings, has put the accolade of intellectual knighthood, but men who have become the unselfish thinkers and planners of a group of people in whose hands lies the economic and social destiny of the darker peoples of the world, and by that token of the world itself.

THE SHADOW OF BEAUTY

Finally, no one may fail to stress before any audience, or on any occasion and on any errand bent, the overshadowing and all-inclusive ideal of Beauty—"fair face of Beauty, all too fair to see"—fitness, rhythm, perfection of adaptation of ends to means. It is hard to mention this intelligently without maudlin sentiment and clouded words. May I speak then in parable?

Last night I saw the Zeppelin sailing in silver across the new moon. Brilliant, enormous, lovely, it symbolized the civilization over which it hung. It rode serene above miles of

Death; like a needle it threaded together clouds and seas, stars and continents. Within its womb were caged eternal and palpitating forces of the universe, and yet without quiver it faced the utter ends of space. Across the city, mute, dominant, magnificent, imponderable—it flew.

And what it did, men and women of Howard, you may do—you must do or die. The Zeppelin is neither miracle nor stroke of genius. It is unremittent toil and experiment and thought and infinite adaptation in the face of every discouragement and failure, in the face of death itself.

I thought as I saw it flying there, of an angel flying low— an angel of steel and silk and of grim and awful human aim. I remembered the word of our own poet, great, but little known:

>   I thought I saw an angel flying low.
>   I thought I saw the flicker of a wing
>   Above the mulberry trees; but not again.
>   Bethesda sleeps. . . . . .
>
>   The golden days are gone. Why do we wait
>   So long upon the marble steps, blood
>   Falling from our open wounds? and why
>   Do our black faces search the empty sky?
>   Is there something we have forgotten?
>   Some precious thing
>   We have lost, wandering in strange lands? . . . .
>
>   There was a day, I remember now,
>   I beat my breast and cried, "Wash me God,"
>   Wash me with a wave of wind upon
>   The barley; O quiet One, draw near, draw near!
>   Walk upon the hills with lovely feet
>   And in the waterfall stand and speak.

Commencement address, delivered at Howard University, June 6, 1930, reprinted from *Howard University Bulletin*, Vol. 9, No. 5, January, 1931, pp. 1–22

The Revelation of Saint Orgne
the Damned (1938)

Saint Orgne stood facing the morning and asked: What is this life I see? Is the dark damnation of color, real? or simply mine own imagining? Can it be true that souls wrapped in black velvet have a destiny different from those swathed in white satin or yellow silk, when all these covering are fruit of the same worm, and threaded by the same hands? Or must I, ignoring all seeming difference, rise to some upper realm where there is no color nor race, sex, wealth nor age, but all men stand equal in the Sun?

Thus Orgne questioned Life on his Commencement morning, in the full springtide of his day. And this is the Revelation and the answer that came to Saint Orgne the Damned as he came to be called, as he stood on his Mount of Transfiguration, looking full at life as it is and not as it might be or haply as he would have it.

"In very truth, thou art damned, and may not escape by vain imagining nor fruitless repining. When a man faces evil, he does not call it good, nor evade it; he meets it breastforward, with no whimper of regret nor fear of foe."

"Blessed is he that reads and they that hear the words of this prophecy for the time is at hand. Grace be unto you and peace, from him which was and which is and is to come and from the seven spirits which are before his throne."

I, who also am your brother and companion in tribulation and in the kingdom and the patience, was in the isle that is called America. I was in the spirit and heard behind me a great Voice saying, "I am Alpha and Omega, the first and the last; and what thou seest write." I turned to the voice. I saw seven golden candlesticks with one in the midst of the candlesticks; and in his hands seven stars and out of his mouth went a sharp two edged sword. And when I saw him I fell at his feet as dead and he laid his right hand upon me saying unto me, "Fear not. Write thou the things which thou has seen; the mystery of the seven stars and the seven golden candlesticks."

So Orgne turned and climbed the Seven Heights of Hell to

view the Seven Stars of Heaven. The seven heights are Birth and Family; School and Learning; the University and Wisdom; the great snow-capped peak of Work; the naked crag of Right and Wrong; the rolling hills of the Freedom of Art and Beauty; and at last, the plateau that is the Democracy of Race; beyond this there are no vales of Gloom—for the star above is the sun itself and all shadows fall straight before it.

Orgne descended into the valleys of the Shadow, lit only by the waving light of single candles set in seven golden candlesticks, struggling through noisome refuse of body and mind. Long years he strove, uphill and down, around and through seven groups of seven years until in the end he came back to the beginning, world-weary, but staunch; and this is the revelation of his life and thought which I, his disciple, bring you from his own hands.

A golden candlestick stood beneath a silver star, atop a high mountain and in the cold gray dawn of a northern spring. There was the first hint of apple blossoms and faint melody in the air; within the melody was the whisper of a Voice, which sighed and said: "Why should we breed black folk in this world and to what end? Wherefor should we found families and how? Is not the world for such as are born white and rich?"

Then Orgne, half grown, lying prone, reared himself suddenly to his feet and shivering looked upward to light. The sun rose slowly above the mountain and with its light spake. Hear ye the Wisdom of the families of black folk:

Gentlemen are bred and not born. They are trained in childhood and receive manners from those who surround them and not from their blood. Manners maketh Man, and are the essence of good breeding. They have to do with forms of salutation between civilized persons; with the care and cleanliness and grooming of the body. They avoid the stink of bodily excretions; they eat their food without offense to others; they know that dirt is matter misplaced and they seek to replace it. The elementary rules of health become to them second nature and their inbred courtesy one to another makes life liveable and gracious even among crowds.

Now this breeding and infinite detail of training is not learned in college and may not be taught in school. It is the duty and task of the family group and once the infinite value of that training is missed it can seldom be replaced through any later agency. It is in vain that the university seeks to cope with ill-bred youngsters, foul-mouthed loafers and unwashed persons who have happened to pass the entrance examinations. Once in the earlier mission schools among American Negroes men tried to do this, knowing of the irreparable harm slavery had done the family group. They had some success right here in this institution; but the day when such effort is possible is gone. Unless a new type of Negro family takes the burden of this duty, we are destined to be, as we are too largely today, a bad-mannered, unclean crowd of ill-bred young men and women who are under the impression that they are educated.

For this task we have got to create a new family group; and a cultural group rather than a group merely biological. The biology and blood relationship of families is entirely subordinate and unimportant as compared with its cultural entity; with the presence of two persons who take upon themselves voluntarily the sacrificial priesthood of parents to children, limited in number and interval by intelligent and scientific birth-control, who can and will train in the elements of being civilized human beings: how to eat, how to sleep, how to wash, how to stand, how to walk, how to laugh, how to be reverent and how to obey.

It is not entirely our fault that we have missed, forgotten or are even entirely unaware of the cultural place of the family. In European and American civilization we have tried to carry out the most idiotic paradox that ever civilized folk attempted. We have tried to make babies both sins and angels. We have regarded sex as a disgrace and as eternal life. We talk in one breath of the Virgin Mary and of the Mother of God. And at the critical age of life for both men and women, we compel them to strain the last sinew of moral strength to repress a natural and beautiful appetite, or to smear it with deception and crime. We base female eligibility for marriage on exotic personal beauty and childlike innocence, and yet pretend to desire brains, common sense and strength of body. If an age thus immolates its ugly virgins, it will crucify its beautiful fools, with the result of making marriage a martrydom that few enter with open eyes. The change from this has got to recognize the sin of virginity in a world that needs proper children; the right of the so-called unfathered child to be; the legal adoption into the cultural family of gifted and promising children and the placing of black sheep, no matter who their parents are, under necessary restraint and correction. Amen.

The Voice ceased. As Orgne walked slowly down the mountain, he brooded long over the word he had heard, wondering vaguely how far the revelation was within or without his own soul; and then turning the message over in his mind, he thought of his own home, of the three small rooms, of the careful, busy mother and grandmother, of the dead father; and he mused: if one's start in life depends on breeding and not on color or unchangeable and unfathomable compulsions before births, surely I may live, even though I am black and poor.

There came a long space of Seven years. Orgne stood by the bank of the Golden River, with the second candlestick in his hand. He could not see the stars above, for it was nine o'clock of a sun-washed morning; but he knew they were there. He was celebrating all alone his entry into High School. None of his people save only his dead grandfather had ever gotten so far; but with the wave of disappointment which comes with all accomplishment, he muttered, "And why should they, why should I, dawdle here with elements of things and mere tools of Knowledge while both I and the world wait." The river flowed softly as he slept in the summer mildness. Daisies and buttercups waved above him. The grey fleecy clouds gathered and swiftly low thunder rolled; a bolt of heat lightning flashed across the sky. He slept on, yet heard the second star as it spoke:

Hear ye! This is the wisdom of the elementary school.

The difficulty and essential difficulty with Negro education lies in the elementary school; lies in the fact that the number of Negroes in the United States today who have learned thoroughly to read, write, and count is small; and that the proportion of those who cannot read, cannot express their thoughts and cannot understand the fundamentals of arithmetic, algebra and geometry is discouragingly large. The reason that we cannot do thorough college work and cannot keep high university standards is that the students in institutions like this are fundamentally weak in mastery of those essential tools to human learning. Not even the dumbest college professor can spoil the education of the man who as a child has learned to read, write, and cipher; so too, Aristotle, Emmanuel Kant and Mark Hopkins together are powerless before the illiterate who cannot reason.

The trouble lies primarily, of course, in the elementary schools of the South; in schools with short terms; with teachers inadequate both as to numbers and training; with quarters ill-suited physically and morally to the work in hand; with colored principals chosen not for executive ability but for their agility in avoiding race problems; and with white superintendents who try to see how large a statistical showing can be made without expenditure of funds, thought nor effort.

This is the fault of a nation which does not thoroughly believe in the education of Negroes, and of the South which still to a large extent does not believe in any training for black folk which is not of direct commercial profit to those who dominate the state.

But the fault does not end there. The fault lies with the Negroes themselves for not realizing this major problem in their education and for not being willing and eager and untiring in their effort to establish the elementary school on a fundamental basis. Necessary as are laws against lynching and race segregation, we should put more money, effort, and breath in perfecting the Negro elementary school than in anything else, and not pause nor think of pausing until every Negro child between five and fifteen is getting at least nine months' a year, five hours a day, five days in the week, in a modern school room, with the best trained teachers, under principals selected for training and executive ability, and serving with their teachers during efficiency and good behavior; and with the school under the control of those whose children are educated there.

Until this is done and so far as it is not done the bulk of university endowment is being wasted and high schools strive partially in vain. Amen.

Again flew seven years. Orgne was far from home and school and land. He was speaking an unknown tongue and looking upon the walls and towers, colors and sounds of another world. It was high noon and autumn. He sat in a lofty cathedral, glorious in the fretted stone lace-work of its proudly vaulted roof. Its flying buttresses looked down upon a grey and rippled lake; beyond lay fields of flowers, golden chrysanthemums and flaming dahlias and further the ancient university, where for a thousand years men had sought Truth. Around rose a symphony of sound, a miraculous blending of strings and brass, trumpet and drum which was the Seventh Symphony with its lovely interlacing of melody and soft solemn marches, breaking to little hymns and dances. He listened to its revelation gazing rapt at candlesticks and gilded star and whispered: "Why should I know and What, and what is the end of knowing? Is it not enough to feel?" The angels in the choir sang No—Hear ye! For Wisdom is the principal thing.

There can be no iota of doubt that the chief trouble with the world and the overwhelming difficulty with American Negroes is widespread ignorance; the fact that we are not thoroughly acquainted with human history; of what men and peoples have thought and done in the seven thousand years of our cultural life. We are especially unacquainted with modern science; with the facts of matter and its constitution; with the meaning of time and space; with chemical reaction and electrical phenomena; with the history of the machine and the tool; with the history of human labor; the development of our knowledge of the mind; the practical use of the languages of the world; and the methods of logical reasoning, beginning and ending with mathematics.

This great body of knowledge has been growing and developing for thousands of years, and yet today its mastery is in the hands of so few men, that a comparatively small death roll would mean the end of human culture. Without this knowledge there can be no planning in economy; no substantial guidance in character building; no intelligent development of art. It is for acquaintanceship with this knowledge and the broadening of its field that the college and university exist. This is the reason and the only reason for its building among American Negroes and the work that it is accomplishing today is so infinitely less than that which with any real effort it might accomplish that one has a right to shudder at the misuse of the word university. Amen.

Orgne stood at twilight in the swamp. In seven more years, all the romance and glamour of Europe had sunk to the winter of America. It was twilight, and the swamp glowed with the mystery of sunset—long shafts of level burning light —greens and yellows, purples and red; the whisper of leaves, the ghosts of dead and dying life. The sun died dismally, and the clouds gathered and a drizzling rain began to fall with slow determination. Orgne shrank within himself. He saw the toil of labor and revolted. He felt the pinch of poverty and wept. "What is this stuff I hear," he cried: "how can we marry and support a family without money? How can we control our schools without economic resource? How can we turn our churches from centers of superstition into intelligent building of character; and beyond this how shall we have time for real knowledge; and freedom of art, and effort toward world-wide democracy, until we have the opportunity to work decently and the resources to spend, which shall enable us to be civilized human beings?"

Suddenly across the swamp and across the world and up from the cotton fields of Georgia rolled a Negro folk song. Orgne saw in music Jehovah and his angels, the Wheel in a

Wheel. He saw the Golden Candlestick and heard the revelation of the Star: Hear ye! This is the teaching of the World of Work.

The most distressing fact in the present world is poverty; not absolute poverty, because some folk are rich and many are well-to-do; not poverty as great as some lands and other historical ages have known; but poverty more poignant and discouraging because it comes after a dream of wealth; of riotous, wasteful and even vulgar accumulation of individual riches, which suddenly leaves the majority of mankind today without enough to eat; without proper shelter; without sufficient clothing.

Nowhere was the dream of wealth, for all who would work and save, more vivid than here in the United States. We Negroes sought to share that vision and heritage. Moreover, the poverty which the world now experiences, comes after a startling realization of our national endowment of rich natural resources and our power to produce. We have the material goods and forces at command, the machines and technique sufficient to feed, clothe the world, educate children and free the human soul for creative beauty and for the truth that will widen the bounds of all freedom.

That does not mean that we could have enough goods and services for present extravagance, display and waste; but if there were neither idle rich nor idle poor; if sharing of wealth were based not on owning but only on effort, and if all who are able did their share of the world's work or starved, and limited their consumption to reasonable wants, we could abolish poverty.

Why have we not done this? It is because of greed in the production and distribution of goods and human labor. We discovered widely in the eighteenth century and the nineteenth the use of capital and it was a great and beneficent discovery; it was the rule of sacrificing present wealth for greater wealth to come. But instead of distributing this increase of wealth primarily among those who make it we left most workers as poor as possible in order further to increase the wealth of a few. We produced more wealth than the wealthy could consume and yet used this increased wealth to monopolize materials and machines; to buy and sell labor in return for monopoly ownership in the products of labor and for further wealth.

We thus not only today produce primarily for the profit of owners and not for use of the mass of people, but we have grown to think that this is the only way in which we can produce. We organize industry for private wealth and not for public weal, and we argue often honestly and conscientiously, that no human planning can change the essentials of this process. Yet the process itself has failed so many times and so abysmally, that we are bound to change or starve in the midst of plenty. We are encouraging war through fear of poverty that need not exist; we face the breakdown of production by persistent overproduction of the kinds of goods which we cannot afford to consume.

What can we do? There is only one thing for civilized human beings to do when facing such a problem, and that is to learn the facts, to reason out their connection and to plan the future; to know the truth; to arrange it logically and to contrive a better way. In some way, as all intelligent men acknowledge, we must in the end, produce for the satisfaction of human needs and distribute in accordance with human want. To contend that this cannot be done is to face the Impossible Must. The blind cry of reaction on the one hand, which says that we cannot have a planned economy and, therefore, must not try; and the cry of blood which says that only by force can selfishness be curbed, are equally wrong. Is it not a question of deliberate guilt but of selfish stupidity. The economic world can only be reformed by Spartan restraint in the consumption of goods and the use of services; by the will to work not simply for individual profit but for group weal; not simply for one group but for all groups; and the freedom to dream and plan.

This reformation of the world is beginning with agony of soul and strain of muscle. It can and must go on, and we black folk of America are faced with the most difficult problem of realizing and knowing the part which we have got to play in this economic revolution for our own salvation and for the salvation of the world. This is not easy, for we are cut off from the main effort by the lesions of race; by the segregation of color; by the domination of caste. And yet nothing could be more fatal to our own ideals and the better ideals of the world than for us with unconscious ignorance or conscious perversity or momentary applause to join the forces of reaction; to talk as though the twentieth century presented the same oversimplified path of economic progress which seemed the rule in the nineteenth: work, thrift and wealth by individual effort no matter what the social cost.

The economic illiteracy prevalent among American Negroes is discouraging. In a day when every thinker sees the disorganization of our economic life and the need of radical change, we find the teachers of economics in colored colleges, the Negro business men, Negro preachers and writers to a very large extent talking the language of the early nineteenth century; seeking to make themselves believe that work for any kind of wages, saving at any sacrifice and wealth on any terms not excluding cheating, murder, and theft, are ways of the world still open and beckoning to us. Selah!

Orgne listened and sat staring at the sodden cotton field beyond the somber swamp. Always the swinging thunder of song surged above—Jordan rolled; the rocks and the mountains fled away, the Way was crowded; and Moses went down, away down among the cabins in the cotton patch to the crazy church and hysterical crowd of penitents all praying madly to escape debt. Orgne talked to the planter and said "let my people go." and worked with the tenants seven long years.

Seven years he toiled and in the end had a little nest of land holders owning one large unmortgaged farm in twenty shares; working their crops and buying their provisions in common and dividing them with equal justice. Poor, Orgne came to them and poor he finally went away leaving them poor too but fed and sheltered. They called him Saint. He smiled and looked upward to the star; but the preacher looked down to the dirt and mortgaged it behind the backs of the trusting flock and ran away with the money.

Saint Orgne cursed and cried how shall we plan a new earth without honest men and what is this thing we call a church. So, angry, disillusioned and weary he came to a land where it was always afternoon, and he laid him prone on the earth and slept.

Seven years he slept and in seven years came a thousand miles and more to Ohio, to teach in college. At high noon he stood before the chapel and heard the singing of a hymn in the haze of early spring time. Around him stretched the wide, undulating valleys of the Miami, the Ohio, and the realm of the Mississippi. He looked up and suddenly hated the walls that shut out the stars; he hated the maudlin words of the hymn quite as much as he loved the lilt of the voices that raised it. He loved the flowers—the violets and morning glory, the blossoming fruit that filled the yards about. Then came the earthquake; then the earth trembled and swayed; far off in San Francisco a city fell and around the nation quivered. In the midst of the rushing, swaying crowd, again Orgne, after seven years, awoke and found the Golden Candlestick in his hands, and heard the low clear revelation of the Star:

Saint Orgne the Damned, behold the Vision of the Seven Black Churches of America,—the Baptist, the four wings of Methodism, the Roman and Episcopal Catholics.

Their five millions of members in 40,000 groups, holding $200,000, in their hands, are the most strongly organized body among us; the first source of our group culture, the beginning of our education—what is this church doing today toward its primary task of teaching men right and wrong, and the duty of doing right?

The flat answer is nothing if not less than nothing. Like other churches and other religions of other peoples and ages, our church has veered off on every conceivable side path, which interferes with and nullifies its chief duty of character building.

It has built up a body of dogma and fairy tale, fantastic fables of sin and salvation, impossible creeds and impossible demands for ignorant unquestioning belief and obedience.

Ask any thorough churchman today and he will tell you, not that the object of the church is to get men to do right and make the majority of mankind happy, but rather that the whole duty of man is to "believe in the Lord Jesus Christ and be saved"; or to believe "that God is God and Mohammed is his prophet"; or to believe in the "one Holy and Catholic church," infallible and omniscient; or to keep the tomb of one's grandfather intact and his ideas undisputed.

Considering how desperately, great and good men have inveighed against these continuing foibles of priesthood for many thousand years, and how little in essence has been accomplished, it may seem /hopeless to return to the attack today, but that is a precisely what this generation has to do. The function of the Negro church, instead of being that of building edifices, paying old debts, holding revivals and staging entertainments, has got to be brought back, or shall we say forward, to the simple duty of teaching ethics. For this purpose the Hebrew scriptures and the New Testament canon will not suffice. We must stop telling children that the lying and deceitful Jacob was better than the lazy Esau, or that the plan of salvation is anything but the picture of the indecent anger and revenge of a bully.

We can do this, not so much by the attacking of outworn superstition and conventional belief as by hearty research into real ethical questions. When is it right to lie? Do low wages mean stealing? Does the prosperity of a country depend upon the number of its millionaires? Should the state kill a murderer? How much money should you give to the poor? Should there be any poor? And as long as there are, what is crime and who are the criminals?

So Saint Orgne preached the word of life from Jeremiah, Shakespeare and Jesus, Confucius, Buddha and John Brown; and organized a church with a cooperative store in the Sunday school room; with physician, dentist, nurse and lawyer to help, serve and defend the congregation; with library, nursery school, and a regular succession of paid and trained lecturers and discussion; they had radio and moving pictures and out beyond the city a farm with house and lake. They had a credit union, group insurance and building and loan association. The members paid for this not by contributions but by ten dollars a month each of regular dues and those who would join this church must do more than profess to love God.

Seven years he served and married a woman not for her hair and color but for her education, good manners, common sense and health. Together they made a home and begot two strong intelligent children. Looking one day into their eyes Orgne became suddenly frightened for their future. He prayed "Oh life let them be free!"

So soon, so soon, Orgne sighed, the world rolls around its sevens of years. It was midsummer and he was sailing upon the sea. He was bound for Africa on a mission of world brotherhood. Behind and waiting were wife and children, home and work. Ahead was the darker world of men yellow, brown, and black. Dinner was done and the deck empty save for himself; all were within the magnificent saloon massed with tall vases of roses and lilies, priceless with tapestry and gilding, listening to the great organ which the master played. The largo whispered, smiled and swelled upward to tears. Then the storm swept down. Then the ocean, lashed to fury by the wind, bellowed and burned; the vast ship tossed like a tortured soul, groaned and twisted in its agony. But Orgne smiled. He knew that behind the storm and above the cloud the evening stars were singing, and he listened to the rhythm of their words: Hear Ye! This is the Freedom of Art which is the Beauty of Life.

Life is more than meat, even though life without food dies. Living is not for earning, earning is for living. The man that spends his life earning a living, has never lived. The education that trains men simply for earning a living is not education.

What then is Life—What is it for—What is its great End? Manifestly in the light of all knowledge, and according to the testimony of all men who have lived, Life is the fullest, most complete enjoyment of the possibilities of human existence. It is the development and broadening of the feelings and emotions, through sound and color, line and form. It is technical mastery of the media that these paths and emotions need for expression of their full meaning. It is the free enjoyment of every normal appetite. It is giving rein to the creative impulse, in thought and imagination. Here roots the rise of the Joy of Living, of music, painting, drawing, sculpture and building; hence come literature with romance, poetry, and essay; hence rise Love, Friendship, emulation, and ambition, and the ever widening realms of thought, in increasing circles of apprehended and interpreted Truth.

It is the contradiction and paradox of this day that those who seek to choke and conventionalize art, restrict and censor thought and repress imagination are demanding for their shriveled selves, freedom in precisely those lines of human activity where control and regimentation are necessary; and necessary because upon this foundation is to be built the widest conceivable freedom in a realm infinitely larger and more meaningful than the realm of economic production and distribution of wealth. The less freedom we leave for business exploitation the greater freedom we shall have for expression in art.

We have got to think of the time when poverty approaches abolition; when men no longer fear starvation and unemployment; when health is so guarded that we may normally expect to live our seventy years and more, without excess of pain and suffering. In such a world living begins; in such a world we will have freedom of thought and expression, and just as much freedom of action as maintenance of the necessary economic basis of life permits; that is, given three or six hours of work under rule and duress, we ought to be sure of at least eighteen hours of recreation, joy, and creation with a minimum of compulsion for anybody.

Freedom is the path of art, and living in the fuller and broader sense of the term is the expression of art. Yet those who speak of freedom talk usually as fools talk. So far as the laws of gravitation are concerned there can be no freedom; so far as the physical constitution of the universe is concerned, we must produce and consume goods in accordance with that which is inexorable, unmoved by sentiment or dream. But this realm of the physical need be only the smaller part of life and above it, is planning, emotion and dream; in the exercising of creative power; in building, painting and literature there is a chance for the free exercise of the human spirit, broad enough and lofty enough to satisfy every ambition of the free human soul. Limited though it be by birth and death, by time and space, by health and mysterious native gift, nevertheless its realm is so magnificent that those who fear that freedom may end with the abolition of poverty or that disease is needed to insure room on the earth or that war and murder are the only handmaids of courage are all talking utter nonsense.

The freedom to create within the limits of natural law; the freedom to love without limit; the freedom to dream of the utter marriage of beauty and art; all this men may have if they are sufficiently well-bred to make human contact bearable; if they have learned to read and write and reason; if they have character enough to distinguish between right and wrong and strength enough to do right; if they can earn a decent living and know the world in which they live.

The vastest and finest truth of all, is that while wealth diminishes by sharing and consuming and calls for control; Art, which is experience of life, increases and grows, the more widely it is shared. Here lie the rock foundations of Democracy. Selah.

So now again pass seven years. It is midnight of an autumn day; and Saint Orgne, risen beatified on the dark frustration of his soul, to the quiet peace of pain, stands in an old forest amid falling leaves, with the starry heavens above him. He knows where, months before, the heavy fragrance of purple wisteria had hallowed this air and dipped great festoons of blooms down into a scented world. But tonight these are gone. All is death. There is no sound; and yet somehow somewhere beneath lies some Tone too deep for sound—a silent chord of infinite harmony. Saint Orgne lifts his hands and waves back to the skies the seven golden candlesticks and the seven silver stars, and speaks, saying, "It is enough!" But the Voice replies:

"I see a new Heaven and a new Earth." "How can that be," wails Saint Orgne. "What is new about War and Murder? What is new in deified and organized race hate? What is new in breadlines and starvation, crime and disease? Is not our dream of Democracy done?"

The stars shine silently on, but in his own heart Saint Orgne's answer comes—Hear ye! This is the Truth of Democracy and Race.

The world compels us today as never before to examine and re-examine the problem of democracy. In theory we know it by heart: all men are equal and should have equal voice in their own government. This dictum has been vigorously attacked. All men are not equal. Ignorance cannot speak logically or clearly even when given voice. If sloth, dullness and mediocrity hold power, civilization is diluted and lowered, and government approaches anarchy. The mob cannot rule itself and will not choose the wise and able and give them the power to rule.

This attack began in 1787 during the French Revolution and it rose to crescendo sixty years later in 1867 when our fathers were enfranchised. The original dictum of human equality and the right of the governed to a voice in their government has never been universally accepted and only seldom has it been attempted. In the world today, universal suffrage is coerced by force as was true here in the South during reconstruction; or by intimidation as was true in the South after 1876; or by economic pressure, either through threat of poverty or bribery of increased income, as has been true in the United States for years. Today finally we have entered the period of propaganda, when people to be sure may vote but cannot think freely nor clearly because of falsehood forced on their eyes and ears; or equally by the deliberate suppression of the whole truth. It is thus that there has arisen in our day, on an astonishing scale, the fascism of despair; the acquiescence of great masses of men in irresponsible tyranny, not because they want it, but because they see no other escape from greater disaster.

Let us then examine anew the basic thesis of democracy. It

does not really mean to say that all men are equal; but it does assert that every individual who is a part of the state must have his experience and his necessities regarded by that state if the state survive; that the best and only ultimate authority on an individual's hurt and desire is that individual himself no matter how inarticulate his inner soul may be; that life, as any man has lived it, is part of that great national reservoir of knowledge without use of which no government can do justice.

But this is not the main end of democracy. It is not only that the complaints of all should be heard, or the hurts of the humblest healed; it is for the vastly larger object of loosing the possibilities of mankind for the development of a higher and broader and more varied human culture. Democracy then forms not merely a reservoir of complaint but of ability, hidden otherwise in poverty and ignorance. It is the astonishing result of an age of enlightenment, when the ruling classes of the world are the children of peasants, slaves and gutter snipes, that the still dominant thought is that education and ability are not today matters of chance, but mainly of individual desert and effort. As a matter of fact the chances of real ability today getting opportunity for development are not one-tenth as great as the chance of their owners dying in child-birth, being stunted by poverty or ending in prison or on the gallows. Democracy means the opening of opportunity to the disinherited to contribute to civilization and the happiness of men.

Given a chance for the majority of mankind, to be educated, healthy and free to act, it may well turn out that human equality is not so wild a dream as many seem to hope.

The intelligent democratic control of a state by its citizens does not of itself and by any mechanical formula mean good government. It must be supplemented by the thrift and unselfishness of its citizens. The citizen of a democracy who thinks of democratic government chiefly as a means of his own advancement, meets and ought to meet disappointment. Only in so far as he conceives of democracy as the only way to advance the interests of the mass of people, even when those interests conflict with his, is he playing the heroic role of a patriot. And whenever he excludes from that mass the inter- ests of the poor and the foolish; the Jew and Negro; the Asiatic and the South Sea Islander; he kills the effort at democracy.

Democracy does not and cannot mean freedom. On the contrary it means coercion. It means submission of the indi- vidual will to the general will and it is justified in this com- pulsion only if the will is general and not the will of special privilege.

Far from this broad conception of democracy, we have increasingly allowed the idea to be confined to the opportu- nity of electing certain persons to power without regard as to whether they can or will exercise power or for what. Even this choice of the voter, in current democracies, is confined mostly to comparatively minor matters of administration; but in the great realm of making a living, the fundamental inter- est of all; in the matter of determining what goods shall be produced, what services shall be rendered, and how goods and services shall be shared by all, there has been deep and bitter determination, that here democracy shall never enter; that here the Tyrant or the King by the grace of God shall always and forever rule.

It is widely in vain that the basic argument for democratic control has here been brought to bear; that these goods and services are the product of the labor of the mass of men and not solely of the rich and talented; and that therefore all men must have some decisive voice in the conduct of industry and the division of wealth. To be sure this calls for more intelli- gence, technical knowledge of intricate facts and forces, and greater will to work and sacrifice than most men today have; which is only saying that the mass of men must more and more largely acquire this knowledge, skill and character; and that meantime its wide absence, is no valid excuse for sur- rendering the control of industry to the anarchy of greed and the tyranny of chance.

This faces us directly with our problem in America. Our best brains are taught and want to be taught in large northern universities where dominant economic patterns and European culture, not only prevail, but prevail almost to the exclusion of anything else.

Naturally these men are then grabbed up with rolling eyes and eager mien by the best Southern Negro schools. Now if these Negro universities have any real meaning it is that in them other points of view, should be evolved. They may or may not be radically different. They may bring something entirely new or be an adaptation of surrounding civilization; but certainly they should logically bring a newness of view and a re-examination of the old, of the European, and of the white, which would be stimulating and which would be real education.

But right here we have not simply little or no advance, but we have attitudes which make advance impossible. On the matter of race, for instance, we are ultra-modern. There are certainly no biological races in the sense of people with large groups of unvarying inherited gifts and instincts thus set apart by nature as eternally separate. We have seen the whole world reluctantly but surely approaching this truth. We have therefore hastened to conclude there is no sense in studying racial subjects or inculcating racial ideals or writing racial textbooks or projecting vocational guidance from the point of view of race. And yet standing in stark contradiction of all this are the surrounding facts of race: the Jim Crow seats on the street cars every day, the Jim Crow coaches on the railroads, the separate sections of the city where the races dwell; the discrimination in occupations and opportunities and in law; and beyond that the widespread division of the world by custom into white, yellow and black, ruler and eternally ruled.

We American Negroes form and long will form a perfectly definite group, not entirely segregated and isolated from our surroundings, but differentiated to such a degree that we have very largely a life and thought of our own. And it is this fact that we as scientists, and teachers and persons engaged in living, earning a living, have got to take into account and make our major problem. In the face of that, we have these young intellectual exquisites who smile if they do not laugh outright at our writhings. Their practical program is, so far as our race or group is concerned: Do nothing, think nothing, become absorbed in the nation.

To which the flat answer is: This is impossible. We have got to do something about race. We have got to think and think clearly about our present situation. Absorption into the nation, save as a long, slow intellectual process, is unthinkable and while it may eventually come, its trend and result depend very largely upon what kind of a group is being absorbed; whether such racial integration has to do with poverty-stricken and half starved criminals; or whether with intelligent self-guided, independently acting men, who know what they want and propose at any civilized cost to get it. No, separated and isolated as we are so largely, we form in America an integral group, call it by any name you will, and this fact in itself has its meaning, its worth and its values.

In no line is this clearer than in the democratization of industry. We are still a poor people, a mass of laborers, with few rich folk and little exploitation of labor. We can be among the first to help restore the idea of high culture and limited income and dispel the fable that riotous wealth alone is civilization. Acting together, voluntarily or by outer compulsion, we can be the units through which universal democracy may be accomplished.

We black folk have striven to be Americans. And like all other Americans, we have longed to become rich Americans. Wealth comes easiest today through the exploitation of labor by paying low wages; and if we have not widely exploited our own and other labor the praise belongs not to us, but to those whites whose monopoly of wealth and ruthless methods have out-run our tardy and feeble efforts. This is the place to pause and look about, as well, backward as forward. The leaders of the labor movement in America as in Europe, deceived us just as they deceived themselves. They left us out. They paid no attention to us, whether we were drudging in colonies or slaving in cotton fields or pleading in vain at the door of union labor factories. The object of white labor was not the uplift of all labor; it was to join capital in sharing the loot from exploited colored labor. So we too, only half emancipated, hurled ourselves forward, too willing if it had but been possible, to climb up to a bourgeois heaven on the prone bodies of our fellows. But white folk occupied and crowded these stairs. And white labor loved the white exploiter of black folk far more than it loved its fellow black proletarian.

Such is the plight of democracy today. Where in this picture does the American Negro come? With few exceptions, we are all today "white folks' niggers." No, do not wince. I mean nothing insulting or derogatory, but this is a concrete designation which indicates that very very many colored folk: Japanese, Chinese, Indians, Negroes; and, of course, the vast majority of white folk; have been so enthused, oppressed, and suppressed by current white civilization that they think and judge everything by its terms. They have no norms that are not set in the nineteenth and twentieth centuries. They can conceive of no future world which is not dominated by present white nations and thoroughly shot through with their ideals, their method of government, their economic organization, their literature and their art; or in other words their throttling of democracy, their exploitation of labor, their industrial imperialism and their color hate. To broach before such persons any suggestion of radical change; any idea of intrusion, physical or spiritual, on the part of alien races is to bring down upon one's devoted head the most tremendous astonishment and contempt.

What to do? We went to school. But our industrial schools taught no industrial history, no labor movement, no social reform—only technique just when the technique of skilled trades was changing to mass industry. Our colleges taught the reactionary economics of Northern Schools. We landed in bitter and justifiable complaint and sought a way out by complaining. Our mistake lay not in the injustice of our cause, but in our naive assumption that a system of industrial monopoly that was making money out of our exploitation, was going voluntarily to help us escape its talons.

On the other hand when we turn to join the forces of progress and reform we find again no easy or obvious path. As the disinherited both of labor and capital; as those discriminated against by employer and employee, we are forced to a most careful and thorough-going program of minority planning. We may call this self-segregation if we will but the compulsion is from without and inevitable. We may call it racial chauvinism but we may make it the path to democracy through group culture. This path includes sympathy and co-operation with the labor movement; with the efforts of those who produce wealth, to assert their right to control it. It has been no easy path. What with organized, intelligent and powerful opposition and ignorant and venal and dogmatic leadership, the white labor movement has staggered drunkenly for two hundred years or more and yet it has given the world a vision of real democracy, of universal education and of a living wage. It is the most promising movement of modern days and we who are primarily laborers must eventually join it.

In addition to this, no matter how great our political disfranchisement and social exclusion, we have in our hands a voting power which is enormous, and that is the control we can exercise over the production and distribution of goods through our expenditure as consumers. The might and efficiency of this method of economic reform is continually minimized by the obvious fact that it does not involve radical change and that without other and more thorough-going changes it can bring no immediate millenium. But notwithstanding for a minority group it is the most powerful weapon at hand and to refuse to use an instrument of power because it is not all powerful is silly.

A people who buy each year at least a half billion dollars worth of goods and services are not helpless. If they starve it is their own fault. If they do not achieve a respected place in the surrounding industrial organization, it is because they are stupid.

Here then is the plight and the steps toward remedy. Yet we are not awake. We have let obvious opportunities slip by during these awful days of depression when we have lost much of the land we used to own; when our savings have been dissipated; when our business enterprises have failed and when if not a majority a strikingly large minority of us are existing on public charity. We have not asked for the advantage of public housing as we should. We have not taken advantage of the possibilities of the TVA. We have not pushed energetically into plans of resettlement and the establishment of model villages. We have almost refused the subsistence homestead. We have not begun to think of socialized medicine and consumer cooperation. We have no comprehensive plans concerning our unemployment, our economic dependence, the profit economy and the changing technique of industry. The day of our reckoning is at hand. Awake, Awake, put on thy strength Oh Zion.

The martyrdom of man may be increased and prolonged through primitive, biological racial propaganda, but on the other hand through cooperation, education and understanding the cultural race unit may be the pipe line through which human civilization may extend to wider and wider areas to the fertilization of mankind.

It is to this use of our racial unity and loyalty that the United States impels us. We cannot escape it. Only through racial effort today can we achieve economic stability, cultural growth and human understanding. The way to democracy lies through race loyalty if only that is its real and consciously comprehended end. Selah and Amen.

This then is the revelation of Saint Orgne the Damned, as given me by his hand; and the philosophy of life out of which he strove to climb, despite the curse, to broader and more abundant life. Bearing this revelation, Men and Women of the Class of 1938, there return to you today, three pilgrims, and the ghosts of three others, whose memories await us. Fifty years ago we stood where you stand and received the Light of the Seven Stars. We return, not all-wise, but wise; for we have seen ten presidents rule in America and five kings reign in England; we have seen the fall of three great empires; a whole world at war to commit 26 million murders; the rise of dark Japan and fall of darker Ethiopia. We have seen our own race in America nearly double in number from less than seven to more than twelve million souls.

We return home today worn and travel stained, yet with the Light which Alma Mater laid upon our hands; it does not burn so high nor flash so fiercely—yet it has lighted thousands of other candles, and it is still aflame. We hand it on to you, that fifty years hence you give it again to others—and so on forever.

Fisk News, November–December, 1938

Jacob and Esau (1944)

We have got to stop making income by unholy methods; . . . to stop lying . . . that a civilization based upon the enslavement of the majority of men for the income of the smart minority is the highest aim of man.

I remember very vividly the Sunday-School room where I spent the Sabbaths of my early years. It had been newly-built after a disastrous fire; the room was large and full of sunlight; nice new chairs were grouped around where the classes met. My class was in the center, so that I could look out upon the elms of Main Street and see the passersby. But I was interested usually in the lessons and my fellow students and the frail rather nervous teacher, who tried to make the Bible and its ethics clear to us. We were a trial to her, full of mischief, restless and even noisy; but perhaps more especially when we asked questions. And on the story of Jacob and Esau we did ask questions. My judgment then and my judgment now is very unfavorable to Jacob. I thought that he was a cad and a liar and I did not see how possibly he could be made the hero of a Sunday-School lesson.

Many days have passed since then and the world has gone through astonishing changes. But basically, my judgment of Jacob has not greatly changed and I have often promised myself the pleasure of talking about him publicly, and especially to young people. This is the first time that I have had the opportunity.

My subject then is "Jacob and Esau," and I want to examine these two men and the ideas which they represent; and the way in which those ideas have come to our day. Of course, our whole interpretation of this age-old story of Jewish Mythology has greatly changed. We look upon these Old

Testament stories today not as untrue and yet not as literally true. They are simple, they have their truths and yet they are not by any means, the expression of eternal verity. Here were brought forward for the education of Jewish children and for the interpretation of Jewish life to the world, two men: one small, lithe and quick-witted; the other tall, clumsy and impetuous; a hungry, hard-bitten man.

Historically, we know how these two types came to be set forth by the Bards of Israel. When the Jews marched North after escaping from slavery in Egypt, they penetrated and passed through the land of Edom; the land that lay between the Dead Sea and Egypt. It was an old center of hunters and nomads, and the Israelites, while they admired the strength and organization of the Edomites, looked down upon them as lesser men; as men who did not have the Great Plan. Now the Great Plan of the Israelites was the building of a strong, concentrated state under its own God, Jehovah, devoted to agriculture and household manufacture and trade. It raised its own food by careful planning. It did not wander and depend upon chance wild beasts. It depended upon organization, strict ethics, absolute devotion to the nation through strongly integrated planned life. It looked upon all its neighbors, not simply with suspicion, but with the exclusiveness of a chosen people, who were going to be the leaders of the earth.

This called for sacrifice, for obedience, for continued planning. The man whom we call Esau, was from the land of Edom, or intermarried with it, for the legend has it that he was twin of Jacob the Jew. But the idea of the Plan with a personality of its own took hold of Europe with relentless grasp and this was the real legacy of Jacob, and of other men of other peoples, whom Jacob represents.

There came the attempt to weld the world into a great unity, first under the Roman Empire, then under the Catholic Church. When this attempt failed, and the empire fell apart, there arose the individual states of Europe and of some other parts of the world; and these states adapted the idea of individual effort to make each of them dominant. The state was *all*, the individual subordinate, but right here came the poison of the Jacobean idea. How could the state get this power? Who was to wield the power within the State? So long as power was achieved, what difference did it make how it was gotten? Here then was war—but not Esau's war of passion, hunger and revenge, but Jacob's war of cold acquisition and power.

Granting to Jacob, as we must, the great idea of the family, the clan, and the state as dominant and superior in its claims, nevertheless, there is the bitter danger in trying to seek these ends without reference to the great standards of right and wrong. When men begin to lie and steal, in order to make the nation to which they belong great, then comes not only disaster, but rational contradiction which in many respects is worse than disaster, because it ruins the leadership of the divine machine, the human reason, by which we chart and guide our actions.

PROFIT AND POWER AS MOTIVES

It was thus in the middle ages and increasingly in the seventeenth and eighteenth and more especially in the nineteenth century, there arose the astonishing contradiction: that is, the action of men like Jacob who were perfectly willing and eager to lie and steal so long as their action brought profit to themselves and power to their state. And soon identifying themselves and their class with the State, they identified their own wealth and power as that of the State. They did not listen to any argument of right and wrong; might was right; they came to despise and deplore the natural appetites of human beings and their very lives, so long as by their suppression, they themselves got rich and powerful. There arose a great, rich Italy; a fabulously wealthy Spain; a strong and cultured France and, eventually, a British Empire which came near to dominating the world. The Esaus of those centuries were the Jews but the chief fact is, that no matter what his blood relations were, his cultural allegiance lay among the Edomites. He was trained in the free out-of-doors; he chased and faced the wild beasts; he knew vast and imperative appetite after long self-denial, and even pain and suffering; he gloried in food, he traveled afar; he gathered wives and concubines and he represented continuous primitive strife.

THE LEGACY OF ESAU

The legacy of Esau has come down the ages to us. It has not been dominant, but it has always and continually expressed and re-expressed itself; the joy of human appetites, the quick resentment that leads to fighting, the belief in force, which is war.

As I look back upon my own conception of Esau, he is not nearly as clear and definite a personality as Jacob. There is something rather shadowy about him; and yet he is curiously human and easily conceived. One understands his contemptuous surrender of his birthright: he was hungry after long days of hunting; he wanted rest and food, the stew of meat and vegetables which Jacob had in his possession, and determined to keep unless Esau bargained. "And Esau said, Behold, I am at the point to die: and what profit shall this birthright be to me? And Jacob said, Swear to me this day; and he swore unto him: and he sold his birthright unto Jacob."

THE LEGACY OF JACOB

On the other hand, the legacy of Jacob which has come down through the years, not simply as a Jewish idea, but more especially as typical of modern Europe, is more complicated and expresses itself something like this: Life must be planned for the Other Self, for that personification of the group, the nation, the empire, which has eternal life as contrasted with the ephemeral life of individuals. For this we must plan, and for this there must be timeless and unceasing work. Out of this, the Jews as chosen children of Jehovah would triumph over themselves, over all Edom and in time, over the world.

Now it happens that so far as actual history is concerned, this dream and plan failed. The poor little Jewish nation was dispersed to the ends of the earth by the overwhelming power of the great nations that arose East, North, and South and eventually became united in the vast empire of Rome. This was the diaspora, the dispersion of, curiously represented by various groups of people: by the slum-dwellers and the criminals who, giving up all hope of profiting by the organized State, sold their birthrights for miserable messes of pottage. But more than that, the great majority of mankind, the peoples who lived in Asia, Africa and America and the islands of the sea, became subordinate tools for the profit-making of the crafty planners of great things, who worked regardless of religion or ethics.

CENTURIES OF EXPLOITATION

It is almost unbelievable to think what happened in those centuries, when it is put in cold narrative; from whole volumes of tales, let me select only a few examples. The peoples of whole islands and countries were murdered in cold blood for their gold and jewels. The mass of the laboring people of the world were put to work for wages which led them into starvation, ignorance and disease. The right of the majority of mankind to speak and to act; to play and to dance was denied, if it interfered with profit-making work for others, or was ridiculed, if it could not be capitalized. Karl Marx writes of Scotland: "As an example of the method of obtaining wealth and power in the 19th century; the story of the Duchess of Sutherland will suffice here. This Scottish noblewoman resolved, on entering upon the government of her clan of white Scottish people to turn the whole country, whose population had already been, by earlier processes, reduced to 15,000, into a sheep pasture. From 1814 to 1820 these 15,000 inhabitants, were systematically hunted and rooted out. All their villages were destroyed and burnt, all their fields turned into pasture. Thus this lady appropriated 794,000 acres of land that had from time immemorial been the property of the people. She assigned to the expelled inhabitants about 6000 acres on the sea-shore. The 6000 acres had until this time lain waste, and brought in no income to their owners. The Duchess, in the nobility of her heart, actually went so far as to let these at an average rent of 50¢ per acre to the clansmen, who for centuries had shed their blood for her family. The whole of the stolen clan-land she divided into 29 great sheep farms, each inhabited by a single imported English family. In the year 1835 the 15,000 Scotsmen were already replaced by 131,000 sheep.

EXPLOITATION OF COLONIES

"The discovery of gold and silver in America, the extirpation, enslavement and entombment in the mines of the Indian population, the beginning of the conquest and looting of the East Indies, the turning of Africa into a warren for the commercial hunting of black-skins, signalized the rosy dawn of power of those spiritual children of Jacob, who owned the birthright of the masses by fraud and murder. These idyllic proceedings are the chief momenta of primary accumulation of capital in private hands. On their heels tread the commercial wars of the European nations, with the globe for a theatre. It begins with the revolt of the Netherlands from Spain, assumes giant dimensions in England's anti-jacobin war, and continues in the opium wars against China."

Of the Christian colonial system, Howitt says: "The barbarities and desperate outrages of the so-called Christians, throughout every region of the world, and upon people they have been able to subdue, are not to be paralleled by those of any other race, in any age of the earth. This history of the colonial administration of Holland—and Holland was the head capitalistic nation of the 17th century—is one of the most extraordinary relations of treachery, bribery, massacre, and meanness."

Nothing was more characteristic than the Dutch system of stealing men, to get slaves for Java. The men-stealers were trained for this purpose. The thief, the interpreter, and the seller were the chief agents in this trade, the native princes the chief sellers. The young people stolen, were thrown into the secret dungeons of Celebes, until they were ready for sending to the slave-ships.

The English East India Company, in the seventeenth and

eighteenth centuries, obtained, besides the political rule in India, the exclusive monopoly of the tea-trade, as well as the Chinese trade in general, and of the transport of goods to and from Europe. But the coasting trade of India was the monopoly of the higher employers of the company. The monopolies of salt, opium, betel nuts and other commodities, were inexhaustible mines of wealth. The employees themselves fixed the price and plundered at will the unhappy Hindus. The Governor-General took part in this private traffic. His favorites received contracts under conditions whereby they, cleverer than the alchemists, made gold out of nothing. Great English fortunes sprang up like mushrooms in a day; investment profits went on without the advance of a shilling. The trial of Warren Hastings swarms with such cases. Here is an instance: A contract for opium was given to a certain Sullivan at the moment of his departure on an official mission. Sullivan sold his contract to one Binn for $200,000; Binn sold it the same day for $300,000, and the ultimate purchaser who carried out the contract declared that after all he realized an enormous gain. According to one of the lists laid before Parliament, the East India Company and its employees from 1757–1766 got $30,000,000 from the Indians as gifts alone.

TREATMENT OF ABORIGINES

The treatment of the aborigines was, naturally, most frightful in plantation colonies destined for import trade only, such as the West Indies, and in rich and well-populated countries, such as Mexico and India, that were given over to plunder. But even in the colonies properly so-called, the followers of Jacob outdid him. These sober Protestants, the Puritans of New England, in 1703, by decrees of their assembly set a premium of $200 on every Indian scalp and every captured red-skin: in 1720 a premium of $500 on every scalp; in 1744, after Massachusetts Bay had proclaimed a certain tribe as rebels, the following prices prevailed: for a male scalp of 12 years upward $500 (new currency); for a male prisoner $525, for women and children prisoners $250; for scalps of

women and children $250. Some decades later, the colonial
system took its revenge on the descendants of the pious pil-
grim fathers, who had grown seditious in the meantime. At
English instigation and for English pay they were toma-
hawked by the red-skins. The British Parliament, proclaimed
blood-hounds and scalping as "means that God and Nature
had given into its hands."

With the development of national industry during the eighteenth century, the public opinion of Europe had lost the last
remnant of shame and conscience. The nations bragged cynically of every infamy that served them as a means to accumulating private wealth. Read, e. g., the naive *Annals of
Commerce* of Anderson. Here is trumpetted forth as a triumph of English state-craft that at the Peace of Utrecht,
England extorted from the Spaniards by the Asiento Treaty
the privilege of being allowed to ply the slave-trade, between
Africa and Spanish America. England thereby acquired the
right of supplying Spanish America until 1743 with 4,800
Negroes yearly. This threw, at the same time, an official cloak
over British smuggling. Liverpool waxed fat on the slave-
trade. Aihin (1795) quotes that "spirit of bold adventure
which has characterized the trade of Liverpool and rapidly
carried it to its present state of prosperity; has occasioned
vast employment for shipping sailors, and greatly augmented
the demand for the manufactures of the country; Liverpool
employed in the slave trade, in 1730, 15 ships; in 1760, 74; in
1770, 96; and in 1792, 132."

A PROMISE UNFULFILLED

Henry George wrote of "Progress and Poverty" in the
1890's. He says: "At the beginning of this marvelous era it
was natural to expect, and it was expected, that labor-saving
inventions would lighten the toil and improve the condition
of the laborer; that the enormous increase in the power of
producing wealth would make real poverty a thing of the
past. Could a man of the last century (the eighteenth)—a
Franklin or a Priestley—have seen, in a vision of the future,
the steam-ship taking the place of the sailing vessel, the rail-

road train of the wagon, the reaping machine of the scythe, the threshing machine of the flail; could he have heard the throb of the engines that in obedience to human will, and for the satisfaction of the human desire, exert a power greater than that of all the men and beasts of burden of the earth combined; could he have seen the forest tree transformed into finished lumber—into doors, sashes, blinds, boxes or barrels, with hardly the touch of a human hand; the great workshops where boots and shoes are turned out by the case with less labor than the old-fashioned cobbler could have put on a sole; the factories where, under the eye of one girl, cotton becomes cloth faster than hundreds of stalwart weavers could have turned it out with their handlooms; could he have seen steam-hammers shaping mammoth shafts and mighty anchors, and delicate machinery making tiny watches; the diamond drill cutting through the heart of the rocks, and coal oil sparing the whale; could he have realized the enormous saving of labor resulting from improved facilities of exchange and communication—sheep killed in Australia eaten fresh in England, and the order given by the London banker in the afternoon executed in San Francisco in the morning of the next day; could he have conceived of the hundred thousand improvements which these only suggest, what would he have inferred as to the social condition of mankind?

"It would not have seemed like an inference; further than the vision went it would have seemed as though he saw; and his heart would have leaped and his nerves would have thrilled, as one who from a height beholds just ahead of the thirst-stricken caravan the living gleam of rustling woods and the glint of laughing waters. Plainly, in the sight of the imagination, he would have beheld all these new forces elevating society from its very foundation, lifting the very poorest above the possibility of want, exempting the very lowest from anxiety for the material needs of life; he would have seen these slaves of the lamp of knowledge taking on themselves the traditional curse, these muscles of iron and sinews of steel making the poorest laborer's life a holiday, in which every high quality and noble impulse could have scope to grow."

This was the promise of Jacob's life. This would establish

the birthright which Esau despised. But, says George, "Now, we are coming into collision with facts which there can be no mistaking. From all parts of the civilized world," he says speaking fifty years ago, "come complaints of industrial depression; of labor condemned to involuntary idleness; of capital massed and wasting; of pecuniary distress among business; of want and suffering and anxiety among the working class. All the dull, deadening pain, all the keen, maddening anguish, that to great masses of men are involved into the words 'hard times' which afflict the world today." What would Henry George have said in 1933 after airplane and radio and mass production, turbine and electricity had come?

BIRTH OF REVOLT

Science and art grew and expanded despite all this, but it was warped by the poverty of the artist and the continuous attempt to make Science subservient to industry. The latter effort finally succeeded so widely that modern civilization became typified as industrial technique. Education became learning a trade. Men thought of civilization as primarily mechanical and the mechanical means by which they reduced wool and cotton to their purposes, also reduced and bent human kind to their will. Individual initiative remained but it was cramped and distorted and there spread the idea of patriotism to one's country as the highest virtue, by which it became established, that just as in the case of Jacob, a man not only could lie, steal, cheat and murder for his native land, but by doing so, he became a hero whether his cause was just or unjust. One remembers that old scene between Esau who had thoughtlessly surrendered his birthright and the father who had blessed his lying son; "Jacob came unto his father, and said, My Father: and he said, Here am I; who art thou? And Jacob said unto his father, I am Esau thy first-born; I have done according as thou badest me: arise, I pray thee, sit and eat of my venison, that thy soul may bless me." In vain did clumsy, careless Esau beg for a blessing—some little blessing. It was denied and Esau hated Jacob because of the blessing: and Esau said in his heart, "The Days of mourning

for my father are at hand; then I will slay my brother Jacob."
So revolution entered—so revolt darkened a dark world.

The same motif was repeated in modern Europe and America in the nineteenth and twentieth centuries, when there grew the super-state called the Empire. The Plan had now regimented the organization of men covering vast territories, dominating immense force and immeasurable wealth and determined to reduce to subserviency as large a part as possible, not only of Europe's own internal world, but of the world at large. Colonial imperialism swept over the earth and initiated the First World War, in envious scramble for division of Power and Profit.

Hardly a moment of time passed after that war, a moment in the eyes of the Eternal Forces looking down upon us when again the world, using all of that planning and all of that technical superiority for which its civilization was noted; and all of the accumulated and accumulating wealth which was available, proceeded to commit suicide on so vast a scale that it is almost impossible for us to realize the meaning of the catastrophe. Of course, this sweeps us far beyond anything that the peasant lad Jacob, with his petty lying and thievery had in mind. Whatever was begun there of ethical wrong among the Jews was surpassed in every particular by the white world of Europe and America and carried to such length of universal cheating, lying and killing that no comparisons remain.

THE IMPASSE OF OUR TIME

We come therefore to the vast impasse of today: to the great question, What was the initial right and wrong of the original Jacobs and Esaus and of their spiritual descendants the world over? We stand convinced today, at least those who remain sane, that lying and cheating and killing will build no world organization worth the building. We have got to stop making income by unholy methods; out of stealing the pittances of the poor and calling it insurance; out of seizing and monopolizing the natural resources of the world and then making the world's poor pay exorbitant prices for aluminum, copper and oil; iron and coal. Not only have we got to stop these practices, but we have got to stop lying about them and seeking to convince human beings that a civilization based upon the enslavement of the majority of men for the income of the smart minority, is the highest aim of man.

THE FAULTS OF ESAU

But as is so usual in these cases, these transgressions of Jacob do not mean that the attitude of Esau was flawless. The conscienceless greed of capital does not excuse the careless sloth of labor. Life cannot be all aimless wandering and indulgence if we are going to constrain human beings to take advantage of their brain and make successive generations stronger and wiser than the previous. There must be reverence for the *birthright* of inherited *culture* and that birthright cannot be sold for a dinner course, a dress suit or a winter in Florida. It must be valued and conserved.

The method of conservation is work, endless and tireless and planned work and this is the legacy which the Esaus of today who condemn the Jacobs of yesterday have got to substitute as their path of life, not revengeful revolution, but building and rebuilding. Curiously enough, it will not be difficult to do this, because the great majority of men, the poverty-stricken and diseased are the *real workers* of the world. They are the ones who have made and are making the wealth of this universe, and their future path is clear. It is to accumulate such knowledge and balance of judgment that they can reform the world, so that the workers of the world, receive just share of the wealth which they make and that all human beings who are capable of work, shall work. Not national glory and empire for the few, but food, shelter and happiness for the many. With the disappearance of systematic lying and killing, we may come into that Birthright which so long we have called freedom: that is, the right to act in a manner that seems to us beautiful; which makes life worth living and joy the only possible end of life. This is the experience which is Art and Planning for this is the highest satisfaction of civilized needs. So looking back upon the allegory and the history, tragedy and promise, we change our subject and speak in closing of Esau and Jacob, realizing that neither was perfect, but of the two, Esau had the elements which lead more naturally and directly to the salvation of man; while Jacob with all his crafty planning and cold sacrifice, held in his soul the things that are about to ruin mankind: Exaggerated national patriotism, individual profit, the despising of men who are not the darlings of our particular God and the consequent lying and stealing and killing to monopolize power.

HOPE FOR A NEW WORLD

May we not hope that in the world after this catastrophe of blood, sweat and fire, we may have a new Esau and Jacob; a new allegory of men who enjoy life for life's sake; who have the Freedom of Art and wish for all men of all sorts the same freedom and enjoyment that they seek themselves and who work for all this and work hard.

Gentlemen and ladies of the class of 1944: In the days of the years of my pilgrimage, I have greeted many thousands of young men and women at the commencement of their careers as citizens of the select commonwealth of culture. In no case have I welcomed them to such a world of darkness and distractions as that into which I usher you. I take joy only in the thought, that if work to be done is the measure of man's opportunity, you inherit a mighty fortune. You have only to remember that the birthright which is today in symbol draped over your shoulders, is a heritage which has been preserved all too often by the lying, stealing and murdering of the Jacobs of the world, and if these are the only means by which this birthright can be preserved in the future, it is not worth the price. I do not believe this, and I lay it upon your hearts to prove that this not only need not be true, but is eternally and forever false.

The Talladegan, November, 1944

Behold the Land! *(1946)*

Delivered in Columbia, South Carolina, October 20, 1946, as the principal address at the closing session of the Southern Youth Legislature, sponsored by the Southern Negro Youth Congress.

The future of American Negroes is in the South. Here three hundred and twenty-seven years ago, they began to enter what is now the United States of America; here they have made their greatest contribution to American culture; and here they have suffered the damnation of slavery, the frustration of reconstruction and the lynching of emancipation. I trust then that an organization like yours is going to regard the South as the battle ground of a great crusade. Here is the magnificent climate; here is the fruitful earth under the beauty of the southern sun; and here, if anywhere on earth, is the need of the thinker, the worker and the dreamer. This is the firing line not simply for the emancipation of the American Negro but for the emancipation of the African Negro and the Negroes of the West Indies; for the emancipation of the colored races; and for the emancipation of the white slaves of modern capitalistic monopoly.

Remember here, too, that you do not stand alone. It may seem like a failing fight when the newspapers ignore you; when every effort is made by white people in the South to count you out of citizenship and to act as though you did not exist as human beings while all the time they are profiting by your labor; gleaning wealth from your sacrifices and trying to build a nation and a civilization upon your degradation. You must remember that despite all this, you have allies and allies even in the white South. First and greatest of these possible allies are the white working classes about you. The poor whites whom you have been taught to despise and who in turn have learned to fear and hate you. This must not deter you from efforts to make them understand, because in the past in their ignorance and suffering they have been led foolishly to look upon you as the cause of most of their distress. You must remember that this attitude is hereditary from slavery and that it has been deliberately cultivated ever since emancipation.

Slowly but surely the working people of the South, white and black, must come to remember that their emancipation depends upon their mutual cooperation; upon their acquaintanceship with each other; upon their friendship; upon their social intermingling. Unless this happens each is going to be made the football to break the heads and hearts of the other.

WHITE YOUTH IS FRUSTRATED

White youth in the South is peculiarly frustrated. There is not a single great ideal which they can express or aspire to, that does not bring them into flat contradiction with the Negro problem. The more they try to escape it, the more they land into hypocrisy, lying and double-dealing; the more they become, what they least wish to become, the oppressors and despisers of human beings. Some of them, in larger and larger numbers, are bound to turn toward the truth and to recognize you as brothers and sisters, as fellow travellers toward the dawn.

There has always been in the South that intellectual elite who saw the Negro problem clearly. They have always lacked and some still lack the courage to stand up for what they know is right. Nevertheless they can be depended on in the long run to follow their own clear thinking and their own decent choice. Finally even the politicians must eventually recognize the trend in the world, in this country, and in the South. James Byrnes, that favorite son of this commonwealth, and Secretary of State of the United States, is today occupying an indefensible and impossible position; and if he survives in the memory of men, he must begin to help establish in his own South Carolina something of that democracy which he has been recently so loudly preaching to Russia. He is the end of a long series of men whose eternal damnation is the fact that they looked *truth* in the face and did not see it; John C. Calhoun, Wade Hampton, Ben Tillman are men whose names must ever be besmirched by the fact that they fought against freedom and democracy in a land which was founded upon democracy and freedom.

Eventually this class of men must yield to the writing in the stars. That great hypocrite, Jan Smuts, who today is talking of humanity and standing beside Byrnes for a United Nations, is at the same time oppressing the black people of Africa to an extent which makes their two countries, South Africa and the American South, the most reactionary peoples on earth. Peoples whose exploitation of the poor and helpless reaches the last degree of shame. They must in the long run yield to the forward march of civilization or die.

WHAT DOES THE FIGHT MEAN?

If now you young people, instead of running away from the battle here in Carolina, Georgia, Alabama, Louisana and Mississippi, instead of seeking freedom and opportunity in Chicago and New York—which do spell opportunity—nevertheless grit your teeth and make up your minds to fight it out right here if it takes every day of your lives and the lives of your children's children; if you do this, you must in meetings like this ask yourselves what does the fight mean? How can it be carried on? What are the best tools, arms, and methods? And where does it lead?

I should be the last to insist that the uplift of mankind never calls for force and death. There are times, as both you and I know, when

> Tho' love repine and reason chafe,
> There came a voice without reply,
> 'Tis man's perdition to be safe
> When for truth he ought to die.

At the same time and even more clearly in a day like this, after the millions of mass murders that have been done in the world since 1914, we ought to be the last to believe that force is ever the final word. We cannot escape the clear fact that what is going to win in this world is reason if ever this becomes a reasonable world. The careful reasoning of the human mind backed by the facts of science is the one salvation of man. The world, if it resumes its march toward civilization, cannot ignore reason. This has been the tragedy to the South in the past; it is still its awful and unforgivable sin that it has set its face against reason and against the fact. It tried to build slavery upon freedom; it tried to build tyranny upon democracy; it tried to build mob violence on law and law on lynching and in all that despicable endeavor, the state of South Carolina has led the South for a century. It began not the Civil War—not the War Between the States—but the War to Preserve Slavery; it began mob violence and lynching and today it stands in the front rank of those defying the Supreme Court on disfranchisement.

Nevertheless reason can and will prevail; but of course it can only prevail with publicity—pitiless, blatant publicity. You have got to make the people of the United States and the world know what is going on in the South. You have got to use every field of publicity to force the truth into their ears, and before their eyes. You have got to make it impossible for any human being to live in the South and not to realize the barbarities that prevail here. You may be condemned for flamboyant methods; for calling a congress like this; for waving your grievances under the noses and in the faces of men. That makes no difference; it is your duty to do it. It is your duty to do more of this sort of thing than you have done in the past. As a result of this you are going to be called upon for sacrifice. It is no easy thing for a young black man or a young black woman to live in the South today and to plan to continue to live here; to marry and raise children; to establish a home. They are in the midst of legal caste and customary insults; they are in continuous mob violence; they are mistreated by the officers of the law and they have no hearing before the courts and the churches and public opinion commensurate with the attention which they ought to receive. But that sacrifice is only the beginning of battle, you must rebuild this South.

There are enormous opportunities here for a new nation, a new economy, a new culture in a South really new and not a mere renewal of an old South of slavery, monopoly and race hate. There is a chance for a new cooperative agriculture on renewed land owned by the state with capital furnished by the state, mechanized and coordinated with city life. There is a chance for strong, virile trade unions without race discrimination, with high wage, closed shop and decent conditions of work, to beat back and hold in check the swarm of landlords, monopolists and profiteers who are today sucking the blood out of this land. There is a chance for cooperative industry, built on the cheap power of TVA and its future extensions. There is opportunity to organize and mechanize domestic service with decent hours, and high wage and dignified training.

"BEHOLD THE LAND"

There is a vast field for consumer cooperation, building business on public service and not on private profit as the main-spring of industry. There is a chance for a broad, sunny, healthy home life, shorn of the fear of mobs and liquor, and rescued from lying, stealing politicians, who build their deviltry on race prejudice.

Here in the South is the gateway to the colored millions of the West Indies, Central and South America. Here is the straight path to Africa, the Indies, China and the South Seas. Here is the path to the greater, freer, truer world. It would be shame and cowardice to surrender this glorious land and its opportunities for civilization and humanity to the thugs and lynchers, the mobs and profiteers, the monopolists and gamblers who today choke its soul and steal its resources. The oil and sulphur; the coal and iron; the cotton and corn; the lumber and cattle belong to you the workers, black and white, and not to the thieves who hold them and use them to enslave you. They can be rescued and restored to the people if you have the guts to strive for the real right to vote, the right to real education, the right to happiness and health and the total abolition of the father of these scourges of mankind, *poverty*.

"Behold the beautiful land which the Lord thy God hath given thee." Behold the land, the rich and resourceful land, from which for a hundred years its best elements have been running away, its youth and hope, black and white, scurrying North because they are afraid of each other, and dare not face a future of equal, independent, upstanding human beings, in a real and not a sham democracy.

To rescue this land, in this way, calls for the *Great Sacrifice;* This is the thing that you are called upon to do because it is the right thing to do. Because you are embarked upon a great and holy crusade, the emancipation of mankind, black and white; the upbuilding of democracy; the breaking down, particularly here in the South, of forces of evil represented by race prejudice in South Carolina; by lynching in Georgia; by disfranchisement in Mississippi; by ignorance in Louisiana and by all these and monopoly of wealth in the whole South.

There could be no more splendid vocation beckoning to the youth of the twentieth century, after the flat failures of white civilization, after the flamboyant establishment of an industrial system which creates poverty and the children of poverty which are ignorance and disease and crime; after the crazy boasting of a white culture that finally ended in wars which ruined civilization in the whole world; in the midst of allied peoples who have yelled about democracy and never practiced it either in the British Empire or in the American Commonwealth or in South Carolina.

Here is the chance for young women and young men of devotion to lift again the banner of humanity and to walk toward a civilization which will be free and intelligent; which will be healthy and unafraid; and build in the world a culture led by black folk and joined by peoples of all colors and all races—without poverty, ignorance and disease!

Once a great German poet cried: "Selig der den Er in Sieges Glanze findet."

Happy man whom Death shall find in Victory's splendor.

But I know a happier one: he who fights in despair and in defeat still fights. Singing with Arna Bontemps the quiet determined philosophy of undefeatable men:

I thought I saw an angel flying low.
I thought I saw the flicker of a wing
Above the mulberry trees; but not again.

Bethesda sleeps. This ancient pool that healed
A Host of bearded Jews does not awake.
This pool that once the angels troubled does not move.
No angel stirs it now, no Saviour comes
With healing in His hands to raise the sick
And bid the lame man leap upon the ground.

The golden days are gone. Why do we wait
So long upon the marble steps, blood
Falling from our open wounds? and why
Do our black faces search the empty sky?
Is there something we have forgotten?
    Some precious thing
We have lost, wandering in strange lands? . . .

There was a day, I remember now,
I beat my breast and cried, "Wash me God,"
Wash me with a wave of wind upon
The barley; O quiet One, draw near, draw near!
Walk upon the hills with lovely feet
And in the waterfall stand and speak.

Freedomways, Vol. 4, No. 1, First Quarter, Winter, 1964, pp. 8–15

Postscript
The University—Leaders—Education and Work (1903)

A university is a human invention for the transmission of knowledge and culture from generation to generation, through the training of quick minds and pure hearts, and for this work no other human invention will suffice, not even trade and industrial schools.

All men cannot go to college but some men must; every isolated group or nation must have its yeast, must have for the talented few centers of training where men are not so mystified and befuddled by the hard and necessary toil of earning a living, as to have no aims higher than their bellies, and no God greater than Gold. This is true training, and thus in the beginning were the favored sons of the freedmen trained. . . .

Do you think that if the leaders of thought among Negroes are not trained and educated thinkers, that they will have no leaders? On the contrary a hundred half-trained demagogues will still hold the places they so largely occupy now, and hundreds of vociferous busy-bodies will multiply. You have no choice; either you must help furnish this race from within its own ranks with thoughtful men of trained leadership, or you must suffer the evil consequences of a headless misguided rabble. . . .

Men of America, the problem is plain before you. Here is a race transplanted through the criminal foolishness of your fathers. Whether you like it or not the millions are here, and here they will remain. If you do not lift them up, they will pull you down. Education and Work are the levers to uplift a people. Work alone will not do it unless inspired by the right ideals and guided by intelligence. Education must not simply teach work—it must teach Life. The Talented Tenth of the Negro race must be made leaders of thought and missionaries of culture among their people. No other can do this work and the Negro colleges must train men for it. The Negro race, like all other races, is going to be saved by its exceptional men.

From "The Talented Tenth" in *The Negro Problem*, 1903, pp. 33–75

Afterthought

The Problem of Humanity—The "Voice of Voices"—The Fusion of Cultures—Not the "Integration" of Colors

BEYOND ALL THIS, and when legal inequalities pass from the statute books, a rock wall of social discrimination between human beings will long persist in human intercourse. So far as such discrimination is a method of social selection, by means of which the worst is slowly weeded and the best protected and encouraged, such discrimination has justification. But the danger has always been and still persists, that what is weeded out is the Different and not the Dangerous; and what is preserved is the Powerful and not the Best. The only defense against this is the widest human contacts and acquaintanceships compatible with social safety.

So far as human friendship and intermingling are based on broad and catholic reasoning and ignore petty and inconsequential prejudices, the happier will be the individual and the richer the general social life. In this realm lies the real freedom, toward which the soul of man has always striven: the right to be different, to be individual and pursue personal aims and ideals. Here lies the real answer to the leveling compulsions and equalitarianisms of that democracy which first provides food, shelter and organized security for man.

Once the problem of subsistence is met and order is secured, there comes the great moment of civilization: the development of individual personality; the right of variation;

the richness of a culture that lies in differentiation. In the activities of such a world, men are not compelled to be white in order to be free: they can be black, yellow or red; they can mingle or stay separate. The free mind, the untrammelled taste can revel. In only a section and a small section of total life is discrimination inadmissible and that is where my freedom stops yours or your taste hurts me. Gradually such a free world will learn that not in exclusiveness and isolation lie inspiration and joy, but that the very variety is the reservoir of invaluable experience and emotion. This crowning of equalitarian democracy in artistic freedom of difference is the real next step of culture.

The hope of civilization lies not in exclusion, but in inclusion of all human elements; we find the richness of humanity not in the Social Register, but in the City Directory; not in great aristocracies, chosen people and superior races, but in the throngs of disinherited and underfed men. Not the lifting of the lowly, but the unchaining of the unawakened mighty, will reveal the possibilities of genius, gift and miracle, in mountainous treasure-trove, which hitherto civilization has scarcely touched; and yet boasted blatantly and even glorified in its poverty. In world-wide equality of human development is the answer to every meticulous taste and each rare personality.

W. E. Burghardt Du Bois, "My Evolving Program for Negro Freedom" in *What The Negro Wants*, 1944, pp. 68–70

Bibliography

Bibliography

Sources of Essays, Lectures and Excerpts Listed
in Order of Classification

Forethought: "On Segregation"—"Postscript" (Editorials), *The Crisis*, Vol. 41, no. 4, April, 1934, p. 115, also no. 6, June, 1934, pp. 182–84; "Race Relations in the United States," *The Annals of the American Academy of Political and Social Science* (Special Issue on the "American Negro"), Vol. 140, no. 229, November, 1928, pp. 6–8; "A Forum of Fact and Opinion," the *Pittsburgh Courier*, August 8, 1936.

AFRICA AND AMERICA—THE AFRICAN BACKGROUND

Prescript: Who Made America?—"Prescript," *The Gift of Black Folk:* The Strafford Co., Publishers, Boston, Massachusetts, 1924, p. 33.

Of Africa—Autobiographical—*Dusk of Dawn: An Essay Toward an Autobiography of A Race Concept:* Harcourt, Brace & Co., New York, 1940, pp. 116–23.

John Brown—Africa and America—*John Brown* (American Crisis Biographies): George W. Jacobs & Co., Publishers, Philadelphia, 1909, pp. 15–20; also new edition, International Publishers, New York, December, 1962.

On the Revolt of San Domingo (Toussaint L'Ouverture)—*Black Folk—Then and Now: An Essay in the History and Sociology of the Negro Race:* Henry Holt & Co., New York, 1939, pp. 175–76.

"American Negroes and Africa's Rise to Freedom"—*The World and Africa:* International Publishers, New York, 1965, pp. 334–38; also 1946 edition, The Viking Press, New York.

Postscript: "Negroes and the World Color Problem," *The World and Africa*, pp. 267–68, originally published in the *Guardian*, 1961.

BLACK CULTURE—"THE BLACK POWER CONCEPT"—"A NEGRO SELF-SUFFICIENT CULTURE IN AMERICA"

Prescript: "The Gift of the Spirit"—*The Gift of Black Folk*, 1924, p. 340, also "Of Our Spiritual Strivings"—*The Souls of Black Folk*, 1903, pp. 11–12.

"The Conservation of Races," in *Negro Social and Political Thought, 1850–1920*, edited by Howard Brotz: Basic Books, Inc., Publishers, New York, 1966, pp. 483–92.

"The Talented Tenth," in *The Negro Problem:* A Series of Articles by Representative American Negroes of Today: James Pott & Co., New York, 1903, pp. 33–75; also in *Negro Social and Political Thought, 1850–1920*; Basic Books, Inc., 1966, pp. 518–33.

"The Field and Function of the American Negro College," An Address Delivered at the Fifty-second Anniversary of the General Alumni Association of Fisk University and of the Forty-fifth Anniversary of the Graduation of Dr. Du Bois, June, 1933: printed in the *Fisk News* (A Monthly Magazine for the Alumni), Vol. 6, no. 10, June, 1936.

"A Negro Nation Within the Nation," *Current History*, Vol. 42, no. 3, June, 1935, pp. 265–70.

Postscript: "The Negro and Democracy"—*The Gift of Black Folk*, pp. 257–58.

AFRO-AMERICAN HISTORY, LITERATURE AND ART

Prescript: "The Propaganda of History"—*Black Reconstruction: An Essay Toward a History of the Part Black Folk Played in the Attempt to Reconstruct Democracy in America, 1860–1880:* Harcourt, Brace & Co., New York, 1935, p. 728; also new edition, Russell & Russell, Inc., New York, 1962, p. 728.

"The Negro in Literature and Art," *The Annals of the American Academy of Political and Social Science*, Vol. 49, September, 1913, pp. 233–37.

"Criteria of Negro Art," An Address Delivered at the Chicago Conference of the National Association for the Advancement of Colored People, June, 1926. *The Crisis*, Vol. 32, no. 6, October, 1926, pp. 290–97.

"The Vision of Phillis the Blessed" (An Allegory of Negro American Literature in the Eighteenth and Nineteenth Centuries); set down for the Seventy-fifth Anniversary of Fisk University, 1941, the *Fisk News*, Vol. 14, no. 7, May, 1941, pp. 10–15.

"The Lie of History as It Is Taught Today" (The Civil War: the War to Preserve Slavery), in the *National Guardian*, February 15, 1960.

Postscript: "What Have You Read?" "On Discussion" "A Negro Book-of-the-Year Club"—"A Forum of Fact and Opinion," The *Pittsburgh Courier*, August 15 and 22, 1936.

RACE PRIDE—"BLACK AWARENESS"

Prescript: "On Blackness"—*The Dark Princess*, A Romance: Harcourt, Brace and Howe, New York, 1928.

"Credo,"—in *Darkwater: Voices from Within the Veil*; Harcourt, Brace and Howe, New York, 1920.

"On Being Black," the *New Republic*, February 18, 1920; also in *Darkwater: Voices from Within the Veil*, pp. 29–52, 221–30.

"Race Pride," *The Crisis*, Vol. 19, January, 1920.

"New Creed for American Negroes"—"Basic American Negro Creed," *National Baptist Voice*, October 5, 1935; also *Dusk of Dawn*, pp. 319–22.

Postscript: "Race Pride: Comments"—"Comments on Negroes in 1960"—*Afro-American Weekly*, Magazine Section, February 27, 1960, Baltimore, Maryland.

SEGREGATION VERSUS INTEGRATION—RACE SOLIDARITY AND ECONOMIC COOPERATION

Prescript: "On the Duty of Whites"—*The Philadelphia Negro: A Social Study:* University of Pennsylvania, 1899, pp. 393–97; also new edition, Schocken Books, New York, 1967.

"On Segregation"—"Postscript" (Editorials), *The Crisis* (W. E. B. Du Bois, Editor), April and June, 1934.

"Where Do We Go From Here?"—An Address Delivered at the Rosenwald Economic Conference, Washington, D.C., the *Baltimore Afro-American*, May 20, 1933.

"The Present Economic Problem of the American Negro,"—An Address Delivered at the Fifty-fifth Annual Session of The National Baptist Convention, New York City, September, 1935, in the *National Baptist Voice*, October, 1935, Nashville, Tennessee.

"The Negro and Socialism,"—*Toward a Socialist America—A Symposium of Essays by Fifteen Contemporary American Socialists,* edited by Helen Alfred; Peace Publications, New York, 1958.
Postscript: "On The Duty of Negroes"—*The Philadelphia Negro: A Social Study,* pp. 389–93.

AFRICAN CULTURE—COLONIALISM—RISE TO FREEDOM—INDEPENDENCE AND UNITY OF THE CONTINENT

Prescript: "Africa's Mighty Past"—*Dusk of Dawn,* pp. 150–51; "The Rape of Africa—Trade in Men"—*Black Folk—Then and Now,* pp. 135–144.
"What Is Civilization?—Africa's Answer"—*The Forum,* Vol. 73, no. 2, February, 1925, pp. 179–88.
"Africa and the French Revolution"—in *Freedomways:* A Quarterly Review of the Negro Freedom Movement, Vol. I, no. 2, Summer, 1961, pp. 136–51.
"Realities in Africa"—*Foreign Affairs:* An American Quarterly Review, Vol. 21, no. 4, July, 1943, pp. 721–32.
"Africa in the Modern World," A Symposium: in *United Asia,* International Magazine of Afro-Asian affairs (Bombay, India), April, 1955, pp. 23–28.
"The Future of All Africa Lies in Socialism"—An Address, Accra Conference, in the *National Guardian,* December 22, 1958.
Postscript: "Young Africa"—from an Address before the National Convention of the Phi Beta Sigma Fraternity, 1950, quoted in *Freedomways* (Du Bois Memorial Issue), 1965, p. 46; "Friends of Africa" —from Message to the Accra Conference, 1958.

THE WORLD OF COLOR—"THE THIRD WORLD CONCEPT"

Prescript: "The Colored Majority of Mankind"—quoted in "W. E. B. Du Bois as a Prophet" by Truman Nelson, *Freedomways* (Du Bois Memorial Issue), 1965, p. 53; "The Dark Workers of the World," *Black Folk—Then and Now,* pp. 382–83.
"The Color Line Belts the World," *Collier,* October 20, 1906.
"Will The Church Remove The Color Line?"—*The Christian Century:* Journal of Religion, Vol. 68, no. 49, December 9, 1931, pp. 1554–56.
"The Vast Miracle of China Today"—The *National Guardian,* June 8, 1959.
"China and Africa"—in *The World and Africa,* enlarged edition, 1965, pp. 311–16; also in *New World Review,* April, 1959.
"India's Relation to Negroes and the Color Problem"—Aptheker's *Du Bois' Unpublished Writings,* in *Freedomways* (Du Bois Memorial Issue), First Quarter, 1965, pp. 115–17.
Postscript: "The Color Line"—*The Souls of Black Folk*—Essays and Sketches; A. C. McClurg & Co., Chicago, 1903, p. 40; "The Modern Labor Problem"—*Black Reconstruction,* pp. 16 and 30; "On Truth"—the *National Guardian,* 1961.

THE IDEALS OF YOUTH—THE CHALLENGE OF TRUTH—HONESTY—INTEGRITY—COURAGE—SELFLESSNESS—SACRIFICE—WORK—KNOWLEDGE AND REASON—(COMMENCEMENT ADDRESSES TO NEGRO GRADUATES)

Prescript: "The Immortal Child"—*Darkwater,* pp. 193–217; "Youth—A Different Kind"—"Criteria of Negro Art," An Address, 1926, in *The Crisis,* Vol. 32, no. 6, October, 1926, pp. 290–97.
"St. Francis of Assissi"—An Address Delivered at the Joint Commencement Exercises of Miner Normal School, M Street High School, and Arm-

strong Manual Training School, Washington, D.C., June, 1907: in *Readings from Negro Authors for Schools and Colleges*, by Otelia Cromwell, Professor of English, Miner Teachers' College, Lorenzo Dow Turner, Professor of English, Fisk University, and Eva B. Dykes, Associate Professor of English, Howard University; Harcourt, Brace & Co., New York, 1931, pp. 273–84.

"Education and Work"—Commencement Address, Delivered at Howard University, Washington, D.C., June 6, 1930, *Howard University Bulletin*, Vol. 9, no. 5, January, 1931.

"The Revelation of Saint Orgne the Damned"—Commencement Address, Fisk University, June, 1938. *Fisk News*, November–December, 1938.

"Jacob and Esau"—Commencement Address, Talladega College, June 5, 1944, in *The Talladegan*, November, 1944.

"Behold the Land!"—An Address Delivered at the closing session of the Southern Youth Legislature, Sponsored by the Southern Negro Youth Congress, Columbia, South Carolina, October 20, 1946; in *Freedomways*, Vol. 4, no. 1, First Quarter, Winter, 1964, pp. 8–15.

Postscript: "The University—Leaders—Education and Work"—from "The Talented Tenth," *The Negro Problem*, 1903, pp. 33–75.

Afterthought (Postscript to Collection): "The Problem of Humanity"—from "My Evolving Program for Negro Freedom," in *What The Negro Wants*, edited by Rayford W. Logan: The University of North Carolina Press, Chapel Hill, 1944, pp. 68–70.

William Edward Burghardt Du Bois was born in Great Barrington, Massachusetts, on February 23, 1868. He received a bachelor's degree from Fisk University in 1888, another degree from Harvard University in 1890, and a Ph.D. from Harvard in 1895. Dr. Du Bois also studied at the University of Berlin. He held honorary degrees from Howard (LL.D., 1930), Atlanta (LL.D., 1938), Fisk (Litt.D., 1938), and Wilberforce (L.H.D., 1940) universities. Dr. Du Bois taught Greek and Latin at Wilberforce from 1894 to 1896 and at the University of Pennsylvania in 1896 and 1897. From 1897 to 1910 he was professor of economics and history at Atlanta University.

During Du Bois' tenure at Atlanta University, he felt he could no longer ignore involvement in politics. Booker T. Washington was the most popular civil rights leader of the time; he was the head (1900–14) of the Tuskegee Institute and an arbiter of black opinion. While Washington felt that blacks could rise best by first developing economically, by pursuing vocational training, and by putting aside academic, educational, and political advancements, Du Bois strongly felt that only a "talented tenth," a well-educated black elite, could lead the black masses toward a greater kind of prosperity. He was outraged that Washington should ask his people to put aside both education and political power in order to advance only economically. In 1903 Du Bois wrote *The Souls of Black Folk*, which helped to further agitate black opinion against Washington, and in 1905 he formed the Niagara Movement in opposition to Washington's teachings.

He later went on to be one of the founders of the National Association for the Advancement of Colored People and was its director of publications and editor of *Crisis* from 1910 to 1932. Many Niagara members followed him to this new organization. In 1933, Dr. Du Bois returned to Atlanta as chairman of the university's sociology department, where he remained until 1944, when he rejoined the NAACP as head of its special research department, a position he held until 1948. In succeeding years, he was vice chairman of the Council on African Affairs and chairman of the Peace Information Bureau. At various times during his life, Dr. Du Bois was also editor of *Atlanta University Studies* and *Phylon Quarterly Review*, founder and organizer of numerous Pan-African congresses, and editor-in-chief of the *Encyclopedia of the Negro*. In 1961, he and his wife, Shirley Graham, immigrated to Ghana, where he served as editor-in-chief of *Encyclopedia Africana*.

Dr. Du Bois was the author of numerous books, among which are *The Suppression of the Slave Trade* (1896), *The Philadelphia Negro* (1899), *John Brown* (1909), *Quest of the Silver Fleece* (1911), *The Negro* (1915), *Darkwater* (1920), *The Gift of Black Folk* (1924), *Dark Princess* (1928), *Black Folk: Then and Now* (1939), *Dusk of Dawn* (1940), *Color and Democracy* (1945), *The World and Africa* (1947), *In Battle for Peace* (1952), and the trilogy *The Black Flame* (1957–61).

Dr. Du Bois died in Accra, Ghana, on August 27, 1963, at the age of ninety-five.